# Phantom in the Sky

## The Paranormal Investigator Series: Book 5

## By

## Christopher Carrolli

Published by
Melange Books, LLC
White Bear Lake, MN 55110
**www.melange-books.com**

ISBN: 978-1-68046-214-2 Print

Cover Art by Caroline Andrus

*As always, this book is dedicated to my mother, Gladys (1937-2011). This time it is also for my Aunt Betty Emanuele (1928-2015), who told me to write, regardless of what anyone thinks. Thanks, Aunt Betty.*

*I want to thank Drew and Toni Lee for their interest in this idea, and to all of my cousins who support me consistently. You know who you all are. Also, thanks to my Dad, Joe; my sister, Micki, and my brother, Joey.*

*I would also like to thank all of my readers for their constant support. Thanks, everyone!*

*Chris*

# Chapter One

## ~ Something Strange in the Sky ~

Dylan Rasche removed his eye from the high-powered telescope lens he'd been looking through. A fast flash of green engulfed his view, obstructing his focus. The large, refracting telescope had been his late father's—that, and the observatory he now sat in, gazing up at the billions of stars in the night sky. He was searching for the aurora borealis, commonly referred to as the "northern lights." It was to be visible in the eastern sky tonight, a rare sight of an infrequent occurrence. He hadn't located the celestial event, but as he searched, something had moved within his projected focal point.

Whatever it was had been fast, flashing a bright flare of green as it moved. Then, it was gone. It couldn't have been the auroras; he hadn't yet fixed the scope into the position he'd carefully calculated earlier. He focused his eye back over the lens.

Now there was nothing; only the constellations he'd noticed when searching for the right position. In his frustration, he began to question whether or not he'd seen anything at all. What could be there and then gone in an instant? It couldn't have been a slight movement of the telescope; it was in its original position. It hadn't moved. Maybe it was his tiring eyes. Still, the quick incident seemed strange.

Taking a moment to look around him, he thought of his father. Dr. Geoffrey Rasche had been an accredited astronomer and professor at the university where Dylan now served as Chief Investigator of the Paranormal Research and Investigative Society. His father had built this private observatory on the property of his vast, stately home after the university declined the commission of such a structure in favor of a new theater. The observatory on the Rasche estate was a small, square building with a set of stairs that led all the way up into the large, bubble-shaped dome that crowned it. The dome sported several openings through which different high-powered telescopes protruded, offering separate views of the nighttime sky. Here, in his private observatory, his father would devote his time to researching, and then teach at the observatory up on Eagle Rock Mountain.

It was from his father that Dylan had inherited his love of astronomy; an infatuation he shared with his fellow investigator, Brett Taylor. He and Brett would often meet here to study the sky, the constellations, and the moon. Here, they'd seen Mars, Venus, and the icy, crystalline rings of Saturn up close. He began repositioning the telescope, and once again, he lost his focus.

*Damn it!*

He knew he should have used the large, reflecting telescope, yet the far more advanced and higher-powered instrument hadn't seemed necessary for the given occurrence. He'd paid for that enormous reflecting telescope with a healthy chunk of the wealth his father had left him. In addition to being a successful astronomer and a highly regarded professor, his father had also been an author who'd amassed quite a fortune writing books on astronomy. But the wealth wasn't the only thing Dylan had acquired. He and his older sister, Denise, had inherited the entire estate. A few years later, Denise had married and moved to Philadelphia, leaving Dylan behind in the mansion he modestly called home. It had been his home throughout his childhood and teen years. Now, alone with his memories, Dylan recalled his father's clandestine activity, one his students had whispered about outside of the classroom—the fact that Dr. Rasche was a UFO researcher and investigator.

What had made him think of that fact at this moment? What had brought that subconscious knowledge to the forefront of his mind? Was it just memories of his father, or was it because of what he'd just seen, or technically, didn't see? Obviously, Dylan had also inherited his father's fascination with the paranormal. Sometimes, he allowed his fascination to run away with him, and he supposed that now might be one of those times.

He sat in the seat behind the reflecting telescope, the size of which dwarfed all others in the small observatory. He gazed back into the black vastness of space, where nothing stirred, or moved, or caught his eye. Only the twinkling stars shimmered back at him. He sighed in frustration, seeing nothing at all of what he'd hoped to see. Finding the auroras tonight was next to impossible.

He should have asked Brett to be here tonight. Between the two of them, they may have seen something. Dylan hadn't even thought to call his old friend and invite him over to try and catch the rare sight. Brett had been through so much during the past year with Uncle Jack's illness; not to mention that the secret he'd kept from the rest of the world his entire life had exploded like a keg of dynamite. Brett's existence as a shape-shifter had been revealed when the strange ability had overwhelmed him to the breaking point, eclipsing his identity, and splitting his soul in two. Throughout his life, Brett had coexisted with this strange phenomenon, and the revelation of it had placed him in the same company with Sidney Pratt and Leah Leeds.

It had all reached a terrifying climax at Uncle Jack's farm during the heat of the past summer. Then, Uncle Jack died, and Brett had nearly shifted into the shape of a murderer. In many ways, Dylan remained thunderstruck by Brett's revelation. He was still amazed at how it all had ended. Lost in thought, he looked down, almost seeing the blood on his own hands. They'd buried a dead body in the woods adjacent to the farmhouse. It was a secret that Dylan would carry to his grave.

Dylan thought of the irony of how he and Brett were now in somewhat of a similar situation; both of them were left to inherit the vastness of a big house—alone. Dylan remained cautious of gold-diggers in his personal life. It was one reason he hadn't married. Yet, Dylan had family. Denise was only across the state. And while his parents had divorced when he was ten, his mother was remarried and living in San Diego. They had always been in close contact. Outside of the team, Brett had no one.

He wondered if Brett was searching the sky tonight, looking for the auroras with his own telescope. Certainly, he hadn't the advantage that Dylan had here in his own observatory with the copious range of modern and updated equipment, but Brett did have the benefit of the vast and open starry sky that loomed above the land unhindered. The backyard at the farmhouse made a superb location for stargazing. Dylan thought to call

Brett and ask if he'd been searching for the auroras, but the question would be a mere front for what he really wanted to know: had Brett seen *anything* in the sky tonight?

He glanced at his watch. It was shortly after midnight, but not too late to call. Brett was notorious for his late hours. The phone rang three times before his old pal answered.

"Well, well, you're up late," Brett said. "Nightmares or ghost hunting?"

"Stargazing," Dylan replied.

"I see."

"I'm searching for the auroras. They're supposed to appear in the eastern sky tonight."

"Yes, I heard," Brett said.

"You've been searching also?"

Brett said he hadn't. He'd been watching the weekly Saturday-night Horrorfest. "Also, I kind of forgot."

Dylan went on to apologize for not inviting him over. He hadn't been sure the search would've been successful, and it wasn't. At least, he didn't think so.

"I couldn't see a damn thing," Dylan said. "The conditions were just right, and I know I calculated correctly. I may've seen *something*, but I don't know, maybe I just bumped the scope."

"That's a bummer, man. Sorry to hear it."

Brett's tone sounded leery, suspicious of him. Dylan was losing his thread. Obviously, Brett had been inside. But Dylan wondered if he'd been outside for even just a moment, though he would've mentioned seeing anything if he had been.

"You didn't happen to see anything at all tonight, did you?"

He bit his lip. The question was too obvious. His attempt at discretion had been blown.

\* \* \* \*

Brett pressed the red button on his phone, ending the call and thinking of how strange Dylan had sounded. While it was not unusual for Dylan to be calling at this hour, the occasions were sparse, usually limited to last minute, pertinent details of emergency meetings in room 208. Simply put,

Dylan's late-night calls were usually alerts that something was going down. Although, Dylan *had* called this late recently, checking up on him in the wake of Uncle Jack's death and everything that happened last summer. But that was over now. The late night calls from Dylan and the rest of the team had gradually ceased, until tonight.

Only moments ago, Dylan sounded distracted, mumbling about possibly bumping a telescope. *"You didn't happen to see anything at all tonight, did you?"*

It didn't make sense. Why would he ask him if he'd seen anything after he'd just told him that he'd been inside, watching TV? Then, Dylan had whimsically changed the subject, segueing into the issue of updating various forms of equipment for the team's future investigations. For a moment, Brett imagined that Dylan sounded as strangely as he had last summer. He felt a slight sense of relief, knowing that the spotlight he'd been immersed in this past year had finally dimmed and died away.

Brett hissed in quiet laughter. Dylan had probably looked at the stars until his eyeballs were dancing. They both had done it several times already, looking up at the sky in Dylan's observatory and studying the splendid array of constellations for hours on end. Who knows how long Dylan had been fooling around in the observatory tonight? His mind was probably playing tricks on him, making him see God knows what out of the corners of his weakened eyes. Brett continued to laugh as he pictured the scenario in his head.

He went back to the sofa and his movie, mindlessly watching it as thoughts of the past year popped back into his head. It was moments like these when he would look around the room at the walls, and at the house itself, realizing that he was here alone. He pressed the mute button on the TV remote. Nothing stirred, no one moved, and no one spoke. Only the emptiness greeted his searching eyes, and silence responded to listening ears. Uncle Jack and Aunt Viv were both gone. A chapter in his life was now a memorable history. Empty chairs where they once sat stared mockingly back at him.

Everything seemed to be gone now, even the inner chaos that had overcome him and induced the climax of his shape-shifting ability. The overwhelming tension of his lifelong secret had nearly destroyed him last summer. Every time it had enveloped him, he became either a willing or unwilling victim of its rapture. The shifting had become uncontrollable. He had almost killed Herb Haller. He *had* killed Claudia, though it was either him or her. The events of that day had led to another secret that he and the team would endure for the rest of their lives.

But now, he felt like his soul was his own, no longer a divided entity between him and the shape that had taken over. Before he died, Uncle Jack had told him everything he needed to know. It was his parting gift, a tale that had led to the end of a mystery, and to the peace he felt right at this moment. In the hours following Claudia's death, calmness had subdued him, permeating through every physical fiber of his being. That tranquility had remained, and he sat in it now, idly staring at the TV screen. Tahoe had told him that he would most likely overcome the cursed side of his strange ability, and he'd been right.

But he *had* shifted since that night. Tahoe had predicted that the wolf would run again, and it had. Although, the furious upwind of emotions, the unbearable tension that eventually stole his identity were no longer factors. The chaos was no more. Now, only the urges to run as the wolf and soar like the mighty hawk remained. They were random, private moments that Brett Taylor secretly enjoyed in the dark remoteness of his rural haven.

For just a moment, he remembered the glossy madness in Claudia's eyes, the crazed inflexion of her tone. He saw himself washing her blood from his body with the hose. He recalled the taste of her blood in his mouth.

He shook himself out of the dark reverie. There was no need to think about it any longer. It was now in the past.

* * * *

It was shortly after midnight when Ursula Masters stepped out onto the balcony of her second-story apartment. She needed a smoke, and smoking wasn't permitted inside of the newly renovated, refurnished apartment she'd been lucky enough to acquire at a fixed price. When at home, it was how she smoked nowadays, slipping out onto the balcony at all hours for a quick nicotine fix. Even in the late evening and wee morning hours, she fired up out here just beneath the treetops and way under the spacious sky, wearing only her sleepwear and puffing smoke into the fresh nightly air. Tonight had been no different.

She stood smoking and basking in the late April breeze that swayed the treetops above her. The aroma from her Marlboro was merely a minor assault, unsuccessfully slicing through the wafting scent of spring. She'd been marveling at the serenity of moments like these, alone in the darkness while the rest of the world slept soundly in their beds. She stood comfortably enjoying the light coolness as it caressed her, and then it happened.

A flood of green light suddenly surrounded her. She let out a gasp, dropping her cigarette to the ground below. She turned her head up toward the bright green light in the sky. The light was rotating, changing from green, to blue, to red, and then green again. It illuminated the strange shape from which it emanated.

She strained her eyes to see and noticed that the shape was circular; it was disc-shaped, shifting and rotating in the sky. It made no sound at all. It hovered in silence, observing, instilling in her a fearful notion that it watched her from leagues above. The wind rustled once more in the treetops, but now it seemed forceful as the limbs swayed in a sudden frenzy. Ursula felt an unmistakable wave of heat surround her. It was invisible, swallowing the cool breeze that bathed her only moments ago. Two words mindlessly escaped her as she watched.

"Holy shit..." She was stunned into speechlessness. Her eyes remained fixed at the sight in the sky. Her heart leapt just as the object jumped southward with an unfathomable speed. Before she could register what she was seeing, it disappeared, as though it were never there. Now, the sky was perfect again, just as it had been a moment ago.

*What that hell was that?!*

Her thoughts provoked a burgeoning fear inside of her, and then she remembered something. She recalled reading on the internet about how some celestial event was supposed to be seen in the sky tonight. She'd even read something about being able to catch it with the naked eye, depending upon one's location. She didn't know much about astronomy, but she'd heard about the northern lights before. And she knew damn well that was *not* what she'd seen.

The incessant and reverberant pounding in her ears was coming from her heart. That thing in the sky—whatever it was—was gone now, along with the cigarette she'd only half finished. She quickly lit another and puffed until her quivering hands had ceased their agitation. Then, she went inside, locking the door behind her.

Having to smoke outside was only a minor drawback to living in the two-bedroom, upper floor apartment of the remodeled duplex. Inside was the comfortable, quiet home she'd established for herself, and she wouldn't have it any other way. She was now a medical secretary since graduating from the university, and affording such a place on her own was no longer an issue. Her feet felt great in the plush of the new white-shag carpeting. The rest of her felt even better sitting on the matching leather sofa her mother had bought her. But her mind was reeling from what she'd just seen.

*What the hell was that?*

She asked herself that question again, and still, she had no answer. It wasn't a plane or a helicopter. It was no type of aircraft she'd ever seen before. It was too rounded and disc-shaped. No modern aircraft could travel at that speed. It had taken off through the sky like a bat out of Hell. *And* it had been silent the whole time—no purring, whizzing, droning, or humming. Its silence was freakish, haunting, and somehow unholy.

She suddenly thought of the paranormal investigators. It had been awhile since she'd seen them. Following their last encounter, she had kept in touch, stopping in room 208 of Levin Hall a few times to say hello. But she'd graduated the following semester and hadn't seen them since. A few years had passed since she'd been unwittingly duped by that psycho Roman Hadley. He'd almost made her an accessory to kidnapping and God knows what else, but she was the one who blew the whistle to the FBI, and the paranormal investigators, as to the boy's whereabouts.

The boy's name was Ryan. He'd been a listener like her, but unfortunately, so was Hadley. Roman Hadley's ability as a clairaudient was strong, much like her own, and that of her twin sister. Hadley had figured out Ursula's plan to help the boy escape, and she'd fled the underground compound just in time. But she'd been followed, and to this day, she was unsure of by whom. It was as if they'd gone up in the same puff of smoke that erupted from that underground compound when it had been blown to bits and pieces.

A maroon sedan had followed her all the way to Ed's Diner, where she'd spoken with Agent Wiley of the FBI. Afterward, she never saw that car again, yet Agent Wiley had remained in occasional contact with her, just in case. She wondered if she should call him and then thought better of it. She would probably sound crazy. She wondered if the FBI even dealt with such issues. This was more of an issue for the investigators. After all, there were five of them, and five heads were better than one. And she always knew where to find them—room 208 of Levin Hall.

She was certain that they would still be there in their headquarters, investigating paranormal occurrences and researching things like ghosts, poltergeists, and probably more. Ursula heard that Leah Leeds had gone back into Cedar Manor. She'd already heard plenty of strange shit about that place. That creepy eyesore had burned to the ground the night Leah led the team inside. The newspaper claimed that the fire was caused by the furnace, but Ursula knew the investigators well enough, including Leah Leeds.

Furnace, my ass, she thought. Ursula guessed that the police and fire inspector came to their own conclusion, and then shoveled that horseshit story to the hungry reporter who ate it up. Isn't that how it usually went? Either way, she knew that the investigators wouldn't doubt her story. She trusted them. For all she knew, there may even be other witnesses to what she'd seen tonight.

She'd have to wait and see; it was getting late. She yawned, slowly trudging her way to her bedroom and climbing into bed.

She lay in bed, her mind reluctantly replaying what she'd seen from the balcony. She tried to focus on sleep, but the slightest wave of nausea washed through her stomach. Her face felt feverish, hot, and then a wave of heat much like the one she'd felt on the balcony swept over her entire body. She threw the covers off of her and leapt from the bed. She was sweating, panting as she ran for the bathroom. She dropped to her knees and hurled into the toilet, the heat intensifying.

Help, she thought. *What's happening to me?*

\* \* \* \*

Something had moved across the sky just as Marv Kinkaid stepped outside to walk his dog; he was sure of it. There were lights high above, bright, vibrant flares of green and blue that lit up the midnight sky. It wasn't lightning; there wasn't a cloud to be seen. He'd heard earlier of the northern lights phenomena, but didn't suspect he'd be able to see such a thing so clearly with the naked eye. And this thing, whatever it was—it moved fast. He'd seen it streak across the sky, trailing yet another flash of florescent green. Then, there was nothing, as if it had been swallowed whole by a darkened sea.

Now, he stood outside of his house in his bathrobe in the dark of night, holding the leash while Duke, his Saint Bernard, yelped endlessly at the sky. Here was his proof that he'd seen something. Duke had seen it too. He was going nuts, sounding the same repetitive, whining bark he extended to strange visitors. Duke's barking spell died away to a final agonizing whimper as the sky was now perfectly intact. Marv felt the pull of the leash as Duke moved forward, closer to the direction of where the lights had been, his pink tongue wagging, his snout pointed up to the sky. Marv's eyes searched above him in all directions, seeing nothing.

What the hell could've moved that fast? Was it a military fighter-jet? Here in western Pennsylvania? He doubted it. Duke quickly jerked the leash in the opposite direction from which he'd pulled Marv. The dog ran across the sidewalk to the other side of the yard, lifted his leg, and pissed quickly in the grass. Then Duke ran back to the front door, hastening on his hind legs, eager to get back inside.

It was unlike him. He usually liked to go for a quick, late-night stroll just before bedtime, but not tonight. Marv looked around and at the sky one last time. Seeing nothing, he slowly opened the front door and entered just after Duke jumped the front stoop and dashed inside. Marv closed the front door and locked it, then peeked out through the curtain. All was quiet and undisturbed, but Marv's instinct as a reporter told him that a story brewed somewhere outside.

He'd been a reporter for the Valley Tribune for forty years and was now somewhat of a celebrity. He'd spent many of those years being a leading investigative-reporter and eventually landed his own column by the time he was forty. His readership ranged widely and extended throughout the state of Pennsylvania. But lately, he'd been thinking about retiring. He'd reached the age of sixty-five, as well as the height of boredom. His job certainly wasn't what it used to be. And how long would it be before newspapers went under completely? He began to think it wiser to jump ship before it sank.

But whatever it was that spooked Duke began to bug the shit out of him. Surely, whatever it was that he'd quickly glimpsed could not have been the result of some astronomical event. He was no astronomer, but he'd heard enough at the paper and read enough in the news to know better. Duke had now curled up in his corner alongside the couch, and Marv lit his pipe, thinking as the cherry-flavored pipe smoke filled his lungs and the living room. He'd thought of something, or more accurately, someone, when the word "astronomer" had popped into his head: Geoffrey Rasche, the astronomer and author, another local celebrity.

He'd known Geoffrey well enough; they'd served together for a number of years on the university's advisory board. Funny thing about Geoff, Marv had always thought that his death was more than a little suspicious. He'd never really believed the conclusion that Geoff's death was an accident. It was just too mysterious, falling from the top of Eagle Rock Mountain the way he did. He'd gone up to the observatory on top of the mountain, as he often had, to work or research.

They'd found his broken body the next morning some one hundred feet below. He'd fallen far, almost to the bottom, and still, it was ruled an accident. It was said that he'd gotten too close to the cliff's edge while trying to maneuver a telescope he'd retrieved from the observatory. It wasn't like Geoffrey to be reckless or careless with telescopes. He was an astronomer and a professor; he knew his profession well. None of it had made any sense.

Marv had even set out to uncover the story back then. People had whispered that Geoff was a UFO researcher, and that he might have discovered something on top of Eagle Rock, but it was gossip that was never proven. Marv had worked secretly to find anything. A cop he once knew told him that he'd heard about signs of a struggle, but that the scene of the incident had later been compromised. Ironically, Marv's cop friend had suddenly moved to Florida and was never heard from again. Yes, Marv had set out to uncover a story, but he'd had to let it go.

Geoffrey had left behind two children, a seventeen-year-old girl and a twelve-year-old boy. At the time, Marv felt for them. Their mother had lived in California and didn't seem to give a shit. He'd had a young family himself back then. The last thing Marv had wanted to do was to drag all of them into what could have been a firestorm of controversy and pain, all when he may not have been able to prove a thing. If there had been a cover-up, or worse, a conspiracy, he had the safety of children to consider.

As thoughts of the past danced back to life inside his mind, he glanced at himself in the mirror above the fireplace mantle. He was completely gray now. His glasses had turned to bifocals. The years had dropped his face into pudgy piles of dough that drooped to his chin. He puffed his pipe, then blew the smoke back at his aging reflection. He turned and looked at Duke, who was staring at him and shaking ever so slightly.

A story flew past him tonight, a scary one by the looks of Duke. Marv was not a fool, certainly not a young fool. He was well aware of why he'd thought of Geoffrey Rasche tonight. There was a story happening; he could feel it. And this time, he wasn't going to let it go.

# Chapter Two

## ~ His Father's Final Words ~

Earlier, Dylan tried to convince himself that he had overindulged his fascination. But his so-called reasonable explanations had slipped away, and now a nagging apprehension kept him awake and alert at 2:00 am. He couldn't deny it anymore. Whatever he'd seen earlier had moved. The northern lights would not have been *that* easy to spot tonight. It would've taken time to set the scope at the right location and search with the telescopic eye.

As that strange moment replayed in his mind, he tossed and turned until finally rising angrily out of bed. He sat up, irritated at his laughable attempt at sleep. Not only was the sight still fresh in his mind, but he kept thinking of his father. He kept seeing his face in his mind. His father's eyes, his curly black hair—all of it he'd passed on to him. Yet his father's face held a more distinguished countenance, the look of a far more educated, accomplished man, even down to the neatly trimmed mustache that had stereotypically tagged him as a professor. Dylan felt like the memory of his father would not let him sleep, as though it was urging him onward.

Light filled the room as he flipped the switch, hoping that the brightness would drown out that which danced in the darkness. He sighed, feeling the frustration of a thousand unanswered questions. He left the light in his bedroom on as he made his way into the hallway and down the staircase to the first floor. He flipped every switch in sight, flooding the stately mansion with light that surrounded him everywhere. His thoughts became clearer and more calculated when he could see everything around him.

He sat down in a chair, though he remained vigilant and almost antsy. He tried to focus as his roaming thoughts began to wind down, opening his mind to a more logical thought process, but the past continued to taunt him. Denise had picked him up early from school on the day his father died. He'd felt surprise and slight trepidation after being given an unexplained early dismissal. Something was wrong. It had been apparent from her bloodshot eyes.

She'd told him that she would explain once they reached home. Standing outside of his school was Timothy Cain, his father's lawyer. He'd been waiting to drive them back home. Young Dylan had just stared through the windshield, wondering as Denise whimpered. Neither she, nor Mr. Cain, said a word. Once they'd made it back here, to the home he'd always known, they told him.

His father had fallen from the top of Eagle Rock Mountain. It was believed that he'd died instantly. It was an unfortunate accident, as Mr. Cain had called it, but his father died doing what he loved most in this world. He remembered Cain's calm, patronizing voice, as if his father had merely gone on a long trip and wouldn't be back for awhile. As though the horrible accident was just some expected part of life. Denise's face had been wet with tears, but her silence was an agonizing acceptance of his words. Dylan hadn't accepted any of it.

He'd leapt from the chair and ran up to his room, slamming the door behind him in blatant defiance of Cain's words. Afterward, Mr. Cain had explained to him that since Denise was now old enough, she would gain custody of him if he chose to remain here in his father's mansion in Pennsylvania. He'd also been given the option of moving to California with his mother. He'd chosen to stay with Denise. He wasn't about to leave his home. Life had changed enough for him in one day.

The funeral viewing had been packed to capacity with people, many of whom he didn't know: students, colleagues, friends, admirers, and even distant cousins among the numerous family members. The funeral itself had been long, tedious, and torturous. Dylan had stayed in his room for almost a year afterward. He just couldn't believe that his father was gone from some avoidable accident. They said he'd fallen while trying to maneuver a telescope close to the edge of the cliff. None of it had made any sense to him.

He and Denise had picked up and moved on; there was nothing else they could've done. They'd lived life as they always had: going to school, associating with friends, and unwrapping gift after gift under the Christmas tree every year. They'd made certain to change nothing. The only difference was the absence of their father. And it had worked for quite a few years, until Denise decided to marry her high-school sweetheart and move away.

But Dylan had been a grown man by then. The estate became entirely his. He graduated from the university as a double major with a degree in Applied Science and another in Education. He taught part-time at the university, but his father's secret love of the mysterious was something he'd inherited. Soon, he became one of the founders of the university's Paranormal Research and Investigative Society. It was just before then that Denise had taken him into his father's study.

"I want to show you something, in the event that you ever need to know," she said.

"Know what?" he asked, following her to the southwest corner of the room.

Denise got down on her knees and ran her fingers through the thick carpeting, searching for something and knocking on the floor with a closed fist. She snatched a patch of carpet with her fingers and pulled a hidden panel upward from the floor. Dylan still remembered his amazement. There, inside the floor, was a steel safe.

"This is Dad's secret safe," she murmured, spinning the dial from right to left as she spoke.

Dylan had known about the safe in the wall behind a painting in his father's bedroom. That had contained the usual stuff: money, deeds, and other important papers. But he'd never known about this safe. It was the first time he'd ever seen it, a safe in the floor. The lock had popped with a *clink* as Denise turned it to the last number in the combination. Then, she pulled back the safe's heavy, steel door.

"What's that inside?" He could see a notebook of some kind.

Denise pulled the contents out of the safe and held them up to him. "These are Dad's journals. You know that he was a UFO investigator, right? Well, he'd kept journals of *everything* he researched." She looked at him, her eyes relaying something unspoken. "Here it is—all of it. In case you ever want to read them."

"Why are you showing me this now?" Dylan asked. He remembered not being able to understand what she'd been implying, what she'd been trying to accomplish.

"Because, Dylan, I've never believed that Dad's death was an accident."

A heat wave of shock had enveloped him on hearing her words. He'd felt the burning of his ears as if he'd been flanked on both sides by invisible torches. Her words confirmed a silent notion that had stayed somewhere buried inside of him, unnoticed, unrecognized. He was too young when his father died to have been able to identify it. Denise had been older. She'd been more capable of zeroing in on that which the back of his mind had never brought forward.

"You think Dad was *murdered*?" He'd felt almost unable to say that word aloud.

"I can't prove that," she said. "I only know what I feel inside. It wasn't like Dad to do something irresponsible or dangerous. I just can't picture him having to venture that far out on the cliff. I think Dad may have *known* something or *saw* something, and someone didn't like it."

She loosed a helpless sigh before continuing. "I don't know, Dylan." "Maybe someday you can prove it; when you're ready." She'd written the combination down on a small piece of paper and handed it to him, offering a slight smile from the pride she felt for him. "Maybe someday when you have a team of paranormal investigators working under you, you can all figure it out."

The memory of her words caused faces to flash in his mind: Sidney Pratt, Leah Leeds, Brett Taylor, and Susan Logan. Dylan had never taken the time to read his father's journals. Much like Denise, the thought of someone having murdered his father had been too painful to contemplate, but he was the investigator, not her. He'd been putting off the inevitable, but now he thought of his father's study, the room that hadn't been touched in years, except by the cleaning lady. It was time for him to re-enter that room, time to use the combination that Denise had left him. It was time to read his father's journals, once and for all.

\* \* \* \*

He spun the dial of the safe to the right, then left, and back again, just as Denise had showed him. The same memorable *clink* greeted his ears once again. He pulled back the door of the safe and stared at the top notebook that awaited his attention. Its withered cover was time worn, but in no way tattered. Now, for the first time, he held the earliest of his father's private journals in his hands and noticed that the cover discreetly displayed only three letters: *GMR*—his father's initials—Geoffrey Morgan Rasche. Beneath the initials were a set of dates: *1973-1980.*

He gently opened the notebook, and immediately, his father's handwriting was a like a visible ghost, raising the hair on his head, and ready to relay pages worth of cryptic messages from beyond. He read the first entry.

*August 1973*

*Pair of BFs sighted in Union following appearance of strange object in the sky.*

Dylan was well aware of what BF meant. It stood for Bigfoot. His father had been a young investigator back in the early seventies when Green Valley and its surrounding territories became the first backdrops for the Bigfoot myth. If this part of the state was famous for anything, it was for the rash of Bigfoot sightings that occurred in the early seventies. Though Dylan hadn't been born yet, he knew that his father was one of the first investigators involved. Union was a town not far from Green Valley, twenty minutes, at most.

Dylan read his father's details of how a young man had witnessed two mysterious creatures walking alongside the edge of a wooded area. The witness had described them as upright, apelike, and over six feet tall with glowing red eyes. He remained captivated by his father's notations.

*Witness claims to have shot one of the creatures, who seemed to be unaffected. BFs reportedly disappeared into the woods. Sounds of breaking trees were heard afterward. Another witness from a separate sighting has suffered slight psychological trauma as a result. It is difficult to communicate with him fully.*

*These incidents follow a series of UFO sightings in the nearby area, only two miles away. Three different sources claim to have seen a disc-shaped craft hovering above a nearby field. Above average levels of radiation detected with Geiger counter during expedition to field. Reports of BF sightings occur two to three days later.*

Dylan continued to read the details of the various witness testimonies, all reporting the same sighting—upright, hairy, bipedal creatures that seemed non-threatening, yet mysterious. His father had written the words "glowing red eyes" repeatedly throughout his notes. As Dylan turned the pages, he realized that the journal was not just comprised of notations, but clippings of newspaper articles as well. The clippings were responsible for the clumsy thickness of the notebook; all had been pasted inside. The old headlines caught his attention.

*"Bigfoot Seen in Green Valley and Surrounding Areas..."*

*"Sources Say UFO's Sighted First, then Bigfoot..."*

Geoffrey Rasche's notes on another witness were fascinating.

*Witness claims BF disappeared in a flash of light as he pulled the trigger. Coincides with earlier witness's claim that BF was unaffected by gunfire. Most witnesses report a foul odor, one that is compared to sulfur, or rotten eggs.*

When Dylan turned the page, a large, browned newspaper clipping folded outward. It showed a sketch of Bigfoot to one side and a picture of a nearby lake on the other. He read the headline.

*"Bigfoot Sighted at Silver Lake."*

Silver Lake was in Green Valley, only a five-minute drive from where he now sat. He'd never known the sightings had been that close to home. He read the article in fascination, learning that several witnesses claimed to have either seen the creature, or smelled the foul, pungent odor nearby before evacuating. Eventually, a group of paranormal and UFO investigators were notified, the names of which were mentioned in the article. His eyes widened at the last of those names—*"Geoffrey Rasche, a young undergraduate from Duquesne University."* He continued reading his father's notes.

*Been to Silver Lake and saw no footprints, though footprints discovered earlier in the surrounding area. Witnesses are correct; the foul stench of sulfur or rotten eggs was overwhelming. It seemed close, as though something was lurking nearby, but nothing sighted or found. Some theorize that BFs may have moved north from Silver Lake.*

As Dylan turned the page, he discovered a sketch of a round, disc-shaped object, more along the lines of the traditional flying saucer, though it was more rounded at the top. He studied the shape of it. It was haunting even in its rough depiction. The sketch also displayed triangular rays of light emanating from the craft. But there was no way he could be certain that he'd seen anything like this tonight. The thing he'd seen had moved too fast. He'd only glimpsed it quickly while fumbling the lens of the telescope. He turned the page and read the written words that followed.

*The sketch on the preceding page was done by a witness known only as Dale T. He and his wife claim to have seen this on their way home from a camping trip last week. They'd seen it lingering in the sky a few miles east of their location. They claimed it seemed to follow them, and then, it was gone. The first of the BF witness testimonies came from approximately the same location as their sighting.*

Dylan continued flipping through the pages and reading until he reached the end. He'd been unaware of the extent of his father's investigations at that time in his life. The books his father wrote had primarily been astronomy textbooks, but he'd written quite a few on the planets, the universe, and space itself. He wondered why his father had never written any books about any of this—his UFO investigations. Had something stopped him? Why the secrecy?

He retrieved a second notebook from the safe and glanced at the cover. Again, the initials GMR were present, but this time, no dates. He opened the lesser worn notebook, and noticed that it was filled with more pasted newspaper clippings, but now, confusion struck him. The second notebook was obviously not as old as the first; but inside, the yellowed newspaper clippings were much older articles. The articles dated back to 1965, a famous year in western Pennsylvania history. The first of the captured headlines caught his eye.

*"Unidentified Flying Object Report Touches Off Probe Near Kecksburg."*

Dylan quickly deduced what it all meant. Sometime in the eighties, his father suddenly began investigating the famous Kecksburg incident. Kecksburg was a small, rural town only ten miles southwest of Green Valley. On December 9, 1965, it became known for one of the most famous UFO incidents in history. Many witnesses had seen a ball of light streak through the sky that day, and other witnesses reported that an acorn-shaped object had been recovered from the nearby woods. Controversy had ensued the day after the incident.

Article after article, page after page, the Kecksburg incident was plastered throughout the notebook. His father had been merely a ten-year-old boy at the time of the occurrence, but by the looks of it, a childhood fascination had never died. Obviously, his father began investigating the Kecksburg mystery many years later. The now browned and nostalgic newspaper clippings posted eerie headlines from the past.

*"Many See Dazzling Light Flash in the Sky."*

*"Orange Ball of Fire Falls Near Kecksburg: Sighted in Seven States, Canada."*

*"Unidentified Flying Object Falls Near Kecksburg—Army Ropes Off Area."*

Dylan read a portion of the article beneath the last mysterious headline.

*"The area where the object landed was immediately sealed off on the order of US Army and State Police officials, reportedly in anticipation of a 'close inspection' of whatever may have fallen...State Police officials there ordered the area roped off to await the expected arrival of both US Army engineers and possibly, civilian scientists."*

The same local newspaper had printed a later edition that read simply...

*"Searchers Fail to Find 'Object.'"*

Dylan was stunned at how far his father had immersed himself in investigating the Kecksburg incident. He'd tracked down witnesses, two, even three decades later. All of them had spoken freely. The determination of their words and testimonies was evident even in his father's notes. One witness, a child at the time, reported seeing wisps of blue smoke from the nearby woods. He and quite a few adults had gone out into the woods, only to be ordered out by the US Army as they'd cordoned off the area.

The next of his father's notes raised the hair on his head...

*Several Kecksburg witnesses reported seeing strange "men in black" near the crash site. I've heard of these men before. They show up out of nowhere after an incident, asking questions and even making threats in some cases. The Kecksburg witnesses I've spoken to reported seeing the men approach just as other witnesses were ordered out of the area. One witness reported being followed; one even described a close encounter with a pair of them.*

*The witness told of how they'd knocked on his front door, asked questions about what he'd seen, and ordered him not to repeat his story to anyone else. He described them as strange in demeanor with the oddest of appearances. Not only were they dressed all in black, but their faces seemed devoid of any lines, wrinkles, or description. The witness said he was unable to see beyond the dark sunglasses they'd worn.*

The pages thrashed about as Dylan flipped them one by one. He stopped on a page where the chronology of articles began to date in the

1990s. Magazines and newspapers from around the country rang out in a chorus. New information had surfaced on an old, yet undying mystery.

*"Photographs, Audio Tapes, and Film of Kecksburg Crash Reportedly Missing"*

*"Kecksburg Witnesses Claim to Have Been Threatened"*

*"US Army Claims to Have Found 'Absolutely Nothing' at Kecksburg"*

The next article was dated in September of 1990, and dealt with a now defunct television show that had discovered new information on the incident and had subsequently done a nationwide exposé. Back then, the show had uncovered and revealed information that Dylan, as a paranormal investigator, had been unaware of until now. The article detailed one of the show's highlights—the story of a man who was once the director of a local radio station. Dylan knew the station well. It wasn't far from the university.

The man had gone to the Kecksburg crash site, and like many others, was told to evacuate. But while there, he'd taken pictures and notes of whatever it was that landed at the site, as well as audio recordings of eyewitness testimonies. The man had later written a documentary on the incident for radio broadcast, but something had stopped him. According to a fellow worker at the radio station, the mysterious "Men in Black" had visited the station, taken the man into a back room, and ordered him not to air the documentary. The female witness reported that the men had confiscated the director's photographs, audio tapes, and notes. Later, the director went on the air with his documentary, but according to the witness, the censored version was nothing close to what he'd planned on broadcasting.

According to other witnesses, the man had become despondent afterward, refusing to even discuss the Kecksburg incident anymore with anyone. Then, Dylan read something that chilled his blood. The station director was killed a few years later in 1969 by a hit-and-run driver while vacationing in California. The driver had never been found. Dylan's heart pounded hard, his eyes trying to ignore the fact that his father had highlighted that part of the article in bright, neon-yellow.

The man's death was probably just a tragic accident, he thought.

Dylan kept telling himself this, but memories of his father played out in his mind: his father driving him to school, his father showing him every part of the small observatory on the estate, teaching him every aspect of the telescope, his father arriving early for his school play. He was seeing his face in his mind again, real and somehow inciting. He read another of his father's notations.

*To this day, witnesses all adamantly claim that on that night they'd seen the military remove an "acorn-shaped" object from the woods, and then load it onto a flatbed truck. Some witnesses later recanted their original testimonies. NASA has officially insisted that they have no records documenting any recovery or removal by the military.*

Dylan closed the second notebook and set it aside. He retrieved the last notebook from the hole in the floor and looked at its cover. Once again, the initials were present along with another date, 1991, two years before his father died. Inside, more witness testimonies of suspected Bigfoot sightings and mysterious objects seen in the sky were documented just like before. He skimmed most of the witness accounts, searching to find anything that hit close to home, yet nothing seemed to be exact.

He noticed that the dates of his father's notations sailed seamlessly through the decade from 1991, through 1992, and into the year of his death—1993. Then, the headline from another pasted magazine article caught his attention.

*"Slew of UFO Sightings Sweep the US and Europe…"*

So, his father had been on top of the wave of UFO sightings that had erupted in the 1990s; he'd figured as much. He just stared at his father's written words when his eye caught the next page. The pounding rhythm of his heart persisted, as if waiting for something to jump out from the pages. If Denise had dared to read these words, her questions may have been answered.

*Several witnesses in the Green Valley area have reported seeing a strange object in the sky above Eagle Rock Mountain. I've spoken to them all, and they all appear as rational, articulate, and in two cases, highly educated people. These sightings have caught my attention on a personal level, as Eagle Rock is a location that I frequently take my classes for lab sessions. My students and I have never witnessed any objects from the top of, or anywhere near Eagle Rock Mountain, but all witnesses have reported their sightings to be within a mile of the area.*

*They all described a strange object lingering in the sky at approximately 9:30 on the evening of June 12, 1993. All accounts concur that lights were emanating from this mysterious craft, lights of various colors, specifically green and blue. Witnesses Michael Haines and Shawna Reed were atop Eagle Rock Mountain that night. They'd gone "sightseeing" (code for "parking") and saw the object hovering high above the mountain. They've described it as "being there one moment and gone the next, like some strange phantom in the sky." They are the closest reported sighting to the mountain itself.*

*However, RJ Bailey's experience was somewhat different. He'd been driving home from work after his second-shift at the glass factory. He'd taken his usual route along the main road that passes the base of the mountain. This was his custom, as every night, but on the night of June 12, something caused him to pull over to the side of the road. He described the light as "overwhelming and blinding." The powerful flash of green blinded him, and then shifted to blue as he'd found the side of the road through squinted eyes. Then, as the light moved farther away, he watched as a saucer-shaped object moved with a speed that he called "unbelievable." Bailey claims the object had moved so fast that it just disappeared.*

*Many things could account for slightly different descriptions of the object's departure: witness angle, position, location, timing, even eyesight. All three of the above witnesses agree that the object had just "disappeared" in either case. The difference was that Bailey actually saw the object move.*

Dylan sat stunned. His heart fluttered as something *did* jump out from the page—those last words. He stared at them in shock. It was too much of a coincidence. It was an eerie message, and it was received. The first words in the next entry kept his eyes frozen to the page, and for just a moment, he wished he hadn't stumbled upon them. But there they were in the continuance of his father's haunting handwriting.

*I went up to Eagle Rock, alone. I wanted to get a glimpse from where each of the witnesses was standing. It was the first time I'd been up there since March, when I'd taken a class up to the observatory. This is late June. I saw something today just as I arrived at the observatory. At first, I couldn't believe my eyes. It was a large dish-antenna belonging to a radio telescope that had obviously been installed within the last three months. There was also what looked like some sort of viewing or recording device I'd never seen before. It was a thin rod, possibly another antenna that protruded up and down from a small circular tower outside of the observatory.*

*I knew nothing of these recent updates or additions to the Eagle Rock observatory. They were not part of it three months ago. They have been quickly and discreetly authorized, but by whom and why? As I'd reached the front of the building, I was astonished to be greeted by a guard. There has never been a guard there before. When I told him who I was, he steadfastly instructed me that all frequenters of the observatory must have their clearances renewed.*

*"What?" I asked him.*

*"Sorry, professor," he said. "That's all I know."*

*I'm taking this up with the municipal authorities as I write this. I'm not sure what has happened up on Eagle Rock, or why the observatory has so suddenly acquired such state-of-the-art technology. But based upon what I know as a professor and an investigator, I can attest to one thing for certain—they are definitely watching for* something *up there.*

Again, Dylan's fingers flashed through the pages, his mind racing, attempting to ignore the repetitive pounding in his chest. He felt the blood pumping through him, the adrenaline arousing the realization of his worst nightmare. Had Denise been right in her suspicions? If so, he now became, once again, the leader left to deal with a deepening mystery; but this time, it was his own. What had his father stumbled upon? He skimmed through the pages, searching for certain words. When his eyes found what they were looking for, he read on.

*I've gotten nowhere in trying to discover what has taken place at the observatory. Since it's not owned by the university, they can only obtain a limited amount of information on the building, which is owned by the city. I've inquired with the Municipal authorities, who've told me next to nothing. I've been told by an anonymous source that the additions to the observatory up on Eagle Rock have been ordered by our own government. I cannot verify this statement, but it would explain the city's reluctance, or lack of knowledge, in discussing the matter.*

Dylan's heart leapt at a later entry written in all capital letters…

*I'M BEING FOLLOWED!*

The rest of the page was filled with only white space, a blankness that taunted him to continue. After wetting the tip of his finger and flipping another flimsy page, he discovered a more cryptic entry. This one included another date.

*June 28, 1993*

*I've been teaching a summer class at the university. I've been followed by a black sedan for the past few weeks. Tonight, I was followed to and from the university. I've seen that same car again and again in the rearview mirror. The stalking has become more frequent. Something is going on.*

The next pages documented Geoffrey Rasche's various inquiries into the mystery surrounding the observatory. Dates, places, questions that were asked, all were written down, but no record of any replies or offhand answers were found anywhere in the journal. Dylan suddenly realized that his father had documented everything that was going on within these pages and stowed them away where no one could find them. He'd secretly kept and hidden these journals in a safe in the floor for a reason—he was being followed. He'd made too much noise.

At the time, only one person knew about this secret safe, and that was Denise. In the unlikely event that any intruders had searched the house, or discovered the main safe in his father's bedroom, they would find only the regular, everyday legal documents. The journals would be safely undiscovered beneath the safe in the floor. Now, he understood as a broader picture began to unfold.

*June 30, 1993*

*I've been trying to have my clearance to enter Eagle Rock Observatory reinstated, still awaiting a response. I've seen the black sedan once more, this time in the distance, but surely following me.*

Two words jumped out at Dylan once again—*black sedan*. Suddenly, he remembered a few years ago when Ursula Masters had helped the team in locating Ryan Quinn. She'd told them of being followed by a sedan, only a maroon-colored one. Dylan was aware that the legends concerning the infamous "Men in Black" included black sedans in which they were said to have traveled. These mysterious men had been reported in this area all the way back to the Kecksburg incident, and Dylan found quite a few articles about them pasted throughout his father's journals.

Could his father have actually been followed by these men? Could this really have been the case? His head began to spin in a whirlwind of thoughts and possibilities as past revelations resurrected from the hidden pages. He read through the remaining notations until he reached what looked like the final entry. It was dated the day before his father's death.

*September 9, 1993*

*For the past two months, I've been attempting to regain my rightful access to Eagle Rock Observatory. I've heard nothing, and have been getting the runaround every time I try to get answers. I've now been told that the observatory has been temporarily closed to the public, and that I will eventually be notified of its reopening. The university has heard this same bogus story meant to stall our inquiries and divert our attentions. Enough is enough; I'm going up to Eagle Rock Observatory tomorrow night. One of my mounted refracting telescopes has been malfunctioning. I will use the excuse that I have come to have someone look at it, should I run into any problems.*

*I also have the feeling that I will be drawing my stalkers out into the light, or should I say, the dark? I'm tired of being followed. It is time for answers.*

Whiteness filled the remaining space on the page. Dylan flipped his fingers through the rest of the notebook, seeing only the same whiteness, page after page. The last entry had in fact been the last. Geoffrey Rasche's final secret words had stopped as though his voice had suddenly become silent forever, and it had.

He closed the last notebook and stared in silence at the wall. He sat on the floor, unable to move. The three notebooks contained not only his father's final words, but a mystery of national, even worldwide, proportions. All of it was right in his hands. He remembered Denise's words.

*"Maybe one day when you have a team of paranormal investigators working under you, you can all figure it out."*

He silently marveled over the phenomenal team he'd assembled over the past few years. Sidney Pratt, the clairaudient who listened as the dead spoke to him in a sea of his own sudden deafness, the one who had come to him out of nowhere when he was still a two-man operation. The beautiful Leah Leeds, whose powerful third eye saw far beyond the reaches of time and space, and had triumphantly stared down a legion of demons. Brett Taylor, the young man whose secret life as a shape-shifter had shocked them all, was his second in command and had been with him from the beginning.

And then there was Dr. Susan Logan, esteemed psychiatrist and parapsychologist, who had replaced their unseen leader, Roman Hadley, a man who had turned her life upside down. Dylan and Susan had endured moments of tension between them. She was obstinate and so was he, but he had no idea what he, or the rest of the team, would do without her. She was their rock. They were a family.

It was abundantly clear from the journals that his father had met with foul play, just as Denise had always suspected. There was no way he could deny it, having read it on the pages in front of him. His father had taken a tremendous risk, luring whoever was following him out of the shadows. Dylan wondered how he could have done such a thing with two children at home. But then again, he knew damn well that it was the investigator inside of him, the same gene he'd inherited from the man he almost criticized.

And he was convinced now more than ever that what he'd seen tonight was real. And if it was, there would have to be other witnesses. All of these factors conspired together to form an inevitable conclusion; he knew what had to be done. It was time to assemble his phenomenal team once again. Together, they would delve into this otherwise forbidden territory and search for the truth.

But it was past 3:00 am. The search for the truth would have to wait until the light of day. Then, he would alert them.

# Chapter Three

### ~ Radiation Exposure ~

Dr. Susan Logan had instructed Brett Taylor to keep a secret journal documenting each and every time he shifted, and to detail his feelings and thoughts following such an event. Brett had begun a new phase of life, not to mention the fact that he was experiencing a new way of understanding his ability as a shape-shifter. The journal was to contain no mention of anything that occurred last summer. It was to make no reference to either of his birth parents: Claudia Taylor and Antonio Anakas. Brett had come through on his instructions. Susan read the journal now in the quiet of her home office on this Sunday morning, as a new spring day showered sunshine through the window blinds.

The words on the page didn't belong to the troubled and uniquely frazzled Brett Taylor who had been the subject of their last investigation. These words belonged to a young man who had overcome, who now understood, and had moved on with a strong sense of serenity, knowing that the worst of his predicament had passed. Brett was adjusting quite well to his new existence, and the words on the page proved it.

*"I ran as the wolf through the woods for what had to have been hours. I've learned to shift in the woods and leave my clothing behind to be retrieved later. No more sneaking into the house in my birthday suit. As I emerged from the woods, I wasn't aware of how much time had passed, but the peace and tranquility that I felt was blissful. The chaos is no more. As Tahoe predicted, I have overcome it."*

Yes, she would always be concerned for his safety when he shifted into these shapes in the dark of night. She worried about hunters with shotguns, a repeat of the situation with Herb Haller. She feared some stranger becoming an unwitting eyewitness to Brett's shifting, and the possibility of his secret being exposed to the public, or worse, the press. She remained concerned over the undeniable aspect of missing time. But there was nothing she could do about the seemingly endless possibilities. They were dangers that came with Brett's ability. Brett had to live with them, and so did she and the rest of the team.

The notes she kept on her sessions with Brett were the most copious and diligent transcriptions she'd ever kept on any patient or subject, though she would never refer to Brett as the latter. As a parapsychologist, and as his close friend, she needed to understand him in every way possible. Tahoe had been so right in his prediction that Brett would be all right, and for that, she was thankful and much relieved, but her watchful eye remained focused on Brett, more than he actually knew. His Uncle Jack was gone, and she and the team were all that remained of Brett's family. But Susan was vigilant to curtail her concern and focus it from afar, careful not to smother Brett in any way.

The bleating electronic blare of her home office phone suddenly distracted her. Who could it be at this hour? The only calls she received at eight in the morning were either from the hospital or distraught patients. All thoughts of Brett Taylor abruptly vanished when she saw the name on the Caller ID—*D. Rasche*. What could Dylan be calling so early about? Susan would soon discover that it would be the first of two strange phone calls.

She answered the phone, bypassing the customary "hello."

"Dylan?" she said. "It's early even for you. Is everything alright?"

"No, not really. Something's up. I'm going to need your help."

She heard the slightest tinge of paranoid fear in his voice. It wasn't like him. The young bastion of a chief investigator had always held it together through any storm they had weathered, even taking the lead with a shovel to bury a dead body. Now, he sounded afraid.

"Relax, Dylan. Clear your mind, and tell me everything from the beginning."

"I saw something last night, something I can't explain."

"You saw something?" she asked. "You mean, like a ghost or something?"

"No. You may not believe me when I tell you."

He began to detail the events of the night before, how he'd been searching the sky from his observatory, seeking out the aurora borealis. Then, he described the flashing green light that had interrupted his focus, and then fled from his line of sight, gone in an instant.

"I can't say for sure what it was," he said. "But it kept bugging me, and then I began going through my father's things." He sighed through the phone, issuing a harsh breath like rushing static in her ear. "I don't want to say anymore over the phone. I don't feel safe."

"Dylan, you're kidding me? Who on earth could be listening?"

"That's not the point. I need to see you, and the team, immediately. We need to discuss this in private. I say we meet as soon as possible. If I'm right, I can't be the only person who saw something last night. I have a feeling that there are other witnesses. Hopefully, there's someone else out there that can confirm what I saw. But there's more, so much more. I'll show you all when we meet."

"Alright, but as I said, relax," she said. "Stay calm, and let me rustle up the rest of the team. We'll all try to meet before noon."

"Fine. I'll be there."

The line went dead.

Curious, Susan thought. But perhaps Dylan was overreacting. She was well aware of the fact that Dylan's father had been a UFO investigator. It was something Dylan had shared privately with her and the team one day when they'd all been having one of their group discussions, pondering the paranormal and talking about why they did what they did. Dylan had obviously inherited his passion for mysteries beyond this world from his father. But she also knew that Professor Rasche's clandestine activities as an investigator had been kept a secret throughout his career.

Could Dylan simply be associating what he'd seen, with his own thoughts of his father? Possible, but it was unlike him. Could he be right that other eyewitnesses were about to come forward? The thought of it made Susan's blood rush in a shameful momentary thrill. But Dylan said there was more. What was he talking about?

She remembered the slight trepidation in his voice, his paranoia of someone listening. Her blood stopped racing as she remembered his seriousness. She thought for a moment.

*Another sighting here in western Pennsylvania…why not?*

Suddenly, her mind went back to 1965. She'd been around the age of fourteen, sitting somewhere in the eighth grade when the Kecksburg incident had occurred. She recalled how her parents, grandparents, and neighbors had talked about it. She remembered the newspaper headlines that followed, and even how her science teacher had led a discussion on the matter.

While she had studied the history of UFOs extensively for her degree, it wasn't really her area of parapsychology. She'd spent her time researching ghosts and psychic children, especially after discovering a five-year-old Sidney Pratt. She spent a few moments drifting in the past, and then suddenly the phone rang. Was it Dylan again? She looked at the Caller ID. No surprise, it was the hospital.

Susan snatched the phone from its cradle and answered. "This is Dr. Logan." The voice on the other end was familiar.

"Dr. Logan, this is Ashlee from the fifth-floor nurse's station. We have a patient in ICU who was brought in last night. She's not one of your regulars, but she's requesting to see you as soon as possible."

"Me?" Susan was taken aback.

"She says she's a friend of yours?"

"Who's the patient?"

"A young woman named Ursula Masters."

"Oh, no." She remembered Ursula immediately. The young, ballsy and brassy clairaudient who'd helped the team find Ryan Quinn a few years ago. "What's happened? Is she alright?"

"She's stable right now. They brought her into the ER not long after midnight last night. She's been diagnosed as having acute radiation sickness."

"What?" It was the last thing Susan expected to hear. She'd automatically assumed something along the lines of an accident, but radiation sickness?

"Yes, but actually, she's doing much better this morning. She's very lucky. Apparently, she'd been exposed to a level high enough to cause vomiting and other gastro symptoms, but she hadn't been exposed long.

Dr. Adams says she'll pull through just fine," Ashlee said.

"How the hell did this happen?!"

"That's where you come in, Dr. Logan. She says that she wants to speak only to you. She says no one else will believe her. It's obvious that she doesn't trust the rest of us. We were hoping that you might come in today and see her?"

Susan hadn't given it a second thought. "I'll be there in twenty minutes."

She hung up the phone, flabbergasted by what she'd just heard. Ursula Masters, exposed to radiation, how? *"She wants to speak only to you..."* Suddenly, she thought of Dylan. *"I saw something last night, something I can't explain..."*

She quickly picked the phone back up and called her chief investigator. When he answered, their exchange was brief.

"Dylan, meet me at the hospital, fifth-floor, now! Something *is* going on." She didn't go into details. Dylan didn't argue. They hung up once more, and in five minutes, Susan was out the door.

\* \* \* \*

The clairaudient ear of Ursula Masters was attuned to a slightly different function than Sidney Pratt's. She was endowed with the technique of remote hearing, being able to hear random conversations from a distance; Sidney Pratt could hear the dead. Ursula thought of that now as she lay in a hospital bed of the ICU unit, gazing through the door's window and watching the nurse behind the desk in the lobby. She was having a phone conversation, and Ursula began listening, catching random clues with her clairaudient ear.

*"She's been diagnosed as having acute radiation sickness..."*

So, the nurse was talking to someone about her.

*"She's very lucky...Dr. Adams says she'll pull through just fine."*

There was a pause.

*"That's where you come in, Dr. Logan. She says that she wants to speak only to you..."*

The nurse was talking to Susan Logan. Ursula felt a wave of relief. Susan would believe her when she told her what she'd seen. That thing in the sky had made her sick. It was why she was here.

She didn't trust these people. They were liable to move her to the eighth floor with the rest of the whack jobs if she told them the truth. Susan would know she wasn't crazy. But Ursula was also aware that the whole thing could have been much worse. The nurse said she was lucky.

All of it had happened so fast. She'd been outside on the balcony, catching a smoke when she saw that thing in the sky with its strange shape and its bright green light above her. She recalled its silence and the rustling warm wind that enveloped her.

*Radiation.*

So that was the sudden heat wave that had rustled the treetops and surrounded her out on the balcony. Then, the strange object had vanished. She remembered hurrying inside. The sight she'd beheld was so mind-boggling that she'd decided to tell the investigators as soon as possible. She recalled the sudden onset of fatigue, and then the nausea, and the rising temperature that had hit her simultaneously. The memory of hurling into the toilet was fresh, but the rest of what happened came to her in bits and pieces.

She remembered crawling toward the phone, the female voice of the 911 responder, and the next thing that entered her mind was being on a gurney. She was slightly roused by the plastic smell of the oxygen mask that gripped the lower part of her face, and observant of the lights in the hospital ceiling that passed one by one above her. After rolling the gurney into an isolated triage unit, they began ripping her clothes from her body and wrapping her in a swaddling of blankets. They'd stashed her ruined garb in a thick, black, lead-lined bag. The next thing she recalled was waking up in the ICU.

The doctor had been standing over her. The nurse had stood at his side, scribbling inside a chart. He'd flashed a light into her waking eyes before he spoke.

"You're awake," he said. "I'm Dr. Adams. Can you tell me your name?"

After he'd persisted, she told him her name, address, date of birth, and even named the current US president.

"It looks like you're going to be just fine, Ursula," he said. "We're going to keep you for a while though. You're going to need as much rest and recovery as possible. You've been exposed to a fair amount of radiation, but for what appears to be only a brief duration, not enough to have caused any permanent or lethal damage. Can you tell us how this happened to you?"

The doctor had been patient, caring, and attentive, and by Ursula's suspicions, the type that would listen and sympathize, and then call her crazy when he left. Both he and the nurse began eyeballing her, waiting for her response, and expecting it to be some sinister revelation.

"I'm not really sure," she lied. "It's really all so distorted."

"It just seems so odd," Adams said. "You were alone in your apartment, where no signs or traces of radiation have turned up. You yourself called 911. Surely, you remember why you did that."

He'd been pressing her. And by the looks on both of their faces, they weren't buying her excuse. They'd asked about her family. Who did she want them to call?

"Look, I don't want to alert my mother just yet," she said. "I don't want her to worry."

"Fine, Ursula," Adams said. "But we're going to have to know how this happened to you. It's imperative. The authorities are also going to want know how this occurred, and they'll want to know soon."

Seconds of silence passed.

"It's up to you," he said, as he started to walk away. "But radiation exposure is a very serious issue. There will be an investigation into how this happened."

"Wait." Ursula stopped him as his back was turned to leave. "There is one person you can call for me—Dr. Susan Logan."

"Susan Logan?" Adams asked. "Are you a patient of hers?"

Ursula had felt a slight twinge of embarrassment. Looking like she was crazy was exactly what she'd been trying to avoid.

"No, I'm not. But she's a friend of mine. She'll help me."

"Alright then," he said. "You just rest. We'll contact Dr. Logan for you."

They'd left the room about ten minutes ago, and now Ursula watched as Adams's nurse hung up the phone. Susan would be on her way.

\* \* \* \*

Dylan trounced the sixty-five mph speed limit, driving as fast as possible while keeping an eye out for hidden cop cars. A tinge of fear had turned into a rising paranoia that seemed to feed his need for speed on the two-lane highway. What exactly had Susan meant by "something *is* going on?" Did it have to do with what he saw? Surely, if something had been wrong with any other member of the team, she would have told him on the phone. Soon, he pulled into one of the hospital's adjacent parking lots.

Susan had already arrived at the hospital, yet she'd had a much shorter drive. He noticed her walking toward the hospital's front doors as he hurried through the parking lot. He called out to her, and she turned and waited for him. He made a shrugging motion with his arms when he reached her.

"What's going on?" he said. "Why are we here?"

Susan glanced around him, careful of anyone else in earshot. She turned her back and walked side by side with him through the hospital doors. She spoke discreetly. "I received a phone call after hanging up with you," she said. "Ursula Masters was brought into the ER last night. She's suffering from radiation exposure and won't tell anyone what happened to her. She's requested to speak only to me."

*"What?!"*

"Keep your voice down," Susan scolded. "But that was my reaction exactly."

Contrary to his response, Dylan *could* believe what he was hearing. Pieces of a strange puzzle were falling together. How ironic that he'd thought of Ursula just last night while he was reading his father's journals.

*Maroon sedan, black sedan.*

Could Ursula be a witness to the same thing he'd seen last night? How else could she have possibly been exposed to radiation? As residents of western Pennsylvania, they didn't live close to any nuclear power plants. Those few installations, including the most famous, Three Mile Island, were situated on the eastern side of the state.

Dylan noticed Susan's silent admonition, the sudden arch of her eyebrows that told him to remain quiet as they walked through the hospital lobby, passing persons unknown. Once the double doors of the lobby's elevator closed in front of them, Susan continued.

"Apparently, she dialed 911 on her own. They found her on the floor of her apartment, semi-conscious but responsive. Ashlee, the nurse, told me that Ursula is stable and very lucky. It looks as if the exposure was not of a prolonged nature. But she won't tell them what happened. That's where I come in, and I'm sure you can gather what that might mean."

"If she confirms what I saw last night, I think we're about to become embroiled in something far bigger than even we could ever imagine."

"I think you're right," she said.

The single peal signaling the elevator's arrival dinged just before the double doors opened, and the fifth floor spread out before them. Dr. Steven Adams was waiting for Susan as they approached the nurse's station.

\* \* \* \*

"What's the situation, Steve?" She asked him directly, one doctor to another.

"Well, the fact that she vomited shortly afterward was not a good sign. Usually when symptoms occur that quickly, they're signs of a serious exposure. But she's had no other symptoms since, outside of fatigue, which is to be expected. Her tests show that any exposure she'd experienced was only of a brief duration. Whatever happened to her could have been much worse, so yes, she's extremely lucky."

Adams had suddenly taken notice of Dylan who listened without speaking.

"Steve, this is my associate, Dylan Rasche," Susan said. "He's also a very good friend of Ursula's. Would it be alright if he joined me when I speak to her?"

"Fine with me, if it's okay with her," he said. "If either of you can get her to tell us what happened, then so be it. But, Susan, you know well enough that I need to file a report on what happened to her. In a case like this, it's mandatory."

"Yes, of course. She'll talk to me. She knows me well."

Seconds later, they stepped through the doors of the ICU. There was that tough young woman she'd met only a few years ago, confined to the hospital bed that somehow dwarfed her. She was still wrapped in the swaddling of blankets that covered her body. Her face was drawn and pale. Her hair was listless. The fatigue had formed a far-off stare in her eyes. She forged a weak smile at seeing both of them.

"Susan, Dylan," she said. "Thank God you're here." A cry of relief escaped her and segued into what sounded like soft sobbing. "I didn't know who else to call. I've seen the looks on their faces. They wouldn't believe me if I told them. I'd decided to call you all, soon after it happened, but then—"

"It's alright, Ursula," Susan said. "Everything's going to be fine now."

She pulled a single chair up to Ursula's bedside, unafraid to comfort her by touching her forehead. Ursula had not been exposed to any transmittable amount of radiation.

"Yeah," Dylan said, still standing. "A tough chick like you fighting radiation sickness, nah, the radiation doesn't stand a chance."

Ursula's smile widened, and a weak laugh escaped her.

"Why don't you tell us what happened, dear?" Susan said. "Take your time."

Ursula took a deep breath and exhaled, rolling her eyes upward in recollection.

"I'd been outside on the balcony, catching a smoke," she began. "It was late, sometime after midnight. Suddenly, there was a flood of green light all around me. It was a brilliant green, and then blue, and red, and I think it was green again. I remember dropping my cigarette when it happened. Then, I saw this thing in the sky above me. At first I thought it was a plane, but it couldn't have been. I saw its shape. It was round, kind of disc-shaped. It just hovered above me with a strange movement."

From the corner of her eye, Susan caught Dylan's reaction to Ursula's story. Her words had confirmed what Dylan had seen, or thought he'd seen. Everything coincided, even the time-frame. Susan kept her attention on Ursula.

"Then, I felt this wave of heat surround me. It wasn't really hot, but warm, warmer than it was last night. Then, just as quickly as I'd seen this thing, it shot southward so fast it freaked me out. It just disappeared; it was that fast. I'd gone back inside, and that's when I remember thinking to call you all as soon as it was possible. I went to bed, and then suddenly, I felt sick, hot all over."

She sighed in disgust before continuing.

"I puked all over the toilet and the bathroom floor," she said. "I wonder who's going to clean that up."

"See, your sense of humor hasn't left you," Dylan said. They laughed lightly, and then Dylan asked a question.

"Ursula, are you sure that the light that came from it was green?"

"Yes, at first," she said. "I even thought it could have been those northern lights that I'd read about, but it wasn't. Like I said, it had a shape."

Susan glanced over at Dylan, a thousand unspoken words exchanged between them.

* * * *

Dylan's heart leapt at her words. Not only had Ursula seen the same thing that he had the night before, but she'd seen more of it. Dylan hadn't been sure what he'd seen, but Ursula was positive. Even through the haze of fatigue, the details of her recollection were consistent.

"You said that its movement when you first saw it was strange," Dylan said. "Can you remember exactly how?"

"It was sort of…rotating," she said. "The bottom part of it was turning; shifting the light's various colors like a set of stage lights."

He felt embarrassed at having so many questions but not knowing which one to ask next. This wasn't his area of expertise. He was a ghost-hunter, a poltergeist tracker, and most recently, he'd even chased a skinwalker. But this was out of his league. What would his father have done? He suddenly felt like the pages of the journals he'd left securely back in the safe were calling out to him, as if his father was trying to coach him from beyond.

"Ursula, the reason I came along with Susan is because I myself saw something similar last night. But, obviously, you saw more of this thing than I had."

He went into detail about his experience the night before with the telescope. The fast flash of green had caught his eye, yet he'd seen no shape. It had moved too fast.

"Yep," Ursula said. "So, do you think it was a UFO?"

"Yes, dear," Susan answered. "I'm afraid that's exactly what it was."

* * * *

After a few more questions, they'd finally let the dozing Ursula slip into slumber, but not before Susan had told her not to worry about a thing;

she would contact her mother. She would also explain to Dr. Adams the circumstances that had brought her here. She would provide Dylan as another witness to this strange and unexplainable sighting. Susan had assured Ursula that she, Dylan, and the rest of the team were going to help her in every way possible.

They walked through the hallway and back toward the nurse's station, where Nurse Ashlee treaded quickly over to Susan.

"Dr. Logan," she said. "Dr. Adams wants you to meet him in his office, STAT."

"Yes, I know, Ashlee. I was on my way there now to fill him in on Ursula Masters."

"It's not just that, Dr. Logan, there's more."

"I don't understand," Susan said, waiting for the young nurse to continue.

"There's been another one brought into the ER. Another unexplained exposure to radiation. It's even more crucial now that we learn what happened to Ms. Masters."

The graveness of Susan's expression matched Dylan's when she turned to him.

"Wait for me in my office," she said. "I'll fill you in when I get back."

# Chapter Four

## ~ Shane Rowe ~

Shane Rowe had worked until midnight, his regular shift at Happy's Restaurant. The restaurant closed at eleven, but he worked an extra hour cleaning up and helping to prepare for the next day's business. Last night at midnight, he was thankful to be out of there, just like always. Being twenty-one and having to work on a Saturday night sucked, but two Saturdays a month was part of his job. He'd fired up the engine of his Ford truck and fled from the scene of his eight-hour captivity—all within a minute of dashing out the door.

He'd let the cool spring air rip through the windows of the truck, bathing him in abandon and fueling the feeling of freedom that he felt. This was his time, the time he spent alone between work and home, and the rest of the world ceased to exist. As usual, he pulled into the all-night convenience store to grab one of the self-serve sandwiches he would wolf down in the front seat of his car. He had sat in the parking lot doing just that, while the neon glare of the store's sign reflected red and green in his windshield. When he finished, he crinkled the sandwich wrapper up into a ball and stashed it in the accompanying paper bag. He'd also bought smokes, so he lit one as he exited the truck and ditched the bag into the outside garbage can.

He loitered in the parking lot, puffing the Pall Mall down to a butt and adhering to his own rule of no smoking in the truck. Soon, he flicked the fiery stub with his fingers, flinging it far away from the store. He hopped back into the front seat and restarted the truck, feeling the momentary vibration that accompanied its mighty roar of resurgence. On the road, yellow stripes disappeared beneath his wheels, and then vanished altogether when he turned right onto one of the back roads. It was the shortcut he always took. He usually stopped at Ted's Bar and Grill on the way home, downed two or three beers on his wasted Saturday night, and then went home to crash in front of the TV.

But last night, something entirely different happened.

The radio had been belting out some old Nirvana tune. He'd been drumming his hands against the steering wheel to the beat and the words while driving.

*Come as you are, as you were…*
*As I want you to be…*
*As a friend, as a friend…*
*As an old enemy…*

The back road had been vacant, devoid of any other vehicles. Under his breath, he sang along to the song, still drumming his hands to the beat until he'd noticed something approaching from behind. It was a green light that grew brighter and brighter, filling more and more of the truck as it moved from the back bed and into the cab. His first thought was of cops, but cops didn't have green lights, and he wasn't speeding.

The light had flooded the truck, increasing in intensity and blinding him as he drove. Then, the light turned from green, to blue, and a quick flash of red. The radio began to flip through stations, twisting sounds and mingling voices into a warped and warbled cacophony. He'd slammed his foot down hard on the brake pedal, causing the truck's tires to screech and squeal as the vehicle swerved and stopped in a sideways stance on the road. The light had moved through the truck, and then he watched it linger not far up the road ahead of him. He opened the door and jumped down from the cab and onto the road.

He would never forget the sight he'd seen not far up ahead. He could see its flat, saucer shape as it oscillated in the sky above him. And then suddenly it stopped its momentary to and fro motion "on a dime," as his father might say. It was hovering high above, yet he was not directly underneath it. It lingered at a distance of some thirty feet in front of the truck. He watched as the bottom part of the thing rotated, opened, and closed again. He'd hardly taken notice that the radio had returned to his station, resuming its undistorted rendition of "Come as You Are." The song blared from the background as he watched, stupefied by the strange phantom in the sky.

*And I swear that I don't have a gun...*
*No I don't have a gun...*
*No I don't have a gun...*

It was motionless, stationary in a setting that seemed almost reluctant to acknowledge its existence. The trees that lined the side of the back road began to sway their branches, and he'd watched as an invisible wind rustled the new green leaves with a light gale force. He felt heat all around him. It had to be coming from the craft; he'd seen it open. What was it? It wasn't a plane or a helicopter, and it didn't look like anything he'd ever seen before. He stood gawking at its presence, waiting for it to acknowledge him. Instinct told him that it watched him just the same.

And then it was gone. The flash with which it had disappeared was faster than he could register, quicker than he could comprehend. He wasn't even sure that he'd seen it move, but it had to have moved; it was no longer in sight. He turned all around him, his eyes searching everywhere. He moved away from the truck, farther into the road, turning this way and that, desperate for any sign that he hadn't imagined what he'd witnessed only seconds before. He walked over and stood in the spot directly beneath where the craft had hovered.

There was nothing now.

The DJ was announcing the end of the song as he ran back to the truck and jumped back into the cab. He revved the engine and sped away from the scene with his eyes moving back and forth from the ascending speedometer, to his right, left, and straight ahead. It took him only seconds to flee the spot and arrive at the end of the back road. He turned onto the highway but didn't feel like going to Ted's. He had no idea how he would explain this to anyone. He felt too freaked-out to sit there and act like nothing had just occurred. Within minutes, he drove hastily past the flashing neon sign belonging to Ted's Bar and Grill.

As soon as he'd arrived home, he stepped into the shower, washing away the workday's grime but not the images that stayed alive in his mind. The flash of green that followed him was just as bright even with his eyes closed under the raging torrent of the showerhead. The silent, rotating disc was still as fresh and vivid as it was less than thirty minutes ago. He'd changed into his sweats and tee-shirt, and then lounged on the couch, watching the Saturday-night Horrorfest on TV. But the movie was only an assemblage of images that passed on the screen, while his thoughts of what he'd seen roamed in different directions.

He would never forget how it moved, how it rotated, how quickly it disappeared. The slight shaking of his hands provoked a sudden surprise. At over six feet tall and one hundred and eighty pounds, he didn't scare easily, but for the first time in his life, he wasn't ashamed to admit that he'd had the shit scared out of him.

As his eyes stared mindlessly at the movie, he felt a peculiar onset of fatigue, something beyond tiredness. He experienced the strangest feeling of being in front of the TV, but not really being there, as if he were lost in some hazy dream state, and the moment itself was not real. Soon, he pressed the power button on the remote, turning off the television and silencing a scream queen with one touch. He rose from the couch and was soon fast asleep in his own bed.

But just after 5:00 am, he awoke, slightly feverish as a nighttime sweat slicked his forehead. A dizzy spell spun in his head when his feet touched the floor. A sea of nausea swept his stomach and was suddenly gone. This wasn't the flu; something was wrong. He felt a strange and almost electrifying jagged edge even through the fatigue that lingered like a fog. The nighttime sweat soon broke as the nauseous churning in his stomach passed. The symptoms seemed to fluctuate, attacking him intermittently, leaving behind the pronounced fatigue in its wake. He returned to bed and allowed sleep to overcome him once more.

The strange and sudden sickness hadn't subsided as the Sunday morning light breached the window blinds and woke him from an unsteady slumber. He hadn't felt this way until after he'd arrived home last night, after he'd encountered that bizarre anomaly in the sky. Somehow, it was connected to what he was feeling right now; he was more than certain of it. But today was Sunday, and his doctor wasn't in. He needed to see someone. He needed to report what he'd seen. Something was not right.

He placed a call to his doctor's emergency service and was then referred to University Hospital's ER for treatment. He hadn't gone into the details of the night before. He merely reported his symptoms and described the sudden onset of them. It had taken less than ten minutes to drive to the hospital, and after describing his symptoms once again, the emergency staff seemed to take a curious interest in him. He watched them exchange glances and noticed how quickly they'd attended to him, setting him up in a triage unit within seconds.

Normally, he would've expected to sit in the ER for hours on end, but several nurses had attended to him in a short time, taking his blood pressure, temperature, and making him repeat the answers to the same questions over and over again. He wasn't about to reveal what he'd seen last night to a nurse who made rounds and recorded information. He didn't feel the need to regurgitate the details to someone who couldn't help him. After the nurses left, he'd waited only minutes for a doctor to arrive, a tall man in his late fifties with glasses and a balding head.

"Mr. Rowe, I'm Dr. Adams," he said. "I want to run a few quick tests on you, if I may."

He'd then been chauffeured by wheelchair to the elevator and up to another floor. The sign on the double doors read, "Radiology Lab." Something was up. Did they know something? He'd remained quiet about last night's event, but they were surely testing him for something, waving some sort of an electrical device over him as he laid face-up on the table, wrapped in a leaden bib. The technician had even worn protective gear. He felt sure now that something *was* going on, but he was too afraid to ask.

They hadn't brought him back to the triage unit in the ER, but to a smaller room nearby, where he waited to be diagnosed. A sudden paranoia swept him and grew larger with each passing moment as he waited. What was taking so long? Was he contagious? Soon, Dr. Adams was shutting the door behind him as he entered. He began flipping through the pages of a folder. When he spoke, his words were unimaginable.

"Mr. Rowe, what you have is a slight case of radiation sickness."

The words stung him and repeated silently through his mind. He remembered the saucer-shaped craft hovering above him, how its bottom opened up with a slight rotation and closed again. *Radiation sickness...*

46

"You're the second case I've seen so far in the past twelve hours."

*The second case...* So, there was someone else; someone who must've seen the exact same thing he had. The doctor continued.

"Your exposure is of a lesser extent. I need to know how this happened to you. I have another patient that's been exposed, and no one's really clear on how any of this happened. But we need to get to the bottom of it, especially if we're about to see more cases."

Shane remained hesitant. What if they thought he was crazy? What if he caused unwanted, widespread attention that would forever be attached to him? He looked at the doctor, then at the floor, at the doctor again, and then up at the ceiling. How would he begin? He sighed and reluctantly spoke.

"I quit working shortly after midnight, last night," he began. "As I was driving home, something seemed like it was following me. It was a blinding green light. I was on one of the back roads when I stopped my truck, got out, and looked up above. I saw something in the sky last night, something I can't explain."

He went on to detail the shape of the craft and how it moved. He related to Adams how it opened and closed, and how the wind picked up around him, rustling and swaying the treetops. Dr. Adams didn't look at him with skepticism, only a willingness to understand.

"Were you able to identify what type of craft it was from where you stood?"

"No," he said. "I'd never seen anything like it before in my life."

Adams's questions continued. How far away was he? How long had he watched the shape in the sky? Was anyone else present, or any other cars? Shane had answered his questions as well as he could through the drifting fog of fatigue. Then, Adams provided him with a slight sense of relief.

"Your exposure is minimal, but enough to cause the fatigue and slight nausea. You'll be fine. I just want to keep you overnight for observation, and most likely, you'll be out of here. But first, there's someone I want you to speak with—her name is Dr. Logan."

\* \* \* \*

Susan hurried to her office where Dylan had been waiting for her. The look of expectancy on his face was the first thing she noticed as she walked through the door. He quickly rose from the chair, his eyes wide in anticipation.

"The patient who came to the ER a short time ago is a young man," she said. "From what Adams has told me, his story sounds like it matches Ursula's almost identically."

"Can we see him?" Dylan asked. Susan shared his readiness. Something unexplainable *was* happening, and it was becoming more and more apparent.

"He's been admitted to a room for observation. Let's go."

They left her office and took the elevator up to the third floor, where Shane Rowe had been admitted. Susan shared the young man's file with Dylan as the elevator doors closed.

"His name is Shane Rowe," she said. "He's twenty-one and lives in Green Valley. He works at Happy's Restaurant and has his own apartment. No history of mental issues, or physical ones for that matter. According to Adams, he seems like a normal, rational, well-balanced young man who claims to have seen something in the sky last night. Something he can't explain, as Adams quoted him. He also claims that the radiation *had* to have come from the object."

"Just like Ursula," Dylan interjected.

"Exactly. But, Adams claims that Mr. Rowe didn't go into any elaborate details. He figured that's where we should come in."

"So, Adams thinks that he'll trust us more and that we'll be able to develop a clearer picture by talking to him." Dylan's surmise had been quick.

"Precisely." Susan snatched the file from his hands as the elevator doors opened.

They passed one hospital room after another, until finally, Susan turned and nodded to Dylan when she read the name posted on the plaque beside the door—*Rowe, Shane.* She entered first and Dylan followed. A tall, stocky, young man stared back at them from the bed.

"Hello, Mr. Rowe, I'm Dr. Susan Logan," she said. "I'm a psychiatrist and—"

"No way, lady, seriously?" The young man in bed scoffed. "I'm not crazy."

"No, no, of course you're not. I'm sorry, Mr. Rowe." Susan quickly apologized. "I'm not here as a psychiatrist, unless, of course, you would feel the need to see me in that regard. What you didn't give me a chance to say was that I'm also a parapsychologist. I'm here to listen to your story from that perspective."

She recognized the slight shame of his silence as he stared at her, obviously unsure of her meaning.

"I study the paranormal," she said. "I'm the director of Green Valley University's Paranormal Research and Investigative Society. I would have thought Dr. Adams had mentioned that to you. This is one of my investigators, Dylan Rasche."

She motioned to her right. Dylan moved closer and shook the young man's hand.

"We are very interested in what you saw last night—" she paused. "May I call you Shane?" she continued as he nodded. "Dylan is not only an investigator with the society, but the society's chief investigator and founder. Ironically, Dylan thinks he witnessed something last night as well, and the young female patient that Dr. Adams mentioned is someone we both know. So, I'm sure you can understand why we're not only interested, but why this hits so close to home for us.

"Believe me, Shane. I've taken a great deal of flack over my decision to become a parapsychologist. My colleagues in the field of psychiatry aren't exactly proud of me. But my interest in the paranormal has stemmed from a time when I was very young. So, I assure you, I will be the last person to call you crazy."

A slight grin cracked across his face, one that told her that the icy, apprehensive exterior that froze this story solid somewhere underneath had melted away. He sighed faintly and then motioned with his open hand.

"Please, sit down."

They positioned the two small visitor chairs alongside the bed and sat.

"Please, take your time, Shane." Susan instructed him. "Relax, and try to envision the night's events in the order of which they occurred."

"I worked my shift until midnight last night at Happy's," he began. "It was a hectic Saturday night as usual: tons of customers, loud noises, and bitchy managers. I couldn't wait to get out of there. I punched my card at midnight and left."

Shane detailed how he'd driven his usual route, stopped at the convenience store, and detoured onto the back road on his way to Ted's Bar and Grill. The mention of Ted's Bar and Grill caused Dylan and Susan to casually glance at each other. The thought of that place stirred what now seemed like ancient memories. Susan redirected her focus back to the young man in the bed who continued his account.

"This strange green light grew brighter until it blinded me. I couldn't see, so I slammed on the brakes and swerved the truck sideways off to the side of the road. That's when my radio went haywire. It began flipping through the stations on its own. There was a sea of green light all around me. Then, I got out of the truck and stood in the road.

"It was lingering up ahead, not far from me, maybe thirty feet or so. I couldn't believe it. It was disc-shaped, like a flying saucer, kind of gray in color, and it was hovering and rotating. I saw its bottom open up and then close. That's when the wind picked up all around me. It was swaying the treetops, and then I felt this warm heat out of nowhere.

Swaying the treetops, heat, Susan thought. *Again, just like Ursula.*

"It wasn't a plane, or a helicopter. It was no aerial object that I'd ever seen before. It was a UFO; I know it was."

His voice was adamant, persistent, slightly tiring from retelling the story.

"And then it was gone, disappeared as though it was never there." He snapped his fingers. "That's how fast it moved. I remember turning and looking all around me, trying to see if it had gone somewhere else, but it just vanished. For a second, I even considered whether or not I was seeing things.

"I didn't stop at Ted's," he continued. "After I saw that thing, I just wanted to go home. It spooked the hell out of me. I went straight back to my place, got in the shower, and washed away the stink of fried onions and Happy burgers."

"That may account for the fact that your exposure level is only minimal," Susan said. "That shower you took may have lessened it. If you hadn't, you could've been much sicker."

"That's what the doctor told me," Shane replied. "Afterward, I sat on the couch watching TV, and I began to feel tired, almost flu-like. I went to bed and felt like that all night."

"And so you ended up here," Susan concluded.

"You got it," he said.

Dylan leaned forward in the chair, his posture adding conviction to what he was about to tell the young man.

"Shane, something you said struck me. You said that for a second, you considered whether or not you were seeing things. That's what I felt like last night at around the exact same time that you're describing."

Dylan detailed his episode with the telescope, how the flash of green had evaded him. "I could swear that it moved. But it was so fast, I couldn't be sure. What you're telling me coincides with all of my suspicions. I should thank you. Now I know that I'm not crazy, either."

"So, what I saw was real?" Shane asked. "There's something really going on here?"

"I'm afraid so, Shane." Susan said. "But fortunately for us, and you, we're paranormal investigators. This looks like it's going to be our next case, and with your help, hopefully, we'll get to the bottom of this."

"Well, yeah, I mean, but I'm not sure what else I can tell you. That's about everything."

"As a doctor," Susan advised, "you get some rest. Don't run away from the memory of it, Shane. The more you recall the more help it is to us."

"That's right," Dylan said. "And if there's anything else you remember, or anything at all you want to know from me about my experience, please don't hesitate to call me, night or day."

Dylan handed the young man his business card.

"Thanks," he said. "I'll do that."

They made their way back through the hospital corridors, and then spoke more privately and discreetly back in Susan's office.

"So, what's our plan of action?" Dylan asked. He and Susan stared at each other from across her desk.

"Obviously, we have to call the team together," she said. "This is going to be a lot for them to digest. But, we have to tell them about Ursula. It's Sunday. So, meeting, tonight at my house?"

"Let's do it."

Susan reached for the phone.

# Chapter Five

### ~ Janette LaRue ~

Marv had just hung up the phone with one of his many "spies," as he called them. The young informant, one of several whom Marv paid handsomely for information, reported that a young woman from Green Valley had been admitted to University Hospital with radiation sickness. In addition, a young man, also from Green Valley, was admitted just today with the same diagnosis, though not as severe. Marv's inner instinct blared much like an alarm. He suddenly thought of what he and Duke had witnessed the night before.

He hadn't actually caught sight of whatever the object was, but he did see the bright lights as they lit up the sky like an endless stage. Brilliant blue and green painted the sky like a canvass. Duke began barking as if he'd spotted an invisible intruder somewhere in the air, somewhere in the sky. Marv knew that something was there, but whatever it was had moved too fast for his aging eyes to catch. And then thoughts of Geoffrey Rasche popped into his head. How odd that now, little Dylan Rasche was the chief investigator of the University's Paranormal Research and Investigative Society. Another remarkable coincidence was Susan Logan.

He'd grown up with Susan Logan. They'd both lived on Winchester Lane as kids and gone to the same schools all of their lives. Marv was a few years older than Susan. He hadn't seen her in years, and she was now the director of the university's paranormal society.

Though he hadn't encountered them, there were two people that he knew on the paranormal team. Granted, he'd only met Dylan a few times when he was a kid, but he was sure that the young man would remember him. He'd also heard of the infamous Leah Leeds. He'd managed to get his hands on a copy of her memoir, a fascinating read written by a mere teenager at the date of its publication. Marv had also heard stories of what happened in Cedar Manor. He'd worked at the paper with that sneaky, somewhat contemptible punk, Cory Chase, though his death was a regrettable tragedy.

Yes, Marv knew a lot of people, and a lot of stories, and a lot of people who provided those stories. He wanted nothing from the paranormal team. He had no interest in Cory Chase's death; it was his own doing, ultimately. Marv only wanted to speak to them about what he saw last night. And of course, it might be the right time to mention his suspicions to Dylan Rasche about his father's untimely demise. It was about time that Dylan knew about the rumor of a struggle on the mountaintop, the rumor provided to him by his cop friend who suddenly disappeared to Florida and was never heard from again.

Two young people were now admitted into the hospital with radiation sickness, and Marv was making a connection in his mind to what he and Duke had seen last night. It all had to be connected; it was far too coincidental not to be. He wondered if the paranormal team knew about any of this. Maybe it was time to fill them in. Susan was also a psychiatrist at the hospital. He would phone the hospital to get in touch with her, but just as he went for the phone, it rang.

\* \* \* \*

Janette LaRue's job as a 911 responder was often a hectic one—domestic violence, heart attacks, strokes and seizures, drug overdoses, assaults, traffic accidents, house fires, and even the occasional nutcase. But nothing had prepared her for the aftermath of two particular calls she received on Saturday night after midnight. The first of which had come from a young woman whose weakened voice had spoken desperately through the phone.

*"Please, help me,"* she said.

*"What is the nature of your emergency?"* Janette asked a question she often hated.

*"Help me. I'm sick."*

She heard the phone fall away from the young woman's grasp.

*"Hello? Where are you located?"*

There was no response.

*"Ma'am, are you there? What is your location?"*

Again, no response.

Janette had called out several more times and realized that the young woman could be unconscious. She looked at the address that flashed on her computer screen.

*328 Falcon Street; Apt 2*

The name registered to the phone user was flashing as well.

*Ursula Masters*

Janette had immediately sent an ambulance to the address and stayed on the line until the paramedics retrieved the subject: a young woman, semi-conscious on the floor of her second story apartment, cause unknown. The paramedics had been taking her to University Hospital, and the call was soon automatically logged into Janette's computer system.

The next call came about five minutes after the young woman's distress call. It was from an elderly woman only a few blocks away from Ursula Masters' address. The woman spoke normally and with an inquisitive tone.

*"I'm sorry to bother you with what you might think is nonsense,"* she began. Janette listened intently. The woman paused before continuing. *"Have you received any calls regarding something strange in the sky tonight?"*

Janette closed her eyes. The woman didn't sound like a nutcase. But she was older, and Janette thought of the numerous, inevitable possibilities that come with advancing age.

*"No, ma'am, we have not,"* she said. *"I personally haven't. Is there something I can assist you with, ma'am?"*

The woman detailed in lucid and descriptive speech, how she'd been looking out the window before bedtime, a habit she'd adhered to for years, when she saw something in the sky.

*"I could almost see the shape of it,"* she said. *"But not that clearly because it was emitting a bright green light, almost blinding. It looked like a disc, but I can't be sure."*

The woman hissed a sigh of obvious embarrassment through the phone.

54

*"Look, I know this sounds crazy. But I couldn't believe my eyes. I know it wasn't a helicopter, or a plane, or anything like that. Then it was gone, like it was never there. Oh, I feel so foolish."*

*"No, ma'am, it's okay,"* Janette reassured her. *"Please don't. We haven't heard anything through here, but if you'd like to leave your name, I'd be happy to pass this information along in case it ends up being useful somehow."*

Janette could hear a pause that sounded like hesitation.

*"Well, okay, yes. My name is Mabel Forrester."*

Janette had already known the woman's name; it had flashed on her screen.

*"And your address is 526 Phoenix Drive?"*

The woman confirmed her address, which also flashed on the screen. Janette assured the woman that if anything were reported on the matter; her name would be kept as reference for the proper authorities.

*"Okay, then,"* she said, the sound of hesitancy and skepticism still lingering in her voice.

She had asked the woman if there was anything else she could help her with, but she declined, and Janette ended the call. That call, like all calls, was also logged automatically into Janette's computer system. And then the strangest thing happened. It was toward the end of her shift, and Janette had been comparing her manual, paper log of calls to her electronic one that she would scroll through, a task she performed before the end of every shift. It was then that another, more mysterious call had reached her line.

*"911 Emergency,"* she said.

*"Janette LaRue?"*

The voice on the other end echoed with an eerie, mechanical drone. No caller had ever referred to her by her name.

*"This is Janette LaRue,"* she said. Her tone of confusion inquired who it was without asking.

*"Look at your electronic log,"* the voice instructed her. *"Remember the calls from Ursula Masters and Mabel Forrester?"*

*"Yes."*

*"No, you don't,"* the voice said. The man's tone was direct, almost threatening. *"Look at the screen; they're no longer there."*

The man had been right. The calls from Ursula Masters and Mabel Forrester no longer appeared on the screen. They were no longer in the computer. It was as if someone had hacked into her system and deleted them.

*They won't be found on the backup log either. You're to say nothing, not a word, especially to your employer. You will destroy the page of your paper log displaying those calls. This call is coming from an untraceable line and will go unnoticed. It will not log into your system."*

*"Who is this?!"* Janette's feisty attitude toward the mysterious caller boasted that underneath the collected composure of the 911 operator, he was messing with a sista'.

*"Don't say a word to anyone, Janette. You have two beautiful children. You don't want to leave them without a mother."*

Her heart sank down to her stomach. She felt the oxygen leave her lungs as she heard the click on the other end. It was over. It hadn't sounded like a prank. She was sweating profusely. She looked around her and saw that her co-workers were leaving their stations. It was time to leave. Alex, her boss, walked over to her.

*"You okay, Janette? Not in a big hurry to get out of here tonight,"* he said with a laugh.

She looked back at her screen. The names of Ursula Masters and Mabel Forrester were gone. It was definitely no prank. She looked back at Alex. She opened her mouth to speak and thought of her children, a boy and a girl. She closed her mouth.

*"No, just a little slow on the draw tonight, that's all."*

She had finished up without saying a word and left the building.

She'd hardly slept at all throughout the night, tossing, turning, and recalling the sound of that strange voice in her head. The voice had been distorted, as if it was mechanically altered. It sounded warped, unnatural. The replay of it in her mind sent a shiver up her spine. The more she thought about that voice, the bigger the ball of tension grew inside of her.

Janette couldn't call her reaction paranoia, because it was all too real. Who could it have been? Who would tamper with such sensitive information and why? But more importantly, who would threaten her life along with the lives of her two precious children? Now, she sat on the front porch watching her boy and girl play in the yard, and a steady stream of dark thoughts kept her mind occupied. Her head turned in every direction, scanning for anything out of the ordinary. What if they were watching her and her children right now? What if they came out of hiding and committed a drive-by right here in her front yard? What if her cell phone was bugged in some way, her internet?

Her eyes shifted at every sound, every approaching car, and then followed her children as they moved through the yard. She closed her eyes and inhaled, hoping to stop the heart palpitations she'd been feeling all night long. She opened her eyes. She couldn't call Alex. She couldn't call the police, or any other authority. She felt sure that they would be watching or listening. What was she going to do? Janette watched her children play in the yard and realized one thing—she didn't like being cornered. When she was cornered, she came out of that corner clawing like a wildcat, especially when it came to her kids.

Then suddenly, a thought occurred to her. She wasn't afraid to throw this whole thing into the spotlight. Maybe, just maybe, casting a light onto this mess would keep them safe. She had to do something or this state of nervous tension she felt right now would cripple her for the rest of her life, not to mention her children's lives. She realized now how right Mabel Forrester had been. The poor old woman *had* seen something. And if something was going on, the world needed to know about it.

She wasn't going to call the police, the FBI, or the FCC. She would call Marv Kincaid. She'd read his column for many years, and he was known in this area as a hero, having exposed so much scandal and wrongdoings committed against the people of this community for so many years. It would put her and her family in the spotlight, but maybe that's exactly what needed to happen. Let the world be aware that two innocent children and their mother had been threatened by some unknown, unseen source. Maybe it would be safer in the light.

She watched her kids playing and decided it was time for them all to go inside.

"Rodney, Cara?" she called out. "Come on, time to go inside."

"Aw, Mom!" The response had been the usual one.

"I said time to go inside, now."

Janette never needed to raise her voice. She need only change it to the sterner, more direct tone that her kids were used to hearing, and they knew that she meant business. They picked up the ball they were playing with in the yard and joined her up on the porch. She ushered them in first and continued to gaze out at the world from the front porch. *Where are you?* She thought. *Who are you? You think I'm afraid?*

She backed up slowly, keeping her eyes focused outward in an almost fixed state of paranoia. Once inside, she shut the screen door in front of her, locked it, and continued to watch. Slowly, she closed the front door and locked it also. Soon, she would call Marv Kincaid.

* * * *

It wasn't his house phone that rang, but the line he kept open using Call-Transfer, which connected the newspaper office to his home office. He answered that phone at any time, day or night. One could never know when an interesting story might pop up. It was only a few steps to the room he used as an office. He sat down in his chair and picked up the phone.

"Marv Kincaid," he answered.

"Mr. Kincaid," said the female voice. "My name is Janette LaRue, and I'm calling you from the car on one of those pre-paid disposable phones. I'm afraid I have to. Um…"

The woman sounded nervous, afraid.

"I'm a 911 Emergency Responder in Green Valley. I really need to see you about something that happened last night. This story may be a big one for you."

Marv suddenly thought once more about what he and Duke had seen.

"I still worry about telling you any of this, even on a pre-paid phone, and if we meet, I don't think I can come to you."

"Are you in some kind of trouble, Ms. LaRue?"

There was a pause.

"Yes, I've been threatened."

Marv sat upright in his chair at her words. Deep inside, he was sure he could guess quite accurately what this was all about.

"Alright, dear. Are you being followed right now?"

"I don't know. I honestly don't know."

"Well, my home is too risky; everyone knows where I live. I have a better idea. I have an apartment duplex that I rent out. No one knows that I'm the owner, and no one is living there at the moment. I can make it there in ten minutes. If I give you the address, how long before you can be there?"

"As soon as possible," she said. He could hear the rise and fall of her nervous breath.

"Alright then." He gave her the address, and they agreed to meet in twenty minutes. He told her to be careful, to act normal, and to not attract attention. He also gave her directions to the house and told her about an alley behind it. "You can park there and come in through the back door. No one will see you."

Marv made it to the two-sided, beige colored, brick house in only ten minutes. He parked in the alley behind the house and used his key for the back door. Inside, there was no electricity, so there were no lights, and the utilities were not turned on. But it was the end of April, and there was no need for heat or air conditioning. The temperature was comfortable. Out of an underlying sense of paranoia, Marv looked around the house as he always did. Usually it was to inspect for the possibility of squatters or burglars, but this time it was so much more, yet he feared admitting it to himself.

The house was dead quiet, the silence reverberating in his ears, and nothing stirred. He peeped out of one of the front windows and looked out at the street. The only cars were the parked ones of the neighbors across the street. No cars were passing by, no suspicious vehicles loitered. He moved away from the window and opened the small bag he'd brought with him. It contained his mini voice-recorder, as well as a pad and some pencils. He sat quietly on the couch—waiting.

Another ten minutes passed before suddenly, a gentle and modest knocking came from the back door. Marv stood slowly from the couch and walked over to it. Through a back window, he spied a young black woman who glanced up and down the alley, as if waiting for someone to abruptly appear out of nowhere. Marv unlocked the door and opened it.

"Ms. LaRue?"

She looked at him, and as she recognized him, her tightened shoulders sagged in relief.

"Mr. Kincaid," she said.

He quickly ushered her through the back door and shut it behind her. After locking the door, he pulled down the blind that shaded its window.

"I insist that you call me Marv."

"Janette," she said.

"Walk behind me, Janette," he said. "We'll go into the living room."

Marv had quickly remembered the window blinds in the front of the house.

"Just stay right there until I tell you to come in," he said.

Janette waited in the windowless dining room as Marv pulled down the living room window blinds one by one, rendering the room even darker than it already appeared. Now, it was a semi-furnished, vacated abode doubling as a safe house, yet someone had banished the sunshine from it. He told her to come in, and she sat in the chair across from him on the couch. A small, oak coffee table stood between them. He set the mini-recorder in front of her.

"Do you mind if I record?"

"Hell no. I have to tell somebody, anybody. I don't know what to do. Marv, I'm on my own. My husband died four years ago."

She began sobbing, and Marv could see that the tension building inside of her had just burst like a broken dam. He stood from the couch and held her where she sat. He was comforting a woman he'd met only two minutes ago.

"There, there," he said. "No one's going to hurt you. I'm going to see to that."

When she'd finished, he asked if she was all right. She nodded, and he sat back down. Marv pressed the red button on the recorder.

"I want you to start from the very beginning. From what or whom are you running?"

"I don't know." She told him again that she was a 911 responder. She described her duties and told how last night, she'd been working her regular shift.

"I got a call from a young woman who was later found semi-conscious," she began. "The paramedics then brought her to University Hospital."

She paused.

"Go on," Marv prompted.

"After that, I got another call from an elderly woman, and coincidently, I noticed that she was only a few blocks away from the young woman. I know because I've lived in this area my entire life. Anyway, she asked me if I, or any of the other responders, received any calls about something strange in the sky. I thought it was odd, but I get nutcases calling in all the time. Yet this woman was elderly and serious. I didn't have any reason to think there was anything wrong with her. I kept her name in case anything should arise, and that was that. The call ended.

"At the end of my shift, an even stranger call came through. It was a man whose voice was indescribable." Janette told Marv about how the voice sounded almost not real, maybe mechanically altered in some way. "He called me by my name, and that never happens. He asked me if I remembered those two specific calls, which I did. And then he told me to forget those calls ever came through. He told me to look at my screen, and sure enough, those calls had disappeared from my log, as though someone had hacked into my system and deleted them.

"Then I was told to destroy the page of my paper log with those calls on it. I was instructed not to say a word to anyone, included my boss, and then he threatened me."

"He threatened you?" Marv asked, probing for specifics.

"He told me that if I said a word, I would be leaving my children without a mother. He said, 'you have two beautiful children Janette.'" She began sobbing again and shaking. "I'm normally a strong woman, Marv, but this has got me scared! Whoever it was, is watching me. I know it! He threatened me and my children outright, and I believe him."

Marv could feel his own concern showing on his face. This story was exactly what he'd dreaded, exactly what he'd been hoping was not possible, but an instinct deep down had affirmed it from the beginning. He remembered standing with Duke in the yard and the lights that he'd seen in the sky. Duke had been going crazy. Obviously, Duke had seen or sensed much more than he had. He was going to have to tell her. It was for her safety. But first, he had a few questions.

"The older woman who phoned in," he asked. "Did she tell you that she saw something?"

"She said she saw something in the sky, and that it was emitting a blinding green light. She said it was disc-shaped and that it wasn't a helicopter or a plane."

Marv felt the sudden and incessant pounding of his heart.

"Can you recall this woman's name?"

Janette rolled her eyes upward, thinking for a moment. "Mabel Forrester," she said. "Yeah, that's it."

"Do you, by any chance, remember her address?"

Janette hesitated for a moment.

"Remember, Janette, this woman's life could be in danger as well."

"I think it was 526 Phoenix Drive."

Marv wrote all of it down on his pad.

"And what about the page from your manual log?" he asked. "I take it you destroyed it?"

"Yes. It's an oversight that I can't explain to my boss. I have a good record."

Then Marv thought about the young woman admitted to the hospital with radiation sickness. She had to be the first of the two callers that Janette was describing.

"Do you remember the name of the young woman who was found unconscious?"

"Her name was Ursula Masters."

She gave him the address. Marv continued to scribble, and then he looked right at her.

"Alright, now I want you to listen to me," he said. "First, I want you to stay calm. You did the right thing in coming to me and not the police. There is nothing they could have done for you anyway. I'm not going to lie to you, Janette; this is very serious."

"You know who it was?"

"No," he said. "I can't be sure of that, but let me tell you a story."

He told her about everything that happened when he took Duke outside the night before. He told her what little he'd seen, how Duke reacted, and why his suspicions rose.

"This area has had quite a few incidents in the past with UFOs."

The expression on her face was a cross between shock and skepticism.

"Obviously, you're not old enough to remember the Kecksburg incident," he said.

"No," she shrugged, "but I've heard of it."

"Well, let's just say that quite a few people were threatened back then to keep things quiet. Many claim that it was the government that enforced the threatening hush-hush, but none of it was ever proven. There was also some controversy surrounding the death of a local astronomer years ago. He was a friend of mine. Nothing was ever proven there either. This area has had quite a few run-ins with the so-called 'Men in Black.' Ever heard of them?"

Janette eyes widened. She'd heard the stories. She simply nodded her head, stunned into silence. Marv was taking notes on the pad of paper while the wheels of the recorder rolled along.

"Janette, whoever these people are, they're very real. I want you to do as they asked, and say nothing to anyone yet. Are you familiar with the paranormal investigators from the university?"

"I've heard of them." She shrugged again.

"I was planning on seeking them out about what I'd seen last night. The pieces of a puzzle seem to be falling together here. You were asked if anyone called in about seeing anything, and, well, *I saw* something. I may want you to repeat your story to the investigators, but there is someone I have in mind to call first. I also want you to rest assured that if you say nothing, they will not bother you. And you could be right about the phone and the computers. Say nothing through those forums either, got it?"

She nodded. He asked for her address, and she gave it to him.

"Janette, I'm going to have one of the people that work for me drop by your house in the near future. That is how we'll communicate. No one will ever see me at your door. Now, I want you to get back in your car, and drive home, and not a word to anyone, got it?"

"Got it."

Soon, Marv was looking out of the back window, checking that the coast was clear before Janette could leave the house. He let her out, waited as she started her car, and watched her drive away. Marv sat back down in the comfortable dimness and thought about everything. So, it was happening all over again. So many memories replayed in his mind: being a teenager during the Kecksburg incident, the Bigfoot sightings of the 1970s, and the mysterious death of Geoffrey Rasche. Now, in this new, twenty-first century world, the mystery was returning to this small neck of the woods once again.

Marv had told Janette that he was going to call someone he knew, before going to the investigators. As he'd been thinking earlier, he knew many people, many connections, and now was the time to utilize them. Back in the nineties, he'd discovered a young man who was a MUFON investigator. MUFON is the famous "Mutual UFO Network." The network is a known group of investigators dedicated to the investigation of UFO sightings all around the world. He'd sought out the young man after he'd gone poking his nose into the mystery of Geoffrey Rasche's death.

That young man would have to be in his late forties by now, easily. Marv still remembered his name—Seth Dornan. Surely, Marv would figure out a way to contact him, even after all these years. This time, there may be proof that something *is* happening in Green Valley. And with two exposures to radiation and at least three witnesses, and possibly countless others, MUFON would have to investigate this. Marv rose from the old, abandoned couch on which he'd been sitting. It was time to get back to his home office. He had phone calls to make.

* * * *

The two men were dressed exactly the same—black sport jackets covering pressed, white dress shirts and stiff, black ties. Low-pressed black pants and black shoes matched the rest of their dark attire. Fedoras donned their heads, and dark sunglasses shaded their eyes from the modest, yet opulent April sun. Their faces were oddly shaped and slightly different from each other's, one a slimmer face, the other more rounded, but they were suited up to match identically. The black sedan they sat in was parked in an area somewhere close to where Janette LaRue had just vanished from their tracking.

They'd watched as she entered Wal-Mart, followed her as she left, and trailed her on the bypass. But then sometime after exiting the bypass, she disappeared. She'd been using a handheld phone in the car, talking to someone as she drove. But when they'd tapped into her cell phone, there was nothing. She was using a different phone, possibly someone else's, maybe a disposable one she'd purchased at Wal-Mart. They couldn't link a wiretap connection to it.

"Who do you think she was talking to?" The heavier man with the rounded face asked. His tone was flat, even, with an almost carefree abandon.

"Hard to say," the other replied, "but we'll find out one way or another. She disappeared into one of these streets. She has to be close by."

Just as the taller man in black who sat in the passenger's side spoke, Janette LaRue's gray Oldsmobile barreled out from a side alley and into the street.

"There's our girl," the man in the driver's seat said. "Should we hunt her down?"

"No, not yet," the other said. "Let's trail her discreetly, find out where she goes. If she *has* told someone, we'll smoke that person out, one way or another." His voice was relaxed, and then it playfully and psychotically crooned with a singsong melody.

"Just a matter of time…"

# Chapter Six

## ~ A Strange History ~

Susan Logan lived in a prominent neighborhood, a sprawling cul-de-sac, where two and sometimes three-story palatial homes towered almost threateningly over the windy, double-wide streets below. No surprise for a girl who grew up on Winchester Lane. "King's Haven" was situated and neatly concealed in the northern section of Green Valley, where peaceful quiet coexisted with aristocratic refinement. The immense, two-story structure she called home seemed like one house stacked on top of another with modern gable windows that looked out upon her vast front yard. Two-stories of copper toned bricks were surrounded by spruce trees, and a walkway was flanked on each side by lamp posts, giving the place its regal and stately appearance. The street lamps in King's Haven began to light, one by one, in the fading daylight.

Inside, where hard oak floors shined beneath a brilliant and overhanging chandelier, marble slabs framed an out-of-season fireplace and formed a catacomb structure that reached all the way to the ceiling. Susan and Dylan sat in the living room, discussing the impending meeting.

"I want to wait until everyone gets here before going into any details," she said. "We'll conduct the meeting as we normally do. It's just that this time, it'll be a little more relaxed."

She raised the glass of wine in her hand, while she poured Dylan one. It would be a festive meeting, one meant to be tackled with a sense of calm and rationality. Susan had provided the wine, as well as the cheese, and other various hors d'oeuvres. She continued.

"There's a lot of history to be told tonight," she said, "much of which I can provide. You all were not even born at the time of the Kecksburg incident. Your father's journals and the history behind his investigations are also important."

Dylan held the journals up in his hand. He'd retrieved them from the safe in the floor before he left. It was essential that the team read every word of them.

"Right here," he said. "I've brought them."

"It may be a long meeting tonight, but at least we can relax. And, this is far more private than room 208. Also, I may have a guest this evening— one who will be able to shed some additional light on the Kecksburg story."

"Sounds interesting," he said. "Anyone we know?"

"No. But, you'll all meet soon enough."

The doorbell distracted her from the cheese cracker she was about to pop into her mouth. "Well, I think we have our first guest." She walked to the front door and looked out of the side window. "It's Brett." She turned the knob and opened the door.

"Mr. Taylor," she said. "So glad you made it."

"What's happening, Suzy Q.?" he asked, standing in the doorway.

"Everything," she said, as he walked through. "But, it all has to wait until the rest of the team is here. You haven't, by any chance, seen our other two esteemed investigators, have you?"

"Nope. Just me." He walked over to Dylan. "Are you okay? You sounded so strange on the phone last night."

Dylan shrugged and then frowned. Susan interrupted.

"It will all be revealed, Brett, as soon as we're all together. Meanwhile, you're the first to arrive. Sit down, relax, and pour yourself a glass of wine." She looked at the clock on the wall behind her. "Sidney and Leah should be here at any moment."

\* \* \* \*

The wheels of his van trekked effortlessly through the winding streets of the cul-de-sac. Susan had called a meeting with the entire team, and he knew all too well what that meant. She hadn't gone into details, only that she and Dylan had much to tell the team. So, Dylan was responsible for this new turn of events, whatever it might be. Susan had also mentioned that she had some news on an old friend of theirs. What old friend? Sidney thought of all this and recent events, as he swerved the steering wheel this way and that.

The voices he'd been so used to hearing had lately been silent to Sidney Pratt. Not since Aunt Vivian had warned him about the shifting shape of Brett Taylor had Sidney heard the voices. He knew nothing of what was going on in that big, fashionable house of Susan Logan's; and not the slightest clue came to him. Only the purr of the van's wheels riding the street reached his ears. But as he drove, little did he know that soon, with his human ears, he would hear things of which he'd never dreamed— things he would never understand.

Now, he wasn't too far from Susan's house, and he smiled as he noticed a blue Mustang convertible in the rearview mirror. It was cruising faster and faster, gaining ground on him, hoping to surpass him on the desolate double-wide street and beat him to the finish line.

* * * *

The brand new, blue Mustang convertible had been a gift from her father. She loved how the wheels on this thing took so smoothly to the streets. Her treasured new gift was a result of her upcoming graduation. It had taken her a little longer to achieve her master's degree than she'd hoped—maybe a year or so. But it was all because of past memories that had begun to haunt her. It was because she'd entered Cedar Manor and discovered that the resurging memories and vivid, haunting dreams were actually psychic, subliminal provocations sent from sleeping demons awakening in the darkness of that house.

The song playing from her CD player reminded her of her life story.

*Oh, I went searching for an answer...*
*Up the stairs...and down the hall*
*Not to find an answer...*
*Just to hear the call*
*Of a nightbird...singing...*
*Come away... come away...*
*Just like the white winged dove...*

Both the chorus and the guitar riff of this song made her step on it, almost flying to the music, and determined to outrun that familiar white van that lumbered solemnly not too far ahead. She knew the van well, and it was time to give Sidney a run for it in her new car. She quickly gained on him, watching as his head moved toward the rearview mirror, so that his eyes could see the speeding car behind him. He knew it was her. His speed picked up in acceptance of her offer. After all, it was getting dark and there were no other cars around.

The Mustang shot ahead until it was side by side with the van. She looked at Sidney in the front seat of the van. His eyes moved back and forth from her to the road in front of him. She would surely outrun the van within the next fleeting heartbeat. She laughed at him and beeped her horn. Sidney's middle finger went up in the air.

She nearly floored the Mustang's pedal and left the van long and far behind. She rounded the corner onto Susan's street and pulled into her long driveway. The van was soon behind her as she pulled in. In the time it took her to check her appearance in the rearview mirror and glance at her iPhone, Sidney had already gotten out of the van and was standing alongside it. He was staring at her, his arms folded. "The Edge of Seventeen" was still blaring from her CD player.

Leah Leeds pressed the off button on the CD player, keyed off the ignition, and stepped out of the car.

"Wow," Sidney said, awed by her subwoofer stereo system. "Don't ya just love Stevie?"

"Damn straight. So what do you think?" She motioned her hand to the car.

"I love it," he said. "Just don't drive like that all the time. You'll be giving us all heart attacks."

She laughed. "I won't." They began walking together through Susan's driveway and up onto the walkway. Leah pointed out Brett's car, already parked in the driveway. "So, why are we here? Do you know? Susan didn't tell me much."

Sidney shrugged. "All I know is that it has something to do with Dylan."

"What's wrong with Dylan?"

"I don't know yet," he said. "You're right, though; Susan didn't say much. But she hinted that it has something to do with his late father."

"Interesting," she said. They walked up a flight of stone stairs that led to the front door. "Susan mentioned not wanting to say much on the phone. This sounds serious."

"Well, we're here," Sidney said. "There's only one way to find out," He rang the doorbell.

* * * *

The ding-dong of the doorbell pealed through the house. Susan set her drink down on the marble and glass coffee table, walked over to the front door, and peeped through the window blind.

"Perfect," she said. "Our infamous duo has arrived together."

She opened the door, and there on the front porch stood Sidney Pratt, as plump as ever and sporting yet a new pair of glasses. These were more refined and set in gold trim, certainly less of the Coke-bottle type that she'd been used to seeing. Next to him stood Leah Leeds, as beautiful as ever, dressed in black pants and a matching blouse.

"The last to arrive," Susan said. She glanced behind Leah to the driveway and the blue Mustang convertible parked in it. "Very nice," she added. "You must take me for a ride soon."

"Not after you see how she drives it," Sidney said.

She opened the door wider, and Leah and Sidney stepped inside.

They all exchanged greetings, poured wine, tasted the appetizers, and even stepped outside to see Leah's new car. Upon returning, they sat in Susan's living room, comfortably situated on her three-sectional, plush leather sofa. The coffee table sat in the middle of their comfortable soiree. Then, the meeting began.

"As always," Susan said, "I'm sure you're all wondering why a meeting has been called. It's as strange as it is a long and complex story, but Dylan and I are going to fill you in from the beginning. Dylan, I think it's best if you speak first."

Dylan cleared his throat and spoke.

"Last night, shortly after midnight, I was gazing through the refracting telescope, searching to find the aurora borealis." He told them about the flash of green that had obstructed his view, how he'd thought he'd seen something move in the sky, but he hadn't been certain. He told how it was there and then gone in an instant. "Then, I called you," he said, pointing to Brett, who sat next to him.

"So, that's why you sounded so weirded out," he said.

"I know I saw something, but it all happened way too fast to be able to identify it. I kept thinking about it all night long. I knew it wasn't me. I knew I didn't bump the scope, and I knew it wasn't the scope itself. Whatever I'd seen was there, and of course, it had to have moved. I couldn't sleep at all last night. I tossed and turned and kept seeing my father's face in my mind."

The three other investigators looked up at Susan, who said nothing. They'd all known that Dylan's father had secretly been a UFO researcher.

"I'd known for quite a while that my father had kept another safe in the house, one that hid the journals he'd kept on his UFO investigations." Dylan described how Denise had shown him the safe, and how their long held but unspoken suspicions about their father's death had led them to that moment. "I'd never looked at those journals, but I decided to last night. I popped the safe open and I starting reading these."

He raised the journals up in his hands for all to see.

"And by what I've read in them," he said. "I'm convinced now, more than ever, that my father was murdered."

The investigators had yet to become accustomed to shock and surprise. Collective gasps and intakes of breath still filled the air around them. Susan watched as Dylan plopped the notebooks onto the coffee table, his eyes unflinching, remaining fixed on the old, worn out covers. When he began speaking again, he outlined the entire contents of the notebook journals: the span of years, his father's childhood fascination with the Kecksburg incident and subsequent study of it, the Bigfoot investigations, and the sightings that had come to his father's attention shortly before his death.

"My father ran into trouble while investigating some sightings that occurred around the Eagle Rock Mountain area. He'd frequented the observatory up there, and then suddenly, it was closed off, even to him. Secretly, he began investigating, but overtly, he was pushing buttons. You must all read the journals for yourselves, and when you do, you'll discover that my father realized that he was being followed. He decided to lure his stalkers out into the open at Eagle Rock Mountain the night that he died."

There was a pause, a somber silence as Dylan swallowed hard.

"After that particular entry, there is nothing but white space."

Susan broke the awkward silence that seemed to linger.

"Dylan had called me after reading the journals. He was reluctant to say much on the phone, as I have subsequently been. The reason for this will become apparent when we've finished. After speaking with Dylan, I received another phone call. It was the hospital telling me that a young woman was rushed to the ER and was asking for me. She wasn't a patient, but she described herself as a friend. And, it is someone we all know."

Brett, Leah, and Sidney stared at her in anticipation.

"The young woman was diagnosed as having acute radiation sickness. I'm afraid that it's our friend, Ursula Masters." Now the gasps were somewhat louder than before. "But she's okay. She's very lucky, since her exposure to the source of radiation was not a prolonged one. Dylan and I went straight to the hospital to see her."

"And Ursula described for us the source of that radiation," Dylan said. "She was extremely adamant in her description and consistently certain of one thing. What she'd seen and had been exposed to was a UFO."

Now, the silence was thick and heavy throughout the room. Susan could almost hear the ticking of her overpriced clock on the wall. She interrupted the persistent stillness.

"Ursula gave us not only a description of what she'd seen, but she confirmed the time-frame to nearly the exact moment of Dylan's sighting through the telescope lens. Ironically, after witnessing this disc-shaped craft looming above her out on her balcony, Ursula had decided to contact us and report the incident. That never happened."

Susan told them how Ursula had become ill after going back inside. "She phoned 911, and the responders found her barely conscious."

"Unbelievable," Sidney said.

"And there's more," Susan said. "As we left the ICU, I was alerted to the fact that there was yet another case of radiation sickness. This time, a young man was admitted after driving himself to the ER. Fortunately for him, his exposure was not to the extent of Ursula's. He is merely being kept for observation."

Susan detailed how she and Dylan had gone to the young man's room, introduced themselves, and got him to discuss what he'd witnessed. Dylan interjected.

"Dr. Adams felt that if he knew who we were, he might feel more inclined to open up to us," he said. "And he'd been right. His story, as well as Ursula's, convinced me that what I'd seen was real, no fumbling of the scope, no unexplainable anomaly, and not a figment of my imagination. I'd only glimpsed what they'd seen with their naked eyes."

Susan continued.

"Mr. Shane Rowe told us that he'd witnessed the bottom of the strange craft open up, and then it rotated, as he called it. He also described the same swaying of trees that Ursula had mentioned. That instance, he believes, was the moment of his exposure. Mr. Rowe is as equally adamant as Ursula; what he'd seen was a UFO."

"What about the possibility of a military aircraft of some type?" Brett asked. Susan answered his question.

"During their experiences, both Ursula and Shane had immediately concluded that it was no type of aircraft they'd ever seen before. They both ruled out helicopters or airplanes. They've also confirmed the bright-green luminescence that Dylan describes, though our two witnesses claim that they watched it change color. And the poignant fact is the disc-shaped description that both of them have confirmed."

"Are there many military aircraft seen in western Pennsylvania?" Leah asked.

"Hardly any at all," Dylan said. "And since we're on the subject of the military, there's something else I'd like to mention as you all begin reading my father's journals. By a strange coincidence, as I was reading through them last night, I suddenly thought of Ursula. In my father's journals, he wrote that his stalkers were following him in a black sedan. Do you all remember when Ursula was being followed a few years ago? She claimed to have been followed by a *maroon* sedan."

Leah and Brett narrowed their eyes; Sidney rubbed his chin with flexing fingers.

"And the connection you're making?" Sidney asked.

"As you'll read in the journals, my father believed that the black sedan following him had belonged to the infamous 'Men in Black.'"

"Seriously?" Sidney asked. In his mystified tone was a slight touch of unspoken trepidation and Susan had caught it.

"We've all heard the stories of the Men in Black," she said. "It's said that they've visited our area quite a few times already. The most famous instance is Kecksburg. And yes, you've all seen the movie satirizing them, but the real story behind the Men in Black is not only odd, but frightening. When they're involved, it's said to be dangerous business. People are said to have been frightened by them, threatened, and possibly even killed. Yet no one knows who they are, or for whom they work.

"We'll discuss more of them as the night wears on, but first, I want to relate to you all what I personally remember of Kecksburg, and fill you in on our local history and affiliation with this sort of mystery. I should also tell you that I've invited a guest to come and speak with us tonight about his connection to the Kecksburg incident. As you're all well aware, we live in a smaller part of the country, where everyone knows everyone. Our entire area was touched by what happened back then.

"It was December 1965, the ninth to be exact," she began. "I was in the eighth grade when it happened." She felt the smile span across her face as thoughts of a happier, more innocent time took her back into the untouchable past. She watched as their faces lit up, and their eyes widened at hearing her recollection of a history they'd only read about. "I'd been helping my mother clear the dinner table when she received a phone call from my uncle.

"My uncle, her brother, had been a fire marshal. He'd called to tell us that about an hour before, around 4:45pm, a blazing blue light had been seen flashing through the sky in Kecksburg, a mere ten miles from us. Blue smoke was seen rising up from a wooded ravine, and a group of townspeople had traversed into it in hopes of discovering what had landed out there. According to my uncle, he'd heard reports that the military and several media outlets had arrived there also. Whatever was happening was big and beginning to make headlines.

"My mother had turned on the television, while my father turned on his radio. The only reports we'd heard were brief mentions of what had already been told to us, but the talk around the town was circulating. In the days that followed, the story unraveled amid myriad rumors and speculations. The townspeople had searched in the woods, discovering busted treetops and billowing blue smoke. They claimed that within minutes, mysterious men in overcoats had arrived and told them to evacuate immediately—that the area was now quarantined. Then, the military was said to have followed, cordoning off the wooded area and restricting it to military personnel only.

"Who were the mysterious men in overcoats? It is the first known appearance of the Men in Black in our area. But as I said, the townspeople were not the only ones to have shown up at the crash site, there were members of the news media, one in particular whose story will forever be connected and associated with what happened in Kecksburg. His name was John Murphy, and he was the director of our local radio station."

When Susan mentioned the station's call letters, she noticed the looks of surprise on the faces of the younger investigators. They suddenly realized how close to home this mystery was. Dylan mentioned that in his journals, his father had elaborated on the story she was about to tell.

"John Murphy had arrived on the scene with at least one photographer. He'd made an audio recording while there, questioning witnesses who'd seen the strange blue phenomenon streaking the sky. They had watched it go down into the wooded area, and then immediately gone out to investigate the strange object that had fallen not far from their homes. A few witnesses had told him that the thing seemed to be flying in a controlled way, as they'd noticed its zigzagged and seemingly planned path. It was said to have made a sharp turn into the Kecksburg ravine. They'd been sure that it was some type of unidentifiable aircraft.

"Murphy had taken pictures while at the site, but of what no one can be sure. His accompanying photographer never had the chance to take any pictures, because as they were about to head down into the ravine, the men in overcoats stopped them. That's when they'd confiscated Murphy's roll of film. However, it wasn't the only one. He'd placed another roll of film in his pocket, and neither the military, nor the men in overcoats had found it. He was told to immediately evacuate along with everyone else. Those who'd taken over the scene cited the quarantine that had now been in effect.

"The usurped radio director later phoned a few of the witnesses he'd spoken to, specifically a young mother who'd made statements based upon what her little boy had seen. When he spoke to her later on the phone, she recanted her story, saying that her son had obviously been wrong or imagining things. Her sudden reversal led to the theory that she'd been silenced by those whose mission it was to keep things quiet and non-existent."

"The Men in Black," Dylan reaffirmed.

"So it's said," Susan said. "And from your father's journals, he was one of many in accordance with that opinion. But Murphy had taken notes while at the scene. Apparently, he'd had enough from those notes, as well as an undiscovered audio tape, to gather enough information that would allow him to do one thing—go on the air and talk about what happened on that late afternoon. Some say he'd planned to reveal all, including the fact that some witnesses had suddenly and unexplainably recanted their prior statements. But somehow, the two mysterious men had discovered Murphy's intention. One night, they showed up at the radio station."

Again, Susan watched their young faces, the awe, the astonishment that these strange men had left their infamous footprints inside the local radio station, a scant mile from the university.

"A worker from the radio station reported that the men advised Murphy that he would go on the air with a significantly altered and edited version of the presentation that he'd written and was about to broadcast. They'd also reportedly confiscated his notes but still hadn't discovered the audio recording. After having a discussion with Murphy in a back room, they left, and the troubled director went on the air with a presentation that had not been his original.

"Many claim that Murphy became despondent after the incident. They insist that he'd never wanted to discuss the Kecksburg event ever again. That was unlike him. He'd been fiercely adamant about the entire situation, and then suddenly, he'd let it go. He'd later appeared to be troubled by any mention of the event.

"A few years after the Kecksburg affair, Murphy had been vacationing in California. At ten-o'clock at night, he'd mysteriously gone across the street to an obscure area, an oil slick. To this day, no one is exactly sure why. As he was crossing the street, he was killed by a hit-and-run driver. The driver has never been apprehended."

Now, all of their faces were staring at her, frozen expressions trapped in the stillness of silence. Leah was the first to break that silence. The sound of her bewildered sigh was as if all of the air had left her.

"This is unbelievable!"

"And there's more," Susan said. "Before his death, Murphy had handed over his secret audio tape to a certain, well-known, paranormal investigator."

"You mean him, the famous one from our area?" Sidney asked.

"Yes," Susan replied, "*him*. He was the Keoksburg investigator. And that audio tape was stolen from the investigator's office after a mysterious break-in."

"These men," Brett said, "they seem to know things immediately and unexplainably."

"Precisely, Brett," Susan said.

"But what ever happened to the roll of film?" Leah asked.

"Apparently, no one knows." Susan's response coincided with the chime of the doorbell. The sudden peal broke the intense immersion of the meeting.

"That is my guest." Susan stood from the sofa. "He'll confirm much of what I've told you. He's closely connected to the situation; I'd say one degree of separation." She continued speaking as she walked over to the door, and once again, peeped through the window curtain. "I think it's important that you all hear as much of this story by those who remember it as you can. After all, I don't want you to just take my word for it."

She opened the door, and there in the doorway, stood a tall man with smiling eyes, a strong, yet friendly face, and a classic Romanesque appearance. He looked about the same as he always had, though now his hair and mustache had turned to gray. They'd graduated from high school together, and it was as if time hadn't stopped. They exchanged greetings and embraced in the doorway, old high-school friends reunited for the strangest of reasons. Susan turned to the team, closing the door behind her.

"Everyone, I want you to meet Drew Michaels," she said. "He's an old friend, one I've known since junior high school. Drew, these are my paranormal investigators."

She introduced each of them by name, and the eye of Susan's guest lingered when it got to Leah Leeds. By now, almost everyone had heard of her.

"Hello, all. Nice to meet you," he said. Words of greeting and small talk bantered between them, until Susan offered him a seat on the sofa next to her.

"Drew and I were in the eighth grade together at the time of Kecksburg," Susan said, turning her head toward her guest. "As I explained earlier, I want you to tell them about your connection to Kecksburg. Tell them what you told us back then."

"Well," he began, "at the time, my father was a photographer for Channel 12. He and John Murphy were close friends. My father was the photographer that accompanied John into the woods that day in Kecksburg."

Drew Michaels related much of what Susan had already told: how his father and John Murphy were ordered to evacuate by the mysterious men, how they had confiscated a roll of film from Murphy, and how the military showed up, quarantining the area.

"My father hadn't taken any pictures," he said. "He and John were ordered out immediately, but John had stashed a roll of film in his pocket that went undiscovered. Later, John told my father how the Men in Black had entered the radio station and confiscated some of his notes. After this intrusion, John had refused to discuss the matter ever again."

Drew Michaels reiterated the mysterious circumstances surrounding Murphy's death, and how beforehand, he had turned over an audio recording to a local paranormal investigator, the famous one. Later, the investigator's office was burglarized by person or persons unknown. He'd gone public about the break-in, claiming that only material related to Kecksburg had been taken.

"You should all meet with that investigator," Drew said. "I'm sure he could fill you all in with infinitely more details about everything that went down."

"True," Sidney said. "But it's so odd; we've never met him yet." The investigators laughed lightly, exchanging glances at each other. "But what I'm hearing is this: if Murphy *didn't* give the roll of film to the famous paranormal investigator, and neither the Men in Black nor the military had discovered it, then—"

"Then there is a roll of film from the Kecksburg site, possibly still out there," Drew said.

The gasps were sudden and came from all of them. The level of surprise denoted a story that was too mind-boggling for words, a truth that could only warrant expressions of shock and disbelief. Susan's guest continued.

"My family had gone through my father's old things after his passing in 2005, but we came across nothing that would have alerted our attention."

They'd spent the next thirty minutes discussing the Kecksburg event and the stories surrounding it. Susan and Drew told of how some witnesses had claimed to see an acorn-shaped object removed from the woods and loaded onto a flatbed truck. A few witnesses reported seeing what looked like hieroglyphic symbols on the side of the craft. It was said that the object was then brought to Lockbourne Air Force Base in Columbus, Ohio, and then transferred to Wright-Patterson Air Force base, where one witness had even claimed to see a body that was not human.

"And of course, that was never proven," Susan said. "I'm not saying that it was untrue, but we, of all people, know how quickly these matters can snowball into wild and often fictional rumors."

Brett spoke up, adding to the discussion.

"I remember reading once about a Russian satellite that had re-entered Earth's atmosphere that day, and that many had claimed that it was the object that landed in the ravine."

"Yes," Susan said. "That year, Russia had launched the Kosmos 96 Venus Probe. It had ironically fallen back to Earth on the same day, and many skeptics were quick to identify *that* as the Kecksburg object. But it was proven that the Russian satellite had landed in Canada earlier that day. And what's more—the now defunct 'Project Blue Book' had classified the Kecksburg mystery as nothing more than a meteor, contradicting the skeptics who'd hoped to pin it on the Russian satellite.

"What was Project Blue Book?" Susan probed her audience. "As I'm sure you're all aware, our government has had intimate knowledge of UFOs as far back as 1947, starting with the famous Roswell incident.

Project Blue Book was a study conducted by our government regarding the existence of UFOs. Its purpose was to determine if UFOs were a threat to national security, or if these strange crafts were in any way extraterrestrial in origin. The study began in 1952 and was ordered shut down in 1969. The termination was based upon the conclusions that UFOs were nothing out of the ordinary, that after the thousands of UFO reports collected, many of those were explainable misidentifications, and that UFOs could not be identified as extraterrestrial entities.

"And yes, some of the reports continued to be classified as 'unexplained,' but those were not substantial enough to compare to those that our government had deemed as 'explainable.' The study was the third of its kind. 'Project Sign' began in 1947, stating fervently that whatever UFOs were, they were extraterrestrial in origin. That study was quickly terminated, and all of its collected information was destroyed. The second study was initiated in 1949. 'Project Grudge' was the direct opposite of Project Sign. It operated on the belief that UFOs could not possibly exist under any circumstances, which was considered a grudge against the theory of their authenticity. That's how the project got its name. It was also short-lived.

"It's a well-known fact that our government has denied the existence of UFOs for many decades, though that doesn't prove any extraterrestrial connection. So, we ask the questions: Why deny their existence? Why work so hard to quash any reports or testimonies of sightings that continue to this day, all over the world? Are these unidentified crafts alien in nature, or are they possibly our own government's top secret aircraft weaponry, as many have hypothesized? I'm sure it's something that we'll probably never learn the answer to, unless there is some type of worldwide revelation."

They continued to discuss the subject at hand, referring to famous sightings in history, especially the Roswell incident, where an unidentified aircraft had crashed in Roswell, New Mexico. The government had persisted that the object was nothing more than a weather balloon, despite contradictions from eyewitnesses who had come forward throughout the years. They talked about the Phoenix Lights, one of several instances where multiple eyewitnesses had watched as a series of lights formed an outline of an unidentified, V-shaped craft. They even mentioned sightings that were said to have occurred prior to the twentieth-century. The discussion rambled on for more than twenty minutes, but the team had been mindful to tailor it to a general and unofficial nature in the presence of their company. Though the conversation was both studious and fascinating, soon Drew Michaels checked the time on his iPhone.

"I want to thank you all for inviting me." He sat up from the sofa. "If I can be of any further assistance, please don't hesitate to call."

"Leaving so soon?" Susan asked.

He gave his apologies, referring to errands and prior obligations. He and Susan walked arm and arm to the front door.

"We must get together again soon," she said. He agreed, and then turned to face her with his back to the front door. The investigators talked quietly among themselves in the background.

"So," he said, "why were we talking about UFOs?"

Susan turned her head quickly to the investigators who hadn't noticed her, and then turned it back toward her longtime pal. She raised her right eyebrow so only he could see.

*"No shit?!"* His words showered out in a sharp stage whisper.

"Shh!" She shushed him, turning her head again and hoping they hadn't heard.

"I have a feeling that whatever is going on is about to come out one way or another," she said. "Keep watch."

They exchanged cheeky kisses as she led him out the front door. She watched and waved as he walked to his car. As he drove away, she rejoined the investigators.

"So, I'm sure that now you all realize how close to home this mystery is for us," she said, rejoining them. "It's one that we are once again confronted with all these years later, and seemingly, it has fallen right into our lap. Dylan, you began this meeting, and I know you wanted to address a few more things before we wrap up. Dylan, you have the floor."

\* \* \* \*

"I wanted you all to read these now," Dylan began. "I'll be keeping them locked up, right where they've always been." The investigators huddled around him on the sofa as he opened his father's journals. He laid them face-up on the coffee table and began with the earliest one. "This one details the Bigfoot sightings that overwhelmed our area back in the 1970s. There are clipped newspaper articles, as well as my father's notes."

The remaining three investigators were wide-eyed and awed by what they read.

"So there were UFO sightings right before the Bigfoot encounters," Sidney said. "I never knew this. And it all happened right here in Green Valley and the surrounding areas."

They basked in an almost elated fascination, discovering the article about Bigfoot and Silver Lake, a place they'd been to so often in their young lives. They read the journal that contained Dr. Rasche's Kecksburg research and memorabilia, and Dylan could almost see the story unraveling a little further in each of their minds. And finally, they'd read the details of the sightings near Eagle Rock Mountain, Dr. Rasche's involvement with the observatory, and his eerie revelations that he was being followed.

Their eyes were unblinking, gripped by unspoken trepidation as they'd read about Dr. Rasche's Men in Black suspicions. Total silence befell them as they'd read of his plans to lure his stalkers out into the open and confront them by going to the observatory up on Eagle Rock Mountain, an excursion he'd made alone and at night. Dylan sensed their undeclared judgments of foolishness on his father's part, and a deep down pity for their chief investigator that would forever remain unspoken. They stared in silence at the gaping white space that ended the last journal.

"My father died shortly after that last entry," he said. "I now believe that he was murdered. My sister believes it also. The timing of these two mysteries before us is more than coincidental. I feel that it's some kind of cosmic nudge for me to find out who killed my father, and why, and that's exactly what I'm going to do. However, I realize that remains our general and long-term mission. The mystery before us now is whatever happened last night, right here in Green Valley. I have a feeling that there may be other witnesses. If so, we need to find them. But our first order of business is for you three to talk to both Ursula and Shane Rowe. Then, of course, we need to investigate Eagle Rock Mountain, especially the observatory.

"Now, if any of you want to back out of that part of the investigation, I certainly understand. I don't expect any one of you to possibly risk your lives for me, so I can find justice for my father. This is my dilemma, and I understand if you're fearful of the risks involved."

"Are you shitting me?" Sidney asked. "I wouldn't miss this for the world."

"Ditto that," Brett said.

"Seriously, Dylan," Leah said. "Did you think we would let you do this on your own? We're investigators; that's what we do. We're faced with some new challenge all the time."

Susan interjected.

"I've always had a feeling that somehow, some way, this mystery that seems to favor our area was never really over, that one day it would start up all over again. And it seems that it has."

"Then we all agree on our two main objectives," Dylan continued, "what happened last night, and what happened to my father years ago. That will be our secret, underlying investigation. This may go public in a big way. If it does, we won't be able to stop it. We need to appear like we're conducting a normal investigation, merely speaking with witnesses."

All agreed, and then Susan spoke up again.

"One last thing before we end tonight, Dylan," she said, raising her glass. "I would like to congratulate Leah on achieving her master's degree from our very own Green Valley University, and I'm proud to say, that she's about to become a Psychology professor." Applause erupted around Leah. She smiled, blushed, and thanked them all. "And next weekend, Leah, we'll all be attending the master's ceremony to watch you graduate, once again. We wouldn't miss it for the world."

"Here, here." Her fellow investigators cheered, and they all raised their glasses to Leah.

Susan was right; they wouldn't miss the ceremony for the world, and the world wouldn't miss it either.

# Chapter Seven

## ~ Seth Dornan ~

Seth Dornan sat behind the small bureau in his quaint, comfortable living room, twirling a pencil between his fingers. His mind was racing because of the phone call he'd just received out of nowhere and on a Sunday night. It was from a newspaper reporter he'd met over twenty years ago, not long after he began his career as a MUFON investigator. Marv Kincaid was his name, a reporter for the Green Valley Tribune.

In 1993, Kincaid had contacted MUFON with dire suspicions over the death of a local astronomer. He hadn't believed it was an accident, but he'd been unable to prove otherwise. Seth remembered how convinced Kincaid had been that his astronomer friend had stumbled upon something and was murdered because of it. Dr. Geoffrey Rasche had fallen from the top of Eagle Rock Mountain, and Marv Kincaid hadn't bought the accidental cause of death. Truthfully, neither had Seth, yet foul play was far from being proven.

Seth no longer lived in Green Valley. He lived in Pittsburgh with his wife, and two boys, ages twelve and eight. Yet somehow, Marv Kincaid was able to track him down after all these years, ringing the phone that sat snuggly atop the bureau.

He'd sounded a little older over the phone but obviously the same man. Seth could tell by the near perfect grammar of his speech. Apparently, something was going down in Green Valley, and Kincaid had seemingly moved through time to find him. And tonight, he'd heard the aging reporter's voice for the first time in over twenty years.

"I'm sorry to have tracked you down and bothered you at home," he said. "But I wouldn't have done so, if it wasn't extremely important."

Seth, now in his late forties, remained an active investigator for the Mutual UFO Network, though he was a far reach from the twenty-something adventurer he'd once been. But secretly, Seth was well aware that his inner fascination would never die. He welcomed Marv's call; it was not a problem.

"What seems to be the trouble?" Seth automatically assumed that some new evidence had come to light regarding Dr. Rasche's death, but even if it had, he doubted it would ever be enough to expose anyone, especially at this late date.

"Something is definitely going on here in Green Valley," Marv said. "I saw something strange in the sky last night. I ignored it. Now, two people have been admitted to University Hospital with radiation sickness. In addition, I received a call from a terrified female 911 dispatcher."

Marv told him the story of Janette LaRue and the details of her shift the night before. "She took the call from the young woman who was exposed," he said. "Then, she received another call from an elderly woman asking if anyone had reported a strange sighting in the sky. The woman gave a brief description of the object. Soon after, *those men* gained entry into the 911 dispatch system and threatened her."

"What men?" Seth lurched forward in the chair, as if being closer to the phone would provide him with a clearer picture of the story.

"No doubt it was the 'Men in Black.' They'd broken into the system using an untraceable source. Somehow, they'd made certain that their call didn't register within the system. First, they asked her about both women: the young woman who'd been exposed, and the older, inquisitive one who'd phoned in."

Seth had heard many stories of the Men in Black from all over the country, including from witnesses that he'd interviewed right here in western Pennsylvania. It was during the Beaver County incident back in 2006, when he was sure he had a near run-in with them. Several of his witnesses described the strange men almost exactly as what had been reported about them: identical black attire, expressionless faces that were "just not right," and mirrored sunglasses to hide their eyes. The witnesses were ordered not to speak to anyone any further, especially him. They'd known about him. And then, he could've sworn that someone had been following him, a black sedan that seemed to turn at every corner behind him. But then it mysteriously ceased, along with public interest in the incident, so he'd never really been certain.

Kincaid related the details of the dispatcher's dilemma, and then uttered a distressing sigh through the phone. "And then they mentioned her kids," he said, "a boy and a girl both younger than ten. Whatever they're covering up must be huge, because they would to go any lengths to suppress this information, including threatening children."

Seth's heart pounded. He often wondered how he'd managed, over the years, to keep a cool and level head while a bubble of emotions ranging from fear, to thrill, to ecstasy burst inside of him. The tone with which he asked the next question was calm, relaxed, a thin veneer that covered a raging passion for danger.

"What exactly did *you* see that evening?"

Marv told him the details of his regular outing with Duke, how he'd seen lights in the sky, how he'd seen *something* streak across its vast expanse, but it had all happened too fast. Yet Duke had seen or sensed much more.

"And what's the story on the other person who was exposed?"

"It was a young man who'd driven himself to the ER after becoming ill. I have no other details on him at this point."

"And the dispatcher," Seth asked. "She didn't see anything, only took the calls, right?"

"Right," Marv affirmed. He told how Janette LaRue had been smart enough to purchase a disposable track phone, and how he'd met with her at a secret location so no one would know she'd spoken to a reporter. Marv didn't think she'd been followed, but he'd been sure to warn her that her phone lines and internet were possibly being monitored. Seth agreed.

"Whatever you do, don't underestimate them," Seth warned. "They have unexplainable means of finding out things."

"So, I've heard," Marv said. "And there's more. Have you heard of the Paranormal Research and Investigative Society that's headquartered at the university?"

"I've heard of Leah Leeds and Sidney Pratt," he said, "although I've never met them. Are *they* involved with this now?"

"Well, the irony of all this is that the director of the society, Dr. Susan

Logan, is an old neighborhood friend of mine. Plus, the young woman that suffered the radiation exposure, Ursula Masters, is a friend of theirs. She helped them out a few years ago on a case. From what I've just discovered, she's some kind of telepath, a clairaudient. So, I'm sure the team is about to become involved. But, do you know what the real kicker in all of this is?"

Seth listened, waiting for more as the aging reporter paused.

"The society's chief investigator is none other than Dr. Geoffrey Rasche's son, Dylan."

"Interesting," Seth said, registering all of the various associations. Yet here was a connection he hadn't expected. He asked the question that had been turning in his mind. "So, do you think any of this has anything to do with Dr. Rasche, all of these years later?"

"I can't say," Marv said. "But I do know this; I plan on meeting with the investigators. I know where Susan Logan lives. I'm going to pay her a surprise visit and ask to set up a meeting with the team. I need to tell them what's going on. I need to tell them about Janette. This young woman has no one else to turn to, and she's come to me for help. And, it's about time that Dylan Rasche learned of my suspicions regarding his father's death. He was only a child when his father died, but he's an adult now. He needs to know about my suspicions then and now."

"Agreed."

Seth was normally cautious regarding the validity of any unofficial call about some random occurrence. But Green Valley had once been his home; he'd been well aware of the area's penchant for such paranormal occurrences. Radiation exposure and at least three possible witnesses were enough to convince him, but when Kincaid had mentioned the Men in Black, Seth knew for sure that a hastened and unexpected jaunt back home was more than necessary.

"The more people investigating this, the better," he continued. "I want you to keep me posted as to your meeting with Dr. Logan. If the investigators know this girl who was exposed, then odds are in favor of them already being involved. It's only a forty-five-minute drive to Green Valley. I'll be in to see you tomorrow afternoon."

"I think it's best if we meet somewhere clandestine," Marv said.

Seth agreed. Kincaid would notify him of their meeting place once he'd spoken with Susan Logan. He would expect his call in the morning. Now, Seth sat contemplating his excursion to Green Valley.

The MUFON network was a non-profit organization, so his work as an investigator was strictly on a volunteer basis. He helped people, and at the same time, he fed his insatiable passion. His real job was with an advertising firm. Luckily, he had some extra vacation time in addition to what he would normally use in the summer—a couple of days at least. He would utilize them and offer an excuse about a family matter back home. He would provide that same excuse to his wife, Lisa. She wouldn't favor the idea of him running back home to investigate what she would either see as a wild-goose chase or a dangerous escapade.

She'd always been able to spot that spark of excitement, those flares for the mysterious and possibly the dangerous inside of him, and she hadn't liked it.

It had taken him only a matter of minutes to reach his boss and provide his cover story. He would leave for Green Valley tomorrow before noon.

\* \* \* \*

Marv remembered how Susan Logan had sold the house on Winchester Lane after her father's death and purchased a two-story home in the heart of King's Haven. He'd never seen the inside of a King's Haven abode, the majestic splendor of which many had spoken, but tonight would be his first occasion. It was not yet 8:00, still early enough to pay a visit to an old friend. He hadn't been exactly sure of the house number, but that's why phone books still came in handy. She was listed. After all, she is a doctor, he thought.

He cruised through the winding streets of King's Haven, marveling at the stately and prestigious homes that sat quietly beneath the soft beam of streetlights. Soon, he pulled up to the house of the same number he'd found in the phone book—1130. As he approached the long driveway, he noticed a number of cars parked there. A white van and a blue, Mustang convertible blocked and hid two other cars parked in the driveway. He couldn't discern their makes or models in the oncoming night.

*Damn! She has company.*

It wouldn't matter. He would be discreet. He would mention being in the neighborhood, and that he decided to drop by on an old friend.

Privately, he would tell her to reach him immediately, that he needed to speak with her and the investigators. Marv parked alongside the street as there was no more room in the long driveway, and soon enough, he rang the doorbell.

\* \* \* \*

The discussion had ended, the meeting had adjourned, and now they sat idly sipping wine and talking about the more ordinary issues in their lives. The investigators would research more on the mysterious subject matter in their own time, but for now, restless bodies and lagging conversation were drawing the evening to a close, until the doorbell rang. The chime of an unexpected guest echoed the surprise on Susan's face.

"Who could that be, unless Drew has forgotten something?" She asked the question, though none of them could answer. She rose from the sofa and walked to the front door, her pace slowed by curiosity. She peeped once again through the window curtain. "It can't be."

Her voice was one of pleasant surprise. The team exchanged questioning glances. Susan anxiously opened the door as they watched.

"Marv Kincaid!" She threw her arms open. "I don't believe it! Come on in!"

The man they'd all known of as 'the People's investigator' stepped into her arms, and they embraced each other, their voices overlapping and interrupting as they greeted one another. He was a little older than she remembered him—okay, a lot older—but still the same Marvin she'd known for years.

"I'm so happy to see you. But what on earth brings you here?"

He was about to answer when she noticed him turn and stare at the team.

\* \* \* \*

Susan Logan, she never seemed to age, he thought, as he embraced her in the doorway. She'd been in her late thirties the last time he'd seen her, but it was as if the clock had slowed for her, allowing only brief snippets of time to escape.

"You look the same as always," he muttered underneath their overlapping exchanges.

"I'm so happy to see you," she said. "But what on earth brings you here?"

He heard fervent whispers from her guests. He'd forgotten that in the presence of her company, he was a celebrity. How strange; for a moment, he'd forgotten that he was *the* Marv Kincaid. Suddenly, something stood out about the small assemblage in the living room; those who comprised it were much younger. And that wasn't the only thing that caught his eye. He noticed the fat kid with the glasses, the girl with the long blonde hair. Were they...?

"Marv, I want you to meet this very special quartet," she said, as she led him to where they'd all been gathered. "Officially, this is the Paranormal Research and Investigative team from Green Valley University."

She extended her open hand to the team and introduced them one by one. Each one rose in turn and shook Marv's hand. Brett Taylor, Sidney Pratt, and then Marv recognized the tall one with the curly black hair. His face was almost the same as his father's. It was Dylan Rasche. Last and definitely not least was the young, blonde beauty whose face he'd recognized from the jacket cover of her memoir—Leah Leeds.

"So nice to meet you, Mr. Kincaid," she said, rising and shaking his hand. "I read your column faithfully."

"It's Marv, my Dear. And it is an honor to meet *you*." The look on her face was slightly puzzled. "I had the opportunity to read your memoir a few years back. What an incredible account you described and so brilliantly written. If you don't mind me saying, sometime later, I would love to hear everything about your return to that horrid place."

"You might want to rethink that one," Sidney said, snorting through his well-known, wiseass chuckle.

"Thank you so much," Leah said. "I never knew that you and Susan were friends."

"Old friends," Susan said. "Marv and I grew up together on Winchester Lane."

Marv sat among them on the sofa, and they exchanged small talk until Susan reiterated her earlier question: what had brought him here?

"Well," he said, sighing and searching for where to begin the long and complex story. He turned his gaze toward the investigators. "It's lucky for me that I've found you all, because you're the reason that I'm here. I came to notify Susan that I needed to meet with you all—at once." He watched their puzzled expressions prompting him to continue. "But first, I need to say something to someone here."

He turned and looked at Dylan.

"Do you remember me, Mr. Rasche?" Dylan studied his face, trying to zero-in on who he was outside of being *the* Marv Kincaid.

"First, call me Dylan." he said. "And I must admit, I've always thought that you looked familiar to me. Have we ever met before?"

"Yes, we have. I'm not sure if you remember, but I was a friend of your father's; although, you were just a boy at the time."

Dylan was roused by this revelation. He stirred in his seat. "Now I remember. You were at the funeral, right?"

Dylan gave the impression that though he remembered, the events and various people of that time remained blurry. That was understandable to Marv. It was also irrelevant.

"I don't expect you to remember me well." Marv turned his gaze toward the rest of the team. "There's much I need to discuss with you all tonight, but there's something I must address first." He turned his attention back to Dylan. "Dylan, what I need to say to you relates to why I'm here, though I'm not certain that the two things are connected."

He sighed once again.

"Your father and I once served on the university's board of directors," he said. "We had been friends for a good many years, long enough for me to know that he was a responsible, dedicated man, not to mention brilliant. When the details of your father's death emerged, I was suspicious. Something hadn't sounded right. I knew that Geoff had been trying to regain his clearance to the Eagle Rock Mountain observatory. He'd told me of his suspicions that something strange was going on up there, yet he never had the chance to go into any details. He said that he would get back to me when he knew more. Of course, that never happened.

"I encouraged him to give me more details, but he insisted on waiting. I warned him to be careful. The next thing I knew, he was gone, and I just couldn't swallow the circumstances. I started snooping around, provoking a conversation with someone I knew on the local police force. This cop revealed to me that there appeared to have been signs of a struggle on top of the mountain that night, but nothing had been definite. That had been enough for me. I started to probe for more information. And within days, I learned that the cop, who I'd also known for a long time, just up and moved to Florida without a word.

"I'd tried to discover where in Florida he'd gone to, but I got nowhere. I was unable to locate any remaining family here in Pennsylvania. I'd even enlisted the help of a MUFON investigator. His search turned up nothing, as if the man had disappeared from the face of the earth. I never said a word to your sister. I felt that she had enough to worry about, raising a young boy. Besides, if there had been foul play, I didn't want to put the two of you in danger. I'd kept silent because there was nothing I could prove."

Marv watched their frozen faces, their unblinking eyes, and their mouths slightly gaping open in awe. He suddenly thought of why the team was congregated here tonight. Maybe Seth was right, maybe they were already on top of things.

"But the past came back to haunt me last night, and that's the main reason for my visit."

"Let me guess," Dylan said. "You saw something in the sky last night?"

Marv nodded his head. His eyes passed over each and every one of them in a show of unspoken sincerity. He asked a question, but by now, he'd already known the answer.

"So, I take it you're already aware of Ursula Masters' exposure to radiation?"

They glanced at each other, suddenly realizing that nothing escaped *the* Marv Kincaid.

"Yes, Marv, we know," Susan said. "I was notified by the hospital, because Ursula wouldn't speak to anyone but me. Dylan and I have already seen her. We informed the rest of the team about Ursula this evening. But first, Marv, tell us what happened to you last night."

"I'd taken Duke, my dog, outside for his nightly walk," he began. "There were green and blue lights streaking the sky. Duke was going nuts. I couldn't tell what it was. And then the lights moved so fast through the sky, the whole display was gone before I could discern what it was. But I saw *something* move. I'd heard about the auroras, and though I'm no expert, I knew it couldn't have been that. Duke did his business, and then made straight for the house. He had no interest in walking, which was completely unlike him."

Marv explained his assumption that Duke had seen more of the spectacle than he had.

"Then, after we'd gone into the house, I suddenly began to think of your father. And today, I heard about two young people being admitted to the hospital for radiation sickness."

"Are you saying that the story is out already?" The worry in Susan's tone hinted at how unready they all were. A circus of media attention would surely disrupt their investigation.

"No, not that I'm aware," Marv said. "It was one of my own spies who reported back to me with the scoop."

"I should've known," Susan said. Relief washed over her face and formed a slight smile.

"But the bigger part of this story came to me after that. I received a frantic call from a young woman requesting to meet with me. She was the 911 dispatcher who took Ursula's call last night. Her name is Janette LaRue."

Marv told how Janette had been speaking to him from a prepaid, disposable phone she'd purchased specifically to call him.

"She'd said that she thought her phone and internet were being monitored, and that she was possibly being followed. I think she was correct in that last assumption. And after hearing what I'm about to tell you, you will all undoubtedly agree. I told her to meet me at a vacant house that I privately own here in town. Obviously, if she was being followed, showing up at the home of Marv Kincaid would have been a serious mistake. So, within minutes, I'd met this petrified young woman."

He revealed Janette's story as closely as she'd told it to him. He told them about the elderly woman who'd phoned in after Ursula, claiming to have seen something. Marv produced a piece of paper from his pocket with the woman's address and handed it to Dylan.

"It's no coincidence that she lives only a few blocks from your friend, Ursula."

"Mabel Forrester." Dylan read the name on the piece of paper and passed it around to the other investigators.

"But the next call that came through is why Janette insisted on meeting me."

Marv recounted the details of Janette's mysterious caller: how the caller had addressed her by her first and last name in a voice that Janette had described as possibly mechanically disguised, because of its strange and unnatural tone, and how he'd told her to forget the calls from Ursula and Mable Forrester, claiming that those calls had been deleted from the computer system.

"She said it was as if someone had hacked into her system and simply wiped away the recordings of those two calls. Part of her job is also keeping a manual log, so she was ordered by the caller to destroy that particular handwritten page. When she attempted to verbally resist him, the caller threatened her and mentioned her children."

Marv had expected the reactions of surprise and disgust that met his ears. Then, Susan asked a question, but Marv could hear in her tone an unspoken opinion that had already formed.

"So, Marv, in your opinion, who do you think is responsible for the mysterious call?"

"Isn't it obvious?" Dylan interrupted before Marv could answer. He plopped his father's journals back down on the coffee table in front of Marv. "It's the same people that had been following my father, the ones who most likely murdered him, the so-called, 'Men in Black.'"

Brief seconds of silence passed. Marv eyed the journals in front of him. So, Geoff was being followed, hunted like a dog. Marv hadn't been aware of this fact. Right in front of him was the proof that Geoff had written down everything that he was investigating. He said nothing in those brief seconds before answering Susan's question.

"I'm afraid that Dylan's right," he said. "And we're about to find out for certain." He faced Dylan and continued. "Tonight, I spoke with that same MUFON investigator that I consulted after your father's death. I tracked him down and told him everything that I just told you all. His name is Seth Dornan. He will arrive here in Green Valley tomorrow."

Marv turned back and addressed them all.

"He wants to meet with all of you, as well as Ursula, and the young man in the hospital. If these men *are* involved, and it seems apparent that they are, we need to figure out a way to meet discreetly, lest any of us end up being followed. Seth stressed how these men have an uncanny way of knowing things and knowing them early. My instinct tells me that they immediately investigated the area where the sighting had most prominently appeared—Ursula's neighborhood, the Falcon street area. They must've seen the ambulance, and then hacked into the 911 system, which pinpointed Ursula."

"Oh, no," Susan said. "Then they already know about Ursula? It hadn't occurred to me."

"*And* Mable Forrester," Marv said. "Understand that even though these men have destroyed the evidence of the 911 calls, there's still the issue of the paramedics, not to mention Ursula's medical records, but destroying as much proof as possible has always seemed to be their agenda."

Sidney finished the thought, illustrating Marv's point.

"And that would make the victim's claims nearly impossible to prove."

"Exactly," he said.

"Yes, but what about the media?" Susan asked. "When and if they discover our involvement, we'll all be thrown into an unwanted spotlight, and these men will be secretly watching. Marv, what are the chances of keeping this story from breaking?"

"It all depends," he said. "We need to ask our exposure victims to keep things between us; that would be a start. Speaking of the young man, what's the scoop on him?"

Susan and Dylan filled Marv in on Shane Rowe.

"Even though they both saw this thing at different angles and under different circumstances, he and Ursula's descriptions coincide almost exactly," Susan said.

Dylan spoke next, in perfect sync.

"And considering everything you've told us, Marv, the witnesses are accumulating. There are those of us that saw this thing but at varying degrees. Each testimony places a piece of a puzzle within a framework, and Shane and Ursula provide the largest pieces."

"So, then what is our course of action?" Brett spoke up. "I know *I'm* not about to be intimidated by these mysterious thugs. Besides, it's only a matter of time before they realize that we're investigating. It may be safer in the spotlight."

"I second that," Leah said.

"And it *may not* be safer," Marv said. "These men are said to be extremely dangerous. As we already know, they are said to be responsible for all sorts of 'accidents.'"

"And there's one particular accident that we're going to get to the bottom of," Dylan said, "come hell or high water."

Marv could hear the mounting anger in Dylan's voice. He instantly thought of Pandora's Box and prayed that he wasn't prompting Dylan to open it, yet the journals in front of him seemed to absolve him.

"Alright, team," Susan broke in. "So, what's our plan?"

"Get an update on Ursula's condition in the morning," Dylan said. "We need to figure out a way for all of us, including Marv, to meet with her. And of course, we have to warn her."

"I also want to meet Shane Rowe," Marv said.

"Then there's the issue of Mabel Forrester," Susan added. "And it's imperative that we meet with Janette LaRue. Marv, you're going to have to make that happen. But now, I say we all go home and get a good night's rest. Tomorrow, in the light of day, we will have a clear plan."

Marv silently agreed, but there was still one more thing. He continued to stare at the three notebooks on the coffee table. He reached out with his hand and touched one of them.

"Dylan, may I?"

Dylan nodded. "You may want to start with the one on the bottom. It contains his last words."

Marv opened the notebook journal. The slight creases on its cover revealed its age, though it did not appear as old as the others, and the pages were still white after all these years. Marv couldn't help but feel haunted. Reading Geoff's written words was as if his old friend suddenly began speaking to him from beyond the grave. Silently, Geoffrey Rasche's voice came alive. The words were secrets he hadn't told anyone. He simply recorded them here on these flimsy pages and dared to covertly explore on his own.

Marv suddenly discovered within the pages that what he'd thought was a rumor back then was a fact; there *had been* UFO sightings in the area above and surrounding Eagle Rock Mountain back in 1993. Geoff had been investigating. He'd even recorded the names of witnesses, people who had seen a disc-shaped craft.

Then, Marv's blood rushed through his veins at the next words.

*All accounts concur that lights were emanating from the mysterious craft, lights of various colors, specifically green and blue.*

Lights, just like he himself had seen last night. Dylan illuminated a point as he read.

"The account given by RJ Bailey is almost exactly the same as Shane Rowe's," he said. "But, obviously, Shane witnessed the craft from a closer stance and a longer duration."

Marv said nothing as he continued reading. The notebook pages made a flapping sound as he flipped them through his fingers. So, there had been secretive upgrades installed at the Eagle Rock observatory around the same time as the sightings. Geoff had been shut out of the observatory, his security clearance revoked. Something *had* been going on up there.

*Damn! Why didn't he let me in?!*

The thought that maybe Geoff hadn't trusted him was disappointing. He also felt regret at not intervening, not pestering Geoff a bit further when he'd made a brief mention of his suspicions. At the time, Marv hadn't dreamed that those suspicions were anything of a dire nature. It wasn't until after Geoff's death that Marv realized the extent of what could have been going on. And now, the details were being laid bare right in front of him. The regret he felt became a dark blossoming as he read the next words...

*"I'M BEING FOLLOWED!"*

He read Geoff's details of the black sedan and his plan to lure his stalkers out into the open by going up to the Eagle Rock observatory. Marv felt an implosion of anger at a dead man who decided to go it alone, and worst of all, at night, risking his life for his passion while his children were most likely at home, in bed. His decision had been a fatal mistake, and now his grown son sat next to Marv, dealing with the hurt and a different kind of anger.

Marv felt the sudden kindling of something deep inside, a dark foreboding that flourished inside of him. He realized how Dylan's life could be in danger if history were now repeating itself. And if it was, all of their lives could be in the same peril. He wondered how strength in numbers would ever help them in a stance against a faceless adversary.

He read Geoffrey Rasche's last words.

*I'm tired of being followed; it is time for answers.*

His hair rose at what appeared next, only white space. He closed the notebook and thought of asking Dylan to borrow it but then thought better of it.

"Be sure to keep these under lock and key," Marv said. "You can't bring them out into the light yet—not until we have some proof." Marv reminded Dylan of the danger.

Dylan assured him of the journals' safety, telling him about his father's hidden safe in the floor. He was well aware of the danger, but Marv knew that the young man's anger over the loss of his father was much greater. Soon, the night wound down as did their discussion, and Susan's earlier suggestion that they retire for the evening was coming to pass. Marv bid his goodbyes until tomorrow, and then he and the investigators left together, striding down the walkway to their cars. Tomorrow, phone calls would be exchanged, and a plan of action would unfold in the morning light.

# Chapter Eight

## ~ Mabel Forrester ~

Monday morning dawned earlier than expected, and Susan was enjoying her second cup of coffee before phoning the hospital. But her ringing phone roused her before she even touched the receiver. Lucky coincidence—*it was* the hospital. Nurse Ashlee sounded as pert and peppy as ever on a Monday morning.

"Hi, Dr. Logan; it's Ashlee. I thought you might want to know that Ursula Masters has been downgraded and moved to her own room."

"That's excellent news, Ashlee. What about Shane Rowe? What's his situation?"

"I hear that he may be discharged later today, but the doctor needs to see him first."

Susan thanked her for the information and replaced the receiver back in its cradle. She finished her coffee, called Marv and the investigators, and gave them the update. Marv would wait for Seth Dornan to arrive before his next plan of action, but Susan and the investigators had another plan. They were going to see Mabel Forrester.

* * * *

Just like always, they packed into Sidney's van. They then drove to Mabel Forrester's address, the one listed on the small sheet of paper that Marv had given them. On the way, Dylan read the address again and realized something that he hadn't before—something that should have been so obvious.

"I just realized something," he announced. "Mabel Forrester lives on Phoenix Drive, a block away from Ursula on Falcon Street, which we already knew."

"Right," Sidney said from the driver's side. "It's that section of town where all the streets are named after birds."

"Yes," Dylan said. "But Phoenix Drive leads to Eagle Rock Road, which—"

"—leads to Eagle Rock Mountain." Leah concluded the assessment with their usual synchronization.

"I hadn't thought of that either," Susan said. "That's way too much of a coincidence."

"Exactly," Brett said. "And to us, there *are no* coincidences."

The silence filled the van, almost on cue. It was a silence they knew well, one that always confirmed for them that they sat in the midst of some unexplainable quandary.

"Yet the witness locations seem to be spread out," Susan said, breaking the silence. "Shane Rowe was out on the back roads, which is not too far away from the area, but what about Marv and Dylan? They were across town in different directions."

"And oddly, both of us caught only glimpses," Dylan said.

"It does confirm the possibility of a wide-range of witnesses." Sidney spoke up. "For all we know, there could be many more witnesses across town, even across state."

"That's why I'm worried about this thing becoming a media circus," Susan said.

"Marv mentioned that this Mabel Forrester sounded iffy to Janette LaRue," Sidney said. "Do you think she could be batty?"

"Sid!" Leah playfully scolded.

"She might be," Susan said. "But if her description of what she saw matches Shane's and Ursula's, she can't be too batty. She'd be witness number three."

Dylan reminded them of something just as important.

"If Marv's right about those men hacking into the 911 system and deleting all record of her call, as well as Ursula's, then we have to warn her."

"What if they're *already* watching her house?" Leah's tone begged for an answer as to why they hadn't considered such a thing before.

"I doubt it," Susan said. "Besides, we'll be on the lookout. And I think we *do* need to warn her, but without scaring her. We need to watch over Ursula as well."

They rode through the winding residential avenues and boulevards, picturesque with two-story houses stacked against a backdrop of rich greenery that reached for the sky. Silently, widened eyes searched the streets for signs of sedans or unmarked cars. They watched for parked vehicles with loitering passengers but noticed nothing. Then, the van turned onto Phoenix Drive.

"Okay," Susan instructed. "Now, let's keep our eyes peeled to both sides of the street."

Houses passed one by one like a fast-moving slideshow. A man with a briefcase was getting into his car, while a woman reached out of her door to check her mailbox, and another man dragged a garbage can down his driveway. Nothing seemed out of the ordinary. The regular, everyday neighborhood displayed the perfect picture of normalcy on a sunny, Monday afternoon. Finally, Dylan leaned forward and pointed to a two-story, bluish-colored house with white shutters. He glimpsed the house number from the passenger's seat.

"There it is." He pointed. "That's it, 526 Phoenix Drive."

Sidney pulled the van up in front of the house. Susan began to advise them.

"As always, let me go first and introduce you all. We needn't be covert this time. We *can* tell this woman that we're paranormal investigators; in fact, she'll be more inclined to talk to us."

Susan and Dylan led the way down the short, paved sidewalk as the van's doors slammed shut behind them. As they reached the front porch, Dylan noticed that the screen door masked the front door, which was slightly ajar, allowing the spring afternoon breeze to waft inside. Susan nodded to him, and he noisily knuckled the metal frame of the screen door. He glimpsed a shadowy reticence as it inched toward the door. Then, the front door slowly opened further. A woman in her early eighties with a white, robust head of hair stood staring at them in wonder, watching with wary eyes that hid behind bifocal glasses.

"Mrs. Forrester, I presume?" Susan was the first to speak.

"I am," she replied in a soft, shaky voice.

"My name is Dr. Susan Logan. I'm not only a doctor, but a parapsychologist. I work at University Hospital." She motioned behind her. "This is my team of paranormal investigators. We've come to talk to you about what you saw Saturday night."

The woman seemed taken aback. She continued to stare. Dylan spoke next.

"Mrs. Forrester, my name is Dylan Rasche. We'd also like to talk to you about the call you placed to 911 shortly afterward."

Susan had taken her identification from her purse and held it up so Mabel Forrester could see it. Aged eyes squinted to focus even behind bifocals.

Leah stepped forward and introduced herself.

"Mrs. Forrester, we were hoping that you might tell us about what you saw," she said. "It seems that there are others who saw the same thing. And of course, anything you tell us is strictly confidential."

Dylan noticed Mabel Forrester's reaction to the pretty blonde girl whose angelic face had obviously won her over, though her name may have also sparked something. The old woman smiled and spoke.

"Yes, the woman who took my call said she would pass on my information. I didn't think she would. I thought that maybe she'd marked me as an old crackpot." She laughed. "Is that how you found me?"

"Yes, Mrs. Forrester," Susan responded. "The 911 responder passed on your information to us, and that's why we're here."

It wasn't much of a white lie, Dylan thought. He'd heard Susan tell much worse.

"That is, if we haven't come at a bad time," Susan said. "May we come in?"

The woman obliged them with a hospitable grace, smiling and using the word "certainly" as she opened the door and allowed the investigators to step one-by-one into the two-story, but quaint, storybook abode. The comfortable living room was a neat and tidy domain unto itself, where the television featured "Family Feud" reruns, and knickknacks and framed memories adorned the walls. A small, old-fashioned kitchen lay just beyond a breakfast nook divider, and a set of stairs spiraled cottage-style to the second floor.

A long couch and a chair with a matching ottoman had been enough to seat everyone in the small living room before Mabel Forrester muted Family Feud. The old woman began by apologizing.

"I don't get much company. I live alone, since my husband passed. And my children all live out-of-state." She offered them refreshments, and the team respectfully declined while exchanging introductions.

"Mrs. Forrester," Susan said, "Can you tell us everything that you can remember about what you saw that night?"

"I like to stay up and watch late-night TV," she said with a guilty smile. "So, around midnight, I decided to go to bed. I have a habit of looking outside through the window before I turn in, you know, just to make sure everything's okay, and to double-check that my door is locked. I peeped through the window blinds that night, and what I saw you'll never believe."

Her hand touched her bosom in disbelief. Dylan took her other hand and gave it a slight squeeze.

"I'll tell ya what, Mrs. Forrester," he said. "We've seen and studied many things. Why don't you let us be the judges of that?"

There were murmurs and light laughs of concurrence.

"Well, when I looked out, there was something in the sky across the street. Whatever it was emitted a flash of green so bright that I could see its strange, flat shape. It seemed slightly rounded on top, and it was kind of spinning or rotating. Then, it just hovered. I watched it. I never saw anything like it before. It wasn't a plane or a helicopter; I could see that. I had no idea what it was."

*Just like all the others,* Dylan thought. *Each one of them swears it wasn't any known aircraft. The personal accounts from all witnesses match up almost perfectly.*

"Mrs. Forrester, did you go outside at all to get a better look?" Susan asked.

"I unlocked and then opened the door slightly, but I didn't go outside. I didn't want to get anywhere near that thing."

Dylan thought about what a wise decision that had been. He asked the next question.

"Before we leave, could you point out where you saw it hovering?"

She agreed. Then, Brett spoke up next.

"Ma'am, were you able to tell how large of an object it was?"

The old woman's eyes rolled slightly upward, viewing a screen that played past images in her mind. They watched her features wrinkle in estimation.

"It was high up above," she said. "But if I had to guess, I'd say it was about fifty to a hundred feet in diameter."

"You sound so sure." Dylan smiled at her.

She laughed and explained. "I'm a retired math teacher. My students hated me when I talked that way."

They laughed with her, and Sidney joined in the questioning.

"Mrs. Forrester, can you recall anything else about this object? Did it make any noise?"

"No!" Her response was quick and adamant. "It never made a sound. As I said, I had the door slightly ajar, and I could hear no sound coming from it at all. Helicopters and planes make noise; we all know that. There was nothing from this. It was silent. And it just sat in the sky hovering!"

Dylan noticed the woman's emphasis as she reiterated that last point.

"And then," she continued, "it was gone. It moved so fast that I'm not even sure if it moved at all."

A single thought jumped into Dylan's mind.

*Bull's eye.*

"I slammed the door shut and locked it," she said. "I found myself unable to sleep. So, that's when I called 911. I was more curious than anything. I wanted to ask first because I thought I was going crazy."

How well Dylan knew what she meant.

"Believe me, Mrs. Forrester," he said. "You're not crazy. Quite a few others saw the same thing that night."

He failed to mention that he was one of them.

"Yes, and you're very lucky that you kept the doors closed and stayed inside," Susan said. "Two people were admitted into the hospital with radiation sickness."

Mabel Forrester's mouth dropped. Dylan's next question was straight to the point.

"Mrs. Forrester, would you describe what you saw as a UFO?"

The old woman closed her eyes and nodded her head in assurance. "Yes, I would."

After more discussion on the subject, the team decided that they'd obtained enough information. There was not much more Mabel Forrester could tell them, but there was something she could show them—the location of the sighting. At the front door she reenacted how she'd stood, peeping outside. Then, they all stepped out onto the small front porch. She stood and pointed across the street, a distance of approximately one hundred feet away.

"It was over there. It wasn't exactly above my neighbor's house, but I would say, above the back yard area."

"Did you mention anything to your neighbors about what you saw near their house?" Dylan asked.

"No." She laughed. "I didn't want to scare them or make them think I was crazy."

"That's what I want to mention." Dylan could hear Susan's discretion as she was about to warn the elderly woman. "Mrs. Forrester, there may be some people who are over-anxious, or aggressively curious to hear what you've just told us. It's important that you don't speak to them about this. If anyone should contact you, it's important that you play dumb. Tell them you know nothing about what they're talking about. You already know us; you remember our names. We may be back to call upon you, but what I'm asking is that you don't trust anyone else."

Mabel Forrester took a sudden, deep breath. "I understand. I was glad to speak with you all about this. If there's anything else I can remember—"

"Please call us." Dylan handed her his card, as well as the team's card. "Mrs. Forrester, please feel free to contact me anytime day or night. I would appreciate it. This whole issue is very close and personal to me, which I will tell you about sometime."

Susan handed the elderly woman her card next.

"And you may contact me also," she said.

A smile swept Mabel's face, and she thanked them all.

They said their goodbyes, leaving Mabel Forrester alone on the front porch. She watched after them as they reloaded into the van. Dylan and the team waved goodbye as Sidney drove away.

\* \* \* \*

On the way to Mabel Forrester's house, they'd been cautious to search for strange sedans, prying eyes, or unlikely characters. They'd forgotten to search with their own prying eyes to the street above Phoenix Drive. On a crested hill above, Skylark Lane overlooked Mabel Forrester's house, and there, sat a sleek black sedan that no one saw. The two men inside watched the investigators drive away. And they watched the old woman on the porch.

\* \* \* \*

Mabel Forrester hadn't been feeling well for quite some time. The strange twitching in the middle of her chest and the occasional numbness of her right arm were enough to concern her, but she hated hospitals—always did. At eighty-three, she'd seen her share of maladies and was keenly aware of how quickly they often passed. She figured that this one would do the same. But when those nice investigators came to visit her, she hadn't expected the slight twitching that made her try to catch a sudden intake of breath. It happened in front of them, but she thought she'd played it off well. After all, she hadn't been feeling *that* poorly.

How friendly they all were, especially the parapsychologist woman and the young man asking her most of the questions, not to mention that beautiful young blonde girl. Mabel was sure she'd heard her name mentioned before. They'd come to talk to her about what she'd seen Saturday night. She was glad that at eighty-three, she wasn't nuts after all.

She remembered how her heart fluttered when she saw that thing up in the sky. She'd been so enraptured by it that she'd almost forgotten the slight numbness of her arm. What a sight that had been. She'd even blinked to make sure it wasn't her eyes. She would never forget the flash of green it emanated, the way it hovered and rotated, as if it were spying on some secret sleeping subject in the night. She told them about how there had been no noise coming from it. Its dead silence was the strangest thing she'd ever witnessed. Its shape was one that her mind told her was not possible. She'd heard of things like that in the 1950s, and then there was the Kecksburg incident and the whole Bigfoot business in the 1970s. The wild stories had continued into the present time, but now, not even her aging eyes could deny what she'd seen plainly across the street.

She'd shut the door and relocked it. Whatever it was could've stayed the hell out there. She was going to bed. But she couldn't sleep; the curiosity was overwhelming her. She dialed 911 and very innocently asked if anyone had reported seeing anything. She felt like a nut, but the responder who'd answered had been nice. She told her that no one had reported anything. She almost regretted disclosing her name and number, but the appearance of those investigators on her doorstep told her that she hadn't been imagining things.

Now, there was another knock at the door.

For a moment, she thought the investigators had returned, but they hadn't. The two men standing on the porch wore matching fedoras, black overcoats, and equally dark sunglasses. Maybe it was her eyes, but they had the oddest shaped faces she'd ever seen. She stared at them for a moment. Something was not right about them.

"Yes?" she asked.

"Mrs. Forrester, may we come in?"

Mabel opened the screen door and stepped outside onto the front porch. Suddenly, the long ago voice she'd often used in addressing her unruly students surprised her. It had shown up again after all these years.

"And *who exactly* might you be?"

They stared back at her—emotionless, expressionless, eerie countenances unmoved by her sudden sternness. She glowered at them, waiting. The one with the fatter, rounder face spoke first.

"Mrs. Forrester, those people that just left here claim to be paranormal investigators. They are not. They're imposters. It's important that you not speak with them any further."

When he used the word "imposters," something swept through Mabel Forrester's mind, like the clearing of cobwebs in an old house. She remembered something. Leah Leeds was that girl that grew up in Cedar Manor, the one who'd written about it. The real liars were right in front of her. She remembered what Susan Logan had advised her of before she left, those who would be over anxious to find out what she saw Saturday night. Mabel played it cool; she wasn't great at playing dumb.

"Well, I told them exactly what I'm about to tell you," she said. "I'm getting old, and my eyes aren't what they used to be, neither is my mind.

I sometimes see things that aren't there, and sometimes I can't see things that *are* there. I told them I wasn't sure that I'd seen anything."

Her tone had ambiguously told them to buzz-off.

"But you did call 911," the skinnier faced one said. "Is that correct?"

He sounded like he was accusing her. The fatter one spoke next.

"Mrs. Forrester, we work for the US government."

Somehow, in some strange way, Mabel knew this wasn't true. They were liars.

"Then, where are your credentials?!" Mabel's tone turned explosive, like the time Michael Porter called her a bitch. "You don't *look like* you work for the government to me!"

They focused on her, silent, staring her down. Suddenly, she was afraid of these men. The skinnier, taller man stepped toward her.

"Mrs. Forrester, don't tell anyone else about what you saw that night, especially those people that just left here."

He raised his voice to her, issuing a sharp, threatening rasp of a warning...

"If you do, we know where you live," he said. "*We know* in what states your children reside. Don't say another word, or we'll be back to visit you."

Her ears burned while she felt her stomach drop. Her knees were giving out from under her. She watched them turn around and walk briskly off the porch, up the sidewalk, and into a black sedan. Her heart was pounding hard, hurting her eardrums. There was that twitching again, though this time, it was no twitching; it was pain, worse than she'd ever felt before. Her arm was dead with numbness. She tried to speak, but the shock wouldn't let her; it was raising the hair on her head and freezing her spine.

She opened the door and hurried back into the house. She wasn't sure who to call first: Susan Logan, Dylan Rasche, or her doctor. Whether she hated hospitals or not, she was convinced it was time. She was sweating. She couldn't breathe as she reached for the phone. The pain skyrocketed up her arm and through her chest. There was only one number she could call now, the one she'd called recently—911. She wasn't sure if she pressed all three digits before the darkness overcame her.

# Chapter Nine

## ~ Threats ~

The two men in matching black overcoats sat in their black sedan, watching the front doors of University Hospital. They had just left Mabel Forrester's house only moments ago. The driver with the fuller face turned to the other and spoke.

"So, it was *them*?"

"It was," the thinner, taller one replied. "The Paranormal Research and Investigative Society—this is a bigger mess than we assumed, and it seems to be getting bigger."

"You mean because of Dylan Rasche?" The heavier man asked.

"Yes, Dylan Rasche," the other man confirmed, "Dr. Geoffrey Rasche's son."

It was then that the thinner man's phone rang. He answered it without speaking.

"I see," he replied into the phone.

Not another word was spoken, and he ended the call with a push of a button. He turned his head and spoke to the driver.

"The young man has been released from the hospital. He's at home."

"Then it's time we pay him a visit." The driver started the engine, and the sleek sedan slithered out from its hiding place.

\* \* \* \*

Shane Rowe was glad to be home and thankful that the entire episode was over, at least as far as he was concerned. He felt much better and was equally ecstatic to get a few days off from Happy's. But the images in his mind of what he saw that night became relentless. They played over and over again like snatches of scenes from a projector film. He would never forget the green light that swept through the truck, and especially that thing he saw in the sky. Its shape, the way it rotated, the way it was so silent, as if it was watching him, all of it was fresh in his memory—too fresh. Whatever it was had flipped the stations on his radio.

He was convinced that it was the source of the radiation that had caused his exposure and put him in the hospital. He'd been sickened by the sudden heat wave that had surrounded him and silently seeped into his system. Later, he'd been visited by two paranormal investigators—unbelievable. They seemed nice enough, but he wasn't sure what more he could tell them. He told them everything he could remember.

His father had come and retrieved his truck from the hospital and later came to pick him up. It was hospital policy that patients were not permitted to drive home after being discharged. His father had offered him to come and rest at home. His mother was insisting. He declined. He wanted to come back here, to his apartment, where normalcy had stopped when he left for work on Saturday.

When he arrived home, he showered to rid himself of the hospital smell and changed into sweats and a tee-shirt. He'd been lounging on the sofa when there was a fast, rapid knocking at the door.

*Who the hell could that be?*

He lumbered toward the door, wondering what kind of emergency waited beyond it. He prepared to tell someone's ass off if there wasn't one. He swung the door open and stared back at two men dressed almost identically: black overcoats, dark sunglasses and what looked like fedoras, but he wasn't sure. His eyes met each of them, something about their faces...

"Man, who are you, and what do you want?"

His lingering fatigue was making him irritable.

"Shane Rowe?" The taller of the two men spoke, while the other glared at him with what seemed like a malicious challenge.

"Yeah, I'm Shane Rowe? Who are you?"

The taller man, doing all the talking, spoke first.

"Since you're being such a smart ass," he said. "We won't bother to ask to come in. We'll just push our way in!"

The heavier man pushed Shane through the doorway and into the living room. He shoved him hard, so hard that he fell to the floor. The taller, thinner man loomed over him in his own living room.

"Now, listen to me, smart ass. I know that those nosy investigators have spoken to you. *I know* they have."

Shane tried to remain calm. He probably couldn't take both of them. They may have been packing heat. He spoke rationally.

"I don't know what you're talking about—"

Then, a fast pendulum movement of the thinner man's boot kicked him in his ribs. The pain shot up to his head and back again. He cried out.

"Don't deny it," he said. "We know everything. We know that you were exposed to radiation, and that's why you were in the hospital. We saw your father drop you off."

Shane's mind was reeling at the mention of his father. That was a veiled threat, but it took his mind away from the pain.

Then, the fatter one spoke. "Consider yourself warned not to talk to anyone, from here on out, about what you saw Saturday night."

The thinner man began again.

"Not the investigators, not your friends, and *definitely not* your family."

Now, the threat was no longer veiled; it was undeniable. Shane stayed on the floor, careful not to anger or provoke them further.

"Are we clear?"

Shane nodded, while holding his side.

"Oh, and one more thing..." The thinner man wasn't quite finished. "The male investigator that came to see you—was his name Dylan Rasche?

Shane went silent. He remembered Dylan; he was a nice guy. He didn't want to get him into trouble, or worse, killed by the looks of it. He was thinking of what to say when suddenly, the fatter man came around to his other side and dealt another blow with his hard, black boot. He screamed, louder this time.

"Well, was it?!" the thinner man asked.

Shane struggled to catch his breath, panting repetitively. He stuttered when he replied. "Yea-yea—YES!"

"Remember your vow of silence, Shane," the thinner man warned.

"You could always disappear, so could your family."

Shane lay on the floor and watched the two men turn to leave. They opened his front door and slammed it shut behind them.

* * * *

As the men in black drove away from Shane Rowe's apartment complex, the heavier man said to the other.

"So, do we pay a visit to Ursula Masters?"

"No," the other said. "Apparently, she's connected to the investigators. We can't make too much noise."

There was a brief silence.

"So, what do we do now?"

"We wait. We watch from the background and see what happens."

The sedan glided smoothly through Green Valley.

# Chapter Ten

## ~ A Meeting of Minds ~

Ursula was hearing again. Right now, her clairaudience was acute, sharpened. It usually happened that way when she was sick. She could hear them coming down the hallway. They were talking about her, and she could hear every word they uttered.

"So, will she be okay, now that she's been moved to her own room?" That was Sidney Pratt.

"Yes," Susan said. "It means that she's well enough not to be in ICU anymore. I wouldn't doubt it if Ursula is released tomorrow or the next day."

Ursula liked the sound of that. She hated this place; it smelled like pee and death.

Dylan spoke next.

"I would like to go to her apartment with our Geiger counter and see what kind of radiation levels we pick up."

"Well, a contamination team has already been inside to search for radiation levels. They found nothing substantial in her apartment. The only levels they found were minor and may have come from Ursula herself."

"Yeah," Brett Taylor said. "But they didn't check outside where she was standing. The back yard of that duplex may still contain higher levels of radiation."

On those last words, they turned the corner and stood in the doorway of her room.

"Come on in, guys and gals," she said, sitting up in bed.

She held out her arms, and from behind the pack, Leah stepped forward and gave Ursula a giant hug. They exchanged warm greetings.

"I'm so glad that you're okay," Leah said.

"Thank you," Ursula said. "I could say the same to you. It's been awhile."

Brett and Sidney stepped forward and hugged Ursula, and for a moment, she felt the embarrassment of looking like hell. She hoped her breath didn't stink.

"Thank you all for being here," she said. "I could hear you all coming down the hallway. And yes, Dylan, you can go to my apartment and search for radiation levels."

They looked at each other and laughed.

Leah sat on the bed with her, Dylan and Susan sat in the surrounding two chairs, and Brett and Sidney stood. When asked, she told them that she felt much better than before, complained about the food, and the need to go home. Then, they got down to business. Ursula recapped the story of her sighting: how she'd been outside smoking, how the object lingered in the sky above her, and the green light that changed colors.

"It was silent," Ursula said. "It was like it was watching me."

She reiterated how the treetops swayed, how it had moved so quickly, how she'd gone into the house, felt ill, and collapsed as she called 911.

"I was one scared bitch," she said, as they giggled. "I had no idea what the hell was happening. I'm just so glad that it's almost over."

"Ursula," Susan began, "I did want to alert you to the fact that someone else came into the hospital Sunday with radiation sickness, someone who saw the exact same thing that you did. His level of exposure was much less, so he was released today. But you are in no way alone."

Ursula was surprised, and secretly a little scared. This thing was more real than she thought.

"Well, I'm glad that he's okay."

"Ursula, you're right," Dylan said. "I do want to check the levels of radiation at your apartment, as you heard. I guess we have your permission?"

She reached over to her small table and opened up the drawer underneath. She retrieved a set of keys and handed them to Dylan.

"Be my guest," she said.

"And I will be taking you home whenever you're released," Susan said. "There's no need to call your mother or sister. I'll return the keys to you then."

Ursula thanked her, and then Dylan explained his plan. He wanted to start with her balcony, and then go to the back yard where the treetops swayed.

"When you saw the treetops swaying," Dylan said. "We think that's when the radiation had been expelled from this object. The other person who was exposed witnessed swaying treetops as well."

She consented to Dylan's plan, and then Susan gave her a warning.

"Ursula, what I'm about to tell you must remain strictly confidential," she said. "We don't mind telling you, since you're an honorary member of our society. I don't mean to scare you, but we believe that the Men in Black are involved at this point."

Ursula was stunned at the words she'd just heard. Her mind tried to deny that the words had even been uttered. She'd heard of the Men in Black, who hadn't? She felt her eyes widen, exposing the black pearls that they were.

"You mean, *the* Men in Black?"

"Yes, but don't breathe a word," Susan said. "They contacted the 911 operator who took your call and threatened her."

"What bastards!"

"Shh," Leah said, holding her hand.

"Ursula, I have a question," Dylan said. "When you helped us a few years ago, you mentioned being followed by a maroon sedan. Do you remember?"

She nodded. Dylan finished his question.

"Do you think it's possible that the Men in Black were following you?"

She'd never thought of it. She hadn't seen any faces, only the sedan. She shrugged.

"I don't know," she said. "I never really saw *who* it was."

"Well, we wanted you to be aware," Susan said. "They may try to contact you. If they do, I want you to play it cool, which means no temper."

"I know that's hard," Sidney said, nudging her arm.

"Seriously, Ursula," Susan said. "These men are not to be messed with. If you encounter them, don't tell them anything. Tell them you don't want to talk about it. That may be exactly what they want you to do."

She nodded her head. "Okay," she said. "I can hold my own."

"That's what we're afraid of," Sidney said. This time, Ursula playfully slapped his hand.

The subject faded, and after a few more laughs, Ursula congratulated Leah on her upcoming graduation.

"Thank you," Leah said. "I'd love it if you can make it," she said.

"If I'm out of here, kid, I will definitely be there," she said.

They exchanged their goodbyes, and Ursula watched them leave.

The Men in Black, she thought. Underneath the tough exterior, Ursula shivered inside. She'd heard and read the stories about them. Could they be after her? Could it have been them following her when she helped that boy, Ryan Quinn? She sighed and tried not to think about it.

* * * *

They walked down the hallway, talking as they neared the elevator. Out of the corner of her eye, Susan spied Nurse Ashlee scurrying towards her and the team.

"Dr. Logan, wait!" she called out.

"What is it, Ashlee?" Susan asked, as she turned to face her.

"There's been another patient brought into the ER," she said. "They found this lying next to her."

Ashlee handed Susan her own business card.

*Susan Logan*
*Psychiatrist, Parapsychologist*
*Green Valley University Hospital*

The card also contained her various phone numbers and email addresses. This was *her* business card. She'd just given one to Mabel Forrester.

"Describe the patient for me," Susan said.

"She's an elderly Caucasian female in her early eighties."

She heard Leah gasp behind her. Susan knew what this meant; they all did. Mabel Forrester was brought into the ER.

"What happened?" Susan asked.

"It looks like a heart attack."

"Let's get down to the ER, now. Thank you, Ashlee."

Ashlee hurried away just as the elevator doors opened and the team stepped inside. Susan pressed the first floor button for the ER. The doors closed, and after a quick jolt, the magnetic pull thrust them downward.

"Now, wait," Sidney said. "Are you certain that she was referring to Mabel Forrester?"

"Sidney, I just gave her this card," Susan said. "Who else would it be?"

"What could have happened to trigger this?" Brett asked. "You don't think it could have been our visit, do you?"

"I doubt it," Susan said. "Who knows, Brett, she may have already had problems."

Their back and forth speculation lasted less than a minute, until the elevator doors parted, allowing them onto the first floor. Susan led the way to the ER, but then stopped as they arrived.

"They're not going to allow all of you into the ER," Susan said. "Why don't you all wait in the lobby, and let me check it out first. I'll meet you all there afterwards."

The team turned around and made their way to the lobby, while Susan stepped through the entrance to the ER. She found the nearest resident doctor, a younger man in his thirties with dark hair and glasses. She'd never seen him before, so she introduced herself and inquired about the patient who'd been in possession of her business card.

"Yes, Dr. Logan," he said. "I'm Dr. Parsons. The patient is an eighty-three-year-old woman who was brought in. They found your card in her possession. Her name is Mabel Forrester."

Susan's heart sank. Dr. Parsons went on.

"We've done an EKG. We're waiting for the results now, but it looks like a massive coronary."

"What's her prognosis?"

"At her age, it's not good."

"Could something have triggered this?"

"Possibly," he said. "But, it looks like she may have had some problems for quite some time. Add to that a trigger, sure, but it would have happened sooner or later, no doubt."

"May I see her?" Susan asked.

The young Dr. Parsons agreed, asking if Mabel Forrester was a patient of hers.

"Not a patient," Susan said. "She's just an acquaintance."

"She's in and out of consciousness," he said. "Maybe you can find out what happened?"

"I intend to," Susan said.

He directed her to the triage unit where Mable Forrester lay with oxygen tubes spiraling up her nostrils and patches sticking to her arms and chest. The old woman's eyes were closed, so Susan tiptoed toward the bed, careful not to alarm her. She stood over her and watched her eyes slowly open. The old woman focused on the figure standing above her. Susan spoke softly.

"Mabel," she whispered. "It's Susan—Susan Logan."

The elderly woman nodded her head. She remembered.

"Mabel, can you speak?" she asked. "If so, don't overdo it. Speak a word or two, or just nod your head if you need to, understand?"

She nodded her head again.

"You seemed fine when we left you," she said. "Were you having problems before?"

"Yes," she replied.

Susan apologized, telling her that she had no idea.

"Was it our visit that brought this on, Mabel?"

"No!" Mable shook her head adamantly.

Susan noticed the look in her eyes, the look of urgency. The grimace on her face was as if she wanted to say something but couldn't spit it out.

"It's alright, Mabel," Susan said. "Relax, and give me a word or two."

Now, the look in Mabel Forrester's eyes had turned to fear.

"Men," she said. "Overcoats...Glasses."

Mabel took a deep breath. The pain of that breath made her cry. "They threatened me," she said.

Susan's heart began to pound, the blood racing through her veins. What was once slight trepidation at the mention of those men had now turned to explosive anger. But at this moment, she needed to smother it.

"They said they worked for the government." Mabel's face winced. "Liars!"

"Okay, Mabel, stay calm," Susan said. "You're here now. You're safe. I will take care of this. I promise you. I am onto this, and I can, and will help you. But right now, you need to get some rest."

The old woman calmed herself and nodded.

"I'll be back to see you as soon as I can," Susan said. "And I don't want you to worry about a thing."

Mabel nodded once more, and soon, she fell back into sleep. Susan kissed her forehead before leaving the triage and finding Dr. Parsons.

"Dr. Parsons, I'm taking over Mrs. Forrester's case until you locate her doctor. When she's admitted to a room, I want two security guards posted outside of it at all times."

"Alright," he said. "Should I call the police?"

"No, don't do that," Susan said. "I'll handle this."

She could feel Dr. Parson's eyes watching her as she turned and stormed out of the ER. She began to realize that everything that was happening was getting harder and harder to accept. This case was provoking both their fears and their anger. She had to find the team, now.

* * * *

The four of them were waiting in the lobby for her, just as she expected. They rose when they saw her. She looked around the lobby before she spoke to them. Discretion was going to be an even greater concern now. The magnitude of what they'd become immersed in had just climbed a few notches. Her tone was low-key as she spoke.

"I want us all to get back in the van and not speak until we're inside. We'll go back to headquarters, but first, I'll tell you everything I've learned in the van. Let's go."

Soon, the doors of the van slammed and slid shut around them. Sidney keyed the ignition, and the van's engine purred to life. The van rolled its way down the slopes of the hospital's parking garage and out onto the street. She sat in the middle with Leah, who stared at her, waiting for her to speak. Dylan sat up front and turned to face her.

"So," he said. "Was it Mabel Forrester?"

She was well aware that the look on her face was displaying the slight fear she felt inside.

"Susan, what is it?" Leah asked.

"Yes, Mabel Forrester was brought in," she said. "They suspect a massive coronary. But there's more. She told me that she was visited by our friends, the Men in Black. They threatened her. They're the reason she's here!"

She heard their astonishment, saw their quick movements to get a closer ear to the story. Brett moved up closer from the back of the van. Sidney eyed her through the rearview mirror.

"They must have shown up right after we left," she said.

"Then they had to have been watching us," Dylan surmised.

"I think you're right, Dylan," Susan said. "Mabel couldn't say much. I told her to speak using only brief words. She described them perfectly. They threatened her. They threatened her because she spoke to us. I'm sure of it."

"This is out of hand!" Leah said.

Sidney, still watching her through the rearview mirror, spoke next.

"I say it's about time that we get one over on those sons-a-bitches!"

"Great, Sidney. If you have a plan, we'd all love to hear it. These men are dangerous, and what's worse, no one knows who they are. They told her they worked for the government. She said they were liars. For some reason, Mabel knows that they don't work for our government. So, who the hell are they?"

"I wonder if they were following us, or watching her house," Brett said.

"That's a good point, Brett," Susan said. "I will never forgive myself if we brought those men to that poor woman."

"No," Dylan said. "She's a witness. They had to have been monitoring her house, just like they're watching Janette LaRue."

"Well, they already know that we're involved," Susan said. "It's only a matter of time before we hear from them. I think we'd better be prepared."

They arrived at the university and went straight to their headquarters in room 208 of Levin Hall. Room 208 looked as it always had: a giant screen television sat in the corner across from the long conference table with its plush, velvet chairs. Computer stations adorned one side of the wall, and various video screens lined the opposite wall. They all took their usual places around the conference table, grateful to relax in the plush, velvet chairs if only for a few moments.

"So, the Men in Black are aware of our involvement," Sidney said. "I wonder how long it will take for them to show up here."

"I don't understand," Leah said. "We looked all around us, all five of us, when we got to her street. We saw nothing. Where could they have been hiding?"

"Anywhere, Leah," Susan replied. "They could've been anywhere. They're origins are unknown. They claim to be from the government, yet many have disputed that over the years, including our government. They're sneaky, diabolical, and mysterious. They could have been watching from who knows how far away."

"Speaking of our government," Sidney said. "If the MIB are *not* part of our government, then what exactly is the extent of our government's involvement?"

"Yeah," Brett interjected. "It's not like they *don't know* about the UFO phenomena that has taken place all over the world, let alone our country."

"They played a pretty dominant role at Kecksburg, I know that," Susan said. "So many people had described the military's presence at the scene, as well as the Men in Black. Yet, many witnesses are adamant that the MIB are separate from our government. Witnesses have given strange descriptions of their faces and among other things, their uncanny ability of knowing things, and they're quick entrances and exits wherever they are. The stories about them go back all the way to the 1940s. And our government claims to know nothing of the Men in Black."

"Our government has consistently denied the existence of UFOs," Dylan said. "Many believe that's because UFO's are made and owned by our government. The hypothesis is that UFOs are top secret weaponry still in development, and that *there are no* extraterrestrial beings. The UFOs belong to our government, as well as Russia, and who knows what other countries."

"Yeah," Brett said. "Tell that to those who claim to have been abducted."

"Has anyone ever considered the possibility that there could be some divine source behind these phenomena?" Leah asked. "I mean, I know that many people have pondered the possibility, but have any of you?"

Susan smiled, knowing that Leah would be the one to lay that card on the table.

"That's an interesting theory, Leah," she said. "And you're right, many have pondered the possibility, yet no one has any proof of anything."

"What has caught my attention," Dylan said, "is the witness accounts are nearly identical, but that's just it, *nearly*. There are slight differences. For an example, Ursula and Shane saw this object's lights change color, but Mabel did not. She remembers only green. Marv saw different colors in the sky; I did not. Is it because of the object itself, or is it just us?"

Susan answered that one as a psychiatrist.

"Dylan, human minds do not work like recorders. How the mind processes information is one thing, but how the person repeats it in their mind, or verbally, is another. Oddly, we all see things differently. Different human minds work in different ways. Then, there's the issue of timing. You, Ursula, Shane, Marv, and Mabel may have all caught different aspects of the same thing that night. It's not unusual.

"What I'm thankful for," she continued, "is that if either Ursula or Shane had been just a little bit closer, or lingered just a little longer, they both could have suffered severe radiation burns. But they were at a considerable distance from the object. Look, we may never solve the nationwide or worldwide UFO phenomena, but we can try to discover how it affects Green Valley. After all, our area has quite a long history with this type of thing. This one's right in our own back yard and has been for some time now. What is it about our area? We'd be remiss not to investigate."

Dylan spoke up.

"We have to find out what this thing has to do with Eagle Rock Mountain. I know this is why my father died. It's there in his journals. The same thing that's happening now was happening then. The MIB were following him, and now they're back, and they know that we're involved. But I'm not afraid of them. I'm ready to find out why they killed my father!"

Susan leaned in closer to him and spoke precisely and deliberately.

"Of course you do, Dylan," she said. "*We all* do, but first things first. Marv told us that years ago, he contacted this Seth Dornan and voiced his suspicions about your father's death. We will wait for him. He may have some insight into this. He's a MUFON investigator. I'm sure he wants to meet you, Dylan, and I'm definitely sure that he wants to read your father's journals. Let's be patient and hear what his plan of action is."

"I think we should also visit Shane Rowe soon," Sidney said. "I think the rest of us should hear his story in his own words."

"Good idea, Sidney," Susan said. "But for now, let's wait for Marv and Seth Dornan. They're expected to contact us soon."

* * * *

Seth Dornan sat in the quiet, comfortable coffeehouse, awaiting Marv Kincaid's arrival. They were to meet at 2:00 pm; it was five minutes till. Seth hadn't seen Green Valley in a while. The ride in brought back many memories: the long stretch of Route 30, green everywhere one looked, the old Maxim Theater, even the library across the street. He sat sipping his espresso, trying not to let memories cause his mind to wander away from the primary concerns that brought him here: the sightings, the cases of radiation sickness, the Men in Black, and ultimately, the mystery surrounding Geoffrey Rasche's death.

He was lost in thought, not even noticing the man that walked through the door, the man he hadn't seen in twenty years. Marv Kincaid was searching around with his eyes, trying to find him. Seth watched him. Marv was older now; his tighter, younger face had now drooped, and his hair was a dirty gray, but it was him. He was sure of it. The older man's head turned in his direction. Seth motioned to him with a wave of his hand.

Marv recognized him immediately and began walking toward the table. Seth rose as he came forward. Marv smiled at him, and Seth extended his hand.

"Seth Dornan," Marv said, taking his hand and shaking it. "Wow, you've gotten older." He began laughing. Seth thought the joke sucked but laughed anyway.

"It's been a long time, Marv," he said. He motioned with his hand again to the other side of the table, and Marv took the opposite seat. After a quick, mundane version of catching up, Marv got down to business.

"So, the young man has been released from the hospital today. The young woman has been downgraded, expected to be released soon."

"Did you track the older woman who phoned in to 911?" Seth asked.

"No, I think the investigators were going to pay her a visit. I haven't phoned Susan back yet. I was waiting for you."

"What about the 911 responder?"

"My spies tell me that there's been no activity at her house. I've continued to speak with her, since she still has the disposable phone. She says everything's been quiet."

"Good," Seth said. "Is it possible to pay a visit to the investigators today?"

"Most likely," Marv answered. "I told Susan to wait for my call today. I told them to expect you."

"Excellent. I'd also like to read Dr. Rasche's journals, since his son is now in possession of them. If what you told me *is* in those journals, all of it may be enough to open up an investigation into Eagle Rock Mountain. Why don't you call Susan Logan now?"

Marv retrieved his phone from his inner jacket pocket and selected Susan's number from the contact list. Seth watched as Marv waited for an answer.

* * * *

Marv waited for Susan to answer the phone, and on the fourth ring, she did.

"Susan, it's Marv," he said. "I'm sitting here with Seth Dornan. We'd like to know if we could visit you and the investigators."

"Of course, Marv," she said. "But first, I need to alert you to something."

"Go ahead." His eyes shifted across the table to Seth.

"Mabel Forrester is in the hospital. After we visited her today, she was paid yet another visit—by the Men in Black. They threatened her. After they left, she had a massive coronary. Luckily, she was able to dial 911. Marv, they had to have been watching her house. There was no one following us; we're sure of it. But they must have watched us leave. They're onto us."

Marv kept staring at Seth, whose narrow-eyed expression begged him to explain.

"What I'm saying is that they may be watching us here at the university."

Marv told her that he would discuss the new developments with Seth and get back to her. He ended the call and told Seth the news.

"Susan feels that they could be watching the university," Marv said.

"Well, that's possible," Seth replied. "But if they are, how do they know where *we're* going? We could be going anywhere. And, I think there's only one way we're going to get to the bottom of anything; and that is if we draw them out. I think we may need to confront them, once and for all. I don't think they're bold enough to confront all of us at the same time. I think drawing them out into the open may be exactly what we need to do."

"Seriously?" Marv said. "That didn't work so well for Geoffrey Rasche."

"But he was one man. There are seven of us," Seth said. "I don't know about you, Marv, but I'm not about to be intimidated by a pair of men who go around threatening old ladies. Enough is enough. We need to fight fire with fire. And if they already know about the investigators, then what's the point in sneaking around? Call her back. Tell her we're on our way."

Marv redialed Susan's number and told her to expect the two of them.

# Chapter Eleven

## ~ A Meeting of Minds (Part II) ~

"That was Marv calling back," Susan said. The four of them waited for her to continue. "They're on their way here. They've decided to come whether we're being watched or not. Listen, everyone; I'm getting the impression that this Seth Dornan is a little more courageous than normal. He doesn't seem to be bothered by the possibility that they could be watching us. He may be somewhat of a daredevil. If that's the case, remember that we as a team stand together and by our own decisions."

"So, Seth Dornan has investigated UFOs in our area before?" Sidney asked.

"As a MUFON investigator, that's his job," Susan said. "It's possible that he knows a lot more about the Men in Black than we realize. We may be getting involved in a serious showdown."

"I think we know enough already," Leah said.

Dylan had remembered to lock the door of room 208. Now, he unzipped a backpack he'd been carrying around. He took out his father's journals and placed them on the table once again. "I'm anxious to show him these," he said. "Years ago, he told Marv that there wasn't enough to go on. I think these journals may change his mind on that."

"And I'm sure you're right, Dylan," Susan said. "We just have to wait and find out."

\* \* \* \*

Seth and Marv pulled up into the Levin Hall parking lot in Seth's car. Marv pondered the possibility of entering through the building's back entrance.

"What does it matter?" Seth asked. "If they're watching, they're watching."

A wave of unease swept through Marv's stomach. He sighed.

"Alright, then," he said. "Here goes."

They stepped out of Seth's Honda Civic and walked toward the front entrance of Levin Hall. Seth noticed Marv looking around him—left, right, and then left again.

"Let's not look too suspicious, Marv," he said. "If they *are* watching, they can see you."

Marv led the way through Levin Hall, up the stairs, and down the corridor to room 208. He knocked on the door. Only silence greeted him in return. Then, Marv recognized Dylan's voice as it projected from the other side.

"Who is it?"

"It's Marv and Seth," Marv answered.

Suddenly, there was a metallic *click* on the other end, and the door swung open. Dylan motioned them to come in, and they stepped inside of room 208. They quickly exchanged greetings, and then Marv turned toward Seth.

"Everyone, this is Seth Dornan. He's been a MUFON investigator for over twenty years now. He's also been anxious to meet all of you."

Seth shook hands with them all, including Dylan, whose identity he correctly guessed.

"You must be Dylan Rasche," he said. "I've seen photos of your father. I can see the resemblance. I hear you have new information regarding your father's death. Is that correct?"

Dylan motioned with an outstretched hand to the notebooks on the table.

"Great," Seth said. "I would like to get a look at them, if I may. But first, I need you all to relate to me everything that's happened. Marv has already informed me about his part in all this. He's also given me the details on Janette LaRue. Now, I want to hear your side of things."

"Please be seated," Susan said, pointing to two empty chairs at the conference table that were set aside for them. "We have so much to talk about."

\* \* \* \*

Seth sat listening as the investigators told him everything from the beginning. Dylan began first, telling him about Saturday night, and how he later retrieved the journals.

"There's no doubt in my mind that my father was murdered," he said. "You'll see what I mean when you read them."

Susan then explained who Ursula was to them, how they knew her, and her experience from her balcony.

"She was intent on paying us a visit over the whole thing," she said. "But, she became ill when she went inside."

Then, she and Dylan filled in the details of Shane Rowe's experience and their visit to him in the hospital. She told him that he'd been released, and that they were planning on visiting him tomorrow.

"And then, there's Mabel Forrester," Leah said.

Susan told him about their visit, how hospitable she was, and how she'd warned her not to speak with anyone else about what she saw.

"We saw no one as we left," she said. "But once we were gone, *they* paid her a visit as well. She had a massive coronary afterward. When I saw her in the hospital, she told me that they threatened her. Those bastards were watching her house, and then they put her where she is. They could have killed her."

"Well, I know all about the Men in Black," Seth said. "I'm afraid I've had a run-in with them myself a few years back in 2012. They are the real deal. They're ruthless and also dangerous, as you've already learned. They've been suspected, and known, to be responsible for deaths, disappearances, and turning enthused witnesses into silent submitters. Dylan, if they *did* cause your father's death, we're going to have a hard time proving it, but at least we can get as close to the truth as possible."

"So, do they work for our government, or don't they?" Brett asked. Seth looked him straight in the eyes.

"Honestly, I don't know," he said. "Many claim yes, and others claim no. Many witnesses have described them as being too unusual to be from our government. They don't bother with identification, they look different, and they even sound different to some. Some have even claimed that they're not human, that they're faces were not human-like. But whoever they are, they're deadly, make no mistake.

"But as I was telling Marv," he continued, "they seem to do their worst when it comes to individuals, little old ladies, like your friend. However, they've never been known to threaten a group of people. There are seven of us. I truly believe that as far as we're concerned, there is strength in numbers. I plan on drawing them out. I think it's the only way we as investigators will get anywhere in this case."

Susan asked the next question. "You said that you had an experience with them a few years ago. Care to fill us in?"

"It was back in 2012," Seth began. "I was called to Beaver County, because many witnesses watched three golden, circular objects make a formation together in the sky. The witnesses claimed that the formation was hovering above Beaver County Power Station. Then suddenly, the formation disappeared."

"You mean the nuclear power station?" Sidney asked. Seth nodded.

"I'd spoken with various witnesses," Seth said. "All of them told the same, or very similar accounts of what happened. I began snooping around. Then, one day, I saw a black sedan in my rearview mirror. It followed me for quite a while, a few days at least. I gave them the slip one time, but I stayed in Beaver County.

"Then, some of my witnesses suddenly clammed up. I'm sure that the MIB were behind it. Afterward, I never saw the black sedan again. They may have stopped following me because their objective had been accomplished; hardly anyone would speak to me any further."

"That's exactly what they did to my father," Dylan said. "They followed him. It's all right here in his journals. But my father must have stumbled upon something serious. He went up to Eagle Rock Mountain alone, and he never came back."

"I think it's time that I take a look at those, Dylan."

"Be my guest," Dylan said, pushing the notebooks over toward Seth.

Seth flipped through the pages of Geoffrey Rasche's journals, stopping at times to read certain passages aloud. He read through the Kecksburg fascination that began in Geoffrey's adolescence. He was fascinated by his investigation and documentation on the Bigfoot appearances that had immediately followed UFO sightings back in the 1970's. He marveled at how Dr. Rasche had drawn a substantial connection between the two events. Then, he read the last journal that detailed the occurrences at the Eagle Rock observatory. The next words that he read aloud chilled his bones.

*"June 28, 1993. I've been followed by a black sedan for the past few weeks. Tonight, I was followed to and from the university. I've seen that same car again and again in the rearview mirror. The stalking has become more frequent. Something is going on..."*

They'd followed him the exact same way in 2012. His heart began to pound. He read more, the most important bits and pieces.

*"September 9, 1993. I'm going up to Eagle Rock Observatory tomorrow night. I also have the feeling that I will be drawing my stalkers out into the light, or should I say, the dark? I'm tired of being followed; it is time for answers."*

Seth stared at the blank white space that left the journal unfinished. He felt the hair on his head rise.

"As you can see by the date," Dylan said, "that was the day before my father never returned."

Seth was alarmed by the blatant controversy of the pages before him. Direct proof lay right in front of him, proof that the MIB were responsible for Dr. Geoffrey Rasche's death. He'd lured his stalkers out into the open, yet they were unaware that he'd been keeping a journal that recorded their every movement toward him, and named them as his aggressors. The white space at the abrupt end of the last journal would be enough to convince any courtroom, any public, and any media that Dr. Geoffrey Rasche had been murdered. But still, as disturbing as it was, the secret thrill of excitement caused the blood to rush through Seth's veins. He tried not to let it show.

"So, do you think they're watching Levin Hall?" Susan asked Seth.

"It's possible," he said, "but maybe not. As I said, there may be too many of you, or us."

"What do you suggest?" Dylan asked.

"Right now, I'd say go about your business, and continue to be discreet," he said. "Don't seek them out. Let them find us. Did you all say that you were going to see the young man, Shane, tomorrow?"

Susan affirmed this.

"Great," he said. "I'd like to go with you, if I may. I'd like to hear his story."

"You're both welcome to come," Susan said. "But we'll have to take two vehicles." She explained how it was usually cramped with all of the team riding in the van.

"Not a problem," he said. "Also, Dylan, I'd like to photograph a few of these pages, if that's alright with you."

Dylan agreed. Seth took his iPhone from the inner pocket of his light suede jacket and snapped pictures of the pages in question, the final few from the last journal. Then, he mailed them to his home computer.

"I'm going to file these with my report for Hangar 1," Seth said. "You're all familiar with Hangar 1, aren't you? Hangar 1 stores the largest archive of UFO files on earth. It is owned and operated by MUFON. And I assure you, Dylan, these pages will remain strictly confidential while in our possession. MUFON answers to no government or any set of individuals."

Dylan thanked him and shook his hand, and within minutes, Seth and Marv were back in the parking lot in front of Levin Hall. Marv continued to look around him as they spoke. Seth did the same but with more discretion. They got back into Seth's car and talked about what interesting personalities dwelled beyond the door of room 208. Seth keyed the ignition, and they rode out of the parking lot and onto the road.

* * * *

Levin Hall was on the lower level of the campus grounds. An upper level of university buildings sat on top of a small hill and across from the Levin Hall parking lot. The upper level parking lot overlooked Levin Hall, and a clear view of it could be seen from atop. But the upper level parking lot was almost hidden, shaded by trees and foliage. Also neatly hidden was the black sedan whose inhabitants surveyed the home of the paranormal investigators and watched as the two recognizable men walked in and out of the building.

The taller of the two Men in Black spoke from the passenger's side.

"Is that who I think it is?" he asked. "Is that him?"

The heavier man, the driver, waited before responding, watching intently through binoculars to be certain.

"Yes, that's him," he said, handing the binoculars to the taller man. "Take a look."

The taller man took the binoculars and watched.

"You're right, it's him—Seth Dornan," he said.

"Seth Dornan," the other repeated.

"Seth Dornan." The taller man put down the binoculars.

"Who's the older man?" the driver asked. "He looks familiar."

"I'm not sure," he said. "I think he's some kind of reporter. We'll worry about him later."

There was a pause, a quick few seconds of silence before the driver spoke again.

"So, what do we do about Seth Dornan?"

The taller, thinner man in the passenger side thought before he responded.

"I think this time we're going to have to take him out."

\* \* \* \*

Seth dropped Marv off in front of his house. He waited and watched as the elder man waved and closed the front door behind him. Now, Seth had a quick moment alone. He kept yet another device in the opposite inner pocket of his suede vest. It was the one thing he always used when he was investigating—his mini voice-recorder. It was his secret tool, one he used to discreetly record his thoughts or conclusions when no one was looking. Marv Kincaid would most likely understand such a thing, being a reporter, but still, Seth wanted this personal ritual to remain private. He took the recorder from his pocket and spoke into it.

"It has now become apparent that Dr. Geoffrey Rasche was most likely murdered," he said. "I've met his son. I've seen the evidence."

He stopped the recording, replaced the recorder in his inner pocket, and drove away.

# Chapter Twelve

## ~A Refusal and a Plan ~

The investigators assembled inside of room 208 in the late, Tuesday morning hours. It was a beautiful spring day, bountiful in warmth and splendid sunshine. Today, they planned on visiting Shane Rowe. Sidney, Brett, and Leah—as well as Seth and Marv—had wanted to hear Shane's story in his own words.

Susan thanked them all for being punctual and began. "I think it's wise to call Shane before showing up on his doorstep, especially since Marv and Seth will be accompanying us."

They all agreed and took their seats once again at the conference table, though this time; Susan had taken the landline phone and placed its cradle in the middle of the table.

"Dylan, when we call, I think we should both speak to him," she said. "He may feel more comfortable with you on the line. He seemed to listen to you."

Dylan agreed. Susan dialed the number and set the call on speakerphone. They began to stare at each other after five rings, and then Shane answered the phone. His voice sounded lower, even tranquil. Susan responded.

"Shane, this is Susan Logan."

There was silence.

"Shane, it's Dylan Rasche; I'm also on the line. Look, we're glad to hear that you're okay. We were hoping that as a team, we might be able to come out to see you today, if that's—"

There was a loud click on the other end. The amplified echoing of a

133

dial tone rang out through the room.

"It sounded like he hung up on you," Sidney said.

"That's exactly what it sounded like, Sidney," Susan replied.

"I don't get it." Dylan looked to Susan for an answer.

"I don't either." Susan stared at the phone, as if *it* would provide the answer.

"What if it was accidental?" Dylan asked. "Should we call him back?"

"Dude, why?" Brett said. "He just hung up on you."

"No, don't call him back," Susan said. "I want to go out there and see what this is all about. I think you all know what I'm thinking."

"So, we're just going to go see him anyway?" Leah asked.

"Yes," Susan said. "I want to see what's going on. He may be in some kind of danger."

Susan had told Marv and Seth to wait for them at the intersection of University Drive and Grayson Avenue. She wasn't wild about Seth's idea of baiting the MIB, especially if it meant them arriving in room 208. She called Marv's phone next. He answered on the first ring.

"Marv, it's Susan," she said. "Where are you?"

"We're at the intersection, waiting for you all."

"Marv, I just called Shane Rowe, and he hung up on us. I still want to go out there. I think he hung up on us for a reason. What does Seth think?"

She could hear Marv turn the phone away from his mouth and speak to Seth. Seth's muffled response was mere mumbling in the background.

"He agrees," Marv said. "He wants to go there. If it's what you think it is, Seth also wants to speak with him."

"Wait for us," she said. "We'll see you within five minutes. Follow us from there."

She ended the call, and within minutes, they were back in the van, heading out from the university. They left the campus grounds and rode the long stretch of University Drive to the very end, where the intersection connected with Grayson Avenue. Dylan spotted Seth's Honda Civic from the corner of his eye.

"There they are," he said. Sidney honked the horn, and they watched as the Honda Civic followed them closely and in perfect distance. They were on their way to see Shane Rowe, and Susan sat hoping that the hang up had been some kind of phone mishap. Ten minutes later, they turned right into Shane's apartment complex.

"He lives in building 'C,'" Susan said.

Sidney parked the van outside of the building, while Seth parked his car across the lot. Susan and Dylan soon led the way inside and up the stairs to the right apartment—C5. They stood cramped inside the hallway, and then Susan knocked on the door. There was no immediate answer, but the trampling of feet suddenly sounded after the second knock. Susan saw the dark shade of an eye pass over the peephole. Quickly, the door opened.

\* \* \* \*

Shane had hung up the phone when they called him. He felt guilty for having done so, but it wasn't half as agonizing as the pain in his ribs. Both of his sides streaked with sharp pain that soared from his chest, to his head, and back again. He couldn't sleep in bed; he slept upright all night in his living room recliner. He couldn't stand waking in misery whenever he rolled over onto either side. He didn't want to talk to anyone again about Saturday night, especially those damn investigators. They're the ones that brought this crazy shit to his doorstep.

Those men were following them. They'd known about their visit to his hospital room. And they were after that Dylan guy. Their mention of him had made that crystal clear. Still, he no longer wanted any parts of any of it. Those men had threatened his father, his family.

Now, there was knocking at his door. If it was those men again, Shane was ready to hit the fire escape and flee down the back alley. But he had a hunch that it was the investigators because this time, there was no incessant pounding at the door, only a patient knocking. Still, he moved quickly to the door, his footfalls falling hard just in case he had to run. He gazed through the peephole and saw six or seven people standing packed in his hallway.

He recognized Susan Logan and Dylan Rasche. His hunch was right; it was the investigators. He flung the door open and stood staring at them. He was shirtless, except for the ace bandage he'd luckily found and wrapped around his torso. The anger was boiling just beneath his surface. Susan was the first to address him. She spoke softly and cautiously.

"Shane, I came by with the rest of the team and two others who would like to meet you," she said. "I wanted to introduce you to the rest of the team. We were hoping you might want to give your side of the story to all of us at the same time. I hope everything's alright?"

He quelled his anger for a moment as a shroud of pain wrapped around his torso.

"Listen," he said. "I have nothing further to say to any of you about Saturday night. I don't want to talk about any of it. In fact, I may have been mistaken."

Susan tried to counteract him over sighs of dismay that filled the small hallway.

"Shane, please wait," she said. "Has something happened? If so, it's important that you tell us. We're aware of the Men in Black. They've threatened quite a few people already. It's vital that we stand together against them."

"Well, to answer your question, Doctor," Shane said, motioning with his hands to both of his sides. "*This* is what happened! I don't know what kind of people they are, but I do know one thing, *you all* should get different occupations."

Seth stepped forward and took over the conversation.

"Shane, my name is Seth Dornan. I'm a UFO investigator with the MUFON network."

"The who?" Shane asked. His eyes squinted, displaying his irritation and confusion.

"Never mind," Seth said. "I investigate these kinds of things. I'm well acquainted with who those men are, and believe me, I can protect you. We all can protect you."

Shane could not only hear, but feel the fallacy of that last statement.

"Look, I don't want any trouble," he said, "for me, and especially not for my family. I can't do this. I'm sorry. He moved backwards to shut the door and then stepped forward again.

"Oh, and by the way, Dylan," he said. "Be careful. Stay safe, man."

He was mindful not to slam the door, but he closed it just as quickly as he'd opened it. He'd been turning a thought over in his mind. He should've gone back with his father when he was asked. Of course, those men may've shown up at his family's home. Now, he thought of going home and convincing his parents to vacate to their cabin in West Virginia. He might end up having to explain himself, but maybe the truth would get them to go along with him.

He went back into his bedroom and unearthed an old suitcase from the clutter that filled his closet. He slammed it on the bed, unlatched it, and then opened his dresser drawers. He grabbed armfuls of clothing and flung them into the suitcase in a frenzied haste. Underwear, socks, tee-shirts, jeans, all of it he stuffed between the suitcase's deep, wide jaws. Once he could fit no more, he folded it and sat on top of it, fastening the clamps that closed it shut.

He grabbed his discarded tee-shirt and slowly pulled it over him. Then, suitcase in hand, he went back to the door and peered into the peephole. They'd left, all of them. He turned the TV off, and then slung his denim jacket over his shoulder. He opened the door, locked it from inside, and looked up and down the hallway. There was no one, no neighbors, no investigators, and no Men in Black. Then, he headed for his truck. Once inside, he keyed the ignition, revved the engine, and took off.

* * * *

All the way back to the university, Dylan had pondered Shane's words over and over in his head. Now, he paced back and forth across the floor in room 208.

"So, what did he mean, exactly?" Dylan asked. "Did they threaten *me*? Why?"

"I doubt that they threatened you, Dylan," Seth said. "I would guess that they may have asked questions about you, specifically. And there could be any number of reasons for that. They could be curious about whether you're trying to find answers about your father. They might also have some foreknowledge of your father's journals, though I doubt it, especially if they were as hidden as you claim. And since you were one of the people who spoke to Shane, maybe they were curious as to what he'd told you. Either way, I would remain extremely careful."

"You know, he could have elaborated a little further before shutting the door in our faces," Marv said. Sidney and Brett agreed; Susan did not.

"Everyone, do you realize that these men attacked Shane? They obviously threatened his family; he basically told us that. Besides, we know the whole story of what Shane had witnessed. We also know what his situation was as a patient. Dylan and I wanted you all to hear the story firsthand from the witness himself, but we have enough to go on as far as the investigation is concerned."

"Right," Marv said. "But it's a shame that he didn't trust us."

"I have to admit something," Leah said. "When he opened the door, I saw visions of him. I saw him fleeing. As we were leaving, I knew that the truck parked in front was his. I was being shown its wheels tearing up the highway. He's going to be alright. I'm pretty sure of that."

"Well, if he *were* to do that," Seth began, "I doubt that would concern me. In fact, it might be a good idea. If the MIB know that he's fled, they'll be more convinced that he's afraid and won't speak any further about what he saw. What does concern me is this—they seem to be going to extraordinary lengths to keep quiet a few, random sightings—why? It's obvious that this thing is much bigger than that, and it's something that they already know about. They aren't just investigating, looking for answers, and ordering people to keep quiet. This time, they're going around and just doing it, threatening whoever they need to hush."

Dylan had already been keenly aware of this fact. His natural instincts as an investigator had already concluded that the current incidents and the sightings just before his father's death were connected. He shared this theory with all of them.

"I'm also convinced that all of this revolves around Eagle Rock Mountain. My father was investigating it then, and what happened then is reoccurring now. I know it's why he's dead. I know that those men killed him. Shane's warning had assured me of that."

"Unfortunately, I think you're right, Dylan," Seth said. "I want to explore the possibility of investigating up on Eagle Rock Mountain. There's got to be a way to get into that observatory."

"And how do you propose to do that?" Susan was blunt and direct. "Especially if those men are watching"

"*If* they're watching," Dylan said.

"And it's most likely that they are, Dylan!" Susan turned to Seth, her voice slightly raised. "Mr. Dornan, if you think that I'll risk the lives of my investigators to go on top of Eagle Rock and break into an observatory, you're sadly mistaken."

"Who said we'd be *breaking* in?" he asked.

"What you're proposing is not only improbable, but illegal," Susan pointed out.

"But there are a couple things we'd have in our favor, Dr. Logan." Seth counted on open fingers. "One is the fact that according to my theory, there is strength in numbers; two is the reality that any one of us could expose what's going on, which would put these men, and whoever else has been covering this up, in a serious and unwanted spotlight."

"There is some reasoning in that," Sidney pointed out.

Dylan spoke to counter Susan's skepticism.

"Susan, if it's possible, I need to go up there, if for no other reason than to get a better look at where my father supposedly fell. I also want to lay my eyes on that observatory. I *have* to try and find out what happened to him, one way or another."

"You've never been up on that cliff?" Susan sounded surprised.

"No, of course not," he said. "But there comes a time for everything."

"And how would you accomplish getting in there?" Susan's question was to Seth. His response was quick.

"Just let me worry about that, Dr. Logan."

Dylan worked harder to convince her.

"Besides, Susan, the observatory may be off limits, but being outside of it to capture the mountain top view is not."

Susan sighed. She looked around at their young, excited faces. She turned her head swiftly and lifted her eyes up to the ceiling. As chief investigator, Dylan spoke for her.

"Team, I think we should plan on a trip to Eagle Rock Mountain."

# Chapter Thirteen

## ~ Geiger Counters ~

Planning a clandestine trip to Eagle Rock Mountain would have to wait—for now. There was still one thing left to be done today. The team, along with Marv and Seth, ventured to Ursula's apartment, where outside, a search for radiation levels would soon begin. The Paranormal Research and Investigative Society were in possession of a handheld Geiger counter, the most modern and often used device for detecting radiation levels. Seth Dornan had brought a slightly different model, one used in his MUFON investigations.

"This is called the 'probe model,'" Seth said. He retrieved it from the backseat of his car, once they were outside of Ursula's apartment duplex. "The difference between what I have, and your model, is the probe." He pointed to the long, tubular mechanism attached to the heavier model. "This thing detects radiation levels deep inside the ground, if there are any. Both models will come in handy when we search for the spot where Shane Rowe's sighting occurred."

"But what are the chances of detecting radiation three days later?" Brett asked.

"It's very likely," Seth said. "Obviously, the levels would have been higher earlier but would still be there, especially if they're the type that we're looking for."

"And what type would that be?" Leah asked.

"Gamma rays," Seth said, "the most harmful, the type that does the most damage."

"You mean the type that comes from space?" Sidney asked.

"Exactly," he replied.

Seth didn't look up from the small machine when he responded. He simply turned around and walked away from them and toward the apartment house. The investigators stared at each other for a few seconds, and then followed him.

* * * *

Ursula had given Dylan the key to her apartment yesterday. He took it from his pocket as they walked through the front door and up the stairs. A perfect fit of the key in the lock, followed by a slight turn, opened the door. They all looked at the white shag carpeting, the floor by the phone where Ursula must have collapsed.

"I'll start right here," Dylan said, nodding his head to the floor, and to the stand that held the phone. The handheld Geiger counter clutched in his hand looked much like a cell phone. He moved slowly with it, motioning his hand over the area. Soon, tiny clicks and bits of static sounded from it. A moving red arrow inched its way right and left in the device's display window.

"There's not much here," Dylan said.

"I suspect that much of the inside of this place has been decontaminated," Seth concluded. "It's likely we'll have better results outside."

They proceeded out to the balcony where Ursula had been standing the night of the sighting. The balcony was wide and supported a modest wooden patio which housed a grill, a small table with an umbrella, and three chairs. The balcony itself ran the length of three-quarters of the house, and Susan walked over to the edge that overlooked the yard, right where Ursula claimed to have been standing. Susan looked up to the trees; they were just to her left in a diagonal direction.

"This must be the spot," she said, and then pointed to her left. "And those are the treetops that would have swayed."

Holding the Geiger counter, Dylan walked over to where Susan was standing and moved his hand around the area. This time, the clicking was faster, and the red arrow moved with more animation. On Seth's device, a beeping erupted.

"Yeah, this is where she was standing," Dylan concluded.

Seth made an observation.

"So, the wind blew this way from those trees and exposed Ursula where she stood—right here." He stood alongside Susan. "Let's go and see what kind of levels we pick up in the yard."

To the left was an equally wooden set of stairs that led down into the yard. Dylan and Seth led the way over to the trees that they now assembled under. Dylan walked in one direction with the handheld device, and Seth moved in the opposite with the probe counter. Simultaneously, an eruption of noise coincided, a technical cacophony that made them wish they were searching for gold. The clicking static and urgent beeping sounded with greater and louder resonance and with a faster, more definite determination.

"There are Gamma rays still lingering in this area," Seth said. "So, Ursula and Shane were right. The radiation was spewed from the object. It was what was swaying the treetops."

Marv had been silently writing everything down as the team conducted their work. Seth drew a final conclusion, which one of the investigators deemed speculative.

"That means, boys and girls, due to the presence of Gamma Rays, the object that Ursula and Shane had witnessed was most likely extraterrestrial."

"Not necessarily," Sidney retorted. "Isn't it possible that this UFO could have been a terrestrial aircraft, made here on Earth, yet capable of achieving distances such as outer space?"

The sour look on Seth's face made it clear that he'd been rebuffed. Sidney's smart ass, superior intellect had brought out a distinctly logical point.

"And who is responsible for creating these aircraft, Sidney, our government?"

"It's entirely possible," Sidney responded. "After all, what we don't know won't hurt us."

Seth didn't respond. He simply stared at Sidney for a moment, and then turned off his device. Dylan was pressing buttons on the handheld.

"I'll be able to get a visual readout of what we found here when we get back to 208."

"I say we all go and try to find the spot where Shane witnessed his sighting," Leah said.

They all agreed, and soon they were out on the road, headed for the back road, where Shane Rowe had travelled.

\* \* \* \*

It was a road they remembered well. Some years ago, Tracy Kimball had travelled on this same road, though a little farther north, with tragic results. Dylan was driving the van now, and when he stopped, Seth and Marv parked behind them. They all got out and surveyed the area.

"This is the best I can estimate of the location from what Shane described," Dylan said. "He would have seen the green light a little farther back, back by the tree that we just passed. He said that he rode about a quarter of a mile from there. That would lead us here."

Susan and Brett were leaning up against the van, while Leah walked around, her eyes closed, trying to see with her third eye. She threw her head back slightly.

A flash of green swept through her mind. "I see a flash of green light. I see him driving, but it's all moving so fast. I see three intertwined trees atop of a hill."

"Leah can you see the object at all?" Susan probed.

She focused her third eye, just as she'd done in the recent past. She saw Shane standing in the road, but what was in front of him was blurred, hidden behind a soft veil of light. She glimpsed the top of a hillside where three trees twisted together in an intertwined embrace. Then, the blackness of closed eyes returned. The vision had ended.

She opened her eyes and looked around. She pointed to an uphill area approximately fifty feet ahead of where they were parked. At the top, three trees morphed together in natural wonder.

"Up there," she said. "Those three intertwined trees on top of that hill—I'm almost positive that it was there." She continued pointing. "The object was up there when Shane saw it."

Seth had already begun walking in that direction, and soon, the familiar beeping sounded. Dylan followed with the handheld, and eventually they stood together. The others walked behind, but slowly and at a distance. Then, they all walked back to the van.

"There are much higher levels here than at Ursula's," Seth said, "As we expected."

"So, we've got our results," Susan said. "What's next, team?"

Brett was the one to answer that question.

"Go home, and wait and see what tomorrow brings."

# Chapter Fourteen

## ~ Hasty Departures ~

Janette LaRue's home lay at the bottom of a long grassy hill that connected with an opposite street. At the top of that hill, the black sedan was discreetly and safely hidden. Their ideal hiding place, and their high-tech HD binoculars, provided the Men in Black with a perfect view of the modest house at the foot of the hill. They'd watched as the mailman arrived early on this Wednesday morning and shared a few friendly words with the subject. They witnessed a neighbor return a casserole dish, and now they watched as an unidentified young man knocked on the subject's door.

The young man caught their attentions. He seemed out of place. He was college-aged and not a neighbor since he drove up in a white, Chevy Cobalt. He wasn't a relative; the subject had no other family. Who was he? He knocked on the door once, and the subject let him in, closing the door behind her. Though their surveillance of the subject had been sporadic, they'd never seen the young man before. Now, he raised their suspicions.

"Who do you think he is?" The heavier man asked from the driver's side.

"I don't know," the taller man responded. "Keep watching."

Ten minutes later, the young man exited the subject's house. The subject watched him until he reached his car and keyed the ignition. Then, the subject closed the door once again. The men continued to watch the unidentified young man. He seemed to take his time.

"Do you think that he's the one she's been talking to?" the driver

145

asked, "the one that helped her evade us?"

"Possibly," the other man responded.

"Should we follow him?"

There was a slight pause before the taller man spoke.

"Step on it," he said.

From a distance of some one hundred yards away, the sedan roared to life while the young man lingered in his car.

\* \* \* \*

They trailed the white, Chevy Cobalt at a distance of some fifty feet. They were close enough that they could see the young man suddenly hold a phone to his ear. The taller man issued an instruction to the other.

"Get in range of him! We can tap into his phone."

The driver pushed the pedal, and the sedan lurched forward another ten feet.

"I think we're in range," the driver said.

The taller man feverishly pushed buttons on a device that looked like a cell phone, but was some type of advanced device, unique and clandestine in its existence and odd in its appearance. The device allowed the taller man to bypass all federal communication laws and conduct the equivalent of wiretapping. Suddenly, two voices were heard through the device's speakerphone when the taller man pushed the last button.

"She says she's okay." It was the young man up ahead who spoke. "She says there's been nothing. And everything looks normal."

The voice of an older man spoke next.

"Glad to hear it, Tristan. You've done a great job. Hopefully, we won't have to do this much longer."

"I hear ya," Tristan said.

"And remember, Tristan, not a word about this to anyone. This woman and her children's lives may depend upon your silence."

"I gotcha, Marv. No need to remind me."

"You can drop by my house," the older man said. "I'll pay you what I owe you."

"Thanks. See you in a few, Marv," Tristan said.

The lines disconnected.

"Keep following him," the taller man said. "I told you it would only be a matter of time. Our subject has told this Marv person everything. We're about to find out who he is."

* * * *

Janette felt her heart drop at what she'd just seen. She'd been washing dishes in the sink when a black sedan raced past her kitchen window. An inner alarm went off inside of her. Tristan Shelton, the young man who was her contact to Marv Kincaid, had just left her house. Tristan would check in on her and report back to Marv, so they didn't have to meet in public and risk the likelihood of being seen. It had also been Marv's idea for her to ditch the old disposable phone and buy another, and to keep repeating the task for as long as necessary.

Tristan had dropped by and asked if she'd received any new threats; she hadn't. Neither had she witnessed anyone following her. The last question he'd asked was the cause of her current alarm.

*"Have you seen any black sedans in the neighborhood, or anywhere near your house?"*

Her plummeting heart began to pound. Tristan had just left, and a minute later, a black sedan raced off in his direction. She'd seen it through the window. She knew who the black sedan belonged to, and in the time it took for her to realize, time began to run out.

*"Oh, no!"*

She yelled as she turned from the sink, not even taking the time to dry her hands. She started for the stairs and then charged up them, calling out to her children.

*"Cara! Rodney!"* Janette was then careful not to let the fear be heard in her voice. "Pack up your things, babies. We're going on a little vacation."

The shouts of elation were instantaneous.

*"Yay!!"*

Rodney and Cara were used to packing their own suitcases. They did so every time she would bring them to their grandmother's in Philadelphia. This time was no different, but as they packed, Janette snuck off to the bathroom to place a call using the disposable phone. She dialed Marv Kincaid's number. It rang until his voicemail answered. He'd instructed her to never leave a message, of which she'd already known better. Janette cursed in frustration.

*Where is he?*

She ran out of the bathroom, saw to it that the kids were getting ready, and then hurried to her own room to frantically pack. Janette thought of where she would go. She could go to her mother-in-law's in Philly, or to her friend Vera's in Pittsburgh, though she feared involving anyone else. Pittsburgh might not even be far enough.

In less than thirty minutes, she and the kids were ready to go.

"Mama, where are we going?" Cara asked.

"Are we going to Grandma's?" Rodney assumed.

"I don't know yet, babies," she said. "We'll find out when we get there."

Janette locked up the house, hurried the kids into the car, and soon, she was on the highway. While she drove, she dialed Marv Kincaid again. This time, he answered.

"Marv, it's Janette," she said, calmly. "Minutes ago, a black sedan rushed past my house and followed Tristan." Rodney and Cara played loudly in the back seat, oblivious to her words. "I took the kids and decided to take them for a vacation, if you know what I mean."

"Janette where are you, now?" Marv's question was quick, ready to act.

"I'm on Route 30, headed east." She described her whereabouts more specifically.

"Listen, Janette. I'm going to book a hotel room about five miles from where you are now. Stay there until I can come to you. I won't be long. I'll call you back with the details, just keep driving."

Janette continued to drive, and when her phone rang again, it was Marv. He'd booked her and the kids a room at the Castaway Inn in Lincoln. She made it there in less than ten minutes.

\* \* \* \*

Marv quickly dialed Tristan back. The young man he'd spoken to had sounded normal just a few moments ago. Now, a louder, more anxious voice answered the phone.

"Hello?!"

"Tristan, listen to me," Marv instructed. "Is there a black sedan following you?"

*"Yes!"* Marv could hear the fear in Tristan's voice, as though he'd become a child once again. "It must've been following me for a while. I only noticed it about two minutes ago."

"Okay, now listen to me, whatever you do, don't come to my house. Try to lose them if you can; if you can't, then drive to the police station."

"You mean that it's *them?* It's really *them? Oh God!*"

"Now listen to me, Tristan, the last thing you need to do is freak out. Stay calm, and stay with me. Do you understand?"

Tristan was breathing heavily, an exhalation so harsh that it sounded like a roaring furnace. Then, there was a pause, a silence long enough to make Marv momentarily nervous.

"Tristan, are you there?!"

"I don't understand," Tristan said. "They're gone."

"What?" Marv asked.

"They're gone. They just turned a corner for some reason. They're no longer behind me."

Now, Marv *was* nervous. They were on to him.

"Okay, Tristan, that's good. Listen to me. I want you to drive straight home. And if you see them again, do what I suggested about going to the police station. I have a feeling they wouldn't follow you there. No need to worry, I think they have what they need."

"Are you sure, Marv?"

"Yes. Go home, Tristan. I'll be sending you what I owe you by mail. Watch for it."

Marv abruptly ended the call. There was no time to waste.

\* \* \* \*

They'd been listening to the call that came through the young man's phone. They looked at each other when the older man mentioned a black sedan. The older man ordered the younger not to come to his house. He'd made a suggestion about the police station. Then, they'd heard the young man's fear.

*"You mean that it's them? It's really them? Oh God!"*

They hadn't listened to the entire conversation; there was no need. The older man had been telling the younger not to "freak out." Then, the

149

taller man in the black sedan received the signal that he'd been patiently expecting. It was a beeping sound. He pressed a button, and the conversation they'd been listening to was cut off. The driver spoke first.

"Did you get a trace on the caller?"

"Affirmative," the taller man said. "The other phone is registered to a Marvin Kincaid. Make that Marv Kincaid, the journalist. That's why the old man with Dornan looked familiar."

There was a pause before the driver responded.

"So, it looks like our problem has become bigger than we ever expected."

"Much bigger," the other replied.

"What are we going to do about it?"

"Mr. Kincaid is just as big of a problem as Seth Dornan," the taller man said. "I say we kill two birds with one stone."

\* \* \* \*

Susan and the investigators assembled in room 208 on this late Wednesday morning. They decided to meet and discuss the case further, as well as the possibilities of snooping around at Eagle Rock Mountain. They also caught up on a vast array of worldwide UFO research. They were sitting around the long conference table, idly talking when Susan's phone rang.

She didn't recognize the number, but something made her quickly answer the phone.

"Susan, it's Marv. I've got big problems, and I need you to listen."

Susan pressed the speakerphone button. "We're all here, Marv. What's wrong?"

"The MIB are on to me." His voice remained calm, hiding the harried storm of emotions that brewed just underneath. "They followed my spy who was checking on Janette, and I think that they tapped into our phone conversation. I'm calling from an unlisted number. Janette has already left. I won't say more, but I'm taking her away, at least temporarily. I'll stay in touch. Tell Seth what's happened."

"Marv, are you sure you want to do this? Running away from these men isn't going to change anything. You're a journalist; you can expose them."

"And I will," he said. "But, Janette could be in trouble, and it's my fault. I have to help her and those two kids. I have to help them get away from here. I can gather more information if they can't find me, and right now, I have no recourse; my back is against the wall. I discovered that they were onto me in a matter of minutes before my contact almost led them to my home. I've already left the house, I've got Duke with me, and I'm now on the highway."

"Will we hear from you?" Dylan asked.

"I will get in touch with you all, as soon as it's safe," he said. "Tell Seth the same. But right now, I have to go. I'm sorry."

"Marv, wait—"

Susan's words were interrupted as Marv's voice was replaced by a dial tone.

"I don't believe this," Susan said. Her expression as she looked at the investigators was one of dismay. "I can't believe how far this has come."

"How sad for those kids," Leah said.

"What are they covering up?" Brett asked. "It has to be serious."

"You're right, Susan," Sidney said. "It has come too far. Since Marv can't expose them, we need to do it. This affects all of Green Valley, probably even our country itself."

"Exposing them is exactly what we're going to do," Dylan said. "If Seth gets us up onto Eagle Rock and into that observatory tomorrow, we are going to expose all of this, along with what they did to my father. This, I swear on my life."

Silence filled the room. There was nothing left to say.

\* \* \* \*

"We can't afford to have the car seen outside of the old man's house," the taller man said. "We're going to have to go about this discreetly."

"Should we park the car away from the house and walk?" the driver asked.

The taller man answered in the affirmative. They parked the sedan down the street and casually walked to the address they'd traced back to Marvin Kincaid. They attracted no unwarranted attention to themselves, yet they offered no apologies for their unusual presence. Soon, they arrived outside the home of Marvin Kincaid, and the taller man recognized the obvious.

"His car is gone."

They looked at each other before walking down the sidewalk. They knocked on the front door. Nothing and no one stirred from inside. They peeped in the windows, stealing minute glances through the curtains at an empty domain.

"Let's bust the door open." The heavier man suggested.

"No." The taller man stepped backwards away from the house, keeping his eyes on the front of it. Behind dark sunglasses, shaded eyes closed, strangely envisioning. He breathed in through his nostrils in an almost maniacal manner, and then exhaled through his mouth. "There's no one inside. The old man is gone. I know it. Let's go."

They walked back to the sedan without another word, started the engine, and drove away.

# Chapter Fifteen

## ~ Slick Pete ~

Seth had finally made it home to see his family. It was good to be home again, yet his mind remained on other things—more sinister things. His family was typical of the middle, working-class, western Pennsylvania brood. His father had been a steel worker, and then later, a machinist. In addition to being a homemaker, his mother was a retired secretary. Once the surprise was sprung and the initial hugs exchanged, his mother called him her, "prodigal son;" his father called him, "stranger."

"So, what brings you home?" his mother asked, "another case?"

His family had never been fond of his passion for chasing UFOs. A waste of time, they called it, yet he wondered if they had any clue as to how dangerous his calling had become.

"Maybe," he joked with his mother. "But you know—top secret."

She rolled her eyes and looked away, yet the day was filled with fun, reminiscences, and a family dinner. He shared the latest pictures with his mother and watched a baseball game with his father. But when it was over, there was one family member he definitely needed to find—his nephew, Peter. Peter was grown now; almost twenty-five. Seth still remembered the little boy that he'd played softball with in the yard. Time had taken the Dornan family in different directions, especially Peter, Seth thought. The little boy who once complained about Uncle Seth's pitching now had one distinct claim to fame—Peter Dornan was a computer hacker.

Seth had heard stories about how Peter was so slick at what he did that he'd even evaded prosecution after certain things had mysteriously "disappeared" from the state prosecutor's computer system. There were no accusations, but Seth knew his brother's son well enough. He would bet his life that Peter could hack into any computer system, completely unnoticed. Marv had recently told him about the young man he'd worked with at the newspaper, the hacker who had died in the Cedar Manor excursion.

"They say he was a genius," Marv had said. But Seth didn't care what kind of genius the dead guy was, he was no match for his nephew—that he knew. Seth had been sure to phone ahead, and now he stood on his nephew's front porch, knocking, and waiting for an answer.

Peter Dornan bore a striking resemblance to his uncle, and Seth was reminded of that as the young man answered the door. He was a tad shorter than his lanky uncle and with broader shoulders. He sported the same greenish-blue eyes and wore his blondish-brown hair slicked straight back. It was this, along with an unequivocal proficiency at a dubious talent that had earned him the nickname, "Slick Pete." His eyes widened when he saw his uncle.

"Uncle Seth!"

He stepped out onto the porch, and they embraced each other in greeting, patting each other's back. The young man stepped back and looked at his uncle.

"So, what brings you home?"

"I'm glad you asked that," Seth replied. "I need your help."

Once inside, they sat in Peter's kitchen. He offered Seth a beer, of which he took, and the small talk of catching up remained brief as Peter's concern came to the forefront.

"You said you needed my help, Uncle Seth. What's wrong?"

"Nothing's wrong." Seth stared at his nephew, suddenly contemplating whether or not to involve him. But Seth knew that Peter could pull this one off. There was no one better for the job. If anyone could hack into the observatory's computer system, it would be his nephew. "I need your help—as a hacker."

Seth watched as Peter's eyes grew wide in surprise and, like his uncle, obsessive fascination. Peter rubbed his fingers over his bottom lip before responding.

"Tell me more," he said.

"I'm going to, but whatever I tell you must stay strictly in this room, understood?"

Peter's eyes got even wider. "Is this UFO business? Are you investigating? Is that why you're here?"

Seth didn't respond. He watched the wildest display of shock and thrill grace Peter's face.

"Are you serious?" Peter threw his head back, astounded that he'd guessed correctly. He looked back at Seth, waiting for a punch line that would never come. He gasped. "Of course I'll help, Uncle Seth. What do you need me to do?"

Seth explained to him why he'd returned to Green Valley without notice: being contacted by Marv Kincaid, the new light shed on Geoffrey Rasche's death, and two people being admitted to the hospital with radiation sickness after witnessing sightings. He mentioned the Men in Black.

"They followed me a few years ago in Beaver County. They never caught up with me. But now, something's going on here in Green Valley, and they've already threatened a 911 dispatcher, a witness, and one of the patients brought in with radiation sickness. By now, I'm sure that they're aware of my current involvement, and it's only a matter of time before they turn their heads in my direction."

Seth saw Peter's enthusiasm deflate from an inner fear that his words had provoked.

"But not if I can expose them first," Seth continued. "I've been working with the paranormal investigators from Green Valley University. Their chief investigator, Dylan Rasche, is the son of the astronomer I told you about. He and I have valid reason to believe that the MIB were responsible for his father's death."

"They murdered him?" Peter asked.

Seth nodded his head.

"And we're convinced that the whole mystery surrounds Eagle Rock Mountain," Seth explained. "That's where his death occurred, and at the time, he was investigating sightings that took place there. This time, two of the sightings were not far from Eagle Rock. Whatever this mystery is, whatever the MIB are so hell bent to cover up is centered on Eagle Rock Mountain and its observatory."

"And I come in where and how?" Peter asked.

"I need you to hack into the observatory's computer system. I want a layout of that place, I want to know what that place is hiding, what it's watching, and most of all, I need you to breach its security."

Seth watched as his nephew's lips parted, exposing a dropped jaw.

Silence sat between them.

"Wow," Peter said. "That's a tall order, Uncle Seth."

"But you're the best, right? You're untraceable. I know it all sounds illegal, but think of it, Peter; these people are hiding something big from the whole nation, from all of mankind. *They're* doing something illegal, immoral, and if we expose it, the world will be on our side."

Peter was nodding his head, saying nothing.

"So, do you think it can be done?" Seth asked. Peter looked at him before answering.

"Why not, I'm the best, right?" Peter's grin stretched across his face like the Cheshire cat's, displaying parenthesized dimples at both cheeks. It was an expression Seth hadn't seen on his face since he was a little boy. Their laughter filled the kitchen like a chorus.

\* \* \* \*

Peter Dornan's basement was not a basement at all, but more of a computer genius's lair. The dark paneled underground contained a plush leather sectional sofa and matching recliners, a fireplace built into the wall, a table and chairs, and like the paranormal investigators' room 208, side by side computers lined one wall of the room, yet for an entirely different purpose. Seth sat at the table, while Peter walked over to a small wooden desk, where he opened a wide drawer and retrieved a laptop from it. He walked over to the table and sat across from his uncle, flipping open the laptop.

"Wait a minute," Seth said. "You're going to use *that* thing?"

"Of course," Peter said. "This is my baby. Plus, it's a lot easier this way; it's an unregistered laptop."

"So, what are all those for?" Seth pointed to the wall of computers.

Peter shrugged. "Different things," he said, coyly.

Safely hidden in Peter's hand was some type of flash drive. He plugged it into the laptop's USB port.

"What's that?" Seth asked.

"*This* is how I stay untraceable." Peter laughed. "Bring your chair over here."

Seth did so, and now they looked at the laptop's home screen filled with icons.

"I'm going to start by hacking into their website," Peter said. "I can bypass into their mainframe from there."

Seth had no idea what his nephew was talking about. He was part of the wrong generation. Computers were never his thing, though he knew enough to get by. After searching for the observatory's public website, Peter and Seth casually observed the site itself: the pictures of the observatory and its many telescopes, pictures taken of space, even short bios of the limited staff. Once they'd checked out all the mundane aspects of the website, Peter turned and asked his uncle a question, his fingertips poised above the keyboard.

"Okay, are you ready?"

Seth's heart pounded as he swallowed hard.

"Yep, let's do this," Seth responded.

Peter's fingers flashed across the keyboard, creating a rapid rat-a-tat-tat that caused Seth to pray. Instantly, an empty red box flashed upon the screen. Above it, two words blinked in red.

AUTHORIZATION CODE

Seth felt the deflation of defeat. Yet his nephew was staring at him.

"Are you sure you're ready?" He asked, grinning.

Seth stared at the screen.

"Do what you have to do."

Peter's fingers flashed again across the keyboard. A black screen with white wording popped up. Before Seth could read any of it, Peter typed the word "Override." Seconds passed as the black screen disappeared, and what reappeared was the observatory's mainframe. It was the part of the observatory's computer system only accessible by high-level employees and possibly, the government. Seth felt his innards drop. He couldn't hold back his astonishment.

"What about the authorization code?" he asked.

Peter scoffed.

"Hah! I don't need any damn authorization code."

What Seth saw next were blocks that filled the entire screen, a multiview panorama of video feed from the security cameras, each displaying different areas of the observatory. They could see the front entrance, as well as a vast room with refracting telescopes, another room that held reflecting telescopes, and a small chamber that housed the radio telescope projecting from the observatory's dome. Another block of live security video showed an inside view of someone's office, but the image in the block next to it caught Seth's attention.

"This one," he said, pointing. "What is that?"

Seth was pointing to an image of a small alcove within a hallway, where he could see the split between double doors. The security camera focused solely on this doorway.

Peter zoomed in on that particular video block. The image came closer to the screen.

"If I had to guess, Uncle Seth, I'd say it was an elevator."

He zoomed in even more, producing the image to a full-screen view. The double doors in the alcove became even with their eyes.

"You're right," Seth agreed. "It's an elevator. I'll be damned. Where could it go?"

"Up and down?" Peter joked.

"I know that, smart ass," Seth chuckled. "It's goes up to the upper level, but the observatory *has no lower level*, so if the elevator also goes down, where does it go?"

There were brief seconds of thought before Peter answered him. "Down inside the mountain."

Seth was speechless. His genius of a nephew was right. The elevator would have to descend down inside the mountain. So, what was down there other than caves? Was this the secret of Eagle Rock Mountain, that it housed some type of underground activity deep inside its natural, massive structure? He suddenly thought of Geoffrey Rasche being shut out of the observatory all those years ago. Was this the top-secret renovation that he'd eventually stumbled upon?

Suddenly, the screen of video blocks was replaced by a white screen that contained blue architectural sketching and diagrams. Peter had brought the screen up with another magic flash of his fingers. Seth stared at it.

"What is this?" he asked.

"It's the official blueprints of the entire observatory. It gives a complete layout of the place."

Seth stared in fascination at the blueprints, the blue diagrams that depicted the observatory's current layout and appearance. All of the sketches perfectly portrayed the areas in the actual footage he'd just seen. It didn't take him long to memorize the entire layout. It was essential for him to record every little detail in his mind for what he planned tomorrow night. Then, Peter held his finger to the left mouse button and virtually moved through the blueprints, as if he was the master of a video game. The picture on the screen advanced wherever Peter directed it, and Seth watched as it moved toward the depiction of an elevator shaft.

"There it is," he said.

Peter removed his finger from the mouse button, and the picture ceased its movement. After studying the videos and the blueprints, Seth knew exactly where to find the elevator from the front entrance area. It was almost hidden, yet monitored on the security cameras. The blueprints depicted the elevator's ascending and descending ability. Blue arrows pointed up and down; Peter's theory had been right. Now, Seth stood from his chair, and Peter watched him nervously pace for a few seconds.

"By the way, Uncle Seth, what gives? What are you planning?"

Seth sat back down and focused face-to-face with Peter. "I need you to get me and a few others into that observatory tomorrow night."

Peter said nothing. He just turned and looked at the screen.

"Do you think you can do it?" Seth asked. "Can you get us in and out, unnoticed?"

"Let me show you something," Peter said.

Seth watched as Peter exited the current screen and brought up another black screen. The young man began typing and choosing options.

"What are you doing?" Seth asked.

"There are rarely any tell-tale signs that anyone has been hacked," Peter said. "But you never know with some high-tech security sites. There *could* always be some type of security alert system, depending upon the source, but unlikely. So, what I'm doing is covering my tracks. I'm setting their computer system back to an earlier time, five minutes before I hacked into it."

"You can do that?" Seth was bewildered.

"Uncle Seth, I can do anything. So, in answer to your question; hell yeah I can get you all in and out, with or without those cameras, but it has to be quick."

Seth couldn't believe his eyes. He was staring once again at the observatory's public site, as if nothing had happened. He was speechless as Peter looked away from the screen and then back at him.

"Here's how it'll happen," Peter said.

Seth listened intently.

# Chapter Sixteen

## ~ Illegal Entry ~

The next day, in the early afternoon, Seth returned to room 208 to meet the investigators. They were sitting at their usual places around the conference table when he knocked, and then walked into the room. They offered him a seat, and all five faces looked at him expectantly.

"Well, I have some news," he said. "It's about our earlier plans regarding Eagle Rock Mountain and the observatory." He looked at them and raised an eyebrow. "I have a plan."

He told them about the meeting with his nephew, and Peter's dubious claim to fame.

"I've told him that I've been working with all of you, and about our observatory plans."

Seth went into the details of how Peter hacked into the observatory's website, and then into their mainframe. He related how they'd watched the security cameras, saw inside the observatory, and the one interesting thing that caused Peter to discover the observatory's blueprints.

"It was an elevator," he revealed.

Susan looked at him curiously.

"I don't get it," she said.

Seth described the blueprint's depiction of the elevator's rise and fall ability, the blue arrows that went up and down. He related the theory that if the observatory had no lower level, then the elevator must descend down inside the mountain. Wide eyes studied him. And then Dylan broke the silence with his astonishment, as though he hadn't thought of it before.

"So, something exists down inside the mountain?"

Seth slowly nodded.

"It's been excavated, hollowed out?" Sidney's question was met with the same nod.

"What could exist down there?" Leah asked.

"That's what I'm hoping to find out," Seth replied.

Brett jumped into the discussion.

"And your hoping that we'll break into the observatory, and discover whatever it is that's being hidden down inside the mountain?"

Susan interrupted before Seth could respond.

"And how in the world do you think that's going to happen?"

Seth revealed Peter's plan and all of its technical details. Shocked expressions stared back at him, all except Dylan. Seth could see the wild excitement in his eyes, a look he shared with the younger man.

"It sounds like a plan to me," Dylan said.

"Isn't that *my* final decision, Dylan?" Susan's response was quick, as always. She turned her attention to Seth. "I told you before that I'm not willing to jeopardize the lives of my investigators. This is also illegal, and how do you know that this plan is foolproof? Do you realize that your nephew's hacking abilities would be vying with that of the MIB?"

Seth told her about Peter turning the observatory's computer system back to an earlier time. "It's going to be the same idea, the security cameras especially."

Susan turned and looked at the faces staring back at her. Seth could see the look of defeat on her face. She stared once again at him.

"Besides," he said. "My nephew may prove useful to you all in the future."

Susan leaned forward and asked another question.

"What about the staff? They do observe the sky late at night, don't they?"

"Not at 2:00 am, they don't," he said.

"And they certainly wouldn't on a night like tonight," Dylan said. "The weather reports are calling for storm clouds and thunderstorms. They wouldn't be able to see a thing."

Susan sighed, looked up at the ceiling, and shook her head. Dylan's persistence in convincing her was unyielding.

"They *may not* have a top-notch security system. They don't even have a guard anymore."

"Dylan, I know this is important to you, and you'll probably go regardless of what I say," she began. "But I don't want *all of you* going down into that mountain, and I want to be consistently updated as to what's going on. If you all get arrested tonight, don't blame me."

The claps of high-fives went up in the air.

"All right, then," Seth turned to Sidney. "I take it all five of us can pack into your van?"

"We do it all the time," Sidney said.

"Great. Then we'll meet tonight at 1·00 am?"

"We'll meet at my house," Susan replied. "It's safest. If you do this, you do this *my* way."

Seth nodded and spoke.

"Agreed," he said. "So, we meet at that time at your house, Dr. Logan. From there, we travel to Eagle Rock by the back roads. Going to the mountain at such a time of night will be the hardest part of this endeavor— I assure you. We'll park the van at a safe, but quick distance from the observatory and walk the rest of the way. I'll be in contact with my nephew the whole time. He'll be directing us when to go in, when to get out, and so forth. Once I get the clear to go inside, we go in, but we go in and out *fast*."

Sidney took advantage of the break in Seth's speech.

"Shouldn't we all be wearing black masks or something?"

His own joke made him chuckle, and Susan gave him a quieting stare.

"As I explained, we won't be seen," Seth continued. "My nephew will be turning the clock backward on the security footage. It will be showing video of an earlier time."

"So, basically, we move in, and the cameras show no one there?" Brett asked.

"Precisely."

"Awesome."

"Dylan, you and I will find the elevator," Seth said. "The rest of you will make a clean sweep of the place and look for anything suspicious or out of the ordinary. It shouldn't take you long. My nephew is now searching the observatory's computer files and has turned up nothing of value. I think our main concern is what is down inside that mountain."

"So, if only you and Dylan can go," Leah asked, "then what about the rest of us? What happens when we've finished?"

"That's a good question. If Dylan and I are not back up by a certain time, you're to go back to the van immediately, wait a few minutes, and then leave without us."

"I don't like the sound of this," Susan warned.

"Don't worry, Dr. Logan. Dylan and I will get back on our own."

"I will be ready in case you need me," she said.

Seth smiled.

"That's another option. So, is everyone clear on what the plan is?" he asked.

All heads nodded.

"Great, then I suggest that everyone get some rest before tonight. We'll all meet at Dr. Logan's at 1:00 am for a final run-down of our strategy. Think of what questions you may have. We'll discuss them then."

On that note, Seth rose from the table and left room 208.

\* \* \* \*

Soon, darkness fell over western Pennsylvania, spreading a murky magenta sky as far as the eye could see. Sidney picked up Dylan, Leah, and Brett in the van, while Seth drove his own car. They met at Susan's house at exactly 1:00 am, just as planned. Now, all were assembled in the living room, just as before. It was Susan's turn to give directions.

"As I said," she began, "I want at least one of you to be keeping me updated at all times." She turned to Seth. "I've done a little research on my own, and you're lucky that the observatory doesn't have sound activated security alarms. Your plan wouldn't be possible if it had."

"Maybe not," Seth said. "But Peter will be disabling not only the cameras, but any and all alarms. Our entrance into the building is a sure thing. There'll be an override."

Susan sighed in frustration once again.

"I pray this works," she said.

Seth reassured her once again, and then asked the team if there were any last minute thoughts or questions. No one spoke except Dylan.

"We're just playing this by ear, and acting as we go along. We don't have much of a choice. *I* don't have much of a choice. We have to get to the bottom of this."

"Since we're all in agreement," Seth said. "I say we have a moment of prayer before we hit the road."

They held hands in a circle with heads bowed, and then prayed. When it was over, they looked at each other, silent, contemplating. Sidney broke the silence.

"Don't you think it's a little weird to be praying for safety while breaking and entering?"

"We're not *breaking* in," Seth said. "But we *will* be entering."

Then, Dylan uttered a saying for which he was well known.

"Then, let's roll."

* * * *

"You know, much of the sightings back in the nineties, and now, occurred along this very road," Dylan commented as Sidney drove on the deserted back road.

The night sky was lessening of its magenta hue and deepening to a thick, impenetrable violet. Soft thunder rumbled above as the dark sky was split by an occasional streak of lightning. A storm was brewing, but they were early for it. Eagle Rock Mountain stood tall, proud, and silent only yards before them.

The main road up the mountain twisted and turned on an upward and spiraling incline. It was silent, devoid of any presence like the peacefulness of a sleeping giant. The van soon arrived at the top, and they came closer to the observatory. Then, Seth spotted a location for the van.

"Over there," he instructed Sidney, "beneath that thicket of trees. That's where we'll park the van. The observatory is only a minute walk from here."

Lightning lit up the sky, and the thunder was louder now, like an explosion.

"This storm may work in our favor," Dylan said. "The thunder should cover any sounds we make. Not to mention who would be out here in this—other than us?"

They bounded out from the van like soldiers ready for action. They shut the doors slowly to prevent the unnecessary sounds of slamming. The paranormal posse began to stride, side by side, through the darkness.

Lightning pierced the purpling sky once again, lighting the ground beneath them as their trek to the observatory began. They stayed silent, one foot in front of the other as light rain began sprinkling down upon them.

Soon, a square building loomed a few feet in front of them at the end of their path. Its appearance was hindered by the clusters of foliage that surrounded them. Another lightning strike illuminated its round, silver dome in the darkness. It was the observatory, and Dylan could see the cliff just ahead of it as the sky flickered and thunder cracked. He stared straight ahead, but the drop-off faded in the returning blackness. It was then that Seth whispered to the four of them.

"I'm going to call Peter now. We're about to make our first move."

\* \* \* \*

Peter Dornan sat nervously waiting in front of his laptop. The thrill of anticipation charged through him when his phone rang. It was Uncle Seth. The moment had come. He answered after one ring.

"Uncle Seth?"

A whisper spoke back to him.

"I can't talk loudly. Can you hear me?"

"I can hear you," Peter said. He readied his fingers above the keyboard, while gripping the phone to his ear with his shoulder.

"Phase one. Can you reverse the images on the security cameras?" Seth asked.

Peter flashed his magic fingers and brought the images from the security cameras up onto the screen. He discovered the images from thirty minutes earlier; they were identical. Suddenly, the current camera images flipped with static. When the static died, the earlier camera images had replaced the current ones. It was a success, except for one thing, the time stamps on the replaced images were not the same.

Peter scrambled, flashing his fingers even faster. His heart was pounding, his blood racing; sweat was breaking on his forehead. The time stamps blinked and were replaced. The images had been successfully forged.

"Phase one complete, Uncle Seth."

"Phase two," Seth whispered. "Enter the security code for the front doors to open."

That one was easy. Peter had done it before when he was younger. He and a friend had hacked a grocery store and splurged on free beer, but he'd never told anyone about that. His fingers brought up the security command to enter. He entered the security code and password that he'd decrypted earlier when Uncle Seth had gone to see those investigators.

"Phase two complete. Hurry, Uncle Seth; the doors are about to open. You have only twenty minutes before the camera images revert back."

"That's all the time we need."

And then, the call went dead.

\* \* \* \*

Five figures ducked and darted across the path. Like rats in the dark they scurried through the foliage. The observatory loomed closer and closer in sight, and once upon its platform, they hurried to the two sliding glass doors of the front entrance. The doors were open.

Silently and stealthily, they moved fast through the open doorway like well-seasoned burglars. Suddenly, the lights came on.

"Oh God, we're busted," Sidney said.

Seth's heart felt like a bomb about to explode. Using his phone, he called Peter back. As Peter answered, Seth spoke a little louder this time.

"The lights are on. What happened?"

"I turned the lights on, Uncle Seth," he said. "How did you all expect to see?"

This was the one thing that Seth had taken for granted, especially since the team had brought flashlights. Seth gave the signal to the others that everything was in check, and as he remained on the phone, Sidney, Brett, and Leah hurried to investigate the various rooms.

"I'll stay on the line with you, so you can find the elevator," Peter said. "I've just enacted its security code. *Go!*"

Seth and Dylan ran through the observatory, their clomping footfalls loud enough to echo. The soft shushing sounds from the others were heard in the distance. Seth hurried in the direction where the blueprints had shown the elevator. Dylan followed closely behind.

Down the hallway and to the left, and then a sharp right after a few more feet; Seth kept repeating the directions in his head. Sure enough, the small alcove was there and within it, was an elevator. The sleek reflective shine of its double doors was immaculate, and to the left of it was a panel with two buttons, the same up and down arrows that Seth had seen in the blueprints. A light was flashing above the buttons.

"Peter, the light above the buttons..."

"It means that the elevator is enacted. You have eighteen minutes, Uncle Seth."

Seth pressed the down arrow, and a whooshing sound came up from below. Seconds passed before the doors slowly parted. They stepped inside the elevator, where another panel displayed buttons depicting up and down arrows. Seth looked at Dylan and then pressed the down button. The doors closed, and a vacuum pull yanked them down.

"Peter, can you still hear me?" Seth asked into the phone.

"Yeah, Uncle Seth; I can hear you."

"I'm inside the elevator now."

In the background, Seth could hear the tapping of keys as Peter typed. The elevator stopped.

Instinctively, Seth looked above his head, somehow feeling the sense of being underground. Once again, seconds passed before the doors slowly parted. The sight before them left them speechless.

\* \* \* \*

Leah, Sidney, and Brett moved as fast as they could through the observatory's rooms. The first was akin to a classroom, where long science class tables filled the room, a refracting telescope stood in one corner, and a reflecting telescope was perched in the opposite. A white-board filled the wall, and a model of the solar system sat atop of a podium.

"This is a classroom," Sidney said. "There's nothing suspicious here. Why waste time?"

Nonetheless, Leah and Brett rummaged through drawers, finding nothing.

"You're right," Brett said. "Let's get out of here."

Their next stop was an office, where once again, rifling through drawers turned up nothing. They opened the doors to other rooms, finding only telescopes.

"Wow, that's suspicious," Sidney said, "telescopes in an observatory."

Quickly, Brett began examining every one of them. He found nothing until he came to one particular telescope. Something was engraved on its base. It looked like initials. He tried to make them out, but the engraving was faded. Letter by letter, the initials became clear—GMR. He lifted his head up slowly. He knew those initials. They belonged to Dylan's father; he'd seen them on the cover of the journals.

"Guys, come over here and check this out," he said. "This one's engraved with initials."

Sidney and Leah walked over to where he stood. They stooped to examine the find, eyeing the initials.

"Those initials belong to Dylan's father," Brett said.

"You think this scope is his?" Leah asked.

"Has to be," he said. "Come on, let's go. Sid, how much time do we have?"

Sidney looked at his watch.

"Twelve minutes," he said.

Outside, thunder crashed.

They hurried back to the front entrance, where a large glass cubicle stood locked in the center.

"We can't try to get in here; it's locked," Leah said, trying to open the cubicle's small door. "Besides, what if it has some kind of security alarm?"

"Then we won't," Brett said.

Leah looked at the time on her phone.

"It's time to give Susan an update," she said. "She's waiting."

* * * *

Susan sat nervously in her living room, mindlessly watching the twenty-four-hour news channel. Her eyes flickered back and forth from the screen, to her phone, but her mind remained on Seth and the investigators. She jumped when the phone rang. Quickly, she pushed the mute button on the television remote and pressed the talk button on her phone.

"Yes," she answered.

"Susan, it's Leah," she said, in a hushed tone.

"What's going on?"

"We assume that Dylan and Seth have found the elevator and gone exploring," she said. "Sid, Brett, and I have finished our search. There's nowhere left to look, nothing suspicious, though we did find something of interest. We'll tell you when we get back."

"Okay. How much time do you all have before getting out of there?"

Susan heard Leah whisper to Sidney for the remaining time.

"Ten minutes," Leah responded.

"Please, be quick."

"We will," Leah said.

Susan became nervous all over again as the call ended.

\* \* \* \*

They stepped off of the elevator, awed by their surroundings. Their eyes were seeing something familiar, but unrecognizable. A conglomeration of engineering technology abounded everywhere. In the ground, straight ahead, lay what looked like a swimming pool, yet it wasn't. Inside of it, some noxious liquid brewed and bubbled like acid. Above the swimming pool structure, a large cranial arm extended over it, obviously a device used to extract the pool's contents. To the far left and right of the pool, stood large, circular spheres, four on each side. Seth pointed to them.

"Those are generators," he said. His voice was a mixture of amazement and curiosity.

"Peter," he said into his phone.

There was no answer. He called out Peter's name again. Again, there was no answer.

"Damn! We've lost the cell signal down here."

They stepped cautiously through the hidden world beneath the mountain, gazing at everything around them like children in a chocolate factory. Soft yellow light glowed all around, betraying the secrets of the dark. While the premises appeared much like a chemical plant, above it, cavernous rock climbed like catacombs all the way to the dizzying top. They walked over to the pool and watched it bubble.

Then, they walked over to the large, circular spheres and read the one word engraved on all of them. Seth had been right.

*Generator*

"What are they for?" Dylan asked.

Something yellow caught the corner of Seth's eye, something far ahead against a wall.

"I think we're about to find out," he said, motioning Dylan to follow him.

They walked a foot away from the generators. The wall that Seth had spotted was man-made, constructed of four rows of yellow barrels stacked one on top of the other. Again, one word was labeled on the barrels.

*Radioactive*

"Radioactive material?" Dylan asked.

"You got it," Seth replied.

Seth didn't like what he was seeing. The puzzle pieces of where they were, and what they'd stumbled onto were starting to fall together. Farther down on the right-hand side, they noticed a large niche carved in the rock. As they approached it, they saw that it was constructed to be a small room, a storage room to be exact. The storage room held the final piece of the puzzle. This time, stacked on top of each other were gray, rectangular metal boxes. One word identified the contents of the metal boxes. Seth swallowed hard when he read the word...

*Titanium*

"Does that say what I think it says?" Dylan asked.

"Yep," Seth replied.

His voice wavered in and out as he spoke.

"Dylan, I think we've just solved the mystery of Eagle Rock Mountain. It's a nuclear storage facility."

\* \* \* \*

Leah called Susan back. Time was running out. The three of them were becoming antsy.

"Susan, it's me," Leah said, as she answered. "They're not back yet, and Susan, there's only three minutes left before the doors close. *What* are we going to do?"

"Get the hell out of there, now!" Susan's voice was louder than she'd ever heard it. "Get back to the van immediately. Wait for them in the van. If they don't show up in five minutes, get your asses back to my house!"

"Gotcha," Leah ended the call. "She wants us to leave."

"I don't see what other choice we have," Sidney said. "If we're not out of here, the doors will close on us. We'll be trapped in here."

"Come on," Brett said.

The three of them turned and bolted out of the double doors. They ran across the path and slowed down once they neared the van. Quietly, they hopped back inside the van and waited.

* * * *

At the same time, Dylan checked his watch and turned to Seth.

"We have three minutes left. We have to get out of here now!"

*"Shit!"* he said.

Seth had been so enraptured that he'd lost all track of time; not to mention the loss of the cell connection with Peter made him also lose his timekeeper.

"Come on," he said. "We have to get back to the elevator, or the front doors will close and trap us in here."

They quickly snapped a few shots with their phones: the pool, the generators, the boxes, and the barrels. Then, they ran to the elevator, pressed the button, and waited for the doors to open. There was a slow, mechanical whooshing sound, and then a pause.

"Come on, holy shit!" Seth yelled.

The doors opened and they ran inside. Seth pushed the up arrow and nearly panicked at the pause before the doors closed. Then, the vacuum pull thrust them back up to the main floor. Dylan was studying his watch.

"A minute and a half left," he said.

After almost five seconds, the doors opened back up in the observatory. Seth and Dylan began to run through the halls, turning corners to get back to the main entrance. Seth called out to Dylan after he'd taken a wrong turn.

"Not that way, this way!"

When they reached the end of the long hallway, they ran side by side, as though racing in a track meet. Their footsteps fell harder and louder than before. There was no time to waste. Ahead of them, they could see that the observatory was vacant. The team had left, just as planned.

But the one sight up ahead of them caused them to run even harder and faster. Their feet pounded the floor; their footfalls boomed. The sweat was pouring from their bodies. They heaved and gasped. The double doors of the front entrance were closing, coming together like lost partners about to be reunited. Faster and faster they raced as the doors would soon meet.

Seven inches spanned between the closing doors when Dylan was the first to make it through. He turned and pulled Seth by the arm, but the doors closed on Seth's left hand and began to squeeze it. Seth wailed in fear more than pain. Having hold of his right arm, Dylan yanked him one more time. Somehow, the doors backtracked and released Seth's hand. A wrist button from Seth's shirt was torn away from the fabric. It fell to the floor, unnoticed.

But they were free.

\* \* \* \*

Inside the van, the three of them waited, their panting breaths now calmed and quieted. They looked out of the back windows, the front windows, and now Brett got out of the van to see if he could see them—nothing.

"Where the hell are they?" Leah asked.

"I don't know," Brett said. "But, Sid, we're going to have to get out of here if they don't get back soon."

Sidney sat at the steering wheel and sighed, knowing Brett was right. "I guess so," he said. "Let's just give them one more minute."

Leah rolled her eyes. Brett turned in a sideways stance away from the van—clear indications to Sidney that they all were becoming jumpy.

Lightning turned the night into day, but only for a moment. The lightning was so much closer up here. Then, the thunder crashed again. But it was a different set of sounds that caused them to suddenly tense. The thrashing of foliage followed by the thudding of approaching footfalls came closer.

\* \* \* \*

They'd made it off of the platform and across the path, running once again and hoping that they hadn't missed the van. If they had, they would trek down the mountain and walk somewhere where Susan could pick them up. They were safe, and the mission had been an overall success. They were running when Dylan spied something white up ahead. It was the van.

"There they are," he said. "They're still here."

The lightning lit their way like a beacon from a lighthouse. They ran even faster, pushing the mass of bushes and branches out of their way. Dylan saw Brett as he approached the van.

"It's them." Brett turned and reported back. Dylan could see Sidney's head drop to the steering wheel in relief.

"Yeah, we made it out," Dylan said. "And you're not going to believe what we found."

"We'll talk about it later. We have to get out of here, now!"

Sidney started up the van, and the engine roared to life as the rain began to pour. Dylan and Seth quickly jumped inside. Then the van drove away down the spiraling incline, safely headed home.

# Chapter Seventeen

## ~ Drawing Conclusions ~

The taller man in black received a notification at approximately 2:45 am. Something was going on within the observatory computer's mainframe. A hacker was a possibility, but there was nothing concrete. The intrusion detection alert of the observatory's computer system was not the best, so the taller man in black linked his laptop with the observatory's mainframe. He studied his laptop screen, watching some indiscriminate action take place within the mainframe.

He watched the image on the screen as it wavered, twisted, and jumped to different locations within the observatory's computer system on its own. The taller man typed several keys, trying to trace a possible IP address. Whatever was causing the disruption to the mainframe was untraceable. If it was a hacker, he or she was a damn good one.

One of the disruptions was to the observatory's security system. He sat back in his chair and wondered if there was something going on at the observatory. He checked the security cameras. Nothing seemed unusual or out of place. He thought for a moment before he lurched forward, and with his finger, pressed three keys on the keyboard. Abruptly, the wavering and twisting of the screen's image stopped. It was most definitely a hacker, and certainly not a sloppy one. But the predominant man in black had just cut off the hacker's intrusive connection, like the stopping of air to someone who somewhere, breathed.

* * * *

Peter had been talking to Uncle Seth when he boarded the elevator

175

inside the observatory. Seth had asked him if he could still hear him, and he could.

*"I'm inside the elevator now."* That was the last thing he'd heard from Uncle Seth. Peter decided that he would snoop around a little more, try to discover something that he may have missed earlier. He was typing on his keyboard at the moment that he no longer heard a background noise. Peter spoke into the phone to test it.

"Are you off of the elevator yet?" he asked.

There was no response.

"Uncle Seth?" he asked.

Again, there was no reply. Peter continued to call out his Uncle's name, but to no avail.

*Of course,* he thought. *They're underground. The cell connection died.*

"Damn it!" Peter cussed. Now, how was he supposed to guide Uncle Seth out of there? Seth had only eighteen minutes left at the time that the connection was lost. Now, there were seventeen minutes before the doors of that place closed, and possibly, locked them in there until morning. He ended the call to leave the line open, in case Uncle Seth tried to call back.

He waited. There was no call back.

Peter continued to search through the observatory computer's mainframe, searching for anything that Uncle Seth might find suspicious. But he could find nothing. Maybe whoever these people were that Uncle Seth was investigating were smart enough to know better. Why would anyone keep top-secret or sensitive material on their computer, where anyone would be apt to find it? But Peter had a feeling that Seth would uncover something down inside that mountain.

Sixteen minutes had gone by. There was still no word from Uncle Seth. Peter began to sweat, enrapt in the heat of nervousness. He prayed that either Seth or Dylan was keeping track of the time. This operation couldn't fail just because of a dropped cell connection.

Peter had watched the remaining minute tick away on the stopwatch he'd set. The minute had dwindled to seconds, until it was gone. He thought of pulling up the footage from the security cameras, but he'd set it back to an earlier time. He checked the security system; the front doors were definitely closed. His heart dropped. He could only imagine whether

Uncle Seth and Dylan, or the rest of the investigators, had made it out in time. But it was time that would tell.

Now, he began searching around inside the system, trying to discover if there was anything he could do, maybe open the doors back up. But he was unsure as to whether or not it was necessary. Suddenly, something happened. His laptop screen turned completely black. There was nothing now, just blackness, and then his desktop page returned.

He was discovered.

Outside, the thunder crashed

His heart pounded harder. The sweat now streaked his face and caused his clothing to stick to him. He'd been caught. He'd spent too much time snooping around. He pulled the plug on his laptop; lest whoever it was try to discover his IP address, if they didn't already have it. Where was Uncle Seth? He should have called by now. Peter felt like a rat trapped in a wheel, as though there was nowhere to turn. He remembered his old room in the attic of his grandparents' house. He would stay there when he would spend time with them. In the midst of his frenzy, he packed up the laptop and headed out the door to his car. He would stash it at his grandparents' house, where no one would find it.

Once on the road, he called Uncle Seth.

* * * *

The van barreled down the winding incline until reaching the bottom. They were off of Eagle Rock Mountain and safe on the back road. Seth and Dylan had taken the time to catch their breaths. They were both about to reveal their discovery when Seth's phone rang. He answered; it was Peter.

"Uncle Seth, where are you?!" His voice was almost frantic.

"I'm back in the van with the investigators," he said. "Don't worry, we made it out of there okay."

"I thought you were trapped in there!" Peter exclaimed. "And I have bad news. I think I was discovered. Well, maybe not *me*, but I think someone knows the observatory's computer was hacked. I'm pretty sure of it."

Peter told him about the screen going black, like he'd been shut out.

"I doubt it will trace to me," he continued, "but I pulled the plug on my laptop just the same. I'm going to stash my laptop at Gram and Grandpa's house, in the attic."

"Okay, Peter, listen to me," Seth instructed. "It doesn't really matter much now, because it's over. We've made it out of there. We've already discovered what we needed to find out. But I want you to stay at Gram and Grandpa's house anyway, at least for a couple of days. Besides, they'd be glad to see you. Be calm and stay cool; you know nothing about anything."

Peter agreed. He was on his way there now. Seth ended the call and spoke up from the back of the van.

"That was Peter. He thinks that someone discovered his intrusion."

"The Men in Black," Dylan concluded.

"Undoubtedly," Seth said. "You all are never going to believe what we found."

The other three investigators listened intently and expectantly.

Sidney broke the tantalizing pause.

"Well? What did you two find down there? Spill it!"

Dylan answered the question.

"Down underneath Eagle Rock Mountain is a nuclear storage facility."

"What?" Leah gasped.

Sidney's jaw dropped, and a stunned Brett swiveled his seat to face them.

"We even got pictures," Seth said.

"We'll explain everything at Susan's house," Dylan said. "We're almost there."

\* \* \* \*

They were driving through the sprawling splendor of King's Haven within minutes. Soon, Dylan and Seth would tell the tale of Eagle Rock Mountain, but Dylan silently realized that it was, most likely, why his father had died. A somber quiet came over him. Leah phoned Susan to let her know that they were on their way—all of them. Now, they pulled up to her house.

They exited the van at nearly 3:00 am. The sky had now darkened to a near pitch black. The deep twilight gave way to a dead silence, broken only by the thunder that had now quieted to a soft rumble. On Susan's walkway, the soft sound of showering rain caught them by surprise. It was raining again, and again, they were briefly caught up in it. They hurried to the front door.

Susan had been waiting for them to arrive. She opened the front door as they reached the porch and began to usher them in. Dylan noticed that a slight paranoia had come over her, as she stood outside on the front porch, looking out and making sure they hadn't been followed. She closed the door behind her once they were all inside.

"I'll get you all some towels," she said.

And soon, she returned with towels. They dried themselves of the night's rain that had besieged them for the past hour. Susan lit a fire in the hearth to counter the chill of the spring storm, and they sat around the living room just as before.

"I see the two of you made it back in time," she said, to Seth and Dylan.

Dylan felt inattentive, detached from the reality of everything that had occurred tonight, but immersed in what exactly it all meant. He could feel Susan staring at him, as his head was lowered, and his eyes were failing to make contact.

"So," she said. "Is anyone going to fill me in on the night's events?"

He felt Susan's eyes focused on him. It was time for him to snap out of it. He lifted his head and answered her.

"Seth was right," he said. "It was an elevator, and it dropped down inside the mountain." He paused, trying to find the right words. "And down inside the mountain is a nuclear storage facility. It's what's being hidden at Eagle Rock. It's most likely why my father is dead."

Dylan watched as Susan turned a pasty white. Her jaw dropped when she spoke.

"My God, Dylan."

"We took pictures," Seth said, retrieving his iPhone and accessing the images. He gave his phone to Susan and showed her the pictures he'd taken. Dylan did the same, showing the investigators, and phones were passed back and forth until all had seen the images.

"Both of you be sure to send those pictures to the society's email address. We need to have them on file." They agreed, and Susan continued. "Titanium, this is bigger than we thought. It's no wonder there's such a high level of secrecy surrounding that place."

"Titanium is used to make nuclear bombs," Brett volunteered.

"I got that," Sidney said. "But what I don't get is what it has to do with this thing that people have seen in the sky?"

"Because, Sidney," Susan said, "UFOs have been largely spotted near nuclear power plants, storage plants, and other nuclear facilities. Those places are like magnets for these unidentified aircrafts, and no one really knows why. Many guess, but no one knows. So, now it looks like we know why so many sightings have taken place near Eagle Rock Mountain."

"And of course," Seth said, "the assumption is that Dr. Rasche, Dylan's father, had discovered the facility beneath the mountain."

Dylan finished the thought.

"And the Men in Black killed him," he said, without looking at anyone.

"And Dylan, that still has yet to be proven," Susan said.

To him, it was proven. Susan changed the subject.

"So, tell me what else happened tonight."

"We searched the observatory and didn't find anything suspicious" Leah said, and then she hesitated. "But Brett found something." She looked to him nervously, extending her hand and signaling him to speak.

"We entered one room that stored multiple telescopes," Brett said. "I thought all of it was just too easy. Leah's right; at first, we found nothing. So, I began to examine all of the telescopes, and soon, I came across one bearing initials on its base."

Dylan quickly glanced at him.

"The initials were GMR," he told Dylan. "I saw those same initials on your father's notebooks."

"They have one of his telescopes?" Dylan couldn't believe what he was hearing. His father had a few that were monogrammed with his initials, but how could the observatory be in possession of the one he was using at the time of his death? He was never aware of what had happened to it. Still, he felt frustration. Susan was right; what did it prove?

Brett described the telescope perfectly. Dylan remembered it well. Still, even he was unaware of what telescope his father had been using that night. He was a child at the time.

Then, Seth began to go into the details of how they narrowly got out as the doors were closing in front of them. He told Susan of how he'd lost cell contact with Peter, and about Peter's near frantic call in the van.

"But my nephew assures me that he's untraceable," he said. "But there is the chance that they know they've been hacked."

"It doesn't matter," Susan said. "As long as you're all safe, and no one can prove that you were there."

"That doesn't matter either," Dylan said. "If we go public with this, many people will have much to answer for. They're not in any position to make us look like criminals."

"How very true," Sidney agreed. "Which makes me ask, esteemed leader, do we go public with this? And when?"

Susan thought for a moment. Deep inside, Dylan was not yet ready for a media circus. She noticed it on his face.

"I say, let's wait," she said. "I believe Ursula is being discharged tomorrow, and then there's Leah's graduation on Saturday. We still haven't heard from Marv, either. I say we take the weekend to let things cool down a bit. We'll decide what we're going to do, and when, after the weekend, agreed?"

All heads nodded back at her. She turned to Dylan and lifted his chin.

"Don't worry, Dylan," she said. "We will get to the bottom of this, one way or another."

# Chapter Eighteen

## ~ A Hot, White Euphoria ~

In the wee morning hours, the taller man in black had scanned the observatory's computer system, searching for any obvious signs of a hacker. There were none, just as he'd expected. There rarely were, and he'd concluded earlier that if it was a hacking job, it was top-notch. But there was one thing he did discover. It was obvious that someone had interfered with the security cameras. He'd discovered a switch in camera images that had occurred only hours before.

Now, he and his cohort parked the sedan behind the observatory. They walked around to the platform and over to the security panel. The taller man in black swiped a card through a slot, and the doors that Seth and Dylan had nearly been trapped behind swooshed open for him. They walked into the observatory and looked around them, shaded eyes roving to the left, right, and as far away as eyes could see. They walked into the various rooms, noticing nothing out of the ordinary. They paced the hallways until the shorter man's hand reached out and stopped his cohort.

"Look." He pointed to the floor. The taller man looked and then crouched down. They were faint, but unmistakable. Shoe prints, two sets of them, streaked the floor side by side.

"I had a feeling that something was going on here late last night," the taller man said. "And if the cameras *had* been tampered with, then anyone could have been in here."

Without a word to each other, the Men in Black walked together toward the same destination. Their concordance was unspoken, but well understood. Down the hallway and to the left, and then a sharp right after a few more feet, the same direction that Seth had taken—toward the elevator. They stood in front of it. The light above the panel was not lit yet, since it was still 6:00 am, and no staff had arrived yet.

The taller man in black took a key from his inner jacket pocket and turned it in the keyhole just below the light on the panel. The light came on, and with it came a whirring sound. He pressed the down arrow, and once again, a whooshing sound came up from below.

"We're going down?" the second man in black asked.

"Don't you think we should?" he asked. "If someone *was* here, we need to find out."

They were descending in the elevator only seconds later. The doors soon opened in the storage facility, a secret place that had been their primary concern for some time. Nothing stirred down here in the dank and dimly lit underworld. Everything seemed in place, untouched: the barrels, the boxes, the pool, and the generators. All of it seemed as it always had been.

"Let's go," the taller man in black said.

Once they arrived back in the observatory, they'd taken one last look around. The taller man in black stood with his hands in his pockets, his head turning from side to side, sensing something out of place and staring once again at the shoe prints. He made a motion with his head, one that told his cohort that it was time to go. They walked over to the doors, and the taller man pressed a few buttons on an inner security panel. The doors opened.

And then something caught the taller man's eye as they stepped through the doorway. It was small and white, but it didn't escape the keenness of his vision. It lay on the floor, signaling his attention like a talisman. He bent down and picked it up, and then rolled it around in his fingers. It was a button, a shirt button to be precise.

"Well, well, well," he said. He pinched the button between his thumb and index finger and held it up toward the light. "Not mine," he said. "I take it it's not yours either?"

The shorter man in black shook his head.

"The cleaning crew does a clean sweep of this place every night," he said. "They wouldn't have missed those shoeprints. You think the button belongs to whoever was in here?" He waited for an answer, while the taller man smiled and chuckled in amusement. "You think it belongs to Dornan?"

Behind darkened shades, the taller man closed his obscured eyes.

"I know it does," he said.

"Then it's time?" the shorter man asked.

There was a pause before the taller man turned his head toward him.

"It's time," he said.

\* \* \* \*

Susan had picked up Ursula from the hospital shortly after 9:00 am. She'd waited with her as the nurses had taken their time with her discharge papers. Ursula had been tired, restless, and anxious to get back home. Finally, Susan wheeled her out to the car, as mandated by hospital policy. Then, she'd brought her home, opening the front door for her before returning her key. She'd helped Ursula settle in, telling her about their search for traces of radiation in her apartment.

"There was nothing here in the apartment," she said. "But outside, in the yard, the Geiger counter showed some significant levels of radiation. I want you to stay away from the yard, at least for now. I also want to warn you that since you were a patient at the hospital, all of the proper authorities have been notified of the radiation levels outside. *That* was out of my hands. It's not only hospital policy, but it's the law. So, it's hard to imagine that this thing we're investigating will stay under wraps for much longer. If you need me or the team for *anything*, please don't hesitate to call."

"I won't," she said. "I'm going to try to make Leah's graduation tomorrow."

"She'd like that very much," Susan replied. "I'll check on you tonight."

Susan left her there, laid up on the sofa and watching television.

Now, it was nearly noon, and Susan and the investigators had reassembled back in room 208. She filled them in on Ursula, but last night's adventure remained the topic of discussion. Susan had retrieved all of the pictures sent to the society's email by both Dylan and Seth, and now she presented them in a PowerPoint slideshow. The first was of the bubbling pool.

"From what I've researched," she said, "This is a spent fuel pool. It's a storage pool for the spent fuel derived from nuclear reactors. That crane-like structure that you see above it could possibly be for the retrieval of any spent fuel rods."

She clicked a hand-held remote that brought up the next picture. It was of the generators.

"These generators *could be* steam generators, though I'm not sure," she continued. "Steam generators are used to transfer heat from a reactor's cooling system. They could also be electrical generators. It's hard to be certain."

She clicked the remote again, and the yellow barrels loomed large on the screen.

"The pictures of these barrels are self-explanatory," she said. "That one word, 'radioactive,' tells us that those barrels obviously store radioactive material. Where is the material from? That's anyone's guess."

Again, she clicked the hand-held remote, and the next picture popped up. A silent pause lingered between them indefinitely. All eyes stared at the single word labeling the gray metallic boxes, standing out like a warning, an omen—*Titanium.*

Susan broke the silence.

"We all know why titanium is used," she said. "We all know why it's in popular demand in our current day and age. Why is it being stored here in a small, quiet town in western Pennsylvania? That, we don't know. But I do think that there's a connection between this storage facility at Eagle Rock, and the sightings that have occurred near there through the years. It's no coincidence. So, what are the MIB trying to cover up—the storage facility, or the appearances of this thing in the sky? That's a better question."

"Maybe both," Sidney said.

"I wonder if they killed my father over this or something greater," Dylan interjected.

There was a somber, silent concurrence.

"I'm afraid that this one is going to take more than us, team," Susan said. "This one has been kept from the entire nation and the world. While we may solve how it affects Green Valley, the bigger part of this mystery is going to take all of us as a community. We need others on our side in this. We're alone right now. I think this one's much bigger than us.

"But while that may be true," she went on, "we can't let it consume us either. Dylan, you've come much further on the mystery of your father's death that you ever have before. You should be proud of your investigations. But you, and the rest of us, need to take a brief time out, and be there for Leah's graduation. Tomorrow is her day; let's enjoy it."

They all agreed, and the male investigators were fist-bumping Leah's shoulders like teasing big brothers. It was a moment away from the tension of their current mystery, but little did they know that tomorrow, the mystery would thicken.

* * * *

Susan had already briefed him on the meeting she would hold with the investigators, so Seth had spent the day with his family. Besides, it was crucial that he meet up with Peter, who'd stayed the night at Seth's parents' house. Today was Peter's day off from work, so after lunch Seth finally had a few moments alone to speak with him.

"So, tell me everything that happened last night," Seth said. They sat on the front porch, keeping their voices low so that they wouldn't be overheard.

"I was panicking," Peter said. "I wasn't sure if you both had made it out of there before the doors closed. We lost the cell connection. I didn't know what was happening. Soon, I was able to see that the doors *had* closed, and you hadn't called back. I thought you both were trapped!"

"We almost were. But we made it out just in time."

Seth didn't want to scare Peter by revealing just how close they'd come to being trapped.

"So, I started searching around, hoping to do s*omething*," Peter said. "I even thought of opening the doors back up. Then my screen just went blank. I *know* someone shut me out!"

Seth tried to stay calm, though his nerves were jittering. He'd mentioned the MIB to Peter earlier, but now he had no intention of telling him that it was most likely *them* who had shut him out. Peter may have suspected, yet he said nothing.

"Like I said," Seth said. "It's over now. Keep the laptop hidden. Don't use it for a while. Don't let anyone know that you're here. You know nothing about anything, as I said."

Peter agreed, and not another word was spoken. Nerves soon settled as the day wore on. Soon, dusk had tinged the sky a reddish-orange as Seth was having dinner alone at his favorite restaurant. He hadn't been to Fire Catchers in at least ten years, and now he was happy to be sitting alone, getting away from it all, downing a few beers, and devouring their deep fried, jumbo cod sandwich and fries. He sat out on the pyre-lit patio, watching the reddish-tinged sky turn purple as nightfall soon approached. He finished eating, and then sat at the bar, downing another three beers before calling it quits. He looked forward to going back to his hotel and falling asleep in front of the television.

He paid his bill, walked out the door and through the parking lot to his car. He revved the engine and drove away from the restaurant, feeling the slight buzz that made him thankful that the hotel was only a mile from Fire Catchers. The alcohol circulated through his blood, and a much needed wooziness took over his mind and body. He drove, oblivious to the cars behind him.

Finally, he arrived at the Oak Terrace Inn where he'd been staying. It was a modest, inn-type of hotel, where outdoor rooms of a bungalow-style semblance were aligned side by side. The inn was surrounded by oak trees, and in the back was a massive terrace for guests to enjoy. It was how the inn got its name.

He parked the car in his space and sat in the front seat for a few moments to gather his thoughts. He planned to spend the day with his family again tomorrow, since the investigators would be wrapped up at the university for Leah's graduation. It would be nice to have another day to relax and contemplate this whole dilemma over again in his mind. How was he going to go about proving that Geoffrey Rasche was murdered? It was something he had to think about. He would hate himself, having to leave Dylan behind with unfinished business. He promised that he would get to the end of this mystery.

He'd forwarded all of the pictures he'd taken with his iPhone. He'd sent the pictures of Geoffrey Rasche's journal to MUFON headquarters, where they would be stored among many other mysterious photos at Hangar 1. He'd also sent the photos of the facility beneath Eagle Rock to Hangar 1 and to Susan. There was now no need to keep them on his phone.

He sat in the front seat, deleting them all, because he'd almost forgotten.

He stepped out of the car and slammed the door shut, locking the doors with his key fob. Wearily, he walked over to his door—room 103. He pulled his wallet from his back pocket and retrieved the keycard for his room, a longer task than expected in the dark. He didn't react to the rustling sound behind him until a sharp pain sliced through the back of his head and shoulder. Someone had hit him from behind. But it was too late; he was down and unconscious.

\* \* \* \*

He awoke in his room, groggy and unsure, and then the wincing pain in the back of his head made him remember. He tried to move, but nothing happened, as if he was paralyzed. He tried to move his hands but couldn't. Seth lowered his eyes and saw that his hands were tied to the chair. He tried to move again and realized that he was bound to the chair not only by his hands, but around his mid-section as well. Saliva dripped from his sore mouth, a mouth that ached at the jaws from the handkerchief that gagged him.

His vision was becoming clearer, but he didn't need perfect eyesight to identify the men in front of him. They stood before him, both of them in black, with black fedora-style hats on their heads. One was taller than the other. They stood with their black gloved hands clasped in front of them, watching him wake to the sight of their presence.

He writhed in the chair to his right, and then to his left, in hopeless efforts to free himself of the ropes. It was a natural instinct, but the task was fruitless. He stopped and stared at them. They had finally tracked him down. The taller man spoke.

"We we're just wondering if you'd found what you were looking for at the observatory?"

They knew. They *were* the ones who'd shut Peter out of the system. Seth silently prayed not only for himself, but for the anonymity of his nephew. A fear for his family sparked a panic inside, one that made him break a sweat as he tried to suppress it.

He noticed that they weren't wearing their shades. But everything seemed to be blurry to him. He wondered if it was from the lump on the back of his head, but his stomach was turning along with the blurriness that clouded his vision. His left shirt sleeve had been undone, and he felt a slight pinch on the open side of his arm. A rubber band was tied around his upper arm. He looked at their faces. Something was strange, not right about them, but he couldn't make them out clearly; the blurriness was unshakable.

Seth tried to focus on the open side of his arm. He could make out what looked like a red mark. They'd injected him with something. He knew it; he felt it. A surge of heat swept through him, and his mind began to drift through a euphoric haze.

"We know you were there," the shorter man said. Then, between two fingers, the taller man displayed the button he'd found in the entranceway to the observatory.

"Look familiar to you?" he asked.

The taller man stepped closer to Seth in order for him to see the button he held up close to his face. Seth's vision was still blurry, but no doubt, it was his. He hadn't realized he'd lost it. Dylan, it was when Dylan had pulled him through the closing doorway. The wrenching must have pulled the button from his shirt.

He looked up to get a closer glimpse of the taller man's face, but the taller man in black quickly turned away. His back was turned to Seth, but Seth could tell that he'd slipped on his shades. *At night, why?* Seth thought. Even through the haze, he realized that the taller man didn't want him to see his eyes or his face too closely.

Seth watched as the taller man lifted something up in front of him, tilting his shades down and his head upward to get a better look at it in the light. A liquid squirted upward and onto the floor beside the man, and then the man turned, holding a syringe upward in his hand. Seth thrashed and wriggled in the chair with a fierce determination to break the bonds. But his efforts were dulled by whatever they'd shot into him and amounted to futile fidgeting. The taller man stepped slowly back over to him. Seth began to yell, but his shouts were muffled by the gag. Desperate cries were reduced to a stifled croaking.

"Take it easy," the taller man almost cooed. "No one can hear you. Besides, your body's already tasted some of this. Just let go and feel the euphoria."

The fear exploded inside of him. His heart was pounding in his throat despite the haze that sought to subdue him. He was helpless, tied to the chair as the taller man in black neared him, armed with a loaded syringe. He would never see his wife or children again, or his parents, or his nephew. He fought hard, the tears cascading from his eyes.

The taller man reached him. Seth tried to tip the chair, but the shorter, heavier man ran across the room and held it back into place. The taller man pinned his left arm down. He felt the pinch, and then the slight pressure. The hot liquid filled his arm as he continued to fight. The men stepped back just as his body stopped fighting.

Calm, the incapacity to fight, and the inability to focus draped over him like a veil. He was drifting, feeling the rush that swept him from inside. He wanted to rest, to continue drifting, at least for now. He closed his eyes and rode the wave that carried him. Seth felt himself sink, but it was okay; the oncoming darkness had turned into a hot white light that enveloped him.

* * * *

The Men in Black watched him sink down in the chair, despite the bonds that secured him. Seth Dornan's head was hung down, and they watched and waited until the color of his skin whitened. The taller man walked back over to the slumped figure in the chair. He unstrapped the rubber band from Seth's upper arm, and then placed his index and middle finger just above the wrist. The skin was cool, clammy. There was no pulse.

The taller man looked over at his counterpart.

"He's dead," he said.

"Let's fix this place up and get out of here," the shorter man replied.

They untied the ropes from Seth's body and the chair, catching the body before it fell to the floor. They propped the body up on the bed, and the taller man placed the needle in Seth's right hand to affix his fingerprints. Then, he left the needle on the nightstand next to the bed, right where the dead man could've reached it. The shorter man dropped two, empty plastic packets of what had once contained heroin onto the floor, making it look like Seth had been careless and then simply overdosed. The men fixed up the room to perfection. Turning the TV on and keeping it low, rustling up the bed a little, painting the picture that a drug addict had died during a private, one-man party.

They'd already discovered and confiscated the mini voice-recorder in his inner jacket pocket. So, Dornan was investigating Dr. Rasche's death, just as they'd suspected. They'd searched through the images on his phone, finding nothing of significance.

Now, they looked back at the scene they'd manufactured. They'd removed all traces of themselves, stashing the rope in a duffel bag, mussing the carpet to cover any footprints, even wiping away the drops of heroin that had shot from the syringe to the floor. There was no need to worry about wiping surfaces; their hands had been gloved the entire time. One closer look showed their handiwork to be complete.

"Satisfied?" the shorter man asked.

The taller man nodded.

"I'm satisfied," he said. "Let's get out of here."

They peered out of the curtains, seeing to it that there were no possible witnesses to their exit. No one was outside. Then, they opened the door and left.

# Chapter Nineteen

## ~ Graduation Day ~

She stared at herself in the mirror, concluding that the choice of a light-blue blouse and white slacks would be fine beneath her green robe and hood. Leah felt excited, nervous, and relieved, all at the same time. This morning she received a call from Ursula, who told her that she would be attending her post-graduation ceremony today with the rest of the team. The most important person, her father, Paul Leeds, was on his way over to see her before she left early for the university.

She turned from the mirror and sat down on the sofa, surfing through the TV channels, but thinking while mindlessly watching. She thought of Dylan, and how lucky she was that her father was on his way here. Dylan had lost his father to this horrible mystery and had spent his life thinking it was an accident. She had lost the woman she'd *assumed* was her mother. Memories of Cedar Manor made her realize just how much she and Dylan had in common.

Susan's words kept reverberating through her mind, about how the mystery they were now wrapped up in may never be solved completely. Again, it made her think of Cedar Manor and the black mirror that was never discovered. How it, along with Angus Marlowe, had simply disappeared. A man and an antiquated occult artifact, both vanished into thin air with no explanation, no trace, and were never seen again. It still haunted her when she thought about it.

Just then, her doorbell rang. She gazed through the curtained window and saw her father, clutching a bouquet of roses. She opened the door, and he extended the bouquet to her.

"For you, my pretty one," he said.

She took them from him, and they embraced in the doorway. Paul had grown balder since the night at Cedar Manor two years ago. And now, only a gray ring rounded his head like a vine on an ancient Roman's. But he looked healthy, happy, and most of all, sane. She thanked him for the roses, explaining that he shouldn't have; his presence was more important.

"Of course I should have," he said. "You're my girl."

He hugged and kissed her again.

"Are you sure you don't mind sitting with the rest of the team, Dad?" She asked, hoping that old memories were not still fresh.

"No, I don't mind. So, I assume you all are immersed in another case again?"

"Yes. And believe me; you don't even want to know."

"That's okay. I know you can't talk about those things."

"Well, it involves Dylan," she said. "And I feel badly for him right now."

"That's because you're an angel, my dear."

She thought about that for a moment; how Daddy's angel could've been arrested the other night for illegal entry, and possibly computer espionage, and right before she was to receive her master's degree. She chuckled but kept her mouth shut.

Paul sat with his daughter until it was time for her to leave. They left her cottage-style home together, and she anxiously hopped into the graduation gift he'd bought her, her light-blue Mustang convertible. They engaged in an interlude of small talk. He would see her grace the stage in two hours. And then, they parted ways.

\* \* \* \*

The university's sprawling south lawn housed a baseball field, a tennis court, and another immense, open field used for commencement ceremonies except for when it rained. When it rained, commencements were held inside, but today was a sunny, summer-like, spring day. A few fluffy white clouds billowed in the sky, forming shapes if one stared long enough. The temperature had even reached seventy-five degrees.

Several stacked tiers of white bleachers were set up on the field for the ceremony. In the center was a vast stage erected a few feet from the ground, and a speaker's podium stood at the end of it. Chairs surrounded the stage for the graduates, while the bleachers were reserved for guests. And guests were now filling those bleachers. Commencement was to begin at 2:00 pm; it was now 1:30.

Susan, Sidney, Dylan, Brett, and Ursula shuffled their way through the crowd and were soon seated in the front row of one set of bleachers to the far left of the stage. They would have a clear enough view of Leah when she walked up on the stage and accepted her degree. They all brought cameras: Susan, a disposable; Sidney, a Nikon; Dylan, a Cannon; and Brett's video recorder was slung over his arm in a carrying case. No blurry phone shots would be good enough for this occasion. It was a special day for one so dear to their hearts and loved by all of them, their sweet, strange angel with the powerful third eye.

A familiar face was staring up at them from ground level. Susan knew the face well; it was Paul, Leah's father. He waved his ticket in the air at her, and Susan motioned with her hand to come up and join them. Paul walked up the few stairs to the front row and sat on the end next to Susan, but not before they embraced in greetings, and he shook hands with the others. Susan had spent a year in therapy with Paul following the night at Cedar Manor. He finished his sessions about a year ago, and that was the last time she'd seen him.

"How have you been, Paul?" she asked.

"I've been great," he said, smiling, "thanks to you. I'm so glad you're all here for her today. It means a lot to her."

Susan reassured him that there was nowhere they would rather be. She was glad that they all had the chance to see each other again, and this time, under normal circumstances. Susan introduced him to Ursula, and the small talk between the six of them went on for a while. They talked and watched the guests amass before them, thankful that they'd taken their seats early. People bustled everywhere, waiting to be seated in the bleachers. Heads turned to find the right direction, voices became louder, and ushers ran to help control a thickening crowd. The ear-piercing whine of someone testing a microphone turned heads and distracted attentions for a quick moment, and then the clamor of voices continued. Minutes later, the university president took the stage, engendering a scattered applause.

He was a middle-aged man in his mid-fifties with dark hair, dressed in a cap and gown that represented his own, doctoral achievement. He began his speech by thanking everyone for attending. He went on to speak about gathering to honor a generation that was making great strides in a difficult and ever changing world. He made a comparison between his day and age, and the current one. He talked about how education was the key in a world persistent to shun it.

Sidney began to make snoring noises, and Ursula kicked him sideways in the leg. Susan looked at him, and then turned her head in the opposite direction to avoid laughing. The president prattled on for another ten minutes, until reaching the most anticipated moment.

"Ladies and gentlemen, please welcome this spring's postgraduate class of Green Valley University."

Roars and thunderous applause erupted as the president introduced the graduates with a beckoning of his left hand. One by one, students clad in identical green hoods and robes followed each other in a unified procession out onto the field. The investigators spotted Leah within seconds and began cheering. The applause continued until all graduates were seated in the chairs surrounding the stage.

The president introduced the first speaker, the dean of the university. Next, was a former alumni member, followed by the guest speaker—a local congresswoman. All of it was monotonously long, making some guests stare at the ground, past the stage, even up at the sky. Eventually, the dispersing of degrees began, and the investigators watched with anticipation.

It wasn't long before the president reached Leah's name. She was among the top postgraduates. They watched her on stage as her name was about to be called.

"Leah Leeds," the president announced, "Master of Arts, Psychology."

A general applause erupted and the proud cheering of the investigators continued. Brett was steady with the video camera, following Leah's stride across the stage, her shaking the president's hand, and accepting her master's degree. The applause grew louder as the president draped Leah's hood over her head. Susan, Dylan, and Sidney were snapping the same shots from different angles. Leah was now off the stage, and the names of those who followed her were called out.

The investigators basked in a moment of relief; the reason they'd attended was over. They would wait until the end of the ceremony, take pictures with Leah, and then go out to dinner. Finally, the moment had arrived when the graduates assembled in the master's procession. Brett zeroed in on the crowd, found Leah, and recorded the moment.

Keeping their eyes on Leah, they scooted through the crowd and met her on a far-off spot on the right side of the field. She exchanged hugs with them all, especially her father. Now, the picture taking began: she with the investigators, then with each of them individually, she and her father, and then all of them together, a picture she asked a friend to take.

It was minutes before 4:00 pm. The beautiful day hadn't changed, and they stood out on the field, enjoying the sunshine and discussing dinner arrangements. Guests and graduates stood around them in groups and droves, talking, taking pictures, and recording videos. Leah was talking about one of her toughest final exams when she suddenly stopped, and all of their heads turned to hear a change in the noise surrounding them.

Gasps were expelled, one after another, as some unfamiliar amazement rippled through the crowd. The investigators looked at each other, unsure as to what the growing commotion was about, unable to see beyond bodies and heads that obstructed their view.

"What's going on?" Leah asked.

"I'm not sure," Susan replied, turning her head around and seeing nothing.

The gasps grew louder, exploding into cries of shock and fear. A young man, a fellow graduate of Leah's, pointed his finger upward.

"Up there!" he yelled. "It's up there, in the sky!"

The cries from the crowd became not only louder, but ongoing, allowing for no pause in the shock and fear and lingering on the brink of pandemonium. The investigators moved together into action to try and gain a closer view of the sky. They ditched and dodged hastening bodies that threatened the scene with mayhem. People bumped into each other, stepping on feet, while others asked unanswerable questions in high-pitched voices.

Heads turned upward to the sky, while index fingers pointed accusingly at the heavens. Standing together, each of the investigators saw it at the same time. Once it was in sight, all eyes failed to flinch. It stood hovering in the sky above the great crowd amassed in broad daylight. The phantom object was undeniably disc-shaped, and a sleek, metallic-gray in color. In the face of an unrelenting sun, it had no lights. The fluffy white clouds served as a backdrop, doing nothing to deter its presence. It was silent, still, as though examining every person in the crowd.

An ascending rumble of fear stricken voices spread throughout the crowd. Many began to flee the scene, which caused people to push and shove each other out of the way. For the less fearful, phone cameras went up into the air, snapping and recording. The curious ones just stared, hypnotized by disbelief.

"My God," Susan said.

Their mouths were agape, except for Brett's; he'd been recording the object from his first glimpse of it. Dylan stared at it like an enemy before a duel. Sidney began snapping pictures with his Nikon, the continuous clicking in sync with many others, like a mass photo shoot. Dylan took his iPhone and held it up to the sky, utilizing the video function and recording additional footage.

"I don't believe it," Leah said. She turned to her father who was staring up at the sky. His face had drained of all color. The pure white shock painted him ghostly, rendering him speechless and shaken. Leah grabbed onto his shoulders. "Dad, are you alright? It's okay, we can leave."

"No, Leah, I'm fine, really. I'm just surprised like everyone here."

It was clear that Leah was worried about her father's mental state since the night at Cedar Manor, but Paul assuaged her fears.

"Is that what I think it is, Susan?" he asked.

Susan kept staring up at the sky, hearing the question, but wordless in response.

Paul asked another question.

"So, is this what you've all been investigating?"

"It is, Dad," Leah said, not taking her eyes from the object.

"That's it!" A silent Ursula, lost in fear, thought, and contemplation, mustered her voice and finally spoke. "I'm sure of it," she said. "That's what put me in the hospital, though it wasn't that high in the sky that night."

Ursula began jerking her head with slight, but sudden movements, as though trying to shake a bug from her ear. The team suspected what was happening to her—Ursula was hearing.

\* \* \* \*

A different set of sounds quickly came upon her, but her clairaudience was not quite like Sidney's. Ursula never succumbed to any type of deafness. The sounds or voices that she heard would become paramount, while the regular noises around her would fade or coexist in the background. She never heard dead people, only live ones in faraway conversations, and the slur of shit-talkers like a built-in alarm system. The panicky rumble of the crowd now became a hushed and irrelevant vibration.

What she heard now was a squeaking, screeching squeal, like mixed signals or someone rapidly spinning the radio dial. The sounds were warbled, jumbled, and intermixed with blips of static. She saw Susan standing in front of her. Susan knew what was happening. Ursula watched as Sidney lowered the camera and looked at her.

The sounds continued, screeching, bleeping, and crashing, all unidentifiable to her ear. She looked at the crowd. Some were scurrying, hastening, but many were calmly watching. The sounds she heard were not coming from the crowd; she was sure of it. She turned her head back up to the sky. The object still loomed above, but it remained silent to the rest of them.

Could the noise be coming from it? She watched and wondered why she hadn't heard the sounds the first time she'd seen the object. She tilted her head slightly, allowing her clairaudience to function at its fullest. The noises became louder. In between the clamor, she thought that she heard the fast flash of random voices, spoken by sources unknown. It was fragmentary, fleeting bits of words she couldn't catch, incomplete statements interrupted by distance and possibly even time.

"What are you hearing, Ursula?" Susan asked.

"Noise," she said, shaking her head. "I almost hear voices, but..."

A series of words spoken together caused the whiplash of her head back up toward the sky. The words were abrupt and unexpected. They were spoken quickly and clearly.

198

*"A time in the future..."*

She froze even in the day's heat and felt her hair rise. She knew the voice hadn't come from the crowd. The voices in the crowd were hushed to her right now, even Susan's. The voice she'd heard was a human voice, but somehow unusual. It was convoluted, coiled amid the other sounds, and its timbre sounded as if it had not spoken orally, as if the words were planted in her mind. The words had been spoken to her *telepathically*, the same way she'd communicated with Ryan Quinn in the compound.

She continued to watch the object in the sky. Then abruptly, just like before, it vanished. The gasps and cries from the crowd no longer stayed hushed in the background. Now, screams erupted all around her.

\* \* \* \*

People were running through the field, hurrying each other in the process, hell bent on a mass exodus from the campus grounds. Those who'd taken pictures, or recorded videos, now phoned the rest of the world to report what had occurred. Brett had watched the entire episode through the viewfinder. Before the object had utterly vanished, an instinctive notion passed through his mind. He'd felt the urge to shift, to soar like the hawk, and pursue the strange object through the sky. But he'd remembered where he was, what he was doing, and the maddening crowd of people around him. He'd felt hindered, suppressed in the object's presence.

But it was a presence he couldn't take his eyes away from, a legend of lore and speculation so vividly revealing itself in their current reality, and he was getting it all on video. Then he watched it disappear, just like it had never been there, just as Ursula had described it. The object's appearance was one thing; its disappearance was even more frightening. And then frenzied panic erupted on the field.

He looked at the time display in the video. Still recording, the video was now twenty-six seconds. He kept his eye to the viewfinder, unable to remove it. He heard Dylan next to him.

"Brett, did you get that? Did you get it disappearing?"

"I got all of it," he said, "twenty-six seconds and counting."

It had been twenty-six seconds since Brett had heard the younger man's voice.

*"It's up there, in the sky!"*

He'd instantly spotted what the young graduate was seeing. Like a reflex, he hit the red record button and shot the image of the object in the sky. It had been hovering, and Brett could see that its bottom was rotating. He'd been careful not to move or let the crowd bump him out of focus.

The object had been stationary, almost like it was watching, and it was silent. But Ursula was hearing something, a thought that secretly spooked him. He never took his eyes, or the camera, away from the sight. He'd recorded all twenty-six seconds of the encounter, and soon the footage would make history for the Paranormal Research and Investigative Society.

\* \* \* \*

They'd shuffled their way through the crowd, making great strides like the many people who sought to get away. They noticed the eyes that watched and followed them, many by those who recognized them, curious and expectant of their responses as to what had just happened. They paid no mind to the unspoken curiosity, keeping close together as they moved, walking a total of two minutes to Levin Hall.

Paul had been parked outside of Levin Hall, and Leah made a quick detour to see him off.

"Are you sure you're alright, Dad?" she asked, as he sat behind the wheel.

"I'm fine, Leah, shocked is all," he said.

"Listen, Dad, if anyone contacts you, like the press, or asks any questions about me—"

"I got it," he said. "Not a word."

She watched him drive away, and then hurried back up the stairs to Levin Hall, holding her robe above her feet as she moved. Leah saw the investigators up ahead at the top of the stairs and thought silently to herself. She didn't understand. After making sure that her father had been alright, she noticed something going on with Ursula. It was then that she'd turned and focused her third eye on the object.

She hadn't seen anything, no vision, no penetration of the object, no clues. It was a phantom in the sky, just as many past witnesses had described it. It was definitely a UFO, and her third eye had failed her when she gazed at it. It was as though the gray, silent object had been aware.

The feeling had sent a chill down her spine even in the warm sunlight. She rejoined the investigators, and soon they were safely inside of room 208.

* * * *

"Dylan, be sure to lock the door behind you," Susan said, as they entered. Dylan closed and locked the door, producing a hollow clunk and a metallic click. Susan took control of their emergency gathering. "Brett, let's see what you've got on video. I want to see yours as well, Dylan. Sidney, we need those pictures scanned immediately."

Brett connected his video camera to one of the many computers in the room. The remaining investigators took their usual seats around the table. Dylan retrieved the video he'd shot from his iPhone. They huddled around the small screen that Dylan held up in his hand.

"I think this video is one second less than Brett's," he said.

They watched the object on the small, wavering screen. The image was not blurred, but the resolution was somewhat fuzzy; yet there was no denying its authenticity. It would become one of many famous UFO videos shot today, right here at Green Valley University. Dylan enlarged the video to full frame, and the object in the sky absorbed most of the screen. They watched as the lower half of the disc-shaped craft twisted right and left.

"There!" Ursula said. "That's what it was doing the night I saw it."

Brett moved away from the computer and quickly joined them, watching the screen.

"I saw that also," Brett said. "I zoomed in on that in my video."

They moved away from the table and sat surrounding the computer, where Brett returned to his seat. His video was paused at the beginning, and he resumed it with a click of the mouse. The gasps and cries from the crowd were heard in the background. This recorded image was of a higher quality resolution, the audio more coherent. They were now watching a different angle of the image, and the spinning of the object's lower half became more visible.

"Is it dispersing radiation on the crowd?" Ursula said. "That's what happened to me."

Susan glanced at her in fear, hearing a possibility she hadn't considered before.

"It also happened to Shane Rowe," Sidney said.

Susan answered Ursula's question, but it was a guess at best.

"Well, possibly," she said. "But Ursula, you yourself said that the craft was much higher in the sky when you saw it this time. If so, the distance may have protected everyone. Does anyone feel ill at this moment?"

No one did. Susan reminded Brett, Dylan, and Sidney about copies of their images for the society's archives.

"This will be hitting the news now, if it hasn't already," Susan said. "We'll be thrown into this. We were all there, and the media will discover that Leah was among the graduates today. I don't think it's wise for us to go public with the entirety of our case just yet. Dylan, I know that you want this out in the open, but I'm thinking of your safety right now. I'm worried about Shane's warning to you."

Dylan nodded, still absorbed in the shock. But his initial sighting last Saturday night, along with his suspicions, had now been vindicated.

"I say we wait a little longer for Marv to contact us, and we still have yet to call Seth. It's impertinent that he be alerted to what's happened here today, especially since we're about to become immersed in a media circus. My prediction is that the university is about to become flooded with not only reporters, but the military as well. We have yet to hear from our infamous MIB. Will they show up? I doubt any of us wants to wait around and find out."

Susan told Dylan to get Seth on the phone.

"Tell him to meet us either here, or at the restaurant. We're not going to let this ruin our plans for today, not only for the obvious reason, but we need to act normally. If the media finds us holed up here, we'll never get out."

Dylan had already pressed the contact button for Seth's number, and then placed the call on speakerphone. Silently, the investigators waited for an answer. One ring, two rings, three rings, and then four, until Seth's voicemail answered. After the tone, Dylan left a message.

"Seth, this is Dylan. Call us back *immediately* when you get this."

He ended the call and set his phone back down on the table. A brief silence did not betray the thousands of unspoken thoughts that lay buried between them.

"Maybe he's busy with family right now," Leah said.

"As *we* should be," Susan said. "Leah, call Paul and tell him that you're picking him up. We'll all meet at the restaurant. This is your day, Leah. I suggest we all save our assessments of today for discussion tomorrow. Seth will call us whenever he gets the message."

They left room 208, assuming that a few moments of celebration would allow them to escape. Their assumptions were correct, but the moments would be brief.

* * * *

Susan's prediction had been accurate. They'd driven Ursula home, and now military vehicles sped past them on their way back to the university. Sidney drove the van, taking Susan, Dylan, and Brett to retrieve their vehicles from the Levin Hall parking lot. The first military jeep passed them, then another, and as the third came into view, Dylan snapped a picture of it with his phone.

"They're coming from the university, boys," Susan said. "You can bet on it."

"Let's hope they don't stop us from leaving," Sidney said.

"If they're leaving, couldn't that be a good sign?" Brett asked.

"Possibly," Susan said. "Dylan, has Seth returned your call yet?"

"Not yet," Dylan said, shaking his head.

"Let's not waste time when we get there," Susan continued. "We'll observe what we can by sight, but let's quickly get into our cars and leave. Let's also hope that the military, or whoever else, has ushered the media out of there. Say nothing, if we're approached."

Sidney drove the van onto campus grounds and within seconds, arrived at Levin Hall. Susan, Brett, and Dylan each had their keys ready, preparing to drive away as soon as they reached their cars. They exited the van, and Sidney watched the three of them from his front seat. As they walked to their cars, they looked downward to the south lawn and the field beyond it.

The field had been cordoned off with barricades. Military, no doubt, Susan thought. She was convinced when she saw two military officers guarding the barricaded field. Somewhere in the field, a camera flash flared from far away. Someone had been taking pictures, but they were unable to see who.

They saw no one else except the guards and whoever was taking pictures in the field. Apparently, they'd been lucky enough to avoid the cavalry, as well any mysterious men dressed in black. Susan, Dylan, and Brett made it quickly to their cars and started the engines. Sidney followed them out until they were off campus grounds.

They drove their separate ways, thankful that the strange day had ended. They kept in touch once arriving home, relieved that they hadn't been drafted for the media circus just yet. It was good to be home. Their bodies were exhausted. Their minds were astounded. Their mouths were speechless. And still, the night wore on with no word from Seth Dornan.

# Chapter Twenty

## ~ Interesting Insights ~

Dylan had called Seth again after he'd arrived home from the university last night. And again, Seth's voicemail had answered. Dylan had left yet another message.

"Seth, call as soon as you can," he said. "It's an emergency. Something happened today at Leah's graduation."

He hadn't known what to say next. He hated talking to machines.

He'd ended the call and wrinkled his brows in wonder. Where could he be? Seth knew that they were attending Leah's graduation. Leah had invited him, but he politely declined, saying that he needed to spend time with his family while he was here. It was more than likely that Seth had no idea what he'd missed. Dylan would never forget the sight as long as he lived; neither would any of them, especially Leah. It was to be her day.

Sleep was next to impossible last night. He'd stayed up until 3:00 am, and still, there had been no word from Seth. Now, in the Sunday morning light, no message tones alerted him on his phone. No one had called or texted. He called Susan as soon as the coffee began to wake him.

"Let me guess," she said, as soon as she answered. "Couldn't sleep last night?"

"You're on a roll," he said, sipping his coffee. "Still haven't heard from Seth yet. I left another message last night. There's been nothing."

"I'm sure we'll hear from him once he sees the morning paper, not to mention the news."

"It's all over the place, *already?*" he asked.

"Yep. The circus has begun."

Dylan stood from his chair at the kitchen nook, and still holding his phone, walked to the front door and opened it. He reached his hand out and grabbed the morning paper from the newspaper slot. He shut the door, unfolded the paper, and read the headline aloud.

*Hundreds Witness Strange Craft at GVU Ceremony!*

He verbally noted the exclamation point, meant to provoke amazement.

"Yes," Susan said. "And that's only the Valley Tribune."

He walked back to the kitchen, reading the paper and listening to Susan as she continued.

"We need to hold a meeting later today. I have a feeling that any one of us may be contacted by the media. I think it's much wiser if we're all together today. Besides, we need to find Seth, and I also want to speak with Ursula about what happened to her yesterday. She was hearing, but we didn't talk about what it was that she heard, if anything."

Dylan agreed upon the meeting. He reassured Susan that no one had contacted him.

"Besides," he said. "If we don't hear from Seth soon, we may have to track him down."

"We'll meet today at my house," she said, "like last Sunday—3:00. I'll contact everyone."

As they disconnected, Dylan continued to read the paper. The lead paragraph reported that after graduation ceremonies concluded; a gray-metallic object had appeared in the sky and that hundreds of witnesses stood in awe, watching as *"an underlying panic erupted on GVU's Commencement Field, Saturday."*

He read through the article, absorbing witness testimonies containing details that he'd already seen with *his own* eyes. Outside of its shape and color, there was not much to tell. It was there in the sky one minute, and then gone the next—literally. Dylan learned from the article that many of the witnesses had contacted the police from their cell phones. The police had arrived and so did the military—the US Army to be exact.

The police had discovered nothing; they'd had only statements from several witnesses. Then, the article reported that once the military had arrived, they'd taken over the scene. Much like Kecksburg, Dylan thought. The military had cordoned off the field and no reporters or photographers were permitted onto the premises.

Dylan skimmed the layout of the paper. The story absorbed the full front page. There was no irritating continuance three pages later. There were no photos. So, who was taking pictures out on the field last night? It obviously wasn't any photographer from the Valley Tribune. Obviously, the military had allowed someone to be out on the field to take pictures last night. The article concluded with one thrown out fact.

*"The Federal Aviation Administration could not be reached for comment."*

The FAA, he thought, realizing how huge this whole enigma was about to become. Maybe it was a good thing. Maybe this media frenzy would uncover some answer as to what happened to his father. He walked into the living room and turned on the television. He switched back and forth between the twenty-four-hour cable news channels, watching and waiting for Green Valley to make history.

\* \* \* \*

Ursula's sleepless night accounted for one more person who'd watched the sun rise this morning. She'd tried to fall asleep, but she kept hearing the strange voice, the distant telepathy that had reached her clairaudient ear. She kept hearing those words over and over.

*"A time in the future..."*

She'd risen from the bed in a fit of irritation, flinging the covers up and away and planting her feet on the floor. What point was there in sleeping? When she didn't hear the voice, she just tossed and turned, wide awake, too energized for sleep. It was useless. She would sleep tomorrow.

In the living room, she'd sat awake in front of the television, flipping back and forth between the Saturday night Horrorfest and the cable news. Nothing about Green Valley had made the news yet. There had been the usual political garbage and terrible stories of crime, murder, injustice, and racism. She'd switched back to the movie, and even though she'd seen it many times, it managed to temporarily distract her. Still, her mind hadn't wandered too far from those five words.

*"A time in the future..."*

What did it mean? Was someone telepathically trying to tell her that whoever or whatever inhabited that UFO would be unveiled at some time in the future? Was it possible that the craft contained telepathic inhabitants from a future time? Had she witnesses the product of time travel?

Those far out questions made her head want to explode. They caused her to think more than she wanted, but after everything that had happened to her, not rehashing it in her mind was impossible. She couldn't get away from it. She needed to ask the investigators those questions. She would call Susan in the morning. She returned to the Horrorfest and tried to forget.

Hours later, the vagueness of faraway voices reached her unconscious mind. They were murmuring incoherently. The sound of them roused her from the unnoticed slumber she'd fallen into on the couch. She opened her eyes and realized that the voices were part of a morning show, engaged in some inane conversation long after the Horrorfest had ended.

Now, she rose from the couch and brewed a pot of coffee strong enough to wake her from the stumble and stagger of half-sleep. She wasn't a subscriber of the morning paper, but she did peruse it online every so often. Today, the Valley Tribune's front page filled her laptop screen in less than a minute. She read the headline over and over, making sure that she was actually seeing it, reaffirming in her mind that all of it had definitely happened.

*Hundreds Witness Strange Craft at GVU Ceremony!*

She ingested the article, along with her coffee, in a little over five minutes, and then her phone rang. It was the person she was just about to call—Susan.

"We'll be meeting at my house at three," she said. "Can you make it?"

"I will *definitely* be there," Ursula said.

"I take it that you want to discuss what you were hearing yesterday?"

"I do. But I don't really understand *what* I heard."

Susan assured her that she and the team would listen and help her.

"That's why we're here, Ursula," Susan said. "We listen, and we understand."

"I've just read the morning paper. There isn't much that's inaccurate." Susan agreed and mentioned the military presence.

"So, I'm sure you realize just how big this thing is about to become."

"That's what I want to address," Ursula said. "I don't want *anyone* else to know what I heard. If what I reveal today goes public, we'll be thrown into a far bigger circus that you ever dreamed."

Ursula listened to the brief silence on the other end. The words that continued to haunt her both scared and fascinated her. She didn't even understand it enough to go public with what she'd heard, and she never planned on becoming famous, not over this.

"Then we'll see you at three o'clock. And Ursula, you already know that anything you say to us is strictly confidential. I would treat you as I would any of my patients."

"I know," she said, relieved. "I'll see you at three."

She set her phone down, poured another cup of coffee, and skimmed through the article once more. She reread the witness testimony of how the object had lingered. Those five words repeated in her mind once again.

*"A time in the future..."*

\* \* \* \*

Susan watched from the window as they arrived one by one. Finally, they were all gathered together in the comfort of Susan's home, ready for a meeting that would plunder them deep in thought. In the hours before the scheduled meeting time, Susan searched online for the various newspaper headlines in many surrounding areas. The press hadn't failed in picking up the story. She'd found quite a few headlines, and all of the articles were based solely upon witness testimony.

She began the meeting by turning her laptop to face them all.

"These are the surrounding headlines that broke this morning," she said. She brought up the headline from the Lincoln Dispatch.

*GVU Crowd Witnesses UFO in Broad Daylight.*

She clicked on another headline, this one from the Keystone Courier.

*Mass UFO Sighted at GVU—Real or Hoax?*

The latter two articles both published pictures that were taken from witnesses. There was the object in the sky, just as they'd seen it, and exactly as it appeared in the videos.

"I wonder why the Valley Tribune couldn't get their hands on any photos," Susan said.

"They must have moved fast on the article," Brett said.

Sidney was the first to respond to the Courier's headline.

"Hoax, are you kidding me?"

"And there will probably be more of those accusations," Susan pointed out.

"Do they realize that people were nearly trampled?" Leah asked.

"They weren't even there," Ursula said. "All they have are blurry witness photos and varying testimonies."

"Sooner or later, the whole world is going to know," Dylan said, "whether they believe it or not."

Ursula looked over at Dylan.

"I think you're absolutely right, Dylan."

Susan's eyes met Ursula's. Ursula nodded, and then Susan addressed the team.

"Everyone, Ursula has something she'd like to share with us about yesterday."

Ursula sat straighter as all eyes focused on her. She took a deep breath and began.

"You all know how my clairaudience works," she said, "especially you, Sidney. I don't hear the dead as you do. I remotely hear the sounds of the living world around me, and my ability has always been tinged with a stain of telepathy. It was how I communicated with Ryan a few years ago. Yesterday, as I watched that object for a second time, I began hearing. It was something that hadn't happened the first time." She hesitated, and then sighed. "And as I told Susan, I really don't understand what I heard."

"But you heard it," Sidney said, smiling at her, one listener to another.

"Yeah, I did," she said. "And what I heard shocked the hell out of me."

She began by telling them about the mysterious sounds that had suddenly come upon her.

"They were noises, like screeching, squealing, radio transmissions and crashing static. I looked around. I knew that the sounds weren't coming from the crowd. Then, I could hear quick bits of spoken words, voices being interrupted, like someone flipping through radio stations and producing that collage of fragmented sounds."

She looked at Susan.

"That was right before you asked me what I was hearing. I told you that I heard noises, but I thought I was hearing voices."

Susan was nodding. "Yes, and then you turned your head up to the sky."

"That's when I heard the voice speak. It sounded different somehow, like it was human, but with a mechanical tone. It spoke telepathically. The words were clear, quick, and then gone. But I've been hearing those words all night, and I don't think I'll ever forget them."

Susan suddenly thought of Janette LaRue's description of the voice that had threatened her. But right now, knowing what Ursula heard was more important.

"What were those words, Ursula?" she asked. "What did you hear?"

It suddenly felt like a session to her as she waited for Ursula, who sat staring into the glass of the coffee table, to answer the question.

"A time in the future," Ursula said. "That's what the voice said to me—'a time in the future.' I've been wracking my brain, trying to figure out what it could mean."

Ursula looked up at Susan and the team.

"I wonder if it means that the truth about this thing will be revealed in the future, or—"

"Or if that UFO was occupied by time travelers?" Sidney interrupted her thought. "There are many who claim that is the case, that these UFOs are boarded by travelers from our own future. The claims have come largely from those who've experienced close encounters of the third kind, those who have seen or heard things. Then there are many who claim to be abductees, reporting to have witnessed the inhabitants of UFOs, face to face, after being taken."

"Many abductees also report being subjected to experiments," Susan said. "But there have been no abductees in this Green Valley mystery. We have a possible murder, combined with the efforts of the MIB to shut everyone up, two people exposed to radiation, and a hidden nuclear storage facility underneath our very own Eagle Rock Mountain. Ursula, it's pretty safe to say that in all of this, you are the only one who's made contact of some kind."

"But I want this to stay between us," Ursula said. "Like I mentioned, I don't really *understand* what I heard. I'd never expected to hear *anything*. I hadn't the first time."

"You *couldn't* understand," Leah said. "None of us can. I looked up at that thing yesterday. I focused my third eye on it. I saw nothing. It was like it was onto me, like it stopped me from seeing, *as if it knew.*

"That's what I sort of felt. It was as if it singled me out."

"These are interesting insights," Susan said. "But let's suppose, hypothetically, that these crafts are manned by time travelers, that somehow in our future, the world has managed to breach the time-space continuum, issuing in the reality of time travel. So, why are they here, to warn of us of our own eventual destruction? That's an interesting theory, but where is the warning? People have seen these things in the sky for hundreds, possibly thousands of years; why haven't they warned us, if that's the intention?"

"In our specific case, the interest is most likely the nuclear storage facility," Dylan said. "If we utilize Occam's razor, then the most logical conclusion is probably the right one."

"So, why not interfere with the facility's activities? Why watch?" Susan countered. "None of it makes any sense. The whole history of these things is devoid of any motivation or outward action, excluding the testimonies of abductees."

"You make it sound like they've been just watching us for centuries," Brett observed.

"And it looks like that is the case," Susan said. She spun a different phrasing on her earlier question. "All of these years and not a word of contact. Why?"

"It's like you said, Susan," Leah said. "We may never know the answer."

Susan noticed as Dylan checked his phone. He looked over at her.

"Still no word from Seth," he said. "It's nearly four-o'clock. We haven't heard from him in over twenty-four hours. The incident is all over the news and the papers, and he hasn't checked in with us."

"I don't like the sound of this," Susan said. She grabbed her own phone, dialed Seth's number, and listened to the peal of four rings before his voicemail answered. Susan ended the call, ignoring the prompt to leave a message. Dylan spoke before she had the chance.

"I think it's time that we go to his hotel room and find him," he said.

Susan looked at him. A nagging pull in the pit of her stomach spawned a sudden anxiety.

"Agreed," she said. "But I'm going with you all. I doubt that Seth Dornan has been so easily scared away."

"Unless something went down with Peter," Brett said.

"There's only one way to find out," Sidney said.

"Then let's find out," Susan said, rising from the chair.

Within minutes, they were packed into the van and on their way to Seth's hotel room.

# Chapter Twenty-One

### ~ Our Dearly Departed ~

It was ten minutes later when the van turned off of the highway and into the entrance of Oak Terrace Inn. Sidney slowly drove past the outdoor cabins, while Dylan's eyes searched for the rooms numbered in the one hundreds. They passed the three hundreds, the two hundreds, and then turned the corner to the wing where Seth had been lodging. An array of flashing lights stunned and blinded them, and Sidney slammed on the brakes just before room 103.

"Something's going on," Dylan said.

The flashing red and blue lights came from three police cars parked outside of Seth's room. Officers stood outside, watching, waiting, and controlling the scene. A stationary ambulance stood in front of room 103, Seth's room. The police motioned for Sidney to back away from the ambulance, so as to not block its exit.

"Oh, no," Susan said. "That ambulance isn't moving. Dear God, what's happening?"

Dylan felt his heart pounding, his blood rushing in panic. But in some odd way, the realization of his worst fears seemed to come as no great surprise.

"Let's not overreact," Sidney said. "We don't know what's happened yet."

"It's time for us to find out," Susan said.

Sidney parked the van, and slowly they all stepped out of it. They walked in the direction of Seth's room. The door was wide open, but they couldn't see inside from where they stood. A plainclothes officer walked over to them, holding his hands up in front of him.

"Excuse me, folks," he said. "But you can't go in there. Can I ask who you all are?"

Susan stepped forward and extended her hand. The officer clutched her hand and spoke before she could introduce herself.

"Detective Braden, Green Valley PD," he said, "And you are?"

He was civil mannered, but straightforward.

"Detective, I'm Dr. Susan Logan, a psychiatrist from University Hospital. We are friends of the man in room 103. Is there a problem?"

"The man in room 103," he said, sighing. "Seth Dornan, a patient of yours?"

"He's contacted me, as of late, in a professional way," Susan issued a half-truth.

"Well, yes, there is a problem, Dr. Logan," he said. "The problem is that he's dead."

Dylan heard Leah, Ursula, and Brett's astonishment. He watched Sidney's shocked silence and saw Susan's hands cover the lower portion of her face. He felt his legs weaken, his shaking knees testing his balance and nearly giving out from under him. Seth was dead. Surely it had been the MIB, just like his father. An inner fury began to burn his skin and soak his hair. He fought to quell the bubbling anger that threatened to burst.

Detective Braden looked at them, nodding his head.

"So, how did you all know him?" he asked.

"This is the Paranormal Research and Investigative Society out of GVU, of which I am the director," Susan said. "You see, I'm also a parapsychologist. Seth had also consulted our society about a case that we're working on."

"I see," he said. "So, Seth Dornan was a paranormal investigator?"

Dylan couldn't help but feel the shock of Seth being referred to in the past tense. Susan told him the truth about that fact and watched as the detective jotted it down on a small notepad.

"What exactly happened to Mr. Dornan?" Susan asked.

A pause lingered before the detective answered. Dylan noticed that it was the team, not Susan that made him seem skeptical to answer, yet he did.

"The maid couldn't get in to clean his room. She'd been knocking all day and got no response. She finally opened the door with the master key and found him dead. It looks like a possible drug overdose."

Now, there were gasps and scoffs of disbelief.

"That's not possible," Dylan said, his voice turning adamant, testy. Susan touched his shoulder, a covert signal to cool it.

"A drug overdose?" Susan asked. "May I ask which drug is suspected?"

"By the looks of it," he said, "It's the drug that's been killing most of the people in this area—heroin."

The overwhelming incredulity caused the other investigators to fidget restlessly and impatiently, turning their backs and throwing their heads up in dismissal, knowing that what Braden was claiming was false, yet they were unable to disprove any of it. They were all thinking the same thing, that whatever scene lay beyond the door had been manufactured by the MIB.

"Detective, I assure you that my younger cohort is right," Susan said. "Seth Dornan was not into drugs. He was healthy, vibrant—"

"He had a wife and two children," Dylan interjected.

Detective Braden had been taking more notes in the small notepad, and then he looked back up at them following Dylan's revelation. Braden had a full head of gray hair and a pair of listless eyes that drooped halfway shut, rendering him unreadable. He seemed to ignore their concerns regarding Seth's character.

"His Pittsburgh address is listed on his identification," he said. "We'll be contacting his wife as soon as possible. Until then, I assume you can identify the body?"

Susan looked at Dylan. They'd been unprepared for such a task. Braden continued before they could answer.

"Doctor, you'd be the best choice since you're a physician, and you were treating him on some level. Two of you would be all that I need for an initial identification."

Dylan volunteered to enter the room with Susan.

"Good," Braden said. "The rest of you can wait out here."

Braden escorted them both into the room. The others retreated to the van, where they somberly stood alongside it, waiting. Inside room 103, a police forensics team dusted for fingerprints near the nightstand. But more noticeable were the two paramedics who stood at both ends of a long gurney covered in a white sheet. They were ready to wheel it out as the trio entered. Braden addressed the two male paramedics.

"Not just yet, guys," he said. "These two are going to identify."

The paramedic at the end of the gurney stepped aside, the other prepared to pull the white sheet down and reveal the body. He waited for Braden to cue him, and when Susan was ready, Braden nodded. Slowly and respectfully, the paramedic lifted and lowered the white sheet from the top of the gurney. A deceased Seth Dornan lay on the gurney, his skin a deepening purple, his bloodless lips unmoving, and his eyes unblinking forever in death.

They stood over the gurney. Susan fought back tears. Dylan wrestled with rage. It was Seth; there was no doubt about it. The man they'd known for less than a week lay before them, reduced to the stone of a statue, silenced for his determination to discover.

*Just like my father,* Dylan kept thinking. Then, the thought of the black-clad aggressors turning their deadly intentions toward his team swept him as he stared at Seth's lifeless face. That was something that he was never going to let happen. He would stop the killing, if he had to become a killer himself. Susan broke the solemn, respectful silence.

"It's him," she said.

Braden looked at Dylan. Dylan responded.

"Yeah, it's him," he said, stifling the rage that continued to fight its way to the forefront.

Once again, Braden nodded to the paramedic, who then lifted the sheet back up over the body. He gave the go-ahead to remove the gurney, and Dylan watched as they wheeled it out into the ambulance. Braden instructed one of his forensic officers to hold up a clear envelope that was labeled as evidence. Inside the larger envelope was a smaller one stamped with black printing.

"It'll be at least two weeks before toxicology tests return and provide us with anything concrete, but this is what was discovered on the floor. I doubt that you prescribed this; am I right, Doctor?"

Without touching, Susan and Dylan looked closely at the larger envelope's contents. Dylan had to squint in order to read the black printing on the smaller, confined envelope. But the word stamped across it was clear enough—*Heroin.*

"This is all hard to believe," Susan said. "Detective, is there any chance that there is some other explanation?"

"Like what, foul play?" Braden leered at Susan with a suspicious turn of his head. His voice was coaxing, a brazen attempt to elicit what she wasn't disclosing. "If so, our testing will reveal that, but until then, Doctor, if there's something you'd like to share with me—"

"I was just wondering about *any* other possibility, Detective," Susan said. "This doesn't make sense. I'm well familiar with people who are addicted, and Seth showed no signs of being one of them."

"Sometimes they never do," Braden said.

Susan was right in keeping quiet about the MIB, Dylan thought. All of it would be wasted breath on Braden. He hadn't even bothered to ask about the case Seth consulted on. Dylan wondered if he'd read the newspapers. If he had, maybe he thought what happened at the university was all a hoax. But it didn't matter. Dylan and Susan were well aware that detailing the events of the past week would be pointless. Besides, Braden seemed to have already made up his mind.

Dylan heard the double slam of the ambulance doors outside. It was then that Braden asked them for their contact information.

"I'd like to keep in touch, just in case I have any questions for either of you," he said.

Susan handed him her card, and Dylan did the same.

"Perfect. Here's my number," he said, handing them his own card. "And Doctor, if you ever decide to elaborate on what was troubling Mr. Dornan, I'm all ears."

"What makes you think something was troubling him?" Susan contested.

"He makes contact with a shrink and later dies of an overdose," he said. "You think that *nothing* was bothering him? With all due respect, Dr. Logan, this is a clear-cut case of unintended suicide. I'm just saying that if *you* could shed light on this, it may be helpful to his family."

Dylan watched Susan's face harden to a stone-like countenance. Her lips were tightly drawn, while her eyes glared at him in stifled contempt. This wasn't an easy moment for Susan. She'd lied about Seth consulting her as a psychiatrist in an attempt to try to keep quiet his role as a paranormal investigator. She'd obviously never considered that the police would automatically fall for this manufactured scene, this fallacy that said Seth had inadvertently committed suicide.

"I'll keep that in mind, Detective," she said.

Outside, the lingering ambulance's engine roared to life. They heard it drive away.

Braden excused them, thanking them for their assistance. Susan and Dylan left the room, exchanging words in hushed voices.

"You did right by not telling him about the MIB," Dylan said. "I don't trust that guy."

"Why would I tell him?" she said. "If the MIB are involved, there's nothing that the police can do to help us."

It was a chilling truth, but Dylan knew that she was right. They walked through the parking lot to the van, where the remaining investigators waited with watchful eyes and mournful faces.

\* \* \* \*

They returned to Susan's house and sat languidly in the somber silence that surrounded them. Boggled minds brainstormed together as the mystery had grown from dangerous to deadly. Susan and Dylan told the investigators everything they'd seen in the hotel room.

"Is there anyone here who believes Seth was a drug addict?" Dylan asked the question, already setting the record that they were all in concurrence.

"Of course not," Sidney said. "Granted, we hadn't known Seth long, but we all know *why* Seth was silenced."

"And by whom," Leah surmised.

"Peter must have been right," Dylan said. "They must have detected a hacker in the observatory's system."

Brett mentioned a fact that had been on their minds but hadn't escaped their lips.

"And we're the ones that were in the observatory. Does that make us next?"

"Like hell," Susan said, reentering the room. She'd been checking the phone in her home office. "Not if I can help it."

"That will be over my dead body," Dylan said.

"Listen to me, team," she said. "I will *not* let anything happen to anyone here." She turned to Dylan. "And there will be no more dead bodies. I swear that I will blow this thing right out of the water! We all know why that hasn't happened yet. We need to wait for Marv. We need to know that he, Janette, and the children are safe.

"And then there's Seth's family," she continued. "We cannot allow them to believe this vicious lie. Seth was murdered; we all know that. Proving it will be an entirely different task. But I'm starting to think that going public is the best possible route we have for solving this mystery. I've just checked the messages on my home office phone. Many were from unlisted numbers, leaving no message. Let's hope that Marv was one of them."

It was then that her iPhone rang. She didn't recognize the number. She answered it via speakerphone. A female voice bombarded her, first with an introduction, then with a question.

"Dr. Logan, this is Charlotte Wills of WJHI," she said. "I was wondering if you, as the director of the Paranormal Research and Investigative Society, would like to issue a comment regarding the incident at yesterday's GVU commencement."

They all looked at one another in contemplation. Susan's eyes lowered back to the phone.

"I'm sorry," she said. "I have no comment at this time."

"But you did see it, right? Wasn't one of your investigators among the postgraduate class? And have you and the paranormal society decided to investigate this?"

A quiet, observing Ursula sat forward from her seat on the couch. She spoke loudly into the speakerphone.

*"She said no comment at this time! Goodbye!"* Ursula's brash response along with the sing-song high note of her voice on the word 'goodbye' sparked brief and unexpected laughter. Susan hung up on the reporter.

"Now I know who the office calls were from," she said, adding that they now had her cell number.

The quick laughter soon died, and as the evening wore on, Susan answered three more calls from reporters. Again, she declined to comment. Appetites had been quashed by the day's events and were nearly non-existent, yet Susan insisted on ordering pizza and eating in. They sat somberly staring at the leftover slices, devoid of words, lost in thought, and experiencing a sense of defeat at the striking hand of tragedy.

Leah lounged back on the couch, surfing sites on her tablet, and then she broke the somber silence.

"I think we just made the national headlines," she said, sitting up. They gathered around her, reading the headline on the screen of her tablet.

### UFO Strikes Terror at Graduation Ceremony

The headline was listed under a link that read, "Trending." Leah clicked on the small arrow that produced a video of the streaming broadcast, just above the article. The female anchor reported the event, repeating the words of the posted article verbatim. She related how a strange, disc-shaped object had appeared in the sky, hovering over a crowd of thousands, and how eyewitness accounts all concurred. Yet some were disbelieving, calling it a possible hoax.

*"Sources say that the bustling crowd broke into mayhem after the object had suddenly disappeared,"* the young, blonde anchor detailed.

But the written article hadn't contained all of the information that was being reported. The anchor continued with a sidebar mention.

*"However, this story does contain a unique coincidence,"* she said. *"A valuable asset to Pennsylvania's Green Valley University is its Paranormal Research and Investigative Society. Among the postgraduate class was locally known investigator and author, Leah Leeds. She is best known for her memoir, "Cedar Manor," published in 2008. Leah Leeds and her fellow investigators could not be reached for comment."*

It was then that the red line of the streaming counter had run its full course. The video stopped abruptly. Leah spoke first.

"This is like a snowball getting bigger in Hell."

"What a bunch of hounds," Ursula agreed.

"Dylan, I think you better prepare yourself," Susan said. "It looks like going public may happen much sooner than we'd anticipated. We may have no choice. If one side doesn't force us, the other one will."

Dylan lowered his face into his hands, and then ran his fingers through his hair, exhibiting useless efforts to rid himself of the past week's tension.

He got up and moved around restlessly, fidgeting and distracted by a thousand thoughts that found no ordered structure. He paced across the living room floor. He needed to be free of this situation, if just for a moment. He needed air; he felt like he was drowning.

"I'm out of here," he said, "at least for now."

"What?" Susan asked. "Where are you going?"

"I don't know—home—maybe for a drink," he said. "I need to unwind. I can't get the sight of Seth's face out of my mind. I'll be back, I promise."

He hurried out the front door before any of them could sway him otherwise.

\* \* \* \*

Dylan wasn't in the mood to be around strangers, so he combined his two options; he went home for a drink. He had a bar all of his own in the lounge area of what was once Dr. Geoffrey Rasche's spacious living room. Here, where his father once entertained friends and colleagues with small but sophisticated parties, Dylan sat behind the bar, pouring shots of bourbon, and chugging Budweiser as a chaser. The alcohol loosened his body, yet his mind still roamed in different directions.

He thought of his father and felt like he was failing him right now. Sure, he and Seth had uncovered the secret of the storage facility, but Seth was dead because of it. Outside of a dead man's final testimony in his father's journals, he was no closer to proving that the Men in Black had killed him. And now they could all add Seth, and possibly Mabel Forrester, to the rising body count. There was also Seth's family to consider. He wished he could contact Peter, but he wasn't sure that he'd been told about his Uncle Seth yet. There was also the possibility that if that hacking job had been traced to Peter, the eyes and ears of the MIB would be watching and listening.

Then, he thought of the telescope that Brett had discovered in the observatory, the one bearing his father's initials. Surely, that had to be proof of something. He sucked down the rest of his beer and stood the empty bottle behind the bar. He grabbed another bottle, and the 'poof' sound when he opened it sounded louder in his solitude. It was a sound followed by the glug, glug, glug of his chugging, a self-prescribed remedy sure to clear the smoky battlefield of his mind. Setting the bottle back down upon the bar, he sat oblivious, while restless thoughts swelled in magnitude and color.

One such thought would be impossible right now. And that would be asking Peter to hack into the observatory's system one more time, so that he could reenter the observatory and search for the telescope. He could do it alone, but Susan would never allow it. If Peter would be detected a second time, it would really be suicide. But if Dylan could find the telescope, it would place him one step further to exposing the men who killed Peter's uncle, and his own father. But even through the settling haze, Dylan was well aware that the move was much too risky to attempt, even foolhardy.

He poured another shot in hopes of purging the anger and bitterness he felt at having to stand aside and wait. The mystery that had now engrossed all of their lives was a deceit so large that it had been perpetrated against all of mankind, and by the looks of it, it was enough to overwhelm it completely. He rebelled against the thought that he was just a microscopic piece of a vast and unsolvable puzzle. This unchangeable reality did nothing to extinguish his anger.

He leapt from the barstool with beer in hand and paced the room, punishing the bottle because of its fullness. When it was empty, he looked at it, his breath heaving heavier in his frustration. Quickly, he threw the bottle across the room and behind the bar, where it landed on the floor with a crash. In that instant, he decided exactly what he was going to do. He was going to flush them out, just like his father had. He would go up to the observatory on Eagle Rock Mountain and wait for them.

He walked back behind the bar, oblivious of his shoes crunching shards of glass beneath his feet. He bent down and retrieved an old cigar box from one of the bar's shelves, then placed the box on top of the bar and opened it. What he kept around the house for protection lay snuggly inside, wrapped in sheaths of tissue paper. It was a Glock 45, clean and shiny in its shimmering blackness. He'd only used it at target practice, but he knew how to shoot, and he shot well.

If the MIB were watching him as they'd been watching his father, they would know his whereabouts. He would wait for them up on top of Eagle Rock, right where his father had been murdered. He realized that he might even end up at the bottom of Eagle Rock, just like his father, but he would get his answers, one way or another.

Dylan packed the pistol in the side pocket of his denim jacket. It was a chilly spring night, and a light fog was forming, but it might end up being an advantage. He wasn't going to call Susan and the investigators just yet. They would talk him out of it, and Brett and Sidney would be on his doorstep within minutes. He had to do this alone, and he would do it now as the false courage ran through his veins and warmed his blood. He would call them when he neared Eagle Rock Mountain. It would be too late to stop him then.

He lowered the lights and locked up the house. Before leaving, he took one last look around, just in case.

* * * *

In a high-tech room where lights blinked and computers bleeped and blurted output, the Men in Black read from one of many computer screens. All of it had come to their attention: the craft hovering above the university, the multiple eyewitnesses, the mayhem that briefly erupted on Commencement Field, and even the discovery of their handiwork in room 103 of the Oak Terrace Inn. The taller man was scrolling a current article. It was an internet item that detailed the occurrence. The headline was synonymous to many others they'd read.

*UFO Strikes Terror at Graduation Ceremony*

But this article went a bit further than the others; this one mentioned a fellow investigator of Dylan Rasche's—Leah Leeds. She had been among the postgraduates yesterday, and the paranormal team had been in attendance. Now, the investigators had witnessed with their own eyes the mystery they'd been seeking. One pair of those eyes belonged to Leah Leeds.

"She sees things," the shorter man said.

"I know," the taller man replied. "I got a fast copy of her memoir."

The shorter man made an observation.

"Regrettably, our prediction has come to pass. This has reached far out of our hands."

The taller man remained silent for a moment and then responded.

"I think you may be right," he said. "But we need to see how this plays out. Dr. Logan has issued no comment at this time."

"Let's hope she's smart enough to keep it that way," the shorter man said.

The men silently examined the various pictures of the craft taken by eyewitnesses and obtained by the media. All of them were fuzzy, blurry, and often distorted claims to infamy. Naysayers had called it a hoax. But the Men in Black remained silent, exchanging no comments between them. And then the taller man changed the subject.

"I wonder where their friend, Mr. Kincaid, has disappeared to with Ms. LaRue," he said.

"At this point, she's no longer a problem," the shorter man answered.

A sinister smirk crossed the taller man's face.

"No," he said. "But he is."

They continued their search through the internet in silence.

* * * *

During his absence, Marv Kincaid had tracked down every article regarding the UFO occurrence at the university's commencement. The Valley Tribune's article had been mostly witness accounts with no photo gracing the front page. Marv knew almost too well that they'd quickly released the first of what would be a series of articles. Soon, there would be another, he guessed, after they'd obtained the best possible photos. He'd searched on his laptop for the headlines of the surrounding areas, and he'd found them. Now, miles away in a wooded hideaway in central Pennsylvania, he'd been reading the same internet article that was currently trending nationwide.

It was then that he received the disturbing news. Another one of his trusted spies had contacted him on the disposable phone that he was now using. Seth Dornan had been found dead in his hotel room. A drug overdose was suspected.

"No, that's impossible," Marv insisted. "Seth was not a user. I knew him well enough."

"From what I'm hearing," his young spy said, preparing him. "It was heroin. The word is that the police have evidence to back that up."

"Of course they have evidence!" Marv yelled. "Who do you think did this? It was the Men in Black!"

His spy provided a few details, like the fact that the paranormal investigators had shown up at the inn while the police were present. Susan Logan was said to have identified the body. That was all of the information that his spy had known at the moment, and so their covert conversation was brief. Now, Marv sat reading, waiting to hear any further word about Seth. He finished the article and thought of Susan. The guilt he felt at having left her and the team amid the chaos was now much more overwhelming.

Before he left, he'd phoned Susan and told her that he was fleeing. He had to get Janette and her children away from Green Valley as soon as possible. Afterward, he drove Janette and the children all the way to Florida. There, he'd booked her and the kids on a two-week, Caribbean cruise and sent them off. He'd explained to Janette that it was her best option, and that going to Philly and involving her mother-in-law could result in dangerous consequences. She needed to be far away, and the lesser people that were involved, the better it would be for everyone.

While in Florida, he found the perfect opportunity to investigate. He searched, once again, for his one-time cop friend who had suddenly disappeared after Geoffrey Rasche's death in 1993. His efforts had been unsuccessful. There were no records anywhere of a Detective, Sergeant, or even Officer Gill Patterson—as though he'd disappeared off the face of the earth.

And then Marv had remembered something about the time when he'd been snooping around, trying to learn more of the circumstances of Geoff's death. He recalled the professor that ran the observatory back then, a man who had avoided all of his questions and any contact with him. He was a small, robust man, approximately late fifties at the time. Marv remembered him being stern, silent, and unapproachable.

*What was his name? Maitland? Mayland? Maynard!*

"That's it!" Marv spoke aloud to himself, cursing his age for not remembering the cranky bastard earlier. Dr. Alfred Maynard ran the observatory in 1993 when Dylan's father was killed. Marv had given up trying to talk to him, not that he could've told him much, but Marv had wanted to cover all aspects. His suspicions had been slightly raised at Maynard's adamant reluctance. But at some point, Marv had backed off.

He wasn't even sure when Maynard resigned from the observatory, or even if he was still alive, but trying to find him was worth a shot. This time, Maynard had no observatory doors he could walk through and stay hidden somewhere inside. Marv would convince him to speak with him, one way or another.

He soon discovered that Dr. Maynard was in fact, alive. He'd tracked him down to a little town right here in central Pennsylvania, all with the help of his spies, and of course, Google. Marv then drove all the way from Miami, to Bedford County, where he now sat at his laptop in a cozy rural cabin he'd rented upon returning. Dr. Maynard didn't live far from here. Maybe he'd even read or heard the news from Green Valley. He would be in his early eighties today. Hopefully, time had softened him.

Marv continuously thought to call Susan, but he couldn't be sure that the MIB hadn't tapped into all of her communication outlets by now: the phone in room 208, not to mention her home, office, and cell numbers. Even if he was overreacting, he didn't want to risk it. He couldn't put her, or the team, in danger. Besides, he was about three hours from Green Valley; he would see her and the team very soon. But there was someone he was going to visit, first thing tomorrow morning—Dr. Alfred Maynard.

# Chapter Twenty-Two

## ~ A Thickening Fog ~

Dylan avoided the same route to Eagle Rock that Sidney had clandestinely taken on Thursday night. He didn't bother with the dark and desolate back road that had led them all to their secret mission of slipping into the observatory. This time, he took the highway, the great wide open where anyone could have seen him, and hopefully, they had. That was his intention, to lure them out once and for all, just like his father. But unlike his father, he was not about to fail.

The sun had long since gone down, and the temperature chilled as a fog thickened like widespread smoke on a battlefield. The highway remained lit up with taillights and headlights that seemed bigger and brighter from the booze-induced buzz. The fog hung heavily far above the highway, but slowly it descended upon the electric luminescence of the moving world below. He gazed behind him in the rearview mirror. From what he could see, there were no sedans, no large or suspicious cars of any kind. No one seemed to be tailing him.

The winding, spiral roads of Eagle Rock Mountain unwound beneath the wheels of his jeep. He felt the sudden drop in temperature as the jeep climbed higher up the mountain. The fog hung thicker and heavier up here, sweeping through the mountain before its final descent to the ground, where it would eclipse everything. He glanced again in the rearview mirror. Still, no one followed him.

He drove to a spot close to where Sidney had hidden the van. He still felt conflicted about alerting Susan and the rest of the team. But if something should happen to him, they needed to know where he'd gone, especially for their own safety. He sat inside the jeep and called Susan. She answered on the second ring.

"Are you alright, Dylan?" she asked. "Where are you?"

He heard the slightest tone of suspicion in her voice. A few seconds passed before he answered her. His eyes were watching the whiteness of the fog as it blanketed the trees and enveloped the foliage, creating an eerie backdrop.

"I'm up at Eagle Rock," he said. "Don't get angry."

"Dylan, what the hell are you doing up there?!" Susan's suspicious tone erupted into anger despite his plea. "*What* do you think you're doing?"

"I'm waiting for them," he said. "I'm going to get to the bottom of this, once and for all."

The slightest slur in his voice had suddenly slipped out.

"How much did you drink after you left here?" she asked, not waiting for an answer. "Dylan, come down from there now; that's an order!"

"Susan, they're killing people. Don't you understand? People have died to cover up these lies, these secrets. Someone *must* be willing to confront them, to go up *against* them."

"And you think that person is going to be you?" Susan demanded. "Dylan, I know that you're still grieving over your father's death, and especially about what happened today. But we cannot add you to the list of casualties. Is that what you want? I *won't* let that happen!"

"It won't," he said, feeling the hardness of the Glock resting across his ribcage as a dangerous reminder. "I'll protect myself. I have to go now. Everything will be fine; I promise. And please don't send Brett and Sid to find me. I'll call back as soon as I can."

"*Dylan, wait!*" Susan yelled through the phone, but Dylan ignored her final words. He ended the call, and then turned off his phone.

\* \* \* \*

"*Dylan! Dylan!*"

Susan continued to yell through the phone, even though she'd heard the tone of a disconnection. He'd hung up on her. Brett, Sidney, Leah, and Ursula still sat in her living room. They were staring back at her expectantly, anxious for details. Brett and Sidney stood up from the sofa, quickly moving toward her as she stood speechless and holding the phone.

"Where is he?" Brett asked.

"Don't tell us he's gone up to Eagle Rock," Sidney said.

"I'm afraid he has," she said. Her voice sank to a low and wispy drawl from the inner fear she felt right now for Dylan. He'd been drinking; she could hear it. And that, combined with his need for vengeful justice was a dangerous combination. "He's been drinking and has decided to follow in his father's footsteps."

"Let's just hope we get to him before that happens," Sidney said.

"He advised me not to send you both on a search party," she warned.

"Of course, he did," Brett said. "That's because we know exactly where he is."

"He's up at the observatory," Leah concluded.

"Then that's where we're going," Brett said, turning and snatching his keys from the coffee table. "Come on, Sid."

"We'll take my van," Sidney said.

"I'm going with you," Leah said.

"No, stay here," Susan implored. "Let them handle this. You girls stay here with me."

Susan advised them to keep her posted, and to remain watchful and careful at all times. She recalled something that Dylan had said on the phone.

"He also said something about being able to defend himself. I hope that doesn't mean what I think it does."

"Sounds like he's packing heat," Sidney said.

"Yes, Sidney," Susan said. "Thank you for that colorful observation."

"No problem," Sidney said. But Brett and Sidney were out the door before she could warn them any further.

\* \* \* \*

After parking the jeep close to where Sidney had parked the van on Thursday night, Dylan walked the same wooded path that led to the side of the observatory. The parking lot around back was visibly vacant on this Sunday night, and for a few seconds, he stood unobserved amid the foliage, watching the observatory in its empty stillness. The fog glided over its platform, eventually surrounding the structure and making a mockery of the powerful eyes that projected from it.

So far, no one had followed him up here, and now he felt the slightest skepticism at the possibility of a confrontation. Yet it did nothing to extinguish his inner rage that simmered inside; nor did it eliminate the need for justice and answers for so many. He moved through the fog and the foliage, eager to see what his father had once seen. The Thursday night expedition hadn't provided him with the time to glance over the cliff where his father had fallen. He'd merely seen the edge from a slight distance. Now, he looked over it, gazing down at its plundering depths.

Rigid crags, rocks, and foliage were ceaseless below, and his feet were inches from the cliff's edge. As he looked outward and beyond, he could see that below the mountain's rugged peak was the freefall void of open space. He wondered how his father had fallen. Had he slid down the crags to his death, or had he been pushed or thrown into that vast, open freefall? The position of the body would've been a clue, but not in the face of a cover up. Marv Kincaid was especially aware of this fact, that it had been too "perfect" of an accident.

The buzz from his binge mixed with a sudden tinge of vertigo. His feet slid. Bits of loose rock and dirt rained over the edge in a brief, gritty shower. He walked backwards, flailing his arms outward at the sides until his feet were firmly planted back on the observatory's platform. His heart pounded against his chest, but the dizziness subsided.

He bent forward, placing his hands against his knees, and took a moment to catch his runaway breath. After straightening himself, he looked out into the fog falling over the edge and down the mountain. Then, he turned and faced the observatory. He thought of how this small structure secretly fostered a nuclear storage facility that lay safely hidden down beneath the mountain, and how Seth was dead because he'd uncovered this fact. He felt certain that his father had died for the same reason.

He looked through the closed double doors of the observatory, noticing not much more than the dim lights that penetrated the vacant darkness. He thought about one of his father's telescopes, discreetly stored somewhere inside behind these glass doors, and by whom and why he had no idea. He turned away from the building and faced back out toward the fog, staring into it, knowing that by some stroke of irony, it was much like the mystery unfolding before him.

And then, a brilliant flash of green beamed through the fog like an impenetrable beacon. His eyes winced in instant blindness. He stood within the green luminescence, enveloped and enraptured, closer than any witness had stood so far. Like no other known light source, it sliced a sharp pain through his forehead. The light became a shifting chameleon, changing from green, to blue, to red. His fluttering eyes focused on the alternating colors, soundlessly parading in a hypnotic light show.

The fog began swirling, moving away from the light, as though it dared not to touch it. The thick murkiness that had just begun its move down the mountain now parted in different directions, evaporating like cotton candy as it touched something unfamiliar. The parting fog reminded him of a stage curtain being drawn. And as the thick curtain was pulled away, it revealed something larger than life and looming directly in front of him.

It lingered silently just over the cliff's edge, immense, disc-shaped, gray and metallic. He stood merely feet away on an even level away from it. Through squinted eyes he saw the lights lessen, but the brightness continued. An invisible heat wave engulfed him, white-hot, yet warm, bearable like the sun. The phantom in the sky that he'd been chasing was now right in front of him, silent and watching.

Strangely, his pounding heart slowed, calmed by a circulating rush of blood that soothed him. He stood frozen, as if his inner instinct to react had been quelled. The anger, the excitement, and the mystery that ignited his investigative spark all seemed irrelevant in this moment, softened by a docile and subdued state of being. He took one last look at the floating enigma.

White light engulfed him, like the brilliant unveiling of the universe. A reverberant drone heard only by him was the magnificent hum of a thousand echoes. Numbness became paralysis. Every muscle of his physical self was frozen, rendered immovable by the light, yet his conscious mind was content, relaxed, and accepting. The bright light overwhelmed him with one final flash.

And then the craft disappeared along with the light. And so had Dylan Rasche.

* * * *

Sidney and Brett discovered Dylan's jeep near the spot where they'd parked the van on Thursday night. The jeep was eerily absent of its driver, yet the keys remained in the ignition.

"He's got to be over at the observatory," Brett said, stepping away from the jeep.

They walked through the thickening fog, along the same wooded path as before. They crept up to the far side of the observatory, until its outer platform came into full view. It was vacant, as if no one had been there.

"If we walk over to the platform, we'll be seen on the security cameras," Sidney said.

"We don't have much of a choice," Brett replied. "We have to go and look for him."

Soon, they stood on the platform, seeing no one as they gazed through the fog that rolled down the mountain. Sidney looked through the closed double doors of the observatory.

"There's no one working in there tonight," he said. "It's desolate."

"No," Brett said. "They wouldn't be working on a night like this."

"Then he definitely can't be in there." Sidney looked out toward the cliff with worried eyes. "You don't think he could've gone over the cliff?"

Brett's face fell at the thought.

"Let's hope not, but if he's been drinking..."

They walked as far to the edge of the cliff as possible and looked over.

"It's hard to see anything," Brett said. "It's too foggy."

They headed back to the wooded path, knowing that somewhere, they were being watched. They'd spent too much time exposing themselves to hidden cameras and unseen eyes. It was obvious that Dylan was nowhere in sight, yet his jeep remained parked not far away with the keys still in the ignition. They'd even called out to him, but no one responded. Now, Sidney phoned Susan as they approached Dylan's vacated vehicle.

When she answered the phone, Sidney put her on speakerphone, filling her in on the jeep and the fact that Dylan was nowhere to be found.

"He's just gone," he said. "We even fear that he may've gone over the cliff."

Susan's response was quick.

"Sidney, you take the van, and Brett, you take Dylan's jeep. I want you both to drive to the base of the mountain below the cliff's edge. See if you can find anything."

"Yeah, but what if he comes back?" he asked. "He'll need his jeep."

"We'll keep trying to call his phone," she said. "He'll call us when he gets back."

Brett spoke up and warned her.

"Neither of us likes the looks of this, Susan."

"I don't like the sound of it, Brett," she said. "I warned him not to go up there. One more thing, be quick, and be careful. Call me when you're back out on the road."

They disconnected, and soon Sidney and Brett were barreling down the mountain in separate vehicles. Within minutes, they arrived at the base of the mountain, just below the cliff's edge. They searched at the rocky bottom, through the dense underbrush, even up an adjoining hillside. They found nothing and no one, much to their relief, yet also to their bewilderment. Their heads turned in all directions. Where was Dylan?

Back out on the road, Sidney called Susan and gave her the news.

"There was nothing," he said. "We searched everywhere."

"Well that's good news," she said. "At least we know he hasn't fallen. I've tried to call his phone three times already and got nothing except instant voicemail."

Then, she instructed Sidney to return to her house, along with Brett. They would wait for Dylan to call and decide what to do if he didn't.

\* \* \* \*

The taller man in black was alerted that something was taking place at the observatory. Earlier, the cameras had been blinded by an incredible light, and now two young men were walking along the platform and peeping through the observatory's doors. The taller man opened his laptop and accessed the observatory's security footage. He watched them searching through the fog for something, or someone. They seemed to be investigating the cliff's edge, why? Then, they turned and walked away through the wooded area.

But what had transpired earlier? That was a bigger concern, a brilliant light blinding the cameras. He could guess where that brilliant light had come from, or what. But right now, he only had access to the current footage. He would have to go through the already recorded discs to access any footage that had taken place prior to the two young men's arrival.

He knew who they were. He recognized the fat one—Sidney Pratt. He and the other fellow were two of the Paranormal Research and Investigative team. He sat and nodded his head. Here was yet another incident involving the observatory. It was now obvious as to who was behind it.

\* \* \* \*

Back at Susan's house, Sidney and Brett retold their stories in detail: how they'd found Dylan's jeep with the keys in the ignition, but no sign of Dylan, anywhere.

"We found nothing at the base of the mountain, either," Brett said.

Leah looked at Susan.

"You don't think that *they* harmed him in any way, do you?"

The sound in her voice was fear that sought consolation.

Susan knew who Leah meant.

"They better not have," she said, "or they'll be hell to pay!"

As the hours wore on, they made repeated calls to Dylan's phone. Each time, it went straight to voicemail. Worried faces searched each other in stifled terror. A plethora of thoughts ran through Susan's mind. What if they *had* found Dylan, and he confronted them with a gun? What if they'd kidnapped or killed him? But she explored an even worse thought, one that made her silently look at Sidney and Brett and wonder.

What if the two of them had overlooked the body at the base of the mountain? After all, it was nighttime. What if Dylan had met the same fate as his father? She closed her eyes and silently prayed. And as the night progressed, the fear worsened.

And then, the phone in Susan's home office rang.

"That may be him," Susan said, nearly leaping from the chair. "Let's find out."

They joined her in her small office. Susan looked at the Caller ID; the number was unrecognizable. She picked up the receiver and spoke. The voice on the other end was warped, distorted, a mechanical disguise of its natural tone. It gave her a sinister ultimatum...

*"Call off your dogs, Dr. Logan,"* the voice said, *"or you'll end up like Seth Dornan!"*

Anger seethed beneath her normally refined composure. Her eyes narrowed into slits that sought out an invisible opponent.

"Now you listen to me, goddamn you! I won't stand for your damn threats against me or any member of my society! I'll be alerting the press that if I don't see Dylan Rasche within the next twelve hours, I'm holding a very important press conference. And I will tell them everything that my team has uncovered. Do you understand me? I'm not some little old lady that you can threaten. I will sound off on everything that I know, and that includes *you!*"

She waited for the voice to speak, but the line went dead. Shocked and widened eyes stared back at her. Those across from her had never heard her voice ascend to that level of anger. She felt her heart pounding as she hung up the phone. Anger and intolerable fear gripped her, but she was not about to let them win, especially if they'd hurt Dylan in any way. Tears formed in her eyes as she thought of him.

"Team, we cannot let this happen," she said. "We have to find Dylan. And I meant what I said. If we don't hear from him or find him in the next twelve hours, I'm holding a press conference. I will expose this entire cover up, as well as that damn storage facility!"

\* \* \* \*

The taller man had obtained the video discs of security footage which would allow him to view last night's events outside of the observatory. He and his partner sat watching endless footage for hours. They watched as the fog had rolled over the observatory's platform. Soon, a figure had appeared on the platform, a different young man than the other two he'd witnessed last night. The taller man leaned in closer to his laptop screen. He studied the moving figure that looked through the double doors, and then walked over to the edge of the cliff.

A realization suddenly dawned on him.

"That's Dylan Rasche," he said to his partner.

"Are you sure?" the shorter man asked.

"I'm positive. He looks exactly like his father."

They watched as Dylan walked over to the edge of the cliff and then backed away. And then it had happened. The brilliant light had penetrated the fog, blinding everything in its path, including the cameras and Dylan

Rasche. Rasche was staring at something within the light. It was impossible to see what had happened next, but the light got brighter, and then the young investigator had disappeared.

The taller man leaned in once again to the laptop.

"What happened?" the shorter man asked.

The taller man turned his head toward him and spoke.

"I think you *know* what happened."

॥ ॥ ॥ ॥

They hadn't devised a plan to search for Dylan that didn't involve returning to the observatory. Today, Sidney and Brett rode past Dylan's house and saw no sign of him. But Leah Leeds had a different plan of her own in mind. It might work, it might not. But it was worth a shot. All day she had utilized her third eye, searching for signs of Dylan. She saw a bright, brilliant green light. She saw him standing on what looked like the observatory's platform. And the vision would cease.

A bright, brilliant green light, she thought. Ursula had described a bright green light. She herself had seen it when she'd had the vision of Shane out on the back road. Could it be? If that green light was associated with that mysterious craft, then...

No, it couldn't be. She didn't want to think about that possibility. Her nerves suddenly felt like a sparking network of electrical wires. She breathed and took a moment to relax, allowing the vision to come back to her.

Abruptly, she jumped at the sound of someone viciously pounding on her front door. A voice as persistent as the pounding and just as demanding called out...

*"Leah Leeds!"*

Another onslaught of pounding banged the door.

*"Leah Leeds! Open the door!"*

Her response was instantaneous.

*"Go to Hell!"*

"Where is Dylan Rasche? Do you see him? *Where is he?"* So, they *knew* that she was a seer. They wanted to use her, so *they* could discover Dylan's whereabouts.

"I don't know," she yelled back at them. "I can't see *anything!"*

But she could, and she knew that she could. She saw through the door...

They wore identical black suits. The taller of the two men was the one who'd been shouting. The other man was shorter, stout. They wore matching sunglasses, and instantly, she saw behind the shaded spectacles. Strange, menacing eyes glowered. They were beady, close together, and there was something...She suddenly gasped and stepped back away from the door. The eyes startled her. And then her third eye showed her their hasty departure, two men turning, fleeing her porch, and striding quickly up the sidewalk.

They were gone.

She grabbed her phone and called Susan. When she answered, Leah didn't waste time.

"I've just been visited by the Men in Black!"

"What, where?" Susan asked.

"Here, at home," Leah explained that she hadn't let them in. "They wanted me to see. They *knew* that I was looking for Dylan with my third eye. I didn't open the door, but I *saw* through it. I *saw* their eyes behind those sunglasses. Susan, you won't believe their eyes!"

Leah told Susan about the questions they'd shouted through the door, and how after she'd seen their strange eyes, they quickly fled from her front porch.

"They knew that I was seeing them," she said. "They didn't want me to see any farther."

"What *did* you see about Dylan?"

Leah explained the incomplete vision, failing to mention the flash of green light. She didn't want to reveal that part of the vision, not yet. She wanted to be sure.

"Then, where is he?" Susan's voice was pleading.

"I don't know," she said. "But I do know one thing. *They* don't have him."

# Chapter Twenty-Three

## ~ Everything Out in the Open ~

Shortly thereafter, the team gathered in room 208. Susan, Leah, Sidney, Brett, and Ursula were present, all except Dylan. Susan sat at her regular place at the head of the long conference table. The look on her face was heated, determined, with a reserve that would tolerate no more.

"Thank you all for being on time," she said. "It's crucial that we meet today, of all days, especially after what happened to Leah this morning. I want to announce that as I'm sure you've all guessed; I'm keeping my promise. I've called for a press conference to be held at 3:00. It is to be downstairs in the Rotunda Room. I would like you all to be there, especially you, Ursula. I'm hoping that you'll tell your story when I'm finished.

"It has been more than twelve hours since Dylan disappeared. We've all been more than patient. This has to come out. It has to be exposed, or I'm afraid that we may never see Dylan again. When we all stand together as a community, as a society, and demand answers, we'll get them; maybe not the ones we want, but the pressure will be there. We cannot allow this intimidation to go on.

"I wish that Marv could be here with us to tell the story of Janette. Having Marv along with us would add extra credibility to what we're saying. But the press has wanted to hear from us ever since the incident at graduation."

She looked at her watch.

"And now, it's 3:00, time to go downstairs and face the media."

\* \* \* \*

The Rotunda Room was a round-shaped addition to Levin Hall. It was where students usually faced off in debate, and clubs assembled for special meetings. Inside, a podium was erected in the far back, and rows of chairs were set up opposite the expected speaker. Reporters from the Valley Tribune, the Lincoln Dispatch, and other regional papers sat side by side, waiting for the speaker to arrive. They whispered back and forth about how Susan Logan was said to be the leader of the university's extremely clandestine paranormal society. Why had she called this press conference? If this was about the incident at graduation, she was going to reveal *something*.

The doors of the Rotunda Room opened. Reporters turned their heads and watched as Susan and the team entered the room and walked to the podium. They kept their heads down, feeling the eyes that watched them as they walked. Susan took the podium and looked out at the invited crowd as the team lined up behind her.

"Good afternoon, ladies and gentlemen of the press," she began. "I'm sure you're wondering why I've gathered you all here today. But first, I would like to introduce the people behind me."

She turned sideways to reveal them. Outstretching her left hand, she introduced them: Sidney Pratt, Brett Taylor, Ursula Masters, and Leah Leeds.

"This is the Paranormal Research and Investigative team."

Cameras flashed as the last name was mentioned. Susan's tone turned somber.

"But we are absent one today," she paused. "However, I will get to that in a moment. I want to begin with the incident that took place here at the university on graduation day. What happened that day was in fact, related to the case that we, as an investigative society, have become involved in. For those of you who reported on it, but remain skeptical or unsure, I assure you that what we all saw in the sky was real. And that's what I want to talk about today.

"There has been an active conspiracy taking place here in Green Valley for many years dating back to at least 1993 or even before that. It all began with the death of Dr. Geoffrey Rasche, a prominent astronomer, author, and once professor here at the university. But secretly, Dr. Rasche was a UFO investigator."

Susan told them how Dylan, their absent investigator, was the son of Dr. Rasche. She described how Dr. Rasche died, and how long ago, Marv Kincaid had become suspicious.

"Dr. Rasche was investigating a series of UFO sightings that occurred near Eagle Rock Mountain in the early nineties. There was that, and the fact that he'd been banned from entering the Eagle Rock observatory without an explanation. Dr. Rasche had become suspicious, and when he went up to the observatory to investigate, he'd fallen to the bottom of the cliff. He'd gone up there to lure someone who was following him. I know all of this because Dr. Rasche left behind journals of his activity. I have those journals right here."

Susan lifted up a small stack of notebooks that she'd carried into the room and held them up to the crowd of reporters. Gasps and whispers mixed together simultaneously. She felt as though fate were responsible for Dylan leaving the journals behind at her house.

"Who, do you ask, was following and threatening Dr. Rasche? Quite simply stated, it was the infamous Men in Black."

The gasps were louder this time, as if shock had a volume dial.

"The MIB have been a part of this conspiracy for a long time, all the way back to Kecksburg. And let's face it, you all know it."

She paused again, and this time, for a few seconds longer.

"Allow me to fast forward to today."

She told them about the series of sightings shared by Dylan, Marv, Ursula, Shane Rowe, and Mabel Forrester, and how it all happened on the Saturday before last. She stepped aside to reveal Ursula to the crowd.

"Ursula and Shane Rowe were exposed to radiation. Although they were both hospitalized, fortunately, they suffered no major injuries. I will give the podium to Ursula in a few moments. I want to tell you why Shane Rowe is not with us today. Shane was severely beaten by the MIB. He and his family were threatened, and so Shane has left town. To where, no one knows.

"And then there's Mabel Forrester. She was threatened by the MIB after they showed up at her home. She was later brought into the hospital after having suffered a coronary. Mrs. Forrester is in her early eighties."

Snorts of disgust were heard.

"But it gets worse," she continued. "We were visited by a MUFON investigator named Seth Dornan. He was brought to us by Marv Kincaid."

Members of the press murmured at the mention of Marv's name.

Susan told them how Marv had sought out Seth because of his continued suspicion regarding Dr. Rasche's death.

"Seth paid with his life. We believe that he was killed by the MIB, and the reason is plain. He uncovered the conspiracy that has been going on here in Green Valley for years. He discovered that deep down within Eagle Rock Mountain is a hidden nuclear storage facility."

The crowd broke into an uproar of alarm and disbelief. Cameras flashed again. Reporters moved fingers fast across tablets, and some scribbled furiously on small notepads. One of them stood up and asked her a question.

"Dr. Logan, how do you know this?"

"Let's just say I have the pictures to prove it," she replied. "Sidney, if you would?" Sidney sat down behind a small desk to the right of the podium and opened up his laptop. Ursula pulled down a white vinyl screen behind Susan, and then Leah and Brett moved off to the side in order for the crowd to see the upcoming slide show. Sidney tapped away on the keyboard of his laptop, and within seconds, an image of the underground facility popped up on the screen. It was an enlarged image of the nuclear waste pool. The crowd was silent.

"This image is of a nuclear waste pool," Susan began. "It is situated in the center of this nuclear storage facility deep down within Eagle Rock Mountain." Susan moved her finger above the image of the pool. "As you can see, the walls are cavernous."

The image of the pool was replaced by another. This one showed the stacked yellow barrels. The word *Radioactive* was recognizable to all. The crowd continued its silence. "These barrels clearly contain radioactive material that is stored within the facility."

The next image was of the generators.

"I'm sure you all know what these are. They're generators."

Whispers of awe filled the room like the chatter of ghosts in confusion. And then with a click, Sidney displayed the next image. The black metallic boxes were the last of the evidence, the final pieces of the puzzle. The word *Titanium* loomed large on the screen.

Uproar of shock rippled the room. Irate, betrayed voices clamored for answers.

"Yes, ladies and gentlemen," Susan continued. "Titanium—and we all know what titanium is used for."

The crowd continued to banter and then slowly settled.

"When Seth was killed, they made it look like a heroin overdose. Seth *was not* a drug user, not by any means. Anyone who knew him can attest to that. I'm sure you're wondering how I know that the MIB are responsible. I know because I myself received a threat last night from the MIB. They told me to 'call off my dogs' or that I'd end up like Seth Dornan."

Now, the crowd oohed in awe.

"Apparently, Seth died the night before graduation day. Yesterday, his body was found in his hotel room at the Oak Terrace Inn. All six of us attended the commencement ceremonies; it was Leah Leeds' postgraduate ceremony."

Cameras flashed once more.

"We were all there when the UFO hovered over Commencement Field. We all watched it in the sky along with thousands of others. So believe me, it was not, nor ever has been a hoax. We believe that the UFO is attracted to this hidden facility beneath Eagle Rock Mountain. It would explain the 1993 sightings.

"Dylan Rasche learned of his father's past involvement when he discovered these."

She held up the journals once again.

"Since finding them, he was obsessed with finding out exactly what happened to his father, and that's how our investigation began. Last night, Dylan went up to the observatory against my wishes. Last night, Dylan Rasche disappeared."

Surprised voices chattered, while cameras clicked and flashed.

She told the crowd how Sidney and Brett had gone to the observatory to search for Dylan and failed to find him.

"I am despondent over not knowing what has happened to him. We have neither seen nor heard from him in over fifteen hours. I fear that the Men in Black may be responsible."

Susan conveniently left out the part about Leah's visit from the Men in Black. She didn't want to shift the unwanted spotlight onto Leah.

A female reporter stood up and asked Susan a question.

"Dr. Logan, you mentioned Marv Kincaid. To what extent was he involved? And where is Mr. Kincaid right now?"

"I'm right here."

A voice called out from the back of the room near the door. It was Marv.

The murmuring crowd continued as he made his way to the front of the room. Susan looked at him and smiled. Just when she needed him most, she thought.

"Susan, may I?" He motioned with his hand to the podium.

"Please do, Marv."

Marv replaced Susan at the podium. Susan stood alongside Leah and Ursula. Marv adjusted the microphone and spoke into it, placing his hands on both sides of the podium.

"I can answer the young lady's question, if I may?" He paused. "The extent of my involvement has been firsthand. I've been working with the investigators from the beginning. Allow me to tell my side of the story. I know that Dr. Logan has already told you about my suspicions years ago regarding the death of Dr. Geoffrey Rasche. All of it is true. Back then, I immediately suspected that his death was not an accident.

"I set out to find anything I could to prove it, but I was unable. I am the one who met with a younger Seth Dornan at that time in hopes of finding something. The reason I contacted Seth was because Geoffrey was a UFO researcher, and I'd also heard rumors about the 1993 sightings. But there was another reason. A friend of mine, who worked as a cop, secretly told me that there were signs of a struggle on top of Eagle Rock that night. Then, my friend disappeared, allegedly to Florida. I soon gave up. After all, there were children to consider at that time."

Like Susan before him, Marv's story jumped into the present. He began by telling them about the night in his yard with Duke when he experienced his own sighting. He talked about green and blue lighting up the night sky and the quick movement he'd seen from the corner of his eye. He described Duke's reaction. Then, he went into the story of Janette LaRue.

"There was a young woman, who will remain anonymous, who came to me for help."

He reiterated how an elderly woman, Mabel Forrester, had called 911 and reported a sighting on the same night. Then, he divulged how the MIB had hacked into the 911 system and threatened the nameless dispatcher.

"They mentioned her children also," he said. "She came to me for help, and so I helped. I got her out of here. And that's why I've been absent the past week. But I feel responsible for the death of Seth Dornan. I'm the one who brought him here yet again."

Then, as a prism bends light, Marv bent the truth.

"Awhile back, I took a trip to Florida. While there, I decided to search for my friend, Sgt. Gill Patterson, the one who told me of the signs of a struggle. If he is still on the face of this earth, he's not in Florida. I suspect that he's another casualty.

"And as of yesterday, I tracked down a person who turned out to be extremely pertinent to this mystery. In 1993, a man by the name of Dr. Alfred Maynard ran the Eagle Rock Mountain Observatory. Back then, I persisted in speaking with him about the death of Dr. Geoffrey Rasche. He had consistently refused to speak to me, avoiding all of my questions and all contact with me. His reluctance stirred my suspicions even more.

"Yesterday, I tracked him down to Bedford County, where he lives today. He's an elderly man now, approximately eighty-four years old and not in the best of health. I convinced him that more lives would be lost if he didn't tell me what he knew about Dr. Rasche's death. I let him know that the casualties were adding up. In his fragile state, he relented.

"He told me that in 1993, the MIB had taken control of the observatory for some unknown reason. They'd ordered him not to speak to anyone, including me, about anything. He had discovered the nuclear storage facility beneath Eagle Rock Mountain and was ordered by the MIB to 'keep his mouth shut about it.' The MIB were following Dr. Rasche not only because he was investigating the 1993 sightings, but because he persisted in entering the observatory. They knew of his suspicions.

"Dr. Maynard told me that Geoffrey Rasche was involved in a scuffle with two of the MIB outside of the observatory. They'd overpowered him and threw him over the cliff's edge. At the time, it was reported that Dr. Rasche fell while maneuvering a telescope he retrieved from the observatory. That was impossible; *Dr. Rasche had been denied access to the observatory.* He couldn't have taken *anything* from there. According to his journals, he'd brought his own telescope with him. He never made it inside.

"But the MIB's intention was to make it look like Dr. Rasche *did* have access to the observatory. If anyone tried to use Rasche's suspicions as a way to investigate his death, those suspicions could be easily contradicted by saying that he *had* access to the observatory, because he was found at the bottom of the cliff with one of the *observatory's* telescopes. If he were found with one of the observatory's telescopes, it would look like he'd been inside. So, the MIB had thrown one of the observatory's telescopes over the cliff and kept Dr. Rasche's. That's why his telescope is still in the observatory today."

The gasps and murmuring resumed as an entire mystery was unfolded for an anxious press and a mystified public.

"So you see ladies and gentlemen, everything that Dr. Logan has related to you is true. Green Valley has been involved in this mystery for quite some time—many years to be exact. And Dr. Logan is right; it does go all the way back to the Kecksburg incident."

Marv fielded a few questions from reporters about the age, health, and mental state of Dr. Maynard. He was also asked if he, or Dr. Maynard, knew when the nuclear storage facility was constructed beneath Eagle Rock Mountain. It was a question Marv could not answer. At last, the reporters seemed almost too speechless for any further questions. At that point, Marv gave the podium back to Susan, who introduced Ursula.

Ursula told them about her sighting. She described the object in detail. She talked about how she fell ill in her living room but dialed 911 before collapsing. She related the experience of suffering from radiation sickness. Then, a reporter asked her a question.

"Were you ever threatened by the Men in Black?"

"No," she said. "But I was waiting."

Then, another reporter stood up.

"Aren't you the one that helped to rescue that boy a few years back?"

Ursula hadn't expected that one.

"Yes, I am."

"So, you've known the investigators in the past?"

"Yes, I have," she said. "That's why I called Dr. Logan. She's a friend of mine."

She began to fret, nervously expecting a question about her clairaudience, if they even knew. But before that could happen, Susan motioned her away from the podium, relieving her.

"Thank you, Ursula," she said. "That will be all, and thank you ladies and gentlemen of the press for attending."

Bodies rose from chairs simultaneously, while Susan ushered the team together so they could leave without being tagged by the press on the way out. The team, including Marv, walked single file out the door The press conference was over, but voices continued bantering in shock and awe. Reporters hurriedly used their phones, readily transcribing details. Others quickly filed out the door behind the investigators, who made their way back up the stairs to room 208.

* * * *

"Well team, everything's out in the open," Susan said, as they sat around the long conference table. Yet it did nothing to relieve them. There was still no word from Dylan, and the dismal silence conveyed fear, worry, and heartache. Marv took advantage of the lack of words.

"Everyone, I want to apologize for hightailing it out of here the way that I did, and rarely phoning, but I didn't want to risk putting any of us in danger."

On the way back to room 208, Susan had quickly welcomed him back with a hug. Now, she answered him.

"We understand, Marv," she said. "We're so glad to see you, but we're terrified about whatever has happened to Dylan. He disappeared last night and hasn't been seen or heard from since, not by *any* of us."

"Yes, I heard the entire news conference," he said. "I stood outside and listened, and then quietly came inside when I wouldn't be noticed."

Then, Marv told them all about his getaway with Janette.

"I drove her to Florida, and then sent her on a cruise."

Ursula's eyes suddenly stared at the ceiling, a quizzical glare on her face.

"Wow, I *shoulda* been threatened by the MIB."

Sidney's eyes were closed as his belly shook with laughter. The others smiled and laughed. It was a joke that broke the nagging thoughts about

Dylan. Then, Marv asked a question, taking a more serious tone.

"So, do you think that the MIB *are* responsible for Dylan's disappearance?"

"No, I don't think so," Leah said. "The MIB showed up at my door, wanting to know Dylan's whereabouts. They were going to use me to try to find him. I'd been searching for Dylan with my third eye. I'd seen a vision. I saw Dylan standing on the observatory's platform, enraptured in a brilliant green light, but the vision stopped short every time. We all know that the green light has been associated with that UFO."

Faces melted in fear as hearts dropped in tension. Any conclusions about Leah's vision remained unspoken.

"All we can do now is pray," Susan said.

"And wait," Brett said.

The somber silence continued.

\* \* \* \*

Having returned home, Leah began to think about the Men in Black. Those frightening eyes she'd seen behind the sunglasses. Somehow, they didn't seem—human. She kept thinking about the vision. If the green light was from the UFO, why couldn't she see the craft itself? What was stopping the vision? She closed her eyes and let her third eye lead her once more.

\* \* \* \*

The Valley Tribune released its evening edition early, and now the taller man in black held the newspaper up before him. There was a picture of Susan Logan standing behind a podium. The headline was big and bold.

*Paranormal Society Leader Exposes Nuclear Storage Facility*

There was also a sidebar article with an implicating headline.

*Investigator Goes Missing; Logan Blames Men in Black*

The taller man read the entire article. He turned to his cohort.

"The bitch did exactly as she said she would," he said. "It's over. It's time to leave here. Everything's out in the open."

"Of course, there's nothing more we can do now," the shorter man said.

"Agreed. This place is riddled by its own mysteries. But, I'm sure we'll be back one day.

# Chapter Twenty-Four

## ~ Missing Time ~

Dylan suddenly discovered himself walking down the road. He hadn't even been aware that he was walking. It was as if the booze had just worn off, but it hadn't, not completely. He stopped and looked around him. He was on the back road at the bottom of Eagle Rock Mountain. How the hell did he get down here when he was just at the top of the mountain, standing on the observatory's platform? He looked up to the top of the mountain and at the night sky. The fog was gone.

But where was his jeep? He must have been so drunk that he'd fallen asleep, awakened, and then walked down here, ignoring the fact that he drove. How was he going to get back up the mountain to get his jeep? Walking the winding roads to the top would take at least an hour. He felt too tipsy for that, not to mention a little queasy.

His jacket felt lighter. His right hand searched the inner pocket for the Glock 45—it was gone. What could have happened to it? He felt his front pockets for his phone. It was there. He'd call Sidney to come and get him, take him up to the top to get his jeep, and then look for the gun. Sidney could be here in minutes; he was the closest in distance. He dialed Sidney and waited as the phone rang.

\* \* \* \*

Sidney sat at home in front of his computer, researching everything he could about UFO abductions when his phone rang. He swiveled his chair around, grabbed the phone, and glanced at the Caller ID. He felt an inner explosion of hope when he saw the name and number...*D. Rasche.*

He quickly pressed the answer button.

"Dylan?"

"Yeah, Sid, it's me."

"Dylan, where are you? We've been scared shitless!"

"Um, I'm at the bottom of Eagle Rock. I don't know how I got here. I was up at the observatory just a little bit ago. I don't know, man; I'm confused. I need you to come and get me, and take me up the mountain to get my jeep."

Sidney didn't like what he was hearing. Not only did Dylan sound disoriented, but he didn't know his jeep was gone. If he was just at the observatory, how did he not see it gone?"

"Dylan, your jeep is not up there. Brett and I brought it back to your house."

"What do mean? Why?"

Sidney preferred not to go into details. The important thing was getting Dylan back as quickly as possible. Sidney asked for his specific location.

"I'm on the back road," Dylan said, "behind the mountain."

"Listen, get off the road, and go to the base of the mountain. I'll be there in five minutes."

Dylan agreed and hung up. Sidney leapt from his chair, called Susan, and began putting on his shoes. When she answered, he blurted it out.

"I found him!"

"Where is he?" she asked.

"He's at Eagle Rock. I'm going to pick him up now."

"Oh, thank God!"

"Susan, I'll call you as soon as I get him." He told her about Dylan sounding disoriented and thinking that his jeep was still at Eagle Rock.

"Sidney, bring him to my house immediately. I'll phone the others."

Sidney agreed and within seconds, he was out the door.

He was doing seventy miles per hour in the van, until the flashing red and blue lights from a cop car flared in front of him.

"Shit!" He loosened his foot from the gas pedal. The cop car sped past him. "Whew!" He rounded the corner to the back road leading to Eagle Rock Mountain. The mountain came closer and closer into view. At night, Eagle Rock Mountain looked spooky, menacing. He made it to the base of the mountain, and soon, saw a figure standing there. It was Dylan.

Sidney parked and watched as Dylan somewhat staggered to the van. He opened the door and hopped in. In the quick light as Dylan opened the door, Sidney could see that his face was wan, tired, and haggard. He reeked of beer and sweat.

"Where the hell were you?" Sidney asked, but didn't waste time. He pulled out and drove, allowing Dylan to answer the question during the ride.

"I went up to the observatory," he said. "I waited for them to come after me, but they didn't. I must have been so drunk that I fell asleep up on the mountain. I can't remember much. I don't understand; how did you and Brett come to get my jeep? And why?"

Sidney looked at him. Obviously, Dylan had no clue. Sidney switched on the interior light and looked him over one more time. Something happened, and Dylan wasn't even aware.

"Dylan, you've been gone for twenty-four hours."

Dylan looked at him incredulously. There was a pause.

"I have not," he said. "I was just up at the observatory. I'm not sure what happened next. That's my fault for drinking."

"No, Dylan, you don't understand." Sidney felt the frustration of trying to explain the unexplainable. "You went up to the observatory *last night.*

Dylan continued to stare at him.

*"I did not,"* he stressed. "I went up there tonight." Dylan checked the time on his watch. "I hadn't even been there that long."

"Dylan, check the date on your phone. You went up to Eagle Rock last night, which was Sunday. This is Monday night."

Dylan checked his phone. Its glowing light illuminated the confusion on his face.

"Sid, how can that be? I couldn't have been asleep for twenty-four hours."

"Think back, Dylan. What do you remember?"

Now, the confusion on his face made his eyes arc in wonder. He would try to speak, and then stop. Then, the words came to him.

"I came up here," he said. "I know that I drank more than a few. I remember being up on the observatory platform. I remember the fog. And then…"

His thoughts and words died away as his mind went blank.

"Never mind," Sidney said. "Don't worry about it now. All that matters is that you're safe. We're going to Susan's house. She wants me to bring you right away."

"The gun that I brought is gone," he said. "I should go up there and look for it."

"Not now, Dylan, later. I've got to get you back. Everyone has been out of their minds with worry and thinking the worst thoughts these past twenty-four hours."

Sidney received no argument from the speechless Dylan who sat silent, trying to remember. As Sidney drove, he glanced back and forth at him, wondering what was taking place in his puzzled mind. Was it amnesia? Susan would know.

Soon, Sidney was turning into King's Haven and parking the van in front of Susan's house. Brett was already here; his car was parked in Susan's driveway. They walked up the front porch stairs, and Susan opened the door, letting them in. She grabbed Dylan and hugged him. Brett followed.

"Dylan, where have you been?" she said. "Let me look at you in the light."

"What is Sidney talking about?" His voice was testy, irritated. "Have I really been gone for twenty-four hours?"

"Dylan, it's Monday night," Susan said. "You left my house last night. Do you remember? Do you remember me telling you not to go up there?"

Sidney could see Susan studying Dylan's face, noticing that look of confusion, of being lost, unaware. He could tell that she knew something was wrong. Something had happened.

\* \* \* \*

Leah placed her phone on vibrate while she engrossed herself in the vision again. Finally, it overcame her. There was Dylan once again, standing on the observatory's platform. She saw the fog surrounding him and spilling down the mountain. Her third eye was searching, watching and waiting for the light's oncoming presence. Suddenly, the brilliant green light pierced through the fog in the vision. She tried to see through it. Her mind was anchoring her in the image, refusing to let go of it.

She envisioned Dylan staring off at something. And then it appeared, enormous, gray and metallic. The thing they were calling the phantom in the sky hovered just across from Dylan at the top of the mountain. Its light was magnificent. She could see Dylan from behind, enraptured.

Then, the UFO and Dylan were gone, and there was only the blackness of her closed eyes.

She jolted herself up from the couch, not noticing the vibrating phone on the coffee table. The vision was clear to her this time. Dylan had been abducted by that thing. The thought that she might never see Dylan again struck her, making her heart sink down to her knees. The sweat was drenching her, mainly from the stress that she felt right now.

Then, she noticed the vibrating phone. She snatched it fast from the table, but it had stopped vibrating. Whoever it was had hung up. She pressed a button and checked the Caller ID; it was Susan. She dialed her back. It was imperative that she talk to her now. Susan answered after the first ring.

"Susan, I just had the vision again." She proceeded to tell her about it, but Susan interrupted.

"Leah, Dylan is here at my house," she said. "We've found him."

"What?"

"Everyone is gathering over here. Are you coming?"

"I'll be right there, but Susan, Dylan was abducted by that thing."

Susan remained silent, and Leah could almost hear her turning her head toward something or someone.

"We'll see you when you get here."

Leah was out the door within seconds.

\* \* \* \*

Susan had just hung up with Leah as she, Dylan, Sidney, and Brett sat in the living room discussing the matter. When she'd examined Dylan's face in the light, she found that Sidney was right. Dylan was pale, haggard, and his eyes were slightly bloodshot. He still smelled of alcohol. His vitals were normal. His heart rate was a little faster, but that could have been from the booze. Blood pressure was normal. Now, as she asked him questions, his words still slightly slurred like the night before. How was that possible?

"Dylan, what do you remember?"

He told her exactly what he told Sidney when he'd asked.

"I don't remember what happened next. The next thing I knew I was walking down the back road behind the mountain. I didn't realize I was walking until it hit me. I noticed the fog was gone."

"Dylan, the fog was gone because the fog was last night," Susan said.

He looked at her with tired, bloodshot eyes, resembling a bat forced from its cave. He said nothing, and then hung his head in fatigue.

"Dylan, do you still feel intoxicated?" she asked.

He nodded his head as he spoke.

"Yeah."

*Again, how is that possible?* Something familiar was finding its way to her mind. She'd learned about it in her studies, and they'd experienced it with Brett last summer. *How could he still be intoxicated twenty-four hours later? Missing time. He has missing time. Leah's right; he must have been abducted.*

She decided to change the subject—for now. He had to be informed about everything that had taken place within the past day.

"Well, we had an interesting twenty-four hours since you've been gone."

He looked up at her, seemingly more alert. She could see a spark of the old Dylan, the vibrant, passionate investigator that would not rest. He was listening. She continued.

"I was threatened by the Men in Black yesterday." She told him about the phone call she'd received after Brett and Sidney had returned from searching for him. "I told them that if I didn't hear from you within the next twelve hours, I would hold a press conference and reveal everything that we knew. And so I did."

She told him everything about the press conference, everything she revealed, including the nuclear storage facility.

"I held nothing back," she said. "We left a roomful of stunned reporters. But then, we went back to room 208 and worried about you."

"Yeah, you gave us quite a scare," Brett said.

"We thought the MIB had taken you," Sidney said.

Dylan shook his head.

"I never saw them," he said. "I thought they would follow me, but they didn't."

Now, Susan felt almost positive that Leah was right. Dylan *had* been abducted, but not by the Men in Black.

"Oh, and by the way, Marv's back," she said. "He has something important to discuss with you. I'll let him do that. He's on his way here."

Just then, the doorbell chimed.

\* \* \* \*

Marv stood on Susan's front porch, ringing the doorbell. He was anxious; Dylan had been found and was safely inside. Marv thought of what Leah had implied yesterday in room 208. If Dylan Rasche *had* been abducted, the story could blow this mystery open even wider. He thought of the irony that this enigma had affected both father and son. He felt for Dylan. He would do anything he could to help him.

Susan answered the door and let him in. He saw Dylan when he entered. He was quiet, forlorn, and fatigued. But he looked alright, and he responded normally.

"I'm so glad to see you, Dylan," he said. "I have much to tell you."

"Thanks, Marv," he said, in a weakened voice. "Yes, Susan told me that you had news."

Marv sat beside him on the sofa and proceeded to tell him about what he uncovered.

"It looks like you were right, Dylan," he said. "Your father was murdered by the MIB."

He told him about tracking down Dr. Maynard, the man who ran the observatory at the time of his father's death. He revealed how Maynard had confirmed the struggle on top of the mountain, and how the Men in Black had thrown one of the observatory's telescopes over the cliff to make it look like his father had free access to the building.

"That explains why his telescope is still there in the observatory," he said. "They kept it."

There was a lingering silence as Marv finished speaking. Then, Dylan sat up, lowered his head, and placed his hand over his eyes as the tears streaked down his face.

"But look at it this way, Dylan," Marv offered. "You can feel vindicated that you solved this mystery. Your father would be very proud of you. You were right; he *was* speaking to you."

The doorbell chimed again. Susan answered it. Leah walked quickly through the doorway and over to Dylan, embracing him in her arms. He stood and clutched her with an equally strong grip.

"We didn't think we'd ever see you again," she said.

"Yeah, but I'm here," he replied.

They sat back down on the couch, and Leah took both of his hands in hers.

"I used my third eye. I was having a vision."

She told him about her visit from the MIB.

"They were looking for you. They wanted to use me to find you."

"They may have wanted to know what you found in the observatory," Marv guessed.

Leah continued, relating how the vision would stop, and how she had to force herself to see to the end of it.

"Dylan, I think you were abducted by that thing. I saw it in the vision, just like we all saw it at my graduation. Then, it was gone and so were you. Do you remember *anything?*"

Marv keenly watched Dylan's face as his eyes narrowed, trying to recall. He shook his head.

"No, I only remember standing on the platform, watching the fog as it rolled down the mountain."

"Dylan, I think Leah could be right," Susan said. "You have what's called missing time. What was twenty-four hours to us were only minutes to you. It would explain the fact that you still feel intoxicated. You need to focus on remembering."

Then, Dylan wiped at his eyes and decided to call it a night. He asked Sidney if he would drive him home.

"Wait, Dylan," Susan said. "I want you to do one thing before going home. I want you to go to the hospital and get checked out. I feel it's necessary."

"No, no hospitals," he replied.

"Dylan, please," Susan pleaded. "I want to make sure that you weren't exposed to radiation like Ursula and Shane. If you were, you would be exhibiting symptoms, but you still need to be sure."

The rest of them had agreed, overwhelming him with their concerns.

"Come on," Sidney said. "Let's go to the ER. I'll wait for you."

"I'll phone ahead and tell them you're coming," Susan said. "If nothing's wrong, you'll be home before you know it."

Dylan sighed, walking out the door. He just wanted to go home and sleep it off.

\* \* \* \*

He'd gone to the ER. Dr. Adams had taken him immediately, especially since Susan reported him as one with possible radiation exposure. They gave him a complete physical exam. He hadn't been exposed to radiation. There were no injuries, no bruises, lacerations, not even a scratch. Sidney had waited for him in the hospital lounge for two hours. Now, after being discharged, Sidney dropped him off at home.

"I'll be alright, Sid," he said. "You heard them."

"Are you sure?" Sidney asked.

Dylan laughed.

"Later, Sid, call me."

Sidney had seemed surprised that he hadn't been exposed to radiation, assuming that Leah's vision was accurate. He got out of the van and walked to his front door. The mail was not taken inside. The morning and evening editions of the paper were stuffed in the newspaper slot. He grabbed the evening edition and looked at the date. They were right. It was Monday, the 30th. He'd been gone for over twenty-four hours. He unlocked the door and went inside.

After showering, he lay in bed, thankful to be there. He thought of the possibility that he'd been abducted. He knew he wasn't that drunk. He couldn't have spent twenty-four hours in a drunken stupor. He thought of his father, and how they killed him to keep a secret. He realized that he would have to call his sister, Denise, in the morning. He wondered about the Men in Black. Had Susan scared them off? According to her, they had not yet responded.

Because of the press conference, reporters would be badgering him soon, asking him questions about where he was, and of course, his father's journals. Dr. Adams had even encouraged him and Sidney to leave through the hospital back doors in case of reporters. He was relieved to be okay, but it bothered him that he couldn't remember a thing. And then there was the gun. What happened to the gun he'd brought with him?

But it was all over now. What could the MIB, or anyone else, do with the world watching? It was time to retire the myriad thoughts that danced in his head. It was time to fall asleep, and so he did.

# Chapter Twenty-Five

### ~ Hypnotize Me ~

Dylan woke to a ringing house phone, the extension of which was in his bedroom. He opened his eyes to the morning light. He looked at his alarm clock—11:30 am. He'd slept in.

"Hello," he answered the phone groggily.

"Dylan Rasche?" the voice asked.

"Yes."

"Dylan, this is Charlie Page from the Valley Tribune. I was just wondering if you'd like to issue a few comments in response to the small item in this morning's paper."

He was still half asleep, yet half awake.

"What item?" He sighed, his eyes not yet fully open. "I'm sorry, I have no comment."

"Well, Dylan, there are a lot of people curious as to your whereabouts within the past day. We thought maybe you'd want to set the record straight."

"Maybe another time," he said. "Thank you."

He hung up the phone, moaning from a mean hangover, and got out of bed.

After setting the coffee to brew, he noticed the flashing red light on his house phone. Someone had left a message. It was probably the same reporter, but he checked the message anyway. He was surprised when he heard the voice.

*"Dylan, this is Shane Rowe. Listen, I saw this morning's Valley*

*Tribune. I just wanted to say that I'm glad you're okay. I'm also thankful that this is all out in the open. Now that this is over, I'll be returning to Green Valley soon. Take care, man."*

Dylan replaced the receiver back in its cradle. *This morning's Valley Tribune,* Shane had said. What was it the reporter had mentioned? Something about the small item in this morning's paper. He went to the front door and grabbed the morning paper out of the slot. He unfolded it and rifled through the local section. There were articles about an investigation into Eagle Rock Mountain, and then the headline of a small sidebar caught his eye.

### Investigator Found Safe and Well.

It was a small item, one that reported his safe return. Sources said that he'd entered University Hospital's ER last evening. He was amazed at how fast news traveled. That's why Dr. Adams shuffled him and Sidney out the back doors. He sat drinking his coffee, thinking about everything that had transpired. The missing time began to nag him even more now in the sober light of day. He had an idea he hadn't thought of before. He would get dressed and go and see Susan.

\* \* \* \*

Susan wasn't at the hospital today; she was home, so that's where he went.

"You don't know how glad I am to see you," she said, opening her front door. "Come in."

They sat drinking coffee in her kitchen. He told her about Shane's message.

"That's good news," she said. "I've had a few interesting calls myself this morning. The first was from the hospital. Mabel Forrester is being transferred to a hospice for complete care. Then, I got a call from Peter Dornan. He thanked me for defending his uncle's character, and for coming out in the open and exposing the MIB. They're taking Seth's body back to Pittsburgh today. Peter said he would let us know about the funeral arrangements."

"So, I guess that's it," he said. A silence lingered between them as Dylan thought of how to say what he wanted to say next. He decided to come right out with it.

"The missing time is starting to bother me," he said.

"As I assumed it would," she replied.

"There's something I haven't told you. I'd brought a gun with me to Eagle Rock. When I found myself walking, it was gone. I had my phone, but not the gun. I don't remember anything except standing on the platform. But I thought of something, a way to remember." The look on her face prompted him to continue. "I want you to hypnotize me."

"What?" she asked.

"Hypnotize me," he said. "I want you to unlock what I can't remember."

"You're sure about this?"

"Yes. It can be done, right?"

"Well, there are no guarantees," she said. "But it's worth a shot."

She paused. He could tell that she was thinking, contemplating.

"Alright then, what about today?"

"That's fine," he said. "But there's one more thing. I want everyone to be there."

She nodded.

"I'll give everyone a call."

\* \* \* \*

The inside of Susan's home office was the setting for Dylan's hypnosis session. Everyone was there, just as he'd requested. In addition to himself and Susan, there was Leah, Sidney, Brett, Ursula, and Marv. Dylan lounged back in a chair; Susan sat opposite him. The other five sat side by side behind Susan. Dylan requested that Brett be videotaping the session. Susan pressed a button on her audio recorder, and then she began.

"Now, Dylan, I just want to confirm for the record that you requested that all of the team be present for this session. Is that correct?"

"Yes, it is," he responded.

"Great," she said. "Now, we'll begin. First of all, I want you to lay back and relax. I want you to close your eyes and think of a beautiful place you've always wanted to visit. I want you to take yourself there. Can you picture it?"

Scenes of snow-capped mountains towering over a deep blue lake entered his mind.

"Yes," he replied.

"Good." Susan's voice became lower, soothing.

"Now, Dylan, I'm going to count backwards from ten. And when I reach one, you'll be fast asleep. Is that understood?"

"Yes," he replied, his voice also becoming lower.

Susan counted backwards from ten.

"...three, two, one," she said.

"Can you hear me, Dylan?"

There was a pause, and finally, he answered with a sleepy drawl.

"Yes."

"He's under," Susan said. "Dylan, I want you to go back to the night before last when you left my house. Do you remember?"

"Yes," he said.

"And you left my house and went home, right?"

"Yes."

"What did you do there?"

"I drank," he said.

"And then where did you go?"

There was another pause.

"I went to the observatory at Eagle Rock."

"Take us there, Dylan. What are you doing?"

"I'm standing on the platform," he said, after another pause.

"Doing what?" she asked.

"Looking out at the fog, looking at the cliff that my father fell over."

"Okay, Dylan. And then what happens?"

He watched the images in his mind play out like a movie he'd seen before. The scene was moving forward. He was now standing on the observatory platform, looking out at the fog. Then, the piercing green light penetrated his eyes. It is beyond bright. It is luminescent brilliance. There is a quick pain in his head, but he feels warm, comfortable, relaxed. He relates it to them as he remembers.

"Dylan, what happens after you see the green light?"

He tries to see beyond the green light, but everything goes black. A fog like the one he stared through that night sweeps through his mind. He is warm and then hot. He twists, turns, and fidgets in the chair.

"I don't know," he says, his voice rising. "I can't see. Everything is black."

Now, he is writhing in the chair. His breath is harder, faster.

"Okay, Dylan, I'm going to count to three. On three, you're going to wake up, understand? One, two, three."

His eyes open wide. He stares at them all, unsure if anything happened. But by the worried looks on their faces, he assumes *something* had happened.

"Did I go under?"

Susan nodded.

"Did I remember anything?"

"You recalled standing on the observatory's platform and seeing a bright green light. After that, everything went black, according to what you told us."

He let his head fall back against the chair in frustration.

"Don't worry, Dylan," Susan said. "There's always next time. I know that this is frustrating, but we'll get you through it. You may not remember now, but I promise, someday you will." The tone of her voice had turned hopeful. Her words sounded strangely enlightened, striking the chord of a sudden epiphany. "It won't stay hidden forever, Dylan. Someday, someday *we'll all* know..."

The End

# Afterword

In 2012, I conducted a questionnaire on Facebook, asking friends and readers the question: *What area of the paranormal, if any, interests you the most?* I was surprised when "UFOs" polled in second place behind "Ghosts and Poltergeists." After speaking with many people, including my readers, I discovered that all of them considered UFOs to be paranormal subject matter. I had always considered UFOs and Aliens to be safely ensconced in the science fiction category. Whether it was my age, or my careful skepticism that barred me from seeing UFOs as paranormal is a question I can't answer. But the more I immersed myself in the facts, the theories, and the witness accounts; I began to see the light (no pun intended.)

I had already written of ghosts and poltergeists in "Pipeline," and I probably will again at some point in the future. So, I decided to give my readers their second place winner, but I took on this idea with caution. I didn't want to transcend suspension of disbelief, that boundary in fiction writing that holds us authors accountable for our believability. I didn't want to cross over into what I instinctively saw as science fiction. I felt that the presence of aliens *would* transcend me over that edge that separates paranormal and sci-fi. It would also hinder the mystery that is the larger part of these real-life occurrences.

And then, a realization came to me.

I have lived in Greensburg, Pennsylvania my entire life. It's a town about twenty miles east of Pittsburgh. This area is the home of several paranormal events, the most famous being the Kecksburg UFO crash, and the rash of Bigfoot sightings that occurred in the early 1970s. A child at that time, I vividly remember the Bigfoot hysteria. I also remember my parents, as well as other parents, making certain that we kids came home before dark by telling us that Bigfoot would get us. As I'm sure you've guessed; it didn't work too well on me. I came home before dark, but sat out on our front porch in hopes of spotting Bigfoot.

Western Pennsylvania is said to be among the top "hotspots" for paranormal activity. So, with its paranormal history, especially with UFOs and Bipeds, I felt that I would've been remiss if I *hadn't* written this book. Does that mean that Green Valley is my fictional equivalent of Greensburg? Not quite. I have taken aspects from my hometown, as well as several of its surrounding areas, and combined them to make one fictional small town—Green Valley.

If I was going to write this book, I wanted to cover all aspects and all theories about the subject. My first task was to incorporate non-fictional, historical events into this work of fiction. After all, how could my investigators be from the said area, never having heard of the Kecksburg incident or the Bigfoot sightings? I had to make it a part of their history as well. Everything you've read about the Kecksburg incident in this book is true and non-fictional. The acorn-shaped object that landing in the Kecksburg ravine, the appearance of the Men in Black, witnesses being threatened, and especially the story of then WHJB director, John Murphy. All of these events are part of the history of what occurred here in December 1965.

Most of the headlines that you read in this book are real and appeared in December 1965. I have cited the non-fictional headlines. Other headlines have been fictionalized by me. Some of the Bigfoot eyewitness accounts are non-fictional and were reported in the 1970s; others have been fictionalized. Including them was meant to bestow credence to Geoffrey Rasche's journals. The 2006 Beaver County occurrence is also non-fictional.

Much of the information amassed through the years on the Kecksburg incident is the result of the persistent work of author and UFO researcher, Mr. Stan Gordon, also of this area. I have also cited his documentaries on the following page and highly suggest them to any of you who are interested. Mr. Gordon has been investigating the incident since the day it occurred. Though I don't know him personally, I would like to thank Stan Gordon for not letting go of the mystery, for striving to uncover the truth to the public, and not succumbing to intimidation.

Merging with non-fictional history was one thing, but I feel that part of the purpose of fiction is to mimic real life. It begs the frequently asked question: Does art imitate life, or does life imitate art? I'm a firm believer in the former; to me, art imitates life. This is the reason that the investigators solve the mystery of Dylan's father's death, but they never really solve the mystery of the UFO, or what exactly happened to Dylan.

Do we, in the real world, ever solve the mystery of these unidentified objects? No, of course we don't. Almost all witnesses walk away knowing that they've seen something, but they don't really know *what* they saw. Unidentified Flying Object means just that, unidentified. So, why should my investigators solve the mystery of the UFO? They would be the first to do so, and that would be illogical. So, they are left wondering, just like the rest of us.

I've researched many stories of those who claim to have been abducted by aliens. I have read an enormity of abductee accounts by those who claim to have seen and communicated with their extraterrestrial abductors, those who've seen the Blues, the Greys, the Reptilians, and the Annunaki. Again, that is not where I wanted to go. The abduction accounts that interested me the most were those that reported missing time. Many have reported that after witnessing an unidentified craft, they'd lost a significant amount of time, or that they'd ended up in another location not far from their original spot. Missing time is a widely reported phenomenon among alleged abductees, and with it comes a lack or loss of memory. I decided that this scenario worked best as far as what I had planned for Dylan.

And then there are the new characters, especially my characterization of the very real Men in Black. Okay, so you've all seen the comedy-satire film starring Will Smith and Tommy Lee Jones. But the real story behind the Men in Black is not only terrifying, but strange and eerie in many ways. They are, in fact, reported to be malicious and threatening, stopping at nothing to silence witnesses. The allegation behind John Murphy's death is a real one.

To discover the true Men in Black, I suggest that you Google all that you can find, read the books that have been written, and research the Kecksburg incident and others. The reports about them will send chills down your spine. When my characters mention the stories they've heard about the MIB, those stories are real. Everything from descriptions of their strange eyes, faces, voices, to claims that they're not human, but disguised extraterrestrials. All of it has been alleged about the infamous Men in Black.

I've brought Ursula back for this book. For those of you who've read "The Listener," I'm sure you remember her. There is also a quick appearance by Paul, Leah's father. There are new characters, as always. Shane Rowe is a victim; so is Mabel Forrester. Drew Michaels is another instance in which I took non-fictional information and allowed a fictional character to provide it. And of course, there is Seth Dornan. Seth represents MUFON, the Mutual UFO Network, again, a real organization. Including MUFON was part of covering all aspects. And yes, Hangar 1 is a real place utilized by the MUFON network.

So, Seth meets the ultimate fate in this book. Someone had to, right? A reader once confronted me with the critique that I tend to introduce new characters and then kill them off. The best way I can answer that is that the greatest mystery author of all time, Agatha Christie, once said that in order to have a good mystery, someone must die. After writing five paranormal mystery novels, I've found this to be blatantly true.

*Phantom in the Sky* is undoubtedly the most challenging book I've written so far in this series, but I'm thrilled to be sitting here, writing the Afterword. I thank all of you who have made it this far in the series. I also thank those of you who have decided to read backwards, though I warn you of spoilers. And by the way, in the third paragraph of Chapter Nineteen: Graduation Day, when Leah is home alone, I've left a hint as to the nature of Book 6. Not to coin a phrase, but keep reading...there's more.

With Love,
Chris

*Christopher Carrolli*
*August 30, 2015*
*6:22pm*

# Legal Disclosures

## Documentaries

*Secrets of UFO's: Kecksburg UFO Crash—What Really Happened at Kecksburg?* Narrator: Stan Gordon. Dir Stan Gordon. Grizzly Adams Productions. Baseline Entertainment. All Media Guide. 2006.

*UFO-TV Special Edition: UFO Crash: Kecksburg—The Untold Story.* Narrator: Stan Gordon. Dir Stan Gordon. New UFO Documentary.The Disclosure Movie Network. 2004.

## Headlines

"US Army Claims to Have Found 'Absolutely Nothing' at Kecksburg." *Project Blue Book File.* Dec. 1965.

Gatty, Bob. "Unidentified Flying Object Report Touches Off Probe Near Kecksburg." *Tribune-Review* 10 Dec. 1965, County edition.

"Many See Dazzling Light Flash in the Sky."*Ironwood Daily Globe* 10 Dec. 1965.

"Orange Ball of Fire Falls Near Kecksburg: Sighted in Seven States, Canada." *The Daily Courier;* Connellsville. Dec. 1965.

"Searchers Fail to Find Object." *Tribune-Review* 10 Dec. 1965, City (later) edition.

"Unidentified Falling Object Falls Near Kecksburg—Army Ropes Off Area." *Tribune-Review*10 Dec. 1965, County edition.

## Music

Nicks, Stevie, "The Edge Of Seventeen" from *Bella Donna.* Stevie

Nicks. Prod: Jimmy Iovine. Modern Records. 1981.

Nirvana, "Come as You Are" from *Nevermind.* Kurt Cobain. Prod: Butch Vig. DGC Records. 1992.

Photographer: Tara Manon

## About the Author

Christopher Carrolli is a full-time writer, who lives in Western Pennsylvania. He is a graduate of University of Pittsburgh at Greensburg and holds a BA in English Writing, and an AA in English. He has also won the Ida B. Wells Prize in Journalism.

www.facebook.com/ccarrolli
ccarrolli@facebook.com (fb email)
www.christophercarrolli.blogspot.com
carrollic@aol.com
www.goodreads.com/carrollic

## Other Works by the Author at Melange

*Pipeline, The Paranormal Investigator, Book 1*
*The Listener, The Paranormal Investigator, Book 2*
*The Third Eye of Leah Leeds, The Paranormal Investigator, Book 3*
*The Skinwalker's Tale, The Paranormal Investigator, Book 4*